# THE SENIOR MOMENT

## EVA HUDSON



VENATRIX

**THE SENIOR MOMENT**

First published 2013 by Two Pies Press
This edition published by Venatrix

ISBN 978-0-9926357-8-7



This book is a work of fiction and, except in the case of historical fact, any resemblance to actual persons, living or dead, is purely coincidental.

# THE SENIOR MOMENT

*For Alkarim and Jonathan*
*I couldn't wish for better friends*

# 1

By the time she'd wheeled her suitcase along the second aisle, a bunch of flowers crushed under her arm, Jean Henderson realised she had absolutely no idea why she'd ventured into the grocery store. She scanned shelves crammed with bottles of sauce and jars of pickles and strained to recall why she had struggled to cross First Avenue only moments earlier.

Drawn to the hum of the fridges at the far end of the third aisle, she spotted quart containers of milk and remembered. Of course: *a nice cup of tea.*

She leaned close to the refrigerated units, enjoying the cool air for a few seconds. Beneath her jacket her blouse was clinging to damp flesh. She lifted dripping locks of hair from her neck and sucked in a deep restorative breath.

From the front of the store came a loud crash followed by muffled shouts; tempers getting short in the August heat, she supposed. As the shouting ratcheted up, she limped toward the counter to see a hunched figure waving his arms in the air. He was shouting and his voice cracked between syllables like a teenage boy's.

'Come on, man,' he hollered, 'I'm not messing around.'

Another youth, this one shorter than the first, stood perfectly still, silently watching events unfold. Jean looked from one boy to the other. There was something peculiar about them. It seemed as if their hair had been moulded to their heads. She shuffled closer to get a better look.

Two miniature Barack Obamas?

It took a moment for her jet-lagged brain to process what she was looking at. Both youths were wearing rubber masks. She felt a sickening shift in the contents of her stomach and watched helplessly as the quiet boy tapped his companion on the shoulder. The shouting youth angrily brushed his hand aside.

'Let me have it,' the quiet one said.

'What?'

'You said I could.'

'What's the matter with you?'

'Come on. Please?'

After a moment's hesitation the first boy lifted his arm in the air and passed something to his friend. When she made out what it was, Jean's stomach lurched again.

'Don't shoot! Please, don't shoot!' The man behind the counter flung his hands into the air and backed away, crashing into the shelves of cigarettes behind him.

'Shut up!' The boy straightened his arm and the gun trembled in his gloved fist.

The first youth vaulted over the counter and swiped the clerk across the face with the back of his hand. The man's head jerked sideways.

Jean's hand flew to her mouth and she let out an involuntary gasp. She glanced at the other customers standing either side of her. A woman was fingering a set of rosary beads, her lips moving rapidly without making a sound. The young man on her left was clutching a skateboard to his chest as he stared at the unfolding drama, open-mouthed and wide-eyed. Frozen to the spot.

'Get down!' the first youth shouted at them. 'Faces against the floor. Now!'

The two people flanking Jean dropped to their knees and quickly slid onto their bellies. Jean stared down at them, attempted to bend her knees and got stuck in a half crouch as a searing pain pulsed up her left leg. She righted herself and lifted her arms above her head. 'I'm sorry… I just… can't,' she said and backed away a few steps, fully expecting important memories to start playing in her head as sixty-odd years flashed before her. 'I'm so sorry. It's my knee. Please…' She held her breath, convinced she was only moments from death.

'Open the register!' The boy with the gun swung it back toward the man behind the counter, whose face was now smeared with the blood gushing from his nose. Jean eased out a jagged breath and slowly edged further away.

Standing on the other side of the counter, the taller boy peered into the drawer of the cash register and plucked out a meagre handful of notes.

'Where's the safe?' he said.

The bloody clerk didn't reply. He pressed himself against the shelves of cigarettes, arms shielding his face from another blow.

'Where. Is. The. Safe?'

'No safe. All money in register.'

'You're lying! Show me the safe.' The youth struck him again, harder this time. The man's knees folded and he crumpled like a crushed can, disappearing from view. Obama twin number one stared at the money in his hand. 'There's only two, maybe three hundred dollars here.' He shoved the cash into a pocket and clambered back over the counter, shaking his head.

Obama number two stretched up on his toes and peered over at the bleeding man. 'He's unconscious. You hit him too hard. How are we going to find the safe now?'

'We're not.' The taller youth spun on his heels and stared up at the ceiling.

Jean felt horribly conspicuous standing between the two prostrate shoppers. She dropped her shoulders and lowered her head, trying to make herself a smaller target.

Obama one snapped his head back and turned to his accomplice. 'Whack him,' he said.

'What?'

'You heard me!'

'What good will that do?'

'Just do it!'

Jean swallowed and tried to speak, but all that came out of her mouth was a pathetic little croak. She swallowed again – if she could just reason with him.

'Give me back the gun,' the taller youth said.

The second youth pulled the gun out of reach. 'All right!' he said in a gulping yelp.

Instinctively, Jean took a step forward, reaching out a hand to the boy.

'Don't be a pussy – whack him!' Obama number one was staring at the gun, bouncing on his toes, waiting to make another lunge for it.

The first boy's thin little arm rose slowly and he pointed the weapon over the counter. His hand shook so much it looked as if he might drop the gun at any moment.

'Come on!' his friend hollered.

Jean's voice had stalled in her throat, and her arms and legs were refusing to budge. Unable to act, she could do nothing but close her eyes. A thunderous crack echoed around the store, rocking her backward. Then a second and a third. She reached out and grabbed at the nearest shelf, tripped over the woman lying on the ground, and clattered into a wall of stacked cans.

Still staggering from the impact of the recoil, the shooter spun round. Through the holes of his rubber mask, Jean could see his eyes darting left and right. Her breath stopped.

The boy ignored her and pointed the gun toward the skateboarder lying on the floor. 'Stay down!' he shouted, his voice surer now.

A smell filled the air, something Jean had never experienced before, a noxious chemical odour, undercut with the ferrous tang of fresh blood. Vomit rose into her mouth.

The shooter ran after his accomplice, who was already through the door and onto the street. Without thinking, Jean hurried after them, the pain in her knee pulsing as she went. She reached the kerb just as the boy with the gun was swinging a leg over the seat of a waiting motorbike, the other youth sitting up front trying to start the engine. The boy with the gun unpeeled his mask and shoved it in a pocket. The motorbike spluttered into life then died again. The youth at the controls planted both feet on the ground and walked the bike into the gutter. He tried the ignition again. Again he was rewarded with a splutter from the engine. Only this time it didn't die.

They were going to get away.

Helplessly Jean looked left and right, but no one was close enough to help. She couldn't just stand there and do nothing. She wrenched her bag from her shoulder and swung it toward the bike, like an athlete tossing a hammer. As soon as it left her hand, and was flying through the air toward the unmasked boy, she came to her senses. What was she doing? She froze.

The bag made contact with the boy's shoulder, knocking him off balance. He jerked around and stared right at her.

'What the…?' He reached under his jacket.

She stared back into his ghostly white face, his curly hair matted with sweat and plastered to his head. As time slowed, Jean thought abstractly how he reminded her of her grandson. He even had the same smattering of freckles across his nose. She watched him pull out the gun and aim it at her chest, his expression blank. The engine roared again and the bike tore away from the kerb. The boy's arm swung sideways, the weapon flailing wildly in his hand. As the motorcycle picked up speed, he kept his eyes fixed on Jean and swung the gun toward her again.

A single shot rang out, the sound swallowed up by the noise on the street.

Jean staggered backward. She lifted a hand to her chest, as a sudden, sharp pain radiated across it. She swallowed down a mouthful of bile, her fingers searching for a wound. She swallowed again, relieved not to have been hit.

Sirens started up in the distance, whooping and wailing over the sound of car horns and shouting voices.

Jean slowly retrieved her bag from the road and walked unsteadily back to the store. The other two customers were still lying face down on the dirty linoleum, both trembling, both breathing rapidly. Jean peered over the counter to see if there was anything she could do to help the clerk.

But it was far too late for that.

# 2

The woman in the crumpled NYPD uniform unclipped a pair of handcuffs from her belt and, before Stanley Rozello had a chance to protest, secured his wrist to the arm of a chair.

'Very funny, guys. No really – you kill me.' Stanley looked up imploringly at his closest colleague in the squad.

Detective Luisa Rodriguez shrugged back at him, wishing there was some way she could help.

The woman with the handcuffs straddled his legs, laid a hand on either side of her tight shirt and with an extravagant yank, unpopped her buttons. She thrust her breasts into Stanley's face, grabbed the back of his head, and held him there for longer than Luisa thought was healthy.

Or entirely safe.

Stanley was nearly sixty-two – that kind of shock combined with prolonged oxygen starvation could kill a man of his age. He let out a low moan and a roar went up around the squad room. The whole team started shouting, urging the stripper to hurry up.

The fake cop let go of Stanley's head and he emerged from the confines of his fleshy prison with damp red cheeks, his brush of half-inch white hair lay flattened against his scalp. He took a big gulp of air.

Luisa's skin prickled, feeling every moment of her partner's embarrassment. She'd done her best to stop the guys fixing up a surprise retirement present, but all her protests had been dismissed and yet again she'd been labelled a killjoy. A spoilsport. Just because she happened to believe ritual humiliation should have been eradicated from the NYPD along with racism and sexual harassment. Who was she kidding?

Stanley tugged hard on the cuffs shackling him to the chair. They held firm. Again he looked at Luisa, his eyes pleading for rescue.

'I'm sorry, Stan – you just got to suck it up.'

'That's what I'm afraid of,' he murmured.

The stripper ripped off her bra and twirled it over her head. Stanley tried in vain to turn his face away from the encroaching tasselled nipples. No doubt sensing his discomfort, the half-naked woman hooked her transparent nylon underwear around his neck and reeled him in. Luisa saw Stanley snatch a quick breath before his oxygen supply was cut off again.

Hang in there, Rozello.

Five years ago, almost to the day, when Luisa was promoted to detective and first joined the 4th Precinct, Stanley had taken her under his wing and shown her the ropes. He reminded her at every opportunity since then how he'd taught her all there was to know about being a good cop. Which was true, in part. Three tough years as a patrol officer working out of the 83rd in Brooklyn had already taught her plenty. And now, after eight years in the department, Luisa was pretty much NYPD down to her bones.

Just like Stanley.

He lived and breathed it every minute of the day. She wasn't sure how he'd survive on the outside. Or, for that matter, how she would get by without him. She swallowed hard against the lump in her throat and blinked away the sting in her eyes as she watched Stanley's face re-emerge. He gulped down another breath, looking up at Luisa with the same pleading expression. All she could do was smile sympathetically.

The stripper started to unbutton his shirt and ran her fingers over his wiry chest hair. Stanley closed his eyes tight shut and mumbled something that sounded suspiciously like a stream of Hail Marys and Our Fathers. Luisa hung her head, still feeling his pain, still powerless to offer assistance. A sharp elbow nudged her in the ribs.

'Bet you can't wait until it's your turn, huh?'

She looked up at her boss's face, fixed in a fake smile. She didn't bother answering.

'Come on. Get into the party vibe, Rodriguez. That's an order.'

'Yes, sir, Lieutenant, sir.' She stood to attention. 'I've got another thirty-two years before I retire – I guess I'll just have to be patient.'

'Assuming you last that long.' He said it under his breath, but she knew he meant her to hear.

The stripper was down to her panties and a pair of laddered fishnet stockings. 'Don't you think he's taken enough punishment?' Luisa said. 'Can't we send this woman away with a shred of Stan's dignity still intact?'

'Rozello's having a ball.' Lieutenant Riley slapped Stanley on the back to reinforce his point. 'You wouldn't understand. It's a guy thing.'

Luisa could feel her cheeks getting hot. 'But wouldn't it be nice for him to look back on his last day in the department with fond memories? Rather than a sick feeling in the pit of his stomach?'

'Lighten up for one goddamn day, will you?' Someone called his name from the other side of the squad room and Riley hurried away, not missing the opportunity to pinch the stripper's butt cheek as he passed.

Stanley was made to suffer another excruciating ten minutes, when finally the stripper unhooked her legs from his thighs and unlocked the handcuffs. She planted a

Cupid's bow of lipstick on his forehead and quickly draped a raincoat over her shoulders. Immediately the assembled detectives started booing. The woman blew them an extravagant kiss and tottered in her high heels toward the door, her departure accompanied by whistling and whooping.

Stanley's face had turned grey. A layer of perspiration covered his cheeks and forehead and dribbled behind his ears. But before Luisa had a chance to ease him out of his chair and steer him toward the men's restroom, another roar started up. From the other side of the long squad room, one of the dispatchers appeared carrying a slab of cake, iced in red, white and blue, a marzipan police shield decorating the top.

'For he's a jolly good fellow…' the dispatcher sang and encouraged her colleagues to join in.

Luisa gave Stanley a big hug and pecked his sweaty cheek. Someone shouted 'speech' from the back of the room and soon everyone was hollering.

'OK, OK.' Stanley waved his big hands to quiet them. 'Boy am I glad to be getting outta here!'

Another cheer went up.

'We know that ain't true,' the dispatcher said and punched the top of Stanley's arm. 'You practically sleep at your desk every night – I seen you one time, snoring like a grizzly.'

'I been working this precinct twenty-seven years,' Stanley continued. 'I know that's longer than some of you have been alive.' He slowly scanned the room. 'Look at you guys – babies still.' He shook his head. 'Anyways… what was I saying?' he asked Luisa.

'Hey – Rozello's finally losing it – not leaving a moment too soon, my man,' someone yelled.

Luisa leaned toward him and whispered in his ear. 'Twenty-seven years at the fourth,' she said.

'Yeah – right, and I seen a lotta change in all that time. Seen a lotta stuff I wish I hadn't, let me tell you.' He pulled a handkerchief from a trouser pocket and swabbed his face and neck. 'What I'm trying to say… Jesus, help me out here, Lu.'

Luisa threw her hands up and shrugged. 'Maybe you want to tell us just how much we all mean to you – how much you're going to miss us when you leave? How life won't be as rich and full without us.'

Stanley made a show of scratching his head. 'Nah… that weren't it.' His face broke into a broad grin – a Stanley Rozello special – the one he reserved for charming female witnesses. 'Seriously fellas – I just wanna say thank you. Thank you for that fragrant lady just now… thank you for this magnificent cake. But most of all, thanks for being the best friends any man could wish for.'

'Now we know you're lying!' The dispatcher poked her tongue at him.

'Hey – I never said I could make speeches. Somebody give me a knife. I got cake to cut, goddammit.'

As Stanley pressed a ten-inch steel blade into the thick layer of icing, another shout went up.

'Armed robbery in a grocery store on First Avenue,' Riley hollered from the other side of the room.

'Anyone hurt?' Stanley shouted back.

'Store clerk. Shot at close range.'

Stanley grabbed his jacket and started for the exit.

'Where are you going?' Lieutenant Riley cut him off before he reached the door.

'Potential homicide. I'm your most experienced detective. Where do you think I'm going?'

'Stand down soldier. No way are you getting into this on your last day.'

Luisa had already grabbed her sunglasses and bag. 'Don't worry, Stan. I'll tell you all about it when I get back.'

'You're staying here too, Rodriguez – you've got too much paperwork to catch up on. Besides – you can keep Rozello company.'

Luisa clamped a mouthful of flesh between her top and bottom teeth to stop herself swearing at him and threw her bag back onto the desk.

'Any witnesses?' Stanley said.

'A couple. We're looking for two black kids.'

# 3

Ninety minutes after she'd watched the killer escape, Jean was sitting outside the grocery store on a plastic fold-up chair, still waiting for a police officer to interview her. An elderly Korean woman sat on the chair beside her. Jean squeezed the woman's hand and continued to make soothing noises. She'd given up speaking as everything she said ended up sounding like a meaningless platitude. What was there to say?

Shortly after the uniformed police officers had cordoned off the corner of the street, a team of men and women, wearing white suits and grim expressions, stepped out of a large truck and swept into the store. Jean could see them from where she sat now, filling little plastic bags with samples of substances they'd scraped off the floor and counter, and taking photographs of the crime scene from every possible angle. They'd already snapped dozens of pictures of the store clerk. Then the poor soul had been wheeled away in a body bag.

Jean squeezed the woman's gnarled, parchment-dry hand in hers a little harder, and quickly loosened her grip, worried she might snap one of her fragile fingers. The gesture seemed to stir her into action. She mumbled something Jean couldn't make out, untangled her fingers, then slowly and deliberately rose from her seat. She ducked past the policeman standing sentry at the entrance to the store. Jean watched in amazement as the grieving woman weaved her way around detectives and forensics people completely unnoticed. Not one of them made any attempt to stop her traipsing through the murder scene.

Jean stretched her left leg, trying to ease the grinding throb in her knee. The dark green awning overhanging the entrance to the store was keeping the sun from roasting her alive, yet determined rivulets of perspiration still found their way down every crevice and fold in her flesh.

A scowling detective hurried past. Jean reached out and tugged on the man's sleeve, only to have her hand swatted away as if it was a particularly irritating insect. 'Excuse me!' she said as loud as her dry throat would allow. The detective didn't even acknowledge her.

Over half an hour ago Jean had listened patiently as the woman with the rosary beads explained what had happened inside the store. Amazingly, given she had been lying face down during most of the robbery, her account was largely accurate. Except for one essential detail.

The woman carefully described the robbers' appearance, paying particular attention to the rubber masks they were wearing.

'And what about their ethnicity?' the detective asked her.

'You mean the colour of their skin?'

'Yes, ma'am.'

'They were both black. Not dark – light-skinned, you know?'

Jean leapt from her seat, eager to correct the woman's mistake. But at that moment a group of forensics people piled out of the store, blocking her path. She watched as the witness was guided into a police car to continue her statement.

Now, sitting alone on the sidewalk, Jean still waited for a chance to provide her own version of events, but no one so much as acknowledged her existence. Had the police somehow decided she was an unreliable witness? Was her age against her? Or her English accent? As she fidgeted on the uncomfortable plastic chair, she searched the sea of faces for the oldest officer on duty, hopeful someone closer to her own age might be more inclined to listen to her. She spotted a uniformed policeman leaning against a squad car chewing on a pretzel. Judging by his paunch and sagging features, he seemed the most likely candidate. She eased herself upright and headed toward him, dodging around his busy colleagues as she went.

'Excuse me,' she said and turned on a smile. 'I need to speak to someone about what happened.'

After a few moments he stopped chewing and finally looked her up and down.

'Hello,' she tried again, 'I was just wondering when someone—'

'Who let you in here?' he said, shoving the half-eaten pretzel on the roof of the patrol car. 'This ain't no tourist destination, lady. You can't just wander into a crime scene. Jeez.' He turned away. 'Hey, Rowlands!' He waved a hand at a young officer standing on the corner of the street. 'What're you doing letting old ladies past the line?'

Jean studied his face, the rheumy eyes, bulbous nose and drooping jowls. He couldn't have been more than a few years younger than her. Who did he think he was, calling her an old lady? She glanced at her reflection in the window of the car, pulled her shoulders back, straightened her jacket and tidied her hair. The glass made her look shorter and wider and more grey than blonde, and she would be the first to admit her Transatlantic flight had left her a little ragged. But *old lady*?

She stomped back to her seat, collected her suitcase then ducked awkwardly under the police tape, throwing a glance back at the flabby officer who was wagging a finger at his young colleague. He pointed toward the police car, saw she was no longer there and threw his hands in the air.

'Keystone bloody Cops,' Jean said to anyone who might have been listening.

The situation called for much more affirmative action.

A short taxi ride later, Jean was deposited at the steps of the nearest police station, the 4th Precinct station house, the cab driver had helpfully informed her. She marched up to the reception desk and grabbed the edge of the counter, standing on the tips of her toes to gain a few inches.

'Excuse me,' she said.

The man on the desk seemed to be engrossed in paperwork. Which appeared to be the sports section of a newspaper.

Jean coughed loudly and tried again. 'I'd like to make a statement.'

Still he ignored her.

She let out a steadying breath. Obviously she was doing something wrong. She slapped the counter with a hand, rustling the top sheet of the desk sergeant's paper. Was that a slight twitching of his bushy moustache?

She raised her voice. 'What's a woman got to do to get some attention around here?'

Nothing.

Less than four hours in New York and it seemed she had become transparent, dissolving into the background wherever she went. Could it be her age? Surely sixty-five was no age at all. Ever since her last birthday she'd told everyone who'd listen it was the new fifty.

A phone rang on the counter and the police officer answered it immediately.

'OK – if that's the way you want to play it, you leave me no alternative.' Jean dragged her suitcase to the other side of the reception area and climbed gingerly onto the long wooden bench bolted to the wall. No one made a move toward her. No one even raised an eyebrow. She yanked off her jacket, dropping it on the bench beside her, untucked

her blouse from the waistband of her skirt and unstuck it from her damp back. With sweating fingertips she struggled to unfasten the first button, but it refused to slip neatly through its hole. After a few moments she gave up and tugged hard on either side of the blouse, sending tiny pearl missiles into the air. They fell like hailstones on the linoleum. Jean peeled off the blouse, rolling it into a tight ball. She pulled back her shoulders and stuck out her breasts, only remembering in that moment she was wearing an underwired balconette bra that plunged precipitously. She stamped her feet on the bench, banging her heavy heels against the wood.

'Hello!' she hollered. 'Can you see me now? Is this conspicuous enough?'

A few visitors turned their heads in her vague direction, but still no police officer came running toward her with a modesty blanket.

'Do you actually want me topless?' she shouted. 'Because I will, you know.' She shook her head and took a deep breath. 'I have to warn you, last time I got these...' She looked down at her chest, choosing her words. 'Last time I got these puppies out I stopped traffic. Practically caused a riot!' She shook the balled blouse from around her fist, flung it toward the high ceiling and reached behind her back to grab the fastening of her bra. The blouse unravelled itself in the air and, like a billowing parachute, gently floated earthwards.

At that moment a tall, silver-haired man emerged from a side door carrying a tray of thickly iced cake. Jean's blouse landed on his head, the sleeves draping decoratively over his shoulders. Blinded momentarily, he staggered forward, snatching the silk garment from his face. He stopped, just inches from Jean, his eyes fixed on her chest.

'What's the matter with you?' Jean hollered at him. 'Never seen a woman in her undies before?' She planted her hands on her hips.

'I… I, uh…' The cake man held up his free hand. 'You gotta get down from there, ma'am.'

'Why? What are you going to do? Arrest me?'

# 4

'Three hundred and twenty-three dollars, man.'

Linus stared down at the bloodstained bundle of bills as Richie finished counting them. 'You were expecting more?' he said and bounced on his toes. Since they'd dumped the bike and made their way on foot to the park, he hadn't been able to keep still for a second. He scuffed the dry grass and dirt under his shoes. Every one of his muscles was flexed tight. He had a pain in his chest and wondered if seventeen was too young to have a heart attack.

'Hell yeah.' Richie roughly divided the bills and shoved half of them at Linus. 'Busy store like that must take five hundred dollars an hour. Easy.'

'Maybe you shouldn't have hit the clerk so hard. We never managed to find out where the safe was.'

'You think you coulda made him squeal?'

Linus shrugged and wrapped his arms around his ribs, anything to stop the shaking in his hands. 'Why let me have the gun if you weren't going to give me the chance to threaten him with it?'

'It's not like I planned to bust his head. It just happened. Anyway – I let you shoot him, didn't I?'

Linus looked at the ground, hugged himself tighter.

'You OK?' Richie said. 'You look a little green. Don't throw up anywhere near me. I can't stand puke. It's disgusting.'

'I'm not feeling nauseous.'

'"Not feeling nauseous."' Richie raised the tone of his voice by an octave and pushed the tip of his nose in the air.

'Screw you.'

'Yeah?' Richie bumped his chest against Linus and Linus felt the gun in his friend's pocket clatter against him.

'Easy, man.' He backed away, unable to take his eyes off the bottom of Richie's jacket.

'What are you looking at?'

'The gun,' Linus said quietly. 'I want it back.'

'What?'

'I need it. There's something I've got to do.'

'Oh yeah?' Richie pulled out the revolver and aimed it at Linus.

'Jesus!' Linus threw a glance around the park. The sunbathers and dog walkers paid them no attention. Everyone was too hot to care. He wiped a sleeve across his cheeks and forehead. His hair was matted slick to his head.

'Man – there's no way I'm giving you the gun again.' Richie shoved the revolver into the waistband of his pants. 'We're doing the stores together. That's the deal. It's my gun. I say how it goes down.'

'Absolutely. I don't want to do this without you. It's just…'

'Come on!'

'You ever killed anyone?'

'Sure – I've cracked some skulls.'

'But have you actually ever shot someone dead?'

'Maybe.'

'Come on. Really?'

Richie shifted on his feet, his hand automatically reaching around his back. 'Came damn close.'

'You have no idea what it's like.'

'What's the matter? You gonna tell me it was so bad you crapped your pants?' Richie spat out the words.

Linus shook his head. Every nerve in his body felt like it had an electric current going through it, his hands and feet were prickling, the skin on his arms and face fizzing as if it might peel right off. But he didn't feel scared. He didn't know exactly what he was feeling, he was just certain it wasn't fear.

'I need the gun,' he said again.

'No way.'

'There's some unfinished business I have to attend to.'

'Uh huh?'

Linus pulled the bills from his pocket. 'Take my share.' He pressed the untidy bundle into Richie's hand. 'Go on – take it!' His voice came out louder than he'd planned. 'Call it a down payment on the gun. Every store we do from now on, you get to keep all the money.'

'You said you needed cash.'

'I need the gun more.' Though his lips were parched, a pool of saliva had gathered underneath Linus's tongue.

'Keep your share and buy your own gun.'

'I need it now!'

'Too bad.' Richie shoved Linus in the chest with both fists. He was taller and heavier than Linus and Linus stumbled backward, struggling to stay on his feet. 'What's gonna stop you robbing your own stores and keeping all the money?' Richie shoved him again. 'Meanwhile you got the gun and all I got is this crappy three hundred dollars.'

'Honour among thieves,' Linus muttered.

'What are you saying? What did you call me?'

'Nothing!' Linus stepped back and held up his hands. 'If this is going to work – our… business enterprise, then we need to trust one another.' His breath was catching in his throat. He wanted so desperately to feel the cold metal of the gun against his skin again, feel the heft of it in his hand. He opened his arms wide. 'Come on, bro. You got to trust me.'

'Bro? You ain't putting those scrawny little white arms around me.'

Undeterred, Linus stuck out his hand. 'Shake on it, then. You loan me the gun for a little while and I'll give you all the proceeds of every hold-up.'

'You'll give it back after?'

'Yep – just as soon as I've finished using it.'

'When will that be?'

Linus shrugged. 'I've still got to work that out.'

'What business do you need it for?'

'Don't worry – I'm not considering going independent. We're a team, right? Stronger together. I'm not about to betray my compadre.'

'You talk crap.'

Linus managed a smile when all he wanted to do was scream at Richie and drag the gun from his pants.

'If we're gonna trust each other, you gotta tell me what you got planned,' Richie said.

'Damage limitation.'

'What?'

'There's a loose end needs tying.'

'Tell me what you mean.'

'Someone saw me at the store.'

'No they didn't – they saw Obama. Two Obamas.' Richie chuckled to himself. 'That was genius, man.'

Linus took a deep breath and the air rattled into his lungs. 'I took off my mask just before we rode away.'

'You did what?'

'I was hot. I didn't think it mattered. We were leaving.'

'You stupid mother—'

'I couldn't breathe.'

'Stupid—'

'It's done, OK?'

'Who saw you?'

'A little old lady. She stared right into my face.'

'And you think she's telling the cops?'

Linus rubbed his clammy hands over his face. 'She saw me.'

'Why didn't you whack her right then?'

'I tried. But we swerved into the road and I missed.'

'I thought you were just firing into the air. Celebrating or something.' He ran a hand over his head and paced in a circle around the dusty patch of grass. 'You shoulda told me about this before.'

'And what? We couldn't exactly go back for her once the cops arrived.'

The scowl on Richie's face made him look ten years older. Linus had never seen him this mad.

'You motherf—'

Linus held up a hand, his index finger stopping just short of Richie's lips. 'It's not a problem, believe me. Give me the gun and I'll take care of it.'

Richie looked Linus up and down, his teeth gnawing at his top lip. 'Just a loan, yeah?'

'Sure.'

Richie yanked the gun from his pants and slipped it to Linus.

'I need more bullets,' Linus said.

'You still got three in the gun.'

'Two.'

'Jesus! How many you think you're gonna need to knock off an old lady?'

# 5

Jean's fingers fumbled with the safety pin as she tried to thread the slim point of stainless steel through the buttonhole of her blouse. It took her a moment to realise she really couldn't see what she was doing and another to work out why. Frustrated at not being able to fasten her blouse across her chest, her eyes had blurred with sudden tears. She snatched a quick breath. An image of the clerk bleeding to death behind the counter of the grocery store loomed large and bright in her mind. She rested both hands on the edge of the filthy sink and steadied herself. She sniffed hard and exhaled slowly; she wasn't about to break down in the insalubrious surroundings of the ladies' restroom in a New York police station. She couldn't let the events of the day catch up with her here, in public, a young detective about to pop her head round the door at any moment to ask if she was all right. Detective Rodriguez had done that three times already.

Jean caught a glimpse of herself in the dirty mirror above the sink, her eyes wet and what was left of her make-up smeared across her face. Her hair was lank and lifeless. Dressed in a bland beige skirt suit and cream blouse it wasn't any wonder everyone had ignored her.

She rummaged in her bag for a lipstick and quickly applied a coat of Estée Lauder *Autumn Blush* to top and bottom lips, correcting the smudged outline with her little finger. She let out another long breath and checked her face in quarter profile, left then right, then pinched some colour into her cheeks. She put her jacket over her gaping blouse, buttoned it all the way to the top and leaned forward to see just how much of her cleavage was on display. Too much for polite company, but it would just have to do. Anymore frustrated fiddling with safety pins and she might break down completely.

On shaky legs, she made her way back to the squad room, stopping outside the door to fill her lungs with air. Her heart was thumping in her chest and pins and needles had started up in both hands. Did that mean something? An imminent heart attack? A stroke? She took another deep breath and opened the door.

Shoulders back, chin up.

The two detectives were sitting at their desks, facing one another. She watched as the sergeant scooped up the last of the chocolate cream from the cake tray, like Pooh Bear sticking his paw in the honey jar and licking it clean. By rights the man should have been the size of a house, all those calories he was putting away. Instead he had the look of a movie star about him, lean and toned. He looked up at that moment and grinned at her. His smile reminded her of someone, she couldn't place who. The female detective turned and followed his gaze. She scraped back her chair, hurried toward Jean, and guided her back to the desk.

'Are you OK, ma'am?'

Jean let out a quiet sigh. She was feeling decidedly matronly with the all the *ma'ams* she'd been getting since arriving in New York. It grated on her nerves every time she heard it. She sat down heavily on the metal and plastic chair between the detectives' desks and did her best to smile at them both. The sergeant cleared away the dirty cake tray and tidied the paperwork that had been hidden underneath. A thick brown smear obscured half the text on the top sheet.

'Someone's birthday is it?' Jean asked.

'That's not until next month.' The white-haired sergeant shifted uncomfortably in his seat. 'It's my last day in the department.' He cast his gaze downward, and exhaled a pitiful sigh.

'Oh no – been given the chop?' Jean smiled sympathetically at him. 'Cutbacks, I suppose? It's the same everywhere.'

'Retiring, actually.'

'No! You look as though you've still got a few fighting years left in you.' As she reached out and squeezed his arm, she studied the skin around his eyes and mouth, trying to gauge his age.

'Sixty-two in three weeks,' he said, as if he'd read her mind.

'Well there you go – positively a spring chicken.'

'Too old for the NYPD.'

'It's a crying shame – we're on the scrapheap just when we're getting into our stride – eh?' She smiled again.

'Tell me about it.'

Jean held his gaze, his dark brown eyes twinkling at her beneath bushy eyebrows. She felt her cheeks warming.

The young policewoman leaned forward in her seat and cleared her throat. 'Ma'am?'

'So, what do you need to know first?' Jean let go of the policeman's arm, only realising she was still holding on to it when she felt his muscles flex under her fingers. 'Shall I just go through what happened, chronologically? Blow-by-blow?' she said.

Jean spent the next ten minutes describing the robbery in the grocery store in as much detail as she could remember. But even as she painstakingly recounted each point she got the distinct impression that neither detective was taking her entirely seriously. More than once she caught the policewoman throw her colleague a sideways glance. At one point she was sure the young detective stifled a yawn.

'White? You're sure about that?' she said when Jean described the boy on the back of the motorcycle.

Jean nodded. 'White as a sheet at that point – all the colour had drained out of his face. He looked like he might pass out.'

'The other witnesses have confirmed that both perpetrators were black,' the sergeant said.

'They're wrong. They didn't see them without their rubber masks. They've jumped to the wrong conclusions.'

'What about the other perp? Was he white too?' Rodriguez asked.

'I've no idea – he didn't take off his mask.' Jean reached into a pocket and retrieved her boarding pass. 'I wrote this down as soon as I could.' She handed the rectangle of stiff card to the young detective. 'I might have got a couple of the numbers wrong – but it should help, shouldn't it?'

Rodriguez stared blankly at the card.

'The other side,' Jean said. 'It's the registration number of the motorbike.'

The detective raised her eyebrows.

'See? Not as useless as you might think!' Jean settled back into the hard chair. 'Can't you… what is it? Run a match on your database or something?'

The older detective nodded to his colleague and thanked Jean for her diligence.

'Just doing what's right,' Jean said.

'We appreciate that, ma'am.'

Jean flinched. 'Please – call me Jean.'

After an awkward moment of silence, he stuck out his hand. 'Stanley,' he said, smiling.

That familiar smile again. A sudden chill crept across her shoulders and she shuddered as she remembered who it was he reminded her of. Someone she hadn't thought of in years.

'Are you OK?' The policeman seemed genuinely concerned. 'Are you cold? The air con in here can get a little aggressive.' He tugged on a sleeve and started to take off his jacket.

'Please, I'm fine.' She folded her arms. 'Just someone walking over my grave. I dare say they'll stop soon enough.' She let out a breath.

'You sure you're OK, ma'am?'

'Please – it's Jean.' She squeezed his arm and was suddenly aware how cold her hands were. She shivered. The events of the morning had finally caught up with her. 'I really should call my son; let him know I've arrived safe and well. His girlfriend was expecting me over two hours ago.'

'You're visiting family here?'

He sounded just like the man who'd scrutinised her passport at JFK. The anxiety Jean had felt as her fingerprints were scanned came flooding back. She struggled to control her breathing. 'My son's having his first baby, or rather his girlfriend is. Will be. Any day now.'

'A grandma, huh? Congratulations.'

'Simon's first baby, my seventh grandchild. I'm here to lend an expert hand.' She peered into her bag looking for her phone, taking the opportunity to avoid the detective's penetrating gaze.

'So, uh, Mr Henderson didn't make the trip with you?' the policeman said.

Jean glanced up at him. His expression had changed. Now he was avoiding eye contact.

'My husband died a few years back now.'

'Oh, I'm sorry to hear that.'

He didn't sound sorry. Was he flirting with her?

At the next desk Rodriguez finished her phone call. 'The bike was reported stolen at nine-thirty this morning,' she told her partner. 'It was taken some time between midnight and then.'

'So no leads there?' Jean asked and managed to extricate her phone from the depths of her bag.

The detective seemed irritated by the question, as if she'd forgotten Jean was still there. 'Can you tell me anything else about the gunman?' she said.

'Gun*man*? I wouldn't call him that – he was barely out of short trousers. Face as smooth as a baby's bum.'

'Do you think you'd be able to ID him?'

'Absolutely – he looked a lot like my grandson. Just a couple of years older. Not a dead ringer, but I'm sure if you put him in a line-up and I'd spot him straightaway, no trouble.'

'I was thinking more of our computer database. Do you feel up to going through it?'

'Now?' Jean's limbs were starting to go numb, asleep before she was.

'It'd be best to do it right away – while the image is fresh in your mind.'

'I'm not likely to forget my own grandson's face, am I?'

'If you'd rather come back tomorrow, fine.' The police officer didn't even attempt to disguise her disappointment.

'Why don't I show you a photograph of him?'

'You took a picture at the scene?'

'Scene? No – I mean a snapshot of my grandson, Dan.'

As soon as Jean switched on her phone it beeped, informing her a new network had been detected. She had a handful of text messages. She read the first one:

*Why aren't you answering? & what's Simon playing at?*

Jean noticed she had a couple of voice messages too. 'Just a message from Caroline – my daughter. In London,' Jean told the detective, feeling the need to explain. 'Some domestic crisis or other I expect – I'll check the others later.' She scrolled quickly through her photo gallery and found the most recent photograph of her grandson; the only one where he wasn't shrinking from the camera with a hand held up toward the lens. 'There,' she said and handed her phone to Rodriguez. 'Dan's fifteen. The boy you're looking for is definitely older.'

The detective squinted down at the colour picture. 'You're certain the shooter is Caucasian?'

'He was almost as close to me as you are now.'

'I guess we should take a copy of this.'

'Absolutely you should – I can Bluetooth it to you. Do you want it on your phone or computer?'

'You can do *what* with it?' The almost-retired policeman leaned forward in his seat, his hand rubbing the back of his neck.

'It's OK, Stan – I got this covered.'

'Got to keep up with technology or you'll get left behind,' Jean said. 'You want to think about that in your retirement. Might keep you occupied.'

The sergeant bristled. 'Hey – I'm not ready for the golf course yet. The NYPD may be kicking me out, but I got a new job to go to Monday morning.' He grabbed the edge of the desk and Jean noticed the muscles rippling in his tanned forearms.

'Good for you,' she said. 'Life in the old dog yet, eh?'

His colleague tapped some keys on her computer, looking embarrassed.

'You will circulate the photo? Put out an…' Jean hesitated for a moment, trying to remember the terminology she'd heard on countless American television shows. 'An APB – that's it, isn't it?'

'I need to speak to Lieutenant Riley about it first.' Rodriguez threw the sergeant another look.

'You do believe me?' Jean said.

There was a long moment of silence before the policewoman answered. 'Of course, ma'am. Why shouldn't I?'

Jean wasn't convinced. 'Plain as day, I saw him.'

'You were involved in a highly stressful situation,' the sergeant said in a low, soothing tone. 'It's easy to get a little confused in the circumstances.'

'I know what I saw.'

'Sergeant Rozello's right. No one knows how they're going to react. It's easy to remember things a little differently after the event. You probably need to get some rest.'

'I don't believe what I'm hearing.'

'We should wrap this up now and let you get to your son's apartment.' The detective shuffled some paperwork on her desk. 'We just need to complete a little housekeeping before I can let you go.'

'Let me go? You make it sound as if I'm in custody.'

'Figure of speech,' the sergeant said.

'Can I see your passport?'

The whole of Jean's upper body twitched suddenly. She wriggled in her seat, hoping neither detective had noticed. 'Passport?'

'Yes, ma'am, and your son's address, to complete my records.'

'I don't have my passport with me.' The lie was out before she had time to properly think through the consequences.

Both detectives glanced toward her large suitcase then at the bag she was clutching on her lap.

'Maybe you should check your purse,' the sergeant said gently.

'I'm not senile! I do know what's in my own handbag.'

The young detective raised an eyebrow and stared at her partner. Jean hung on to her bag even more tightly.

'I must have lost it.'

# 6

Jean stood on the sidewalk and looked up at the drab four-storey building in the middle of a terrace of equally dilapidated houses and let out a disappointed sigh. Simon had given her the impression he was quite a high-flyer on Wall Street. If this was all a six-figure salary could buy him in Manhattan, it was no wonder he and Cindy were planning to look for a house in the suburbs after the baby was born.

She struggled up the front steps and reached the top of the stoop just as a man dressed in a smart suit pulled open the door. They danced clumsily around one another for a moment before he ducked to one side and Jean bumped her suitcase over the threshold.

Once inside she gazed at the narrow staircase leading up to the second floor and exhaled another sigh. Now she understood what Simon had meant by a Manhattan 'walk-up'. She heaved her suitcase onto the first step and, banging each stair as she went, dragged it and herself to the next landing. She stopped and leaned against the wall in an effort to get her breath back, the effects of the jetlag gathering in her aching limbs. She shuffled to the next flight and wondered how Cindy would manage with a newborn and a stroller. It was hard to imagine how her daughter-in-law was coping now, nine months gone and counting.

Finally she reached her son's apartment and banged on the door. After hearing no movement from within, she banged again and shouted, 'Hello, Cindy love. It's only me.' She pressed an ear against the wood and listened again. Nothing stirred. She thumped the door a third time and tried shouting a little louder.

A door behind her creaked open.

'What's with the hollering?'

Jean turned to see a woman in her eighties, at least, dressed entirely in grey, slouching in the opposite doorway. 'Hello,' Jean said, 'I'm sorry if I disturbed you. I'm trying to get—'

'Your name Henderson?'

Jean stepped back, immediately suspicious, her breath catching in her throat. Since the passport incident in the police station, she fully expected every American she met to report her to the authorities. One false move and she'd be on the next plane home. 'It is. Why?' she finally managed, aiming for a nonchalant, casual tone.

The woman thrust a padded envelope into her hands, mumbled something about leaving a pan of milk on the stove, and retreated back into her apartment.

'Nice to meet you too.' Jean reached into the packet and pulled out a set of keys attached to a beer opener key fob. It had to be Simon's. She peered into the envelope expecting to see a note. It was empty. Then she remembered her daughter's text message. What *was* Simon playing at?

After a frustrating five minutes trying all three keys in various combinations in the many locks on the door, Jean heard a satisfying clunk as the final bolt yielded. 'Hello? Anyone home?' she said, not really anticipating a reply. It was possible Simon had left the keys with his neighbour to save Cindy being disturbed. Unlikely, though, given her son's track record on thoughtfulness.

Dragging her suitcase inside, she glanced down the narrow interior hallway toward a door at the other end, a vertical sliver of light shining like a beacon in the gloom. She closed the apartment door quietly behind her, edged down the cramped hallway, and stepped into the living room, blinking rapidly as her eyes adjusted to the sudden light.

Sunshine flooded through a large undressed window, illuminating a vibrating shaft of dust motes. A beaten-up leather couch took pride of place in the centre of the room, a purple and blue batik throw hung over one arm and spilled onto the floor. Cushions had been arranged in a curve across the wide wooden floorboards, like an archipelago of islands stretching from the couch to the adjacent wall, discarded newspapers and magazines scattered in between. Jean supposed Cindy was finding it difficult to get comfortable. She scanned the rest of the room. A collection of dirty plates and cups sat on a narrow table beneath the window, which explained the distant aroma of soy sauce and garlic. She turned on her heels and checked the kitchen and bathroom, both untidy, both unoccupied. The next door along the hallway was shut. She tapped lightly on it. 'Cindy? Are you there, love?' She turned the handle and edged open the door. A tangled sheet lay across the small double bed, a pile of Simon's clothes on the floor beside it.

She pushed open the final door leading off the hall, not hopeful she'd find her daughter-in-law within. Sure enough, apart from a bright lemon crib and the painted wooden mobile suspended above it, the room was empty.

Jean sucked in and let out a slow breath. She told herself there was nothing to worry about. Cindy had probably just popped out for something. Perhaps she was attending an anti-natal class. Though Jean might have expected her to have stayed in the apartment to wait for her arrival. Or at least left a note. Unless she'd been forced to leave in a hurry. Perhaps Cindy was at the nearest hospital giving birth.

Someone would have called. Surely.

Remembering the messages on her phone, Jean rooted around in her bag for it as she returned to the living room. She shifted the bags contents from side to side, then tipped the lot onto the couch and hurriedly sifted through the pile.

No phone.

She stared in disbelief at the heap of useless items, struggling to recall where she'd used the phone last. Then she spotted her passport poking out at the bottom of the pile. Now she thought about it, she couldn't actually remember retrieving the phone from the detective's desk.

An unexpected sob escaped from her mouth, then another. The feelings she'd only just managed to keep in check at the police station erupted suddenly as one sob followed straight on from the last without space in between for breath. Her tears were falling faster than she could wipe them away. She leaned forward and struggled to gulp down air. After a few moments, the light-headedness began to recede and she lifted her head and scanned the room, looking for Simon's home phone. She finally spotted it hidden behind the pile of unwashed crockery on the table. She forced herself to her feet and crossed the room, cursing as she tripped over the edge of the throw. Then she noticed something that hadn't registered before. Propped up against the phone was a used envelope, a note scribbled on the back of it. She snatched it from the table and held it at arm's length, trying hard to focus, wiping the remaining tears from her eyes with the back of her hand. Simon's spidery handwriting hadn't improved since primary school.

*Mum*

*Tried calling to stop you having a wasted trip, but got your voicemail. Apologies for garbled message – just delete it. I was talking nonsense. Can you get your ticket changed? You should go home just as soon as you can. Cindy's gone to have the baby at her folks' place. Won't be back for a couple of weeks. Maybe longer.*

Jean read the last line again. *Folks*? Cindy never spoke about her family. In fact she was so reluctant to reveal any information about them, Jean had assumed the girl was an orphan.

*Really sorry you've come all this way for nothing. I have to leave town for a while (emergency at work) so I probably won't get a chance to see you before you go home. There's no need to worry – Cindy and the bump are just fine. Honestly.*

In Jean's experience, as soon as Simon started using words like *honestly*, *truly* or *truthfully* there was absolutely no doubt he was lying. She could imagine him crossing his fingers as he wrote.

What *was* he playing at? She grabbed his home phone and closed her eyes, hoping his long cell phone number would come back to her. She tapped a string of digits into the keypad and held her breath. The call was transferred immediately to voicemail. She left him a terse message after the bleep and hung up. Then she closed her eyes again and tried to conjure Cindy's number. But hard as she tried she couldn't get beyond the first three digits. She wasn't entirely sure she'd ever committed the number to memory.

There was nothing else to do. She would just have to return to the police station and rescue her phone.

She collapsed onto the couch. Exhaustion had crept into her arms and legs, leaving them leaden. She was still clutching Simon's note in her fist. She flipped over the envelope to discover more writing on the other side. Barely able to keep her eyes open, she read the remaining lines.

*Don't leave the apartment, not until the cab comes to pick you up for the airport. And whatever you do,* DO NOT ANSWER THE DOOR.

# 7

Detective Luisa Rodriguez watched Stanley Rozello slurp the final strand of spaghetti into his mouth, leaving a trail of tomato sauce snaking up his chin.

'Good?' she said.

Stanley pulled the red and white checked napkin from his collar, delicately dabbed the corners of his mouth and leaned back in his chair looking satisfied.

And tired.

It was the first time Luisa had seen him look this wrecked at the end of a shift. But then this was no ordinary day. Forty-one years on the force. She wasn't sure how Stanley would cope with life as a civilian. He was pretty much institutionalised.

'How about another glass of wine?' She waved the empty bottle at the owner of the restaurant, who was standing behind the bar wiping down the counter, one eye on the final few minutes of a ball game playing on a TV suspended from the ceiling. The half dozen remaining members of Stanley's party had drifted from the long, unbussed table to the bar, and were drinking beers with bourbon chasers.

'I've had enough booze for one day,' Stanley said and let out a surreptitious belch from the corner of his mouth. 'Unlike my former colleagues.' He nodded to the rowdy gang throwing back their heads and slamming shot glasses onto the bar. 'I guess they need to let off a little steam. They were telling me the medical examiner practically had to scrape the store clerk's stomach from the floor.'

Luisa pushed away the remains of her cannelloni and only just managed to suppress a reflux squirt of acid that was on its way up into her mouth.

'What about you, Lu? When are you going to let your hair down?'

'Me? I'm fine.' She had to look away. All night she'd been waiting for the opportunity to talk to Stanley privately, away from the station house and the flapping ears of the detective squad. Now she finally had the chance, she'd lost her nerve.

'If you don't mind me saying, you don't look fine.' Stanley squeezed her hand in his, the warm calloused palm pressing against her knuckles.

'I've got some stuff I need to work through. Maybe you could give me some advice.'

'Me? Sure – if you think there's anything I know that you don't – fire away.'

Luisa took a deep breath. 'I don't know where to start.' She exhaled.

'Jesus, Lu, you're worrying me now – what is it?' He wrinkled his forehead, the horizontal lines forming deep grooves in the flesh.

'I can't believe I'm doing this – getting heavy on your last day. Let's forget about it, huh?'

'You haven't even told me what I'm supposed to be forgetting.'

Luisa picked up the empty bottle and started to scrape the corner of the label with a fingernail.

'Hey! How about some dessert, Sergeant Rozello?' the owner shouted from behind the bar. 'I have some fresh baked apple pie.' He slung a dishtowel over his shoulder and started cleaning his ear with a corner of it.

Stanley patted his flat stomach with both hands. 'Not for me, Tony – I've eaten too much chocolate cake.'

'Please yourself.'

Stanley leaned in close to her. 'Now, are you going to tell me what the hell is going on with you?'

'It can wait.'

The ball game ended and the proprietor switched channels. The tanned face of a middle-aged man filled the screen. Desperate to deflect Stanley's attention from her, Luisa pointed up at the TV. 'Look at that bastard! Like butter wouldn't melt.' Chuck Conner's dazzling white smile was almost mesmerising. 'Doesn't matter how good he is at his job, nobody's worth nineteen million dollars.'

'Hey, come on, Tony,' Stanley hollered. 'I'm meant to be celebrating my retirement here – I don't want to bring my meatballs back up. Get rid of that guy's ugly mug, will you?'

The restaurant owner shrugged and flipped through a half dozen channels before settling on some noisy game show.

Stanley lowered his voice. 'What were you going to ask me?'

'It doesn't matter.' She looked away.

'But I want to help.'

She screwed up her face and shook her head. 'It's just a stupid work thing – you've left all that behind you.' She clinked her empty glass against his. 'Here's to a healthy and happy retirement.'

Stanley's mouth curled into a sad smile. 'Sure.' He half-heartedly lifted his glass in the air.

'What did I say?'

He closed his eyes.

'Stan?'

'Jeez – I don't know. For years I dreamed of buying a little cabin in the Catskills for when I retired. Maria and me living up there for a few months every summer. Me fishing. Her baking.'

'Fishing?'

'Maybe a little hunting. Something.' He rubbed his eyes. 'Maria sure could bake a mean focaccia.'

Luisa couldn't remember the last time Stanley had mentioned his late wife. Maria had died a couple of years after Luisa joined the squad at the $4^{th}$. Stanley never spoke about the accident. Lu raised the subject a few months after the funeral and quickly learned never to bring it up again. She rested a hand on his wide back, gently tracing a circle, when really she wanted to throw her arms around his neck and tell him she understood. But she didn't understand, not really. 'It's a big thing you're doing today,' she said. 'It's only natural to be thinking about the past. About what might have been.' She bit her lip. Five years she'd known him and that was the best she could do?

'Would you listen to me?' He nudged her with his elbow. 'Hunting? I never shot a damn thing in my life. Not even a perp.' He managed a smile and Luisa smiled back. 'You want another glass?' he asked her.

'I should be getting back.' She pushed out her chair. 'Wanna share a cab?'

Before Stanley could answer, the door swung open on the other side of the restaurant.

'Hey hey heaayyyy! Where's my favourite cop in the whole world?'

Luisa would have recognised that voice anywhere. She turned to see Dolores O'Brien careening toward their table in heels so high a woman half her age would think twice before strapping them to her feet. Luisa couldn't help but marvel at the woman's determined hold on gravity. She was wearing a moth-eaten fur coat, a skimpy dress lurking beneath.

'Stanley Rozello – it's the moment you've been waiting for all day! I got your retirement present right here – don't tell me you're not pissing your pants with excitement.' She reared up when she finally registered Luisa standing by the table. 'Oh – *you're* still here.'

'Hey, Dolores – it's been a while.'

The woman ignored her outstretched hand and made a beeline for Stanley. She threw her arms around him and landed a wet kiss on his lips before he had a chance to offer his cheek. He wiped his mouth with the back of a wrist as soon as she pulled away, and managed to smear her cherry red lipstick halfway across his face. He glanced toward Luisa with a look of naked terror in his eyes.

'Betcha can't guess what it is,' Dolores said, shaking a small cube wrapped in gold paper.

Stanley held up both hands, as if he was surrendering to a superior opponent. Which was pretty much what Dolores was. 'That's so thoughtful of you, Dee. How did you even know I was here?'

'Let's just say a little bird told me.' She flashed a wink at the owner who was busy trying to hide himself behind the bar. Dolores had a regular menagerie of little birds spread right across the city. There was no other way to explain how she kept popping up at inappropriate moments, catching Stanley off guard. 'Besides, you been coming here after work for centuries now. Wouldn't take a detective to work it out.'

Stanley gazed cross-eyed at the small golden box Dolores was holding under his nose.

'Why don't I take it home and open it later?'

Dolores slapped his arm with her free hand. 'Now, now, Stanley – are you suggesting I go home with you? And you haven't even bought me a drink yet? What kind of girl do you think I am?'

Stanley knew exactly what kind, but was always too polite to tell her. Luisa stared at the sixty-year-old divorcee as the woman spun on her high heels, demanding Stanley tell her just how gorgeous she looked in her new dress. It was less a dress and more a strip of aluminum foil barely covering an over-cooked turkey.

Dolores completed her spin, staggered a step then pressed the gift at Stanley and ordered him to open it. He looked down at the package as if it was giving off a noxious smell. He shook it.

'Come on, Stan – open it,' the restaurant owner hollered from the safety of the bar.

Stanley lifted it to his ear. 'It's ticking.'

'Of course it's ticking, for crying out loud; it's a gold watch, goddammit. What else is it gonna do?'

Stanley's second retirement wristwatch of the day. Luisa nudged his arm. 'Hey, Stan – at least you got two arms.'

'What's that supposed to mean?' Dolores swivelled on her heels and pointed a long-nailed finger in Luisa's face.

'Nothing,' Stanley said quickly. 'Nothing at all.' He shot Luisa a look, ripped off the gift-wrap, opened the velvet box and quickly slipped the slim dress watch onto his right wrist. 'It's beautiful, Dolores – it's really… ah… golden.'

'It should be beautiful – what it cost me. But that doesn't matter, just as long as you like it. Come here – give me a kiss, you sexy S-O-B.'

Stanley quickly turned his head and snatched a breath, the way he had hours earlier when he'd been assaulted by the stripper.

He looked like a drowning man going down for the third time.

# 8

Linus pushed a hand into the small of his back and felt the hard metal of the gun press into his flesh. Instantly an intense thrill spread through his veins. He had the gun. He had a mission. And no one could stop him.

When Richie had reluctantly handed over the gun and Linus weighed it in both hands, the surge of excitement that rocked through his body felt as though it might explode out of the top of his head. Exactly the same feeling he'd had in the grocery store. He felt as if he'd been sleepwalking his whole life, only waking up the moment he first pulled the trigger.

He stood at the intersection of Lafayette and Houston and looked east, scanning as many of the faces on his side of the street as he could, looking for the old lady. He wondered if he should aim for her head or her chest. A bigger target would be easier, but a bullet to the brain would be deadlier.

He'd been searching the streets of the East Village and the Lower East Side for hours, even straying close to the projects near the river a couple of times. Richie's neighbourhood. As he waited for the lights to change he wondered what Richie was doing right now and who he was doing it with. He thought about calling him, maybe suggest they score some more meth, hang out for a while. Talk a little. He felt an urgent need to discuss the robbery, rerun it beat by beat. Talk about what it felt like to watch the bullets slam into the clerk's body. How they could do it better next time. But then he knew exactly what Richie would say: 'Not take our masks off.' He couldn't hang out until he'd whacked the old lady.

The lights changed and he let the surge of movement carry him across the road, keeping his eyes trained on the faces of the people coming the other way.

It was properly dark now. He wasn't even sure if old ladies came out at night. At this time in the evening his own grandmother would probably be playing bridge with her cronies, taking a cab all the way to a friend's house and another all the way back. He'd be surprised if she dirtied her feet on the sidewalk at all.

Houston was busy, tired pedestrians walked with their heads down, their mouths mostly pulled into scowls, foreheads pinched into deep grooves. All of them looking as if they wanted the day to be over so they could begin again tomorrow. As if tomorrow would be any different for them than today.

Losers.

Linus didn't want the day to end. He wanted to stay out all night, riding on this electric feeling for as long as he could.

His cell squawked from his pocket. He reached in for it and his hand hit the bullets he'd persuaded Richie to give him. Not nearly enough to have fun, but plenty to do some real damage. He pulled out his phone and glanced at the screen, hoping it might be Richie, but instead discovered his mother was calling. He stared down at the phone, squeezing it hard in his hand, wondering what mood she would be in. Whether it was needy mom or angry mom on the other end. He didn't want to speak to either, but ignoring the call would only cause more trouble. He stabbed the call answer key, lifted the phone to his ear and said nothing.

'Honey, are you there?'

Linus curled his lip.

'Linus, honey, answer me.'

'Hey.'

'Where are you?'

'Out.'

'Clearly. What are you doing? I was expecting you for supper. You promised me. We need to sit down, you and I, and have a proper conversation about college. We need to make some plans. I can't watch you just fritter your life away.'

'Later.'

'I've been thinking about contacting a few of your old tutors, perhaps we could arrange for some intensive study, get you through your S-A-Ts?'

'I don't need to go to college.'

'Of course you do. Who was that sweet history teacher of yours? I may still have his number somewhere. He always said such positive things about your work.'

'No way.' Linus had managed not to think about Mr Redmond for years. Why did she have to rake all that up? He yanked the gun from his waistband and shoved it in the front pocket of his hoodie.

'Why don't I give him a call?'

'I said no!' His index finger felt for the trigger.

'OK! Someone else then. Just get back home so we can talk about it.'

Linus let out a noisy breath. The euphoria he'd felt only moments before was leaking out of him as surely as if someone had knocked a hole in the top of his head with a hammer and nail. He saw black dots before his eyes. 'I'm busy,' he said, his voice suddenly sounding like it had never broken.

'Don't be ridiculous. Whatever you're doing can wait. This can't.'

'But I've got to… do something. Something important.'

'This is more important. Your father and I think—'

'You've spoken to dad?'

'It does happen occasionally.'

'What's it got to do with him?'

'For God's sake, Linus, like it or not, he's still your father.'

'Unfortunately.'

'Stop behaving like a child and come home. Now. Unless you want me to reduce your allowance again. To zero.'

She hung up.

Needy mom *and* angry mom, all in the space of a few seconds. That had to be some kind of record. He shoved his phone back into a pocket and stopped at the lights on the corner and turned his head to look up First Avenue. He had skirted this end of First all day, ducking down the cross streets, figuring the area would be swarming with cops, just waiting for him. Hadn't he read somewhere that murderers return to the scene of the crime to relive the experience? He did feel drawn to it suddenly. Surely the cops would have disappeared by now? Maybe the owners had even reopened the store. He started walking north. The old lady might be there right now.

He picked up his pace. Eager to finish what he'd started.

# 9

By the time she woke up, the apartment was dark except for dull electric light filtering in from the street. Jean pulled her damp cheek from the saliva-soaked cushion and sat up slowly, struggling to reorient herself in the unfamiliar surroundings. Her neck and back were stiff and her right foot had gone completely numb. She shook it at the ankle and pulled a crumpled piece of paper from under her thigh. Simon's note. She could just make out the capital letters scrawled on one side: *DON'T LEAVE THE APARTMENT.* Then she remembered her phone languishing on the detective's desk at the police station. That was assuming it hadn't already gone walkabouts. She had to get down there. She rose quickly and immediately regretted it. The combination of her bad knee and dead foot forced her back down, and she cursed her carelessness with the phone all over again.

After a quick change of clothes, and another unsuccessful attempt to reach Simon, Jean left the apartment and stood at the bottom of the stone stoop searching 2nd Street for a cab. No bright yellow vehicle approached from either direction, so she stepped onto the sidewalk and headed for First Avenue, supposing she'd have more luck there. She reminded herself with every step that New York was at least as safe as London. She regularly ventured out after dark at home without a second thought.

But then in London she'd never witnessed a fatal shooting at the cornershop. Despite the oppressive heat and the thickness of the air, a shiver ran up the back of her calves as her muscles tensed. She felt a sudden urge to whistle. Perhaps a happy tune in the vein of Deborah Kerr in *The King and I* would help. She resisted puckering up, but nevertheless couldn't shake the melody from her head as she made her way to the corner.

First Avenue was much busier than the little side street and she immediately felt safer. She spotted a cab at the next set of lights and started waving at it. She stepped into the road as it approached, only to narrowly miss being run down as it accelerated past her. She scooted back onto the sidewalk and carried on in the direction of the main street.

She reached the hustle and bustle of Houston without seeing another cab and immediately got caught up in the jet stream of New Yorkers pushing relentlessly in both directions. Before she'd left the apartment, Jean had checked on her mini Manhattan atlas. It was six blocks from the intersection of Houston and First Avenue to the station house at the northern end of Elizabeth Street. In the relative comfort of Simon's apartment, six blocks seemed no distance at all, but right now, being bumped and jostled in the middle of the sidewalk, six blocks felt like a lunar expedition.

Sweat was dribbling between her breasts and her hair clung determinedly to the nape of her neck. August in Manhattan. Why couldn't Cindy and Simon have planned for a spring baby? She let out a weary sigh as she waited to cross the street. In all likelihood they hadn't planned for a baby at all. And where was Cindy now? With her *folks*? Jean needed to speak to that girl. The sooner she laid hands on her phone, the faster she could solve the mystery. Despite the sharp pain in her knee, when the lights changed she sprang into action and hurried across the road.

She'd only managed to advance a few yards further west when a motorcycle carrying two riders roared to a stop and mounted the kerb in front of her. Jean's heart lurched and a gasp escaped her mouth as the helmeted figure at the back dismounted. Not for a moment had it occurred to her that the boy with the gun might live locally. Her mouth fell open as the leather-clad figure approached. Jean's feet were stuck fast to the pavement. Breathless, she watched the helmet lift to reveal the drawn, tear-streaked face of a woman.

A woman. Thank God. Jean exhaled and scanned the faces of people nearby, belatedly searching for a boy resembling her grandson.

The other figure on the bike snapped up his visor and called after his passenger. 'Come on, baby! Don't get all uptight. You know I didn't mean it.'

The scrawny woman waved a middle finger at him and held her head high, barely avoiding Jean as she weaved along the street, swaying dangerously from side to side on four-inch stilettos.

'Are you all right, love?' Jean asked. The woman ignored her and staggered away, turning an ankle every few steps.

The man jumped off the bike and hollered at her again. 'Baby – don't be mad at me.'

The skinny woman stopped abruptly and turned back. 'You can't treat me like that,' she said, a sob escaping from her mouth. 'I ain't your whore!' she screamed.

'I never said you were.' He started to run after her.

'Stay away from me!'

Without pausing to consider the consequences, Jean stuck out a leg. The hollering man tripped over it, staggered awkwardly for a couple of steps, then fell heavily onto the sidewalk.

'What the…?'

Jean smiled down at him, but he didn't see her; he was too busy staring at his retreating girlfriend. 'Hey, baby!' he said. 'Come back here. I need you.'

The woman turned, saw him sprawled on the pavement and in a flash pulled off her shoes and ran back to him. She helped him to his feet.

'You know I love you, don't you, baby?' He wrapped his arms around her bony shoulders.

'I love you too.'

'Well that's gratitude for you,' Jean said. They both ignored her. To her horror, she seemed to have precipitated a reconciliation, the couple quickly shoving their tongues down each other's throats. Not the outcome Jean had intended at all. She leaned in close to their conjoined heads. 'Get. A. Room.' Again, they took no notice. 'Young love, eh?' she said, but none of the small crowd that had gathered to watch the spectacle shared a smile with her. 'I say – love's young dream!' Jean searched the blank faces as one by one the gathering dispersed. She wondered if this was the way it was going to be for her from now on: transparent and inaudible. Getting older had never bothered her, she actually quite enjoyed the licence it gave her to behave badly and get more of her own way, but this new invisibility thing was becoming tiresome. No one had paid her any attention since the moment she'd arrived. A shiver spread across her shoulders as she remembered the one person who had noticed her. And he could be just yards away from where she was standing right now. She quickly checked the surrounding faces, her heart rate quickening, the memory of the gun pointing at her chest still fresh in her mind. Perhaps the shooter wouldn't recognise her again. He had looked at her for the briefest of moments. How much detail could he have taken in? She shook off another shiver before it ran down her arms and decided to press on.

Banged and buffeted, she continued along Houston toward Elizabeth Street, peering over her shoulder now and then to look for an approaching taxi. A block or so ahead she noticed pedestrians ducking around an obstacle on the sidewalk. As she drew closer she saw what was causing the diversion.

A picnic blanket had been spread across the middle of the pavement, a woman sitting at its centre hugging her knees. She must have been in her late twenties, maybe even early thirties, her hair plaited in uneven bunches, her face tanned and grimy, grubby hands wrapped around an open book. A small cardboard sign sat on the blanket next to an upturned trilby, which was empty.

*NEEDED: Beer, cigarettes, Tampax.*
*All donations gratefully received.*

'I'm sorry, my love,' Jean said. 'I can't help you with any of those.' She smiled at her, but didn't really expect the woman to take her eyes from the pages of her George Orwell. 'Gave up all three quite a while back.' She glanced around at the passers-by who, though they were carefully navigating around the edge of the picnic blanket, seemed to be ignoring the woman as studiously as they were disregarding Jean. She felt a sudden affinity for the well-read beggar.

A shout went up a little way down the street. Jean looked up to see a handful of men and women smoking outside a busy bar, one of them waving his arms around. His friends started laughing at him. Just inside the bar, behind floor to ceiling windows that had been flung wide, well dressed patrons crowded round high metal tables. She glanced back at the beggar with her ragged tee shirt and threadbare jeans. Just like London – the haves and the have-nots both existing cheek by jowl.

Jean wandered to the nearest table covered with bottles of beer, expensive cocktails and packs of cigarettes. She glanced back at the beggar, at the empty trilby and the frayed edges of the blanket.

Without giving herself time to change her mind, Jean quickly reached up for a pristine pack of cigarettes seemingly abandoned in the middle of the table. Just as her fingers brushed the edge of the cellophane, one of the noisy beer drinkers snatched the pack in his fist and tore off the wrapping. Jean withdrew her trembling hand, wondering what had come over her. She'd never stolen so much as a bar of chocolate her whole life. What did she think she was doing? A waitress appeared at the table, delivering fresh drinks and removing empty bottles. The man holding the cigarettes thrust a twenty-dollar bill at her without looking, then pulled it away again, whispered something in her ear and pushed the bill into the front of her blouse. Impressively, the waitress managed to convert her grimace into a smile before she withdrew. The man flung the cigarettes back onto the table and high-fived his nearest companion.

Convincing herself what she was about to do was closer to sharing than stealing, Jean slid the pack of Marlboros from the sticky beer-stained table and slipped it into a pocket. She held her breath and brazenly stared at the owner of the cigarettes, willing him to look at her.

He didn't.

*Might as well be hanged for a sheep as a lamb.*

She reached up to the table again and relieved another customer of a full bottle of Budweiser. She glanced at each of the group in turn – no flicker of a reaction from any of them. She stood perfectly still for a moment, just waiting for the batting of an eyelid, the twitch of a cheek muscle.

Nothing.

She scurried back to the woman on the blanket and threw the pack of cigarettes into the trilby. The woman didn't stir, so Jean bent down and tugged at her ragged sleeve. Finally the woman wrenched her gaze from the book and looked straight into Jean's eyes.

'I can't help with feminine hygiene arrangements, I'm afraid,' Jean said. 'But have a beer and a smoke on me.' Jean handed over the bottle and glanced back toward the bar. 'I didn't think to get matches.'

'I got matches. Thanks – 'preciate it,' the woman said. 'Wanna, like, share it with me?' She wrapped the bottle in a crumpled plastic bag and waved it in Jean's face.

'Share?' Jean dipped into her handbag, pulled out a few dollar bills from an inside pocket and dropped them in the hat. 'No, love – it's all yours. Enjoy it.'

The woman shrugged, took a sip of beer, thanked Jean again then went back to her book.

When Jean passed the bar again, a heated argument had broken out. Someone shouted something about stolen cigarettes and a flailing elbow knocked a bottle from the table. Jean quickened her pace and didn't look back.

After enduring another ten minutes of struggling against the never ceasing tide of bodies, Jean reached the corner of Elizabeth Street. She crossed the road, toward the smell of garlic bread. She hadn't noticed the Italian restaurant next door to the station house on her earlier visit, eating hadn't been a top priority at the time, but now her stomach started to growl. She'd had nothing since the tray of plastic food on the flight over. The growling grew more insistent. Just as she drew level with the door of the little trattoria, someone backed out onto the street.

'Watch it!' Jean shouted and ducked nimbly to one side, only just avoiding getting her toes crushed by a pair of highly polished size twelves.

The man turned quickly, spreading his arms wide. Then his face broke into a rapturous smile.

'Sergeant Rozello!' Jean smiled back at him, relieved to see a friendly face.

'Hey, what happened to you?'

She lifted a hand to her sweat-soaked hair and glanced down at her dirty linen pants. She had the look of a bag lady. 'I… I don't really—'

'Are you OK?' The female detective stepped from behind Stanley Rozello and supported Jean with a firm grip.

'I'm perfectly fine. There's no need to fuss.' Jean extricated her arm and pointed toward the station house next door. 'I left my phone here – it's on your desk, I expect.'

'I'll go get it for you.' Detective Rodriguez bounded up the stairs to the main entrance.

The sergeant held out his arm. Jean gratefully leaned her weight against him, her earlier exhaustion engulfing her once again like a heavy blanket. He felt solid and reassuring. She was surprised how comforted she was by his touch.

A high-pitched shriek erupted from the doorway of the restaurant.

'Hey, Stanley! Aren't you going to introduce me to your *lady*-friend?' A woman dressed in a scabby fur coat and high heels dodged around the ex-policeman and extended her hand.

The merest flicker of a grimace passed over Stanley Rozello's face, as if he'd only just remembered the woman was with him.

'I'm Dolores O'Brien – one of Stanley's dearest and closest friends,' she said, her gaze running up and down Jean unapologetically.

Jean narrowed her eyes. 'Jean Henderson, nice to meet you.' She stood up straight and thrust her bosom toward the unnatural redhead.

'Charmed, I'm sure.' The woman's lips curled at the corners like drying ham neglected at a picnic. 'You're English? How quaint.'

'Is it?' Jean found herself wondering what a nice man like Stanley Rozello was doing with a woman like this. She felt a twinge of something that could only be described as jealousy. Which was ridiculous, she'd only met him a few hours ago.

'Sure it is. I love that accent. Though I could tell where you came from before you said a word.'

'Is that right?'

The woman nodded. 'Tell me, I've wondered about this,' she said. 'I watch a lot of BBC America… What is it with you Brits and dentists? Don't you have anyone properly qualified looking after your teeth?'

# 10

The noise was as insistent as it was annoying. It took Jean a few moments to recognise the source of the sound. She flung out an arm and grappled for her phone on the bedside table. Through half-opened eyes she stabbed the call answer key, but the noise didn't let up. Only then did she realise the irritating chirrup was the alarm she'd set the night before. Finally locating the right button she switched it off and exhaled a disappointed breath. She sat up and dialled Simon's number, the call diverting to voicemail, just as it had the night before. She left a short message and tried Cindy with the same result. Then she listened again to the incoherent message her son had left the day before, imploring her to turn back if it wasn't too late. His voice sounded thick and congested, as if he had a blocked nose.

As if he'd been crying.

She puffed out another breath and swung her legs onto the floor, spotting her open suitcase in the corner of the room, the once neatly folded clothes now tangled and creased where she'd rifled through them in search of her toilet bag and pyjamas. She decided unpacking could wait just a little longer, and retrieved the laptop she'd discovered the night before, jammed between the mattress and the bed frame.

She carried the computer into the kitchen and fired it up. While she waited for the icons to appear on the screen, she wrestled with the unfathomable workings of Simon's coffee machine. She gave up and filled a kettle, hoping to find a teabag lurking in a cupboard somewhere.

The laptop came to life faster than the kettle boiled, so she delayed tea in favour of rattling off a non-committal email to her daughter back in London. She didn't want to call her – Caroline would doubtless bombard her with questions about Simon and the baby that Jean wouldn't be able to answer.

She hesitated before looking at Simon's various mailboxes. He'd probably never forgive her if he found out she'd been looking at his private correspondence. But what else was she supposed to do when he wasn't answering his phone?

She searched all three mailboxes, entering a combination of search terms based on what he'd said in his phone message and note. But the words 'work', 'Fisher Krupps' and 'emergency' yielded no useful information. Neither did 'reservation', 'tickets' or 'receipt'. In desperation she selected 'New' from the menu bar and typed a second email, beginning by explaining who she was, why she was writing, and asking if anyone knew where Simon had taken himself off to. When she'd finished she hesitated again. This really was invading his privacy. But what if he was in trouble? She wondered if she should have had a quiet word with the detective about Simon's disappearance. Perhaps he could have suggested another way of contacting him. The cursor hovered a moment longer over the send button before she clicked it, sending the email to Simon's entire contact list.

After only a few seconds the in-box filled with a dozen or so replies. All of them 'address not recognised' automated responses. The laptop pinged again. Jean quickly opened the new mail.

*wtf Si? whrs my $$$?*

It seemed the sender, Lenny J, had fired off his response without reading Jean's message first. The email was signed at the bottom with the ubiquitous *Sent from my iPhone.* Jean didn't hold with that kind of boastfulness and for a few months last year drove the point home with a signature that announced her email had been *Sent from my 7-year-old Dell.*

She read Lenny P's short message again and wondered how much money Simon owed him. Could that be the reason for his unexpected departure?

The email alert pinged again.

*Ma'am, pls accept my apologies. Just read yr mail. No idea whr Simon is. Gd luck finding him. When you do, pls tell him to call me. Urgently*

She typed a quick reply and hit the *Send* button, staring at the screen, willing another incoming email to appear. After a long few moments of unblinking concentration she rubbed her eyes and got to her feet. She couldn't sit around all day in the hope someone might get in touch. She wandered over to the television and found the remote. After zapping through dozens of channels she came across a news programme that seemed local to New York. The weather report had just ended. She gingerly attempted a few gentle yoga stretches to unkink her back while she waited for the financial news to finish. The CEO of Simon's company flashed a perfect set of white teeth at the camera, explaining just how well he'd run the corporation in the last twelve months and was worth every penny of his nineteen million dollar bonus.

'*Nineteen*? Who needs that much money?' Jean said as she tried to touch the ground with her fingertips. A sharp pain stabbed at her knee, forcing her to stop stretching and collapse onto the nearest chair. On the screen the tanned face of the multi-millionaire executive was replaced by a street scene, the exterior of a grocery store. Jean stiffened.

*The* grocery store. A detective was standing in the middle of the sidewalk, his expression set in a rigid mask of grief. It wasn't a face she recognised from the day before. She listened to his version of the incident, nodding her agreement as he described the whole robbery, from the moment the two masked youths entered the store to their departure on the stolen motorcycle. The reporter asked him for a description of the two perpetrators. He went through height, weight, dress and approximate age, exactly as Jean had described them during her interview at the station house. Then the detective stared straight into the camera, as if he was looking directly at her, and confirmed that both the robbers were African Americans.

'What?'

The reporter appealed to viewers for information that might help the police with their inquiries, then handed over to the anchor in the studio. Jean felt like throwing something at the television. Had the two detectives just ignored what she'd said about the boy with the gun? She found her phone and had just located the female detective's number in her contacts list when a loud buzzing started up in the hallway, as if an angry swarm of bees was invading the apartment. Jean muted the volume on the television and listened. The noise stopped, then a moment later started up again. She padded out of the living room and walked the length of the hallway before she realised the entry buzzer mounted on the wall next to the apartment door was responsible for the racket. She lifted the ancient intercom receiver and held the grimy earpiece a couple of inches from her ear.

'Yes?' She heard a sucking breath at the other end and the distant echo of street noises.

'Oh,' a man's voice said. 'I'm sorry ma'am. I must have pressed the wrong buzzer.' He hung up and a second later the buzzer sounded again.

'It seems you pressed it right the first time,' Jean said.

'I'm looking for Sim-on Hend-er-son.' He broke up the syllables as if he was speaking to a child or a very old, very deaf person.

'I'm his mother.'

'His what?'

'It's not that peculiar – people do have them. Even Simon Hend-er-son.'

'I'm sorry. I just wasn't expecting—'

'Never mind. Who are you?'

'A uh… friend.'

'You don't sound too sure.'

'I work with your son. Is he—'

'You'd better come up.' Jean pressed the stiff plastic button on the intercom and opened the apartment door.

Loud thumps sounded on the wooden stairs as Simon's colleague bounded up the steep flights at a canter. It wasn't until a flushed-faced young man appeared at the other end of the landing that Jean remembered her son's instruction not to answer the door. She looked her visitor up and down, quickly taking in the pinstriped suit, starched collar and sombre tie. His shoes were polished to a military sheen.

Harmless enough. Wasn't he?

He stopped in his tracks. 'Ma'am, I'm sorry – I didn't realise I'd gotten you out of bed.'

Jean folded her arms across her pyjama top. 'You didn't.' She stepped to one side when he reached the door and directed the floppy-haired man down the hallway to the living room. As she closed the door behind her she searched frantically for some heavy or sharp object she could use to protect herself, but compared to the chaos in the rest of the apartment, the hall was remarkably tidy, and Jean was forced to join her visitor in the living room empty-handed.

'Sit down, if you're stopping,' she said and gestured to a low leather armchair. 'Is there some emergency at work?'

'Emergency? What makes you say that?' Awkwardly, he shifted forward in the chair, both hands gripping his knees.

'Just something my son said.'

'What did he say?' He looked around the room, his head jerking left and right. 'Where is he? Could you go get him? It's pretty urgent.' The man flicked his lank hair from his forehead.

'I'm surprised you didn't try phoning first.'

'I've been calling his cell non-stop for the past twenty-four hours.'

'And getting voicemail?'

'Yes. That's why I'm here – I really need to speak to him.'

'Join the queue.'

'Ma'am?'

'You'll have to get in line – he's not answering my calls either.'

'He's not here?' Simon's colleague struggled to get out of the chair.

'Stay exactly where you are.'

He wriggled to the edge of the seat and stopped.

'Who are you?' she asked.

'I work with your—'

'That much I've managed to glean, I'm supposing you have a name?'

Again his gaze darted about the room, like a cornered animal. 'Oliver,' he said after a long silence. 'Malcolm Oliver.'

'Well, Malcolm…' Jean let out a breath and relaxed onto the couch. 'Why don't you tell me what's so urgent you've come here looking for my son?'

'I just need to speak to him.'

'About?'

'Some business matters.'

Jean stared into the young man's face, studying his expression. 'Does Simon owe you money?'

His face seemed to contract, his upper body stiffened. 'He *told* you that?'

An increasingly familiar shiver passed across Jean's shoulders. She glanced down at her pyjama top, and noticed a couple of buttons were missing. Feeling suddenly exposed, she stood up. 'Don't move a muscle.' She wagged an admonishing finger at her guest.

Malcolm Oliver pushed a hand against the arm of the chair and glanced toward the door.

'You're going nowhere until you've told me everything.'

Jean hurried to the closet in the bedroom for a dressing gown of Cindy's she could borrow. She opened the narrow door and groped for a light switch. A dim naked bulb hanging from the ceiling flickered into life. She peered into the gloom, not quite believing what she saw.

On one side of the closet, hanging off a long metal rail, were a dozen or so ironed shirts still wrapped in dry cleaners' plastic. Just opposite the door was a shelving unit stuffed with jeans and sweatshirts. Attached to the wall on the other side of the shallow space were three more rails, stretching all the way from the door to the other end. Jean stepped inside and examined each rail more closely. Apart from a tie-die maternity dress hanging on its own in the middle of the top rail, this side of the closet was completely empty. If Cindy only planned to stay with her parents for a couple of weeks, why had she taken all her clothes?

Jean rushed back to the living room and found Oliver on his feet, straightening his jacket.

'I'm sorry, ma'am. I've got to be going. When he gets in touch, please tell Simon to contact me. It really is urgent.'

'How much?' Jean said, taking up position in the doorway to prevent Oliver's escape.

'Ma'am?'

'How much does he owe you?'

Malcolm Oliver looked at his feet and his hair dropped down across his forehead, partially obscuring his face. 'He doesn't owe *me* the money.'

'Then why are you—'

'We both owe… a business associate.' He let out a long sigh. 'Repayment is overdue.'

'What kind of business associate?'

'You don't need to know.'

'My son's gone God knows where and he's not answering his phone – don't you think I should decide what I need to know? What kind of business—'

'A moneylender.'

'A loan shark?'

He nodded.

'How much money do you owe?' Jean leaned a hand against the doorjamb and prepared herself for whatever he had to say.

'I can't… I mean I shouldn't…'

'I've got some savings tucked away. I could help.' She could feel her throat tightening. 'Whatever it takes for Simon to come home.'

'I can't tell you.'

Jean marched over to him, grabbed both his arms and squeezed hard. 'Tell me!'

He puffed out his cheeks. 'More than your savings account.'

'You don't know that.'

'Ma'am, all due respect, it's only natural you'd want to help, but no one has that kind of money in the bank.'

'For God's sake – just tell me!' She shook him as hard as she could.

'One hundred thousand dollars.'

# 11

The door of the station house shut behind her with a bang. Jean hurried down the steps and stopped on the sidewalk, unsure suddenly exactly where she was hurrying to. She snatched a breath, the words of the detective still ringing in her ears.

'Come back in a few days if they don't turn up,' was the only advice he'd given.

Initially Jean had asked to see Detective Rodriguez, but had been promptly informed Rodriguez was too busy dealing with an *important* investigation. As if her request for help was a dreadful waste of time. It seemed missing adults didn't warrant any investigation at all. Even if one of them was nine months pregnant.

Jean looked back up at the entrance and considered for a moment whether she should march straight back in and demand to see a senior officer. But before she started up the steps she heard someone calling her name. She peered in the direction of the voice, raising a hand to shield her eyes from the glare of the sun, and saw Stanley Rozello hurrying toward her. Her heart beat a little faster. Why was she feeling this pleased to see him? As if she had some teenage crush. She told herself to get a grip. She hardly knew the man.

'Forget something else?' he said.

She glowered back at him.

'What did I say?'

'I thought you'd retired.'

'I did. I'm a free man – 'til Monday.'

'Then what are you doing here?'

He pulled a baseball cap from his head and ran a hand over his brush of hair. 'I got a few personal items to collect.'

'Don't let me stop you. At least you won't be wasting their time.'

'I don't understand. What's happened?'

'You wouldn't be interested.'

'How about you try me?'

Ten minutes later Jean sat opposite the ex-cop in a diner on the other side of the street from the station house, waiting for his reaction after she'd described her frustrating interview with the disinterested detective.

'I hate to say it, but he was playing it pretty much by the book. Your son's a grown man,' Stanley said to her, tearing a narrow strip from a paper napkin he'd grabbed from the dispenser on the table. 'Besides which, he left you a note saying he was going away.'

'So?' Jean tried to catch the waitress's attention, but every time the girl passed the table she seemed to get a faraway look in her eyes. 'I still don't know where he is. He's still not answering his phone.'

'We got other priorities,' Stanley said.

'We?'

The former detective dropped his head. 'I mean the police department. Forty-one years on the job, it's gonna take a while for me to adjust.'

The knot of irritation in Jean's chest untangled a fraction. She didn't have to take it out on him. 'OK – but how do you explain Cindy's disappearing act?'

'I guess she feels more comfortable with her folks. If your son planned to go away, maybe she didn't want to be alone.'

'But she knew I was coming – she wouldn't have been alone. And anyway, Simon didn't plan anything. Don't you think he might have got in touch with me sooner if any of this was planned?'

'But he's not officially missing. What the officer told you was correct.'

'Why isn't he answering his phone?'

The ex-detective shrugged. 'Maybe the battery died. Or he lost it.'

'And Cindy? She's not picking up either.'

'Tell you what – why don't we spend a little time to think this through – maybe work out where he could have gotten to.'

'So you can fob me off just like your ex-colleague did?'

'Listen, I've found more runaways than you've had hot dinners – I betcha.'

'Yes, but how many of them were lying on a slab in the morgue when you did eventually discover them?' The thought set off a chilling tingle in the back of her legs. In an attempt to distract herself, she grabbed the huge laminated menu propped up against the sugar dispenser.

It seemed the diner provided all day breakfast, all day lunch and all day dinner, twenty-four hours a day. Jean supposed this close to a station house there was a steady supply of police officers willing to clog up their arteries. She wondered how many short-order cooks the diner got through in the space of a year. The waitress passed the table again, her shoulders slumped, chin resting on her chest.

'Hello, miss?' Stanley leaned into the aisle.

Still the waitress showed no sign of responding.

'It's not just me then,' Jean said after the girl had made it all the way back to the counter with not so much as a backward glance.

'Pardon me?' The retired policeman raised his bushy black eyebrows at her.

'Ever since I arrived I've felt as if I've melted into the background, no one seems to notice me. Looks like it's happening to you too.'

'I never heard anything so dumb.'

Stanley coughed loudly. 'Miss,' he hollered, 'we'd like to get some service here.'

The waitress shuffled to another table, managing a smile for the family who had just come through the door.

'Welcome to my world,' Jean said in a whisper.

Stanley Rozello shook his head.

'There's no point denying it. People saw the man and the badge before. You had an identity. Now you're insignificant. You've entered the ranks of seniors – the faceless old wrinklies. The grumpy old gits.' She smiled at him and he scowled back at her, mumbling some obscenity under his breath. 'Charming,' she said.

He got up and marched over to the waitress, tapped her on the shoulder, stood back and folded his arms. The waitress turned around and for a moment seemed at a loss.

'When you're ready, miss. We're sitting right over there by the window.'

The waitress's blank gaze eventually focused on him and she responded with a curt nod. 'I'll be right over, sir.'

Stanley strode back to his seat, head held high.

Jean pushed the menu away, the thought of food suddenly turning her stomach.

'What was I saying?' Stanley sat down.

'I think you were about to tell me where my son has "gotten to".'

'We just need to put our heads together, work it out.' He spread his hands on the tabletop and started to drum his fingers. 'You've contacted his friends?'

'Via email. So far the only response has been from someone he owes money to.'

'How much money?'

'I'm not sure.' During the recounting of her tale, Jean had left out the part about Malcolm Oliver's visit. 'But he's not the only one.'

Stanley's fingers stopped drumming. He clasped his hands and leaned forward. 'How many people we talking about?'

'At least two.' Should she mention Oliver? If Simon was in trouble, she wasn't sure she wanted the fact broadcast. She hadn't mentioned it to the detective at the police station. She looked into Stanley's eyes, registered the earnest expression on his face.

*In for a penny.*

'He and a colleague owe someone an awful lot – and they're late with the repayment.'

'How much?'

Jean hesitated. Could she trust this man?

'OK – so much you'd rather not tell me,' Stanley said. 'I'm guessing this someone is not your regular moneylender. We're not talking about a bank loan here. So – it's a loan shark maybe?'

Jean nodded and stared down at the chipped red laminate.

'Do you know what he needed the money for?'

'Simon's colleague wouldn't tell me.'

'You spoke to his colleague?'

She nodded again.

'Are we talking thousands?'

Another nod.

'Tens of thousands?'

Jean looked out of the window without answering and Stanley let out a low whistle.

'I'm guessing your son maybe doesn't want to be found.' He ran a hand over his head. 'If he's buried deep enough, no amount of searching is gonna dig him out.'

'But he could tell his own mother.'

'Why share that information when it could put you at risk?'

'Me? What do you think is going to happen? Someone'll break into the apartment and torture me?'

Stanley reached his hands toward hers and stopped halfway. 'I'm not saying that, not exactly.'

'You can't be serious.'

'It all depends on the kind of people he owes money to. What they're prepared to do to get it back.'

Jean sighed, remembering the haunted expression on Malcolm Oliver's face when he told her. 'I get the impression they don't want to see him to discuss renegotiating the loan.'

'Your son left a note telling you not to leave the apartment or answer the door, right?'

Jean nodded. 'Until I sort out my return flight.'

'Maybe you should think about doing just that. Have you contacted the airline?'

'Of course not – it'd cost me a fortune to change the flight. Besides, I'm not going anywhere until I know Simon's safe and well.'

Stanley Rozello shook his head. 'You might be waiting a long time if he's determined to stay hidden.'

'How can I leave?' She could feel the inside of her eyelids prickling. She sniffed and dabbed at her nose with a paper napkin. 'Do you have children?'

'A daughter.'

'Are you telling me, in the same situation, you would just walk away?'

His big shoulders sagged. 'Not if I still had breath left in my body.'

Jean reached out and grabbed his hands, realised how intimate the gesture was, and quickly pulled away. 'Can't you have a word with your friend, Rodriguez? Isn't there something she could do to track Simon down? Or at least find Cindy – she must be in touch with him.'

Stanley stared into her eyes for a long while before shifting his gaze to the busy sidewalk outside. 'I'm not sure how much influence I would have.'

'But Rodriguez was your partner, wasn't she? Surely that has to count for something. Please – as one parent to another. Help me.'

'I guess she could look at the cell phone records. Maybe credit card transactions.'

'Anything, please.' Relieved to have convinced someone to take her seriously, she slid sideways along the vinyl seat. 'How do you take your coffee?' She swung her legs out of the booth.

'Black – strong as they can make it. Hey – why don't I call Lu right now?'

Jean strode over to the waitress, a lightness in her step she wasn't anticipating. She glanced back at Stanley and her heart beat a little faster, forcing her to snatch a breath. He nodded back at her, his phone raised to his ear. Jean reached the waitress and tapped her on the arm. 'We really are ready to order now.' The girl blinked as if she'd been dragged from a dark cave into daylight. 'Table by the window? Remember?' Jean said, and looked at Stanley again as he put down his phone. A moment later the strains of a Dean Martin song filled the diner. The ex-detective snatched up the phone from the table.

Jean turned back to the waitress. 'We'd like two coffees, one weak with milk, one strong without,' she said. The girl stared at her blankly. 'Have you got that?'

Stanley started shouting behind her. Jean turned to see him on his feet and heading toward the door. 'I'll be there,' she heard him say. 'For Christ's sakes, just stop him doing anything stupid.'

She reached him as he hung up.

'I'm sorry,' he said. 'I've got to go.'

'But what about Simon?' She grabbed her bag from the table. 'I need your help.'

'I left Lu a message. It's the best I can do. Look – I gotta go.'

'What happens next? I'm not sure I can do this on my own,' Jean said, surprised by her own neediness.

'I can't… I don't have… Jesus.' He stared at her, his expression softening as he searched her face.

'Take me with you,' she said in a half-whisper as her breath caught in her throat.

He took her hand in his and dragged her out of the diner.

# 12

They arrived in the Financial District less than fifteen minutes later. Stanley had managed to wrangle a favour from one of his former colleagues to take them in a patrol car with the siren wailing and the red lights flashing all the way. He jumped out of the car leaving Jean to make her own way to the two police vehicles blocking the street. When she caught up with him, he was chatting to a flushed-faced uniformed policeman, both of them peering up at the roof of a ten-storey office block on the other side of the road. A lopsided banner was hanging from a low rail that ran the length of the roof. In clumsy black letters someone had painted on a bed sheet: *Fisher Krupps – USA's top home wreckers.* That name again. Simon's company.

'Thanks for calling me.' Stanley clapped a hand on the policeman's back.

'I did the right thing?'

'Sure.' Stanley shielded his eyes from the sun. 'I don't see him. Where is he?'

'He was there just a minute ago tying that dumb sign to the rail.'

'How many men you got up there?'

'I don't have any men up there – this is all we got. Priority's keeping the road and the sidewalk clear.' He pointed to the patrol cars blocking traffic and the four officers manning lines of yellow tape stretched across both ends of the street.

'There's no one on the roof with him?'

'I didn't want to spook him. That's why I called. If anyone's gonna talk him down, it's you.'

Stanley rubbed both hands over his face. 'Jeez – I don't know. I never negotiated more than a discount off the ticket price on a new car.'

'No one else will be here for at least a half hour.' The policeman looked at Stanley then back up at the roof. 'Might be all over by then.'

'You actually heard him threaten to jump?'

'Not in so many words.'

'Don't seem like a thing Jimmy would do.'

'None of us know what we'll do if we're pushed hard enough.' The policeman turned and noticed Jean standing next to Stanley. 'Hey, lady – who let you in here?'

'It's OK – she's with me.' Stanley bowed his head and whispered to her. 'Stay right here until it's over. This officer will look after you.'

'I'll do no such thing.' Jean started toward the entrance of the building. 'I used to answer the phones at the Samaritans. I know how to speak to people in this situation. I've had proper training. I can talk him round.'

'We don't know what kind of situation we've got here,' Stanley said. 'Jimmy's not gonna jump.'

'You know that for sure?'

Stanley shook his head, his gaze still fixed on the roof.

'Then I don't think we want to take that risk, do we?' She crossed the street and called over to him when she reached the door. 'Are you coming or what?'

They took the elevator to the tenth floor and walked the final flight of stairs up onto the roof. Stanley flung open the door and stepped outside, Jean close behind. The air was a little cooler up there; a slight breeze ruffled her hair.

About twenty yards away she spotted a stooped figure standing right at the edge of the roof. Her heart thudded in her throat. 'That's him?' she whispered. Stanley nodded back at her and crept closer to the man.

'Come out and speak to me!' the man hollered. 'Come on, Conner, you coward! Come and face me like a man.' His throat caught on the last word and he started coughing. Each cough shook his body so violently Jean thought he might knock himself clean off the roof.

'Hey, Jimmy!' Stanley kept his voice low and even. Jimmy spun round to face him. His face was grey with a hint of yellow, like dirty candle wax. He had a ravaged look about him, the same wary expression as Malcolm Oliver.

'What the—?'

'I got a call,' Stanley said.

'They had no business calling you.' The man rubbed a shirtsleeve across his forehead. 'Don't come any closer, Stan. I'm warning you.'

Stanley stopped and held up both palms to Jimmy. 'You're the boss. Whatever you say goes.'

'Oh yeah?'

'We do things your way.'

'OK… Get that sonofabitch out of his penthouse office to come speak to me.' He dabbed his face again, a large damp patch spreading across his frayed cotton sleeve.

'Which sonofabitch is that, Jimmy? They ain't short of them round here.'

'Conner – the man who's stealing my house.'

Stanley moved closer, his gaze fixed on his friend standing just a few inches away from the edge of the roof. 'Stealing your house?'

'I got the final foreclosure notice.'

'But you already paid for your house. We celebrated at Antonio's. Don't you remember? You and Marge and me and Maria.'

Jimmy turned away. 'Course I remember. I ain't losing my mind – just my house. I remortgaged.'

'Jesus, Jimmy – why didn't you tell me this was happening? I could have helped.'

'You got thirty thousand bucks just lying around, huh?'

'How much?'

Jimmy glanced in Jean's direction for the first time. He lost his balance and staggered one or two steps then looked back at Stanley. 'Who the hell is she?'

'Hello, Jimmy. My name's Jean. I'm just tagging along with your friend here.' She stuck out a hand and strode toward him.

'Stay back!'

As Jean got closer she could see the sweat streaming down his face. 'Of course. I can just stand here. That's fine – we can do the formal introductions later.'

'Stan?'

'She's… uh… she's a friend of mine.'

'She's English!'

'We don't bite.' Jean smiled. 'Honestly.' She folded her arms behind her back and shifted her weight onto one leg, trying to look unthreatening. 'I nearly had my house repossessed. In the eighties. We got it sorted in the end. Rescheduled the payments. Perhaps you could do the same?'

'It's way too late for that.'

'For God's sake, Jimmy. Why'd you remortgage?'

'Had some bills to pay.'

'What kinda bills cost thirty thousand dollars?'

Stanley's friend coughed into his sleeve, the rattle in his lungs echoing around the rooftop.

'Hey, buddy.' Stanley rushed forward, his arms outstretched.

'Stay away from me, Stan! I mean it!' Jimmy took a step back, as he did, his right calf hit the foot-high metal rail at the edge of the roof. The blow knocked him off-balance, his arms windmilled frantically as his upper body lurched toward the eighty-foot drop. Stanley lunged toward him and managed to grab a fistful of shirt. He yanked hard and pulled him back toward the roof. But Jimmy couldn't have weighed more than a hundred pounds, and he banged into Stanley, bouncing off him, losing his footing. He dropped to the floor as his legs buckled beneath him. His head struck the low metal rail as he fell. A bloody gash opened across his temple.

Stanley dropped to his knees and put a hand on Jimmy's face. 'Buddy! Hey, come on.' He slapped him lightly, but Jimmy was out cold.

# 13

The paramedics shoved the gurney into the waiting ambulance. As the doors slammed shut, Jean saw Stanley's forlorn face staring out at her. He was holding his friend's hand. The ambulance accelerated away and Jean made her way to the nearest corner not cordoned off by the police. She weaved her way north through the streets of the Financial District, asking for directions on every corner.

When she finally arrived at All Saints Hospital she saw Stanley sitting at the end of a row of seats bolted to a wall in the emergency department. She watched him jump up when a woman in scrubs passed. The woman quickly shook her head and pointed toward a long line of people standing at the reception desk. Stanley slumped back down, only to jump up again as another member of staff walked by. They too pointed to reception and Stanley sat down again, dejected.

Jean couldn't help but feel sorry for him. She wanted to help, overwhelmed by a disproportionate desire to make everything better. She rushed over to him. When he saw her his weary face brightened.

'Thought you could do with some company,' she said, pushing him back down as he started to get up.

'There was no need to come all the way—'

'I'm here now, so let's just make the best of it, shall we?' She gazed up and down the long corridor.

The seat next to Stanley's had a pair of crutches leaning against it. A pregnant woman occupied the next seat along. She looked up at Jean.

'Sorry – I'll move them.' She grabbed the crutches and awkwardly shifted her leg out of the way.

'Let me help.' Jean held out her hands.

'It's OK, I've got it.' The woman balanced the crutches between her knees and reached out with her spare hand to a small boy running up the corridor. 'Stop that. You need to be a good boy. Sit down for mommy.' The boy started whining. 'Not long now, honey. I promise.'

Jean smiled at her and sat down next to Stanley. 'How's Jimmy?'

'They took him into the operating room as soon as we arrived. Now no one'll tell me anything.'

Jean sighed. 'I expect they'll give you news when they have any.'

'Why is it taking so long?'

Jean was suddenly aware the little boy was staring at her. He tugged at her arm.

'Why'd you talk so funny?' he asked.

'Don't be rude,' his mother said. 'I'm sorry.'

'It's OK, love. He's not doing any harm.' She looked at the woman's domed belly, her bony hand wrapped around the crutches. 'Waiting for someone to pick you up?' The woman nodded.

Two nurses ran past, one pushing an electronic contraption on a trolley. They burst through the doors at the other end of the corridor.

'Looks like someone's in a bad way,' Jean said, staring at the doors swinging back and forth in their wake.

'Maybe it's Jimmy.' Stanley stood up. 'I got to speak to somebody.'

'You stay right where you are.'

The line at the reception desk had disappeared. Jean marched up to the counter, but before she got the chance to speak to the nurse standing the other side, a man barged past her.

'Two hours I've been here,' he said to the nurse. 'What the hell is going on?' He pointed over his shoulder. 'My wife is in pain. She needs to see a doctor.'

'I'm sorry, sir. We operate a triage system. We'll get around to seeing your wife just as soon as we can.'

'Get around? Do you know how much money my family have donated to this hospital over the years? And this is how we get treated?'

'Other people are in greater need – it's as simple as that. If you're not happy you can fill out a comments form.'

'Oh sure. That's going to help my wife.'

The nurse turned to Jean. 'How can I help you, ma'am?'

'A man was brought in earlier. Head injury. Unconscious.'

'Name?'

'Jimmy…' Jean looked over at Stanley who was walking over to her.

'Kapowski,' he said.

'That's right,' Jean said and leaned her elbows on the counter.

'And who are you?' The woman in pink and yellow scrubs started tapping a keyboard.

'Me? I'm his wife.'

'Mrs?'

Jean hoped she'd heard Stanley correctly. 'Ka-pow-ski.'

'How are you spelling that?'

'I just want to know how he is.'

The nurse tapped some more keys and the whirr of a printer started up just behind the desk. She snatched a handful of sheets from the tray, then thrust them at Jean.

'What's all this?' Jean said, looking at the pages, the tiny type impossible to read without a magnifying glass.

'Forms for you to fill out. As next of kin.'

Jean held the paperwork at arm's length, but still the content remained unintelligible.

'We need the patient's insurance details.'

Stanley grabbed the sheets from her. 'For Christ's sakes – we don't even know if Jimmy's alive or dead and you want us to fill out forms?'

'And who are you?'

'I'm his friend. Please check on that computer of yours and tell me how Jimmy's doing.' The nurse narrowed her eyes, instantly triggering a smile from Stanley. 'He's my buddy – please, miss. I really would appreciate your help.'

After more seconds of rapid typing, the nurse flashed a sad smile at him. 'He's still in surgery. He has a subdural haematoma – a swelling – on his brain. The doctors are draining the fluid.'

'Jesus.' Stanley closed his eyes.

'We really do need those forms, ma'am,' the nurse said.

The man who'd barged past Jean earlier reappeared, his face still an angry shade of red. Before he had a chance to speak, the nurse behind the counter handed a bundle of paperwork to him.

'We need your wife's insurance details.'

'I have my card. It covers the whole family.' The man reached into his jacket. His hand came out empty. He patted his pockets. 'For God's sake, what kind of place is this? Someone's stolen my wallet.'

Jean turned to see Stanley looking blankly down at the paperwork he was holding. She eased the forms from his hands and steered him gently back to the seating area.

As they approached the line of plastic seats Jean spotted a fat wallet lying on the floor. She looked over her shoulder at the angry man at reception. He was prodding a finger at the nurse behind the counter. Jean quickly kicked the wallet under the row of seats and she and Stanley sat down.

'I'm sure Jimmy will be just fine,' she said and put her hand over Stanley's, lightly brushing his knuckles.

'I've known Jimmy most of my life. He doesn't have a real good record of coming through things unscathed.'

'He's got this far, hasn't he?'

'I guess.' He looked down at her hand for a moment before lacing his fingers through hers. The unexpected intimacy sent a charge up Jean's spine. She wasn't sure how to interpret it. She drew down a long quiet breath through her nose and tried to compose herself. She hadn't felt this way about anyone since her husband died. She looked up at Stanley's troubled face and resisted the urge to plant a reassuring kiss on his cheek.

'I can't believe he could get himself in so much trouble. Thirty thousand dollars… Jesus, they're gonna take his house away.'

Jean squeezed his fingers a little tighter. 'He'll work something out. Perhaps we can speak to the bank on his behalf.'

'*We*?'

'I'll help if I can.'

'It's not your problem.'

'I suppose not.' She snatched a breath. 'While we're waiting, why don't you tell me about how you and Jimmy met?'

Stanley slipped his fingers from hers and cupped both hands round his knees. 'There's not much to tell.'

'When was it?'

'I can't remember a time when I didn't know him – we grew up in the same neighbourhood.'

'Here in Manhattan?'

'Nah – Queens – not so far from where Jimmy lives now.'

'You went to school together?'

'School, church, Police Academy.

'Jimmy's a policeman?'

Stanley closed his eyes again, his body slumped against the wall. 'Not anymore.'

'Retired – like you?'

Stanley's chest was moving in shallow pulses. 'Jimmy…' He squeezed his eyes tighter and tears appeared at the corners. 'He uh… left the department back in the seventies.'

'Oh.' Jean didn't know whether changing the subject now would be welcome or not. Perhaps it would be good for the tough ex-cop to let his emotions out. 'Why did he leave? Was he ill?'

Stanley ground his fists into his eyes and sniffed. 'Look,' he said, turning to Jean. 'I appreciate what you're trying to do – distracting me and all – but I'd rather not talk about it.'

An orderly approached them and Stanley quickly stood up. But the man ignored him and spoke to the pregnant woman still waiting with her small son. She gathered her bag and started to get up.

'I'm sorry, miss, there's no more space on the bus.'

The woman's face fell. 'When's the next one?'

The orderly looked at the floor. 'Tomorrow.'

'What am I supposed to do?'

'Try the subway?'

'To the Bronx?'

Jean peered into her bag and fished out her wallet. She had less than ten dollars in cash. The orderly walked away and the pregnant woman pulled her little boy toward her. Her eyes were welling with tears. Jean turned to Stan, but he was on his way back to the reception desk. Then she remembered the fat wallet she'd kicked under the seats. She bent down, shoved her hand between her feet and groped for the wallet. She snatched it up and pulled out all the bills.

'Here,' she said and handed the thick wad of cash to the woman.

'What's this?' The woman looked down at the money then up at Jean.

'Get yourself a cab home.'

'I can't take your money.'

'Of course you can. I have more than enough.' Jean glanced over at the owner of the wallet, he was pacing up and down by the counter, a phone glued to his ear.

'I won't be able to pay you back,' the woman said, her hand reaching tentatively for the money.'

'Good – because I wouldn't hear of it.'

'Thank you. So much.'

'My pleasure.' Jean dropped the wallet onto the floor and back-heeled it under the seats. She looked up to see what the wallet owner was doing and saw Stanley marching toward her.

'What *was* that?' he said as he drew close.

'I don't know how much you saw.'

He lowered his voice. 'You've got to get that money back from her.'

'I'll do no such thing. You can see what a state this poor girl is in. Right now she needs the money more than he does.'

Stanley reached into a pocket and withdrew his wallet. 'Jesus.' He pulled out two tens.

Jean put her hand over the bills. 'It's not enough.' She glanced over at the man by the counter. 'Besides, it's not just the money. It's the principle.' She tugged on Stanley's hands until he sat down.

'Mary, Mother of God,' he said.

The woman had struggled to her feet and was making her way slowly down the corridor toward the exit.

'How much did you take?' Stanley demanded when the mother and her son had disappeared around the corner.

'I didn't exactly have a chance to count it.'

'You still have a chance to get it back.'

Jean folded her arms. 'You get it back. You take that woman's cab fare from her. You watch her little boy cry.'

'Jesus Christ.'

'I don't see that I've done anything that wrong. One person has too much. The other not nearly enough. I just balanced things up a bit. It's just a spot of wealth redistribution,' Jean said.

'What are you? Some kind of communist?'

'Why? What are you – some kind of Republican?'

'It's still a crime.'

'Go on then – arrest me.' She raised her hands to his face, pressing her wrists together. 'No wait a minute… you can't. You're not a policeman anymore.'

'I can find one easy enough.'

'Oh come on, you're really prepared to hand me over to the police?'

'I'm an accessory if I don't.'

She looked into his face. He was serious.

'It can still get you twelve months in the city jail.'

'Only if I get caught.'

Stanley shook his head, clearly still not believing what he had witnessed with his own eyes.

'Would it help if you thought of me as a modern day Robin Hood? Robbing from the rich to give—'

'You're sitting there trying to justify a Class A Misdemeanour?'

'But really – where's the harm?'

Before he could answer, Jean's phone started ringing in her bag. She dug around for it, only just managing to answer before the voicemail kicked in. She listened in silence to what Detective Rodriguez was telling her, not daring to take a breath, the air stalling in her lungs and throat. When she hung up she fell against Stanley, suddenly unable to support herself.

'What is it?' he said.

'The police have found a body.' Her voice sounded thin and unfamiliar. 'Same general description as…' She snatched a breath and swallowed. 'They think it's Simon.'

# 14

Luisa Rodriguez was running late. She squealed to a stop right outside the entrance of the blue-tiled building on 30th and First, the nearside fender and passenger door of the decrepit departmental pool car scraping against a fire hydrant.

'Crap.'

She shoved a 'Police On Call' sign onto the dash, fully expecting the car to be towed before she'd even halfway finished her business inside the Chief Medical Examiner's office.

She jumped from the car and inspected the damage. The dark blue paintwork had picked up two fresh battle scars. Fortunately they were no worse than the existing network of scratches and gouges. Luisa rubbed her sleeve over the new marks, redistributing dirt and grime so they looked a little less obvious. Then she gave the hood an affectionate pat and ran through the highly polished chrome entrance of the building. She flashed her shield at the man on the security desk and pushed through to the hallway beyond the main reception.

One floor beneath the sidewalk, down a maze of fluorescent-lit corridors, Luisa made her way to the waiting area. She froze in the doorway when she saw who was sitting next to the English woman.

'Stan?'

He threw her a dirty look. 'What time do you call this?' he said and jumped to his feet. 'You know how long we've been waiting?'

'What are you doing here?'

'Jesus, Lu, what's that got to do with anything? This lady has been going out of her mind. They wouldn't let us look at the…' He lowered his voice. 'The *body* until you arrived.'

Luisa glanced over at Mrs Henderson, who was clutching her purse on her lap, staring so intensely at the tile floor Luisa thought there must be some important message written there. 'I don't understand why you're with—'

'I'll explain later. Right now I want you to go over there and be nice to her.' He levelled his gaze, staring hard in Luisa's eyes. 'Do you think you can do that?'

'Jesus, Stan. I'm always nice.'

He grabbed her firmly by the arms, turned her around and gave a gentle shove in the direction of the vacant-eyed woman. 'Mrs Henderson,' Luisa said in her most sympathetic voice.

The English woman snapped her head quickly toward her; her eyes focused suddenly, her face pinched into a frown. 'Can we get this over with?' she said and started to get up. Immediately Stanley hurried across the room and shoved a supporting arm under her elbow. 'It's the not knowing,' she said. 'Better to find out, one way or the other.'

Luisa was dreading the next part. She'd rehearsed what she was going to say on the drive uptown. Each time she'd tried a new approach it sounded more crass and unfeeling than the one before. This wasn't even her job, a cop from the 7$^{th}$ should be doing it. The body was found in their precinct. But after she'd listened to Stanley's message about Mrs Henderson's missing son and then heard about the corpse turning up in the park down by the river, she felt a personal responsibility to the woman.

She tried to soften her voice. 'Mrs Henderson – I'm really sorry to have to tell you this…' Luisa glanced at Stanley. 'But you need to prepare yourself.'

'I have seen a dead body before.'

'This is a little different.' She exhaled and felt a chill creep up her arms. After eight years in the department she would have expected this to have gotten easier. 'The body you're about to see… well, the man didn't die of natural causes.'

'I didn't think he had.'

'He suffered some major trauma to the head.'

Mrs Henderson grabbed onto Stanley's arm. 'What does he look… I mean, his face. Is it…?'

'His face is bruised and grazed.'

The woman gulped noisily.

'The head injury is at the back of the skull.'

'So he's recognisable?'

'Yes, ma'am.' Luisa led the way down another corridor. She opened a door at the end and waited for Mrs Henderson and Stanley to enter ahead of her. She closed the door quietly then pointed to another. 'I'll let you have some privacy.'

The woman let go of Stanley's arm and pulled back her shoulders, taking a deep breath. 'I want to do this alone.' She walked slowly to the door and opened it, her head down, eyes trained on the floor. She took another deep breath and stepped into the room.

Luisa threw a glance toward Stanley, but his eyes were focused on the doorway and the woman beyond. Luisa moved closer to the inner room, maintaining a respectful distance. From where she was standing she could see the orderly fold down the green sheet covering the corpse to expose the head and shoulders.

'Oh my God,' Mrs Henderson murmured.

Luisa joined her. 'I'm sorry ma'am. I have to ask you to formally identify—'

'It's not Simon.' The woman held out her hand and Stanley hurried to her side. 'Thank God.'

'Ma'am?' Luisa looked at Mrs Henderson's face; it was colourless. She looked just as distressed as she had on the way in. 'You seem a little—'

'I know him,' the woman said.

'You do?' Stanley tilted his head and peered more closely at the waxy face.

'I met him.' Mrs Henderson took a breath. 'What is it I can smell?'

'Maybe we should get out of here,' Stanley said.

'Ma'am – you're sure this isn't your son?'

'What do you think?' She shook her head. 'I'm not bloody senile – no matter how much you might want to believe I am.'

'I just need for you to be sure.'

'You said you know him,' Stanley said and started to lead Mrs Henderson from the room. 'That you met him? Was this in the grocery store yesterday?'

'It was just this morning.' She turned to Stanley. 'It's the lad I told you about – the one who came looking for Simon.' She let out a noisy breath. 'No wonder he seemed so bloody scared.'

They were all back in the outer room, the smell of death seemed to have followed them out. Luisa pulled a menthol-scented ChapStick from her bag and applied it generously to her lips. 'Do you remember his name?' she asked Mrs Henderson.

'Of course I do – Malcolm Oliver. He works with… he *worked* with Simon.'

'And he looked scared when you saw him?' Stanley said.

'Turns out he had every right to be.' She pulled a handkerchief from her purse and blew her nose. 'I thought Simon was exaggerating when he said in his note I shouldn't leave the apartment or open the door.' She glanced over her shoulder toward the viewing room. 'He's always done it – exaggerate, I mean. He can get carried away. But now this has happened…' She gripped Luisa's hand. 'You've got to find him. You have to. Otherwise… otherwise the same thing…' She sniffed and exhaled a ragged breath.

'Sorry, ma'am, I'm a little confused. What does his colleague's death have to do with a note your son wrote?'

Mrs Henderson glanced at Stanley. He nodded encouragingly. 'My son and Malcolm Oliver were having financial… difficulties.'

'Ma'am?'

'A loan. They owe a lot of money.'

'And you think this has something to do with Oliver's death?'

The woman nodded. 'What if they've done the same thing to Simon?'

'They?'

'The loan sharks – that poor boy was terrified.' She gripped Stanley's arm. 'Where did you find Oliver?'

'I'm not sure that's relevant, ma'am. I can't really tell you that.'

'Why the hell not?' Stanley glared at her.

Why was he taking sides with this woman against her? Luisa glared back at him. 'A dog walker found the body in a park on the East River.'

'Are you searching the area?'

'Detectives at the Seventh Precinct have the whole area sealed off. Police divers are in the East River as we speak. If they find anything connected to your son – anything at all – they'll be in touch.'

That seemed to satisfy her. Stanley put an arm around the woman's shoulders and squeezed. Luisa had never seen Stanley so much as look at another woman since his wife died. He only met this lady yesterday. He didn't know anything about her. She was a foreigner for God's sakes, fresh off the plane. And she'd acted really weird when Luisa had asked for her passport.

Luisa scrutinised the stranger's face, hoping to read something there she had missed before. Stanley needed someone looking out for him. He should at least have some idea what he was getting himself into. Luisa decided to do a little digging on his behalf. If she found out something she would pass it on, if she didn't, he'd never need to know about it.

The woman started sifting through the contents of her purse. 'I'm sure I put it in here.' She handed a hairbrush and a wallet to Stanley, then a packet of Kleenex and a round silver compact. Finally she plucked out a scrap of paper. 'Here we are!' She waved the small slip in the air. 'For some reason Oliver didn't want to give me his business card, so he wrote a private mobile number on here for me.' She handed it to Luisa. 'Might it help?'

'You said he worked with your son?'

The woman nodded, her eyes taking on a far away look.

'But you haven't told me where that is.' Luisa flipped the paper over. It was blank on the other side.

'But I told the police officer this morning where my son works. Haven't you spoken to him?'

'If you could refresh my memory?'

'He made it quite clear he wasn't taking me seriously.'

'Please, ma'am, if you could just—'

'Fisher Krupps,' Stanley interrupted.

'Which one?'

'Not a branch,' Mrs Henderson said. 'He works at their headquarters. On Wall Street.' She grabbed her things from Stanley and threw them back into her purse.

'It's on Nassau,' Stanley corrected.

'How do you know that?' The woman strapped the purse across her chest, squeezing it tight, like a child with a security blanket.

'It's my job to know.' Stanley ran a hand over his head, looking embarrassed suddenly. 'My new job. Fisher Krupps is one of our biggest clients.'

'You never mentioned it.' Mrs Henderson turned sharply toward him. 'What is your job exactly?'

'I'll explain later.'

*Later*? Luisa looked from Stanley to Mrs Henderson. How much time was he planning on spending with this woman?

The treacly smooth voice of Dean Martin suddenly filled the room. 'Sorry,' Stanley said and answered his cell.

'You will look for my Simon now, won't you?' The woman held on tight to Luisa's hand. She was stronger than she looked. 'Simon's in a lot of trouble. He needs your protection.'

'Ma'am – you can be sure the department will do everything we can to find him,' Luisa said, certain the guys at the 7th would be very interested to speak to Simon Henderson about the murder of Malcolm Oliver.

Stanley strode back into the room. 'That was the hospital,' he said. 'I've got to get down there.'

'I'll come with you.' Mrs Henderson dropped Luisa's hand and held onto Stanley's. 'How is he?'

'He came round a little while ago.' Stanley slipped his cell back into a pocket. 'He hasn't stopped talking. Unfortunately, he's not making any sense.'

'Who's in the hospital?' Luisa grabbed Stanley's other hand.

'My oldest buddy – Jimmy Kapowski.'

'Jimmy? Jesus, Stan, why didn't you tell me? What happened?'

Stanley wriggled his hand free from hers. 'I don't have time to explain. The doctor needs to speak to us urgently.'

# 15

At just after three-thirty that morning Linus had crept into his bedroom, changed his clothes and snuck back out without disturbing anyone inside the apartment. By the time he'd taken the elevator down to the lobby and walked undetected onto the sidewalk he felt a sense of achievement, triumph even.

His mother was a light sleeper, and often roamed around in the dark between four and five in the morning with a bottle of vodka in one hand and a handful of blue pills in the other. But he had been so quiet, so stealthy; she couldn't even have stirred in her bed.

He was made for this stuff.

Standing at the intersection of Houston and First, after more hours of trawling the streets of the Lower East Side and Alphabet City, retracing his steps again and again, the electric energy that had kept him bouncing on his toes for the last thirty hours was wearing off. He could sense the world returning to the drab dull place it had been before.

He must have covered miles looking for the old lady. His disappointment in not finding her felt as sharp as a pain, jabbing under his ribs. His eyes were sore after so many hours searching the sea of faces passing by. She had to be here somewhere. He carried on north up First and slowed when he reached the grocery store.

The first two times he'd returned, the store had been shuttered, a big hand-written sign stuck to the door: *Closed due to family emergency*. Linus had read the words and felt an unexpected surge of emotion flood through his stomach and into his chest. It had taken him a moment to recognise it.

It felt an awful lot like pride. The store was closed because of him.

On this visit, though the shutters were up and the door was open, a big section of the interior was still cordoned off with yellow police tape. Outside a display of fruit and vegetables and a plastic tub of ice stuffed with containers of milk crowded the sidewalk. A wrinkled old Korean lady was sitting on a fold-up chair in front of the display. She was watching an ancient portable TV propped on a wooden stool beside her. Linus stared at her face. He didn't remember seeing her in the store yesterday.

'Hi,' he said and smiled at her.

She dragged her attention away from the tiny screen.

'This your store?'

She eyed him suspiciously and tightened her grip on a black leather fanny pack strapped to her waist.

'I heard about what happened yesterday. May I offer my condolences?' he said, concentrating hard on sounding sincere.

The old lady checked him out from head to kickers. He looked down at his feet. He had on the same sneakers he'd been wearing the day before. A spike of panic rushed through him. Suddenly the electric charge was back. The colours of the apples and mangoes and bananas stacked up behind the old lady all seemed a little brighter.

'What happened to the clerk…' He paused for a moment fighting to control the squeak that had crept into his voice. 'What happened to him was a tragedy. I'm sure the police are doing everything they can to find the people responsible.' He picked up an apple and threw it in the air. The old lady snatched it before it landed back in his hand.

'You an want apple, you pay.'

'Did you see it happen? That must have been so traumatic for you.' He leaned closer to her. 'How are you feeling now?'

She twisted on her chair to get a better a view of the TV. She'd obviously decided he wasn't a threat. *Stupid old bitch.* He turned to see what was so interesting she couldn't even answer a perfectly polite question. On the screen was a long shot of a busy street. The sidewalk was full of people, cops mostly, heading to and from a grocery store.

This store.

'Hey that's you,' he said and pointed to the tiny version of the old lady on the TV screen, on the same chair she was sitting on right now. Next to her was a second woman. Another spike of adrenalin, much bigger than the last, pulsed through him. 'And who's that with you?'

She didn't answer. Then the scene changed and the old lady seemed to lose interest.

'Who was that?' he said again, more forcefully this time.

'Nice lady.'

Linus nodded enthusiastically. 'She sure looks nice. She a friend of yours?'

'Why do you want to know?'

'Just curious. She uh…' Without even trying, a story presented itself to him fully formed. 'She reminds me of an old school teacher I once had. She was real nice too. I just thought maybe it was her.'

The old lady shook her head. 'No way.'

'She's about the right age. And she used to live round here.'

'Not possible.'

'Why not? I'd love to see her again. Do you know her well?'

'She's visiting her son. From England.'

'Hey – it must be her. My teacher left school to go back to England when she retired. Her son live anywhere near here?'

The old lady shrugged. 'She said I can call her anytime.' She nodded approvingly. 'She's a very kind lady.'

'Sure sounds like my old school teacher. Why don't you give me her number so I can surprise her?'

'Why would I do that? I don't know you.' She screwed up her nose. 'If you don't want groceries, maybe you should go.'

Linus reached a hand to the back of his waistband and wrapped his fingers around the handle of the gun, not taking his eyes off the woman. She turned away suddenly and started waving, a broad smile spreading across her face. Linus followed her gaze to see a woman cop climbing out of a patrol car.

As soon as the cop saw the old lady waving, she waved right back, keeping her eyes trained on Linus.

'Anyway,' he said, moving away slowly. 'Real nice talking to you. I'm sorry for your loss.' He nodded toward the cop, making sure he smiled just as broadly as the old lady as he pulled his sweat top over the gun. 'Good afternoon, officer. I was just saying to this lady here, what a terrible thing it was that happened yesterday.'

The cop ignored him and turned to the storekeeper. 'Are you OK, ma'am?'

The old lady nodded.

Linus persisted. 'I mean – it's not something that happens every day, is it? Thank God. Must really shake up the whole neighbourhood.'

The policewoman scrutinised his face. 'You're not from round here?'

'Sure – just a few blocks away. Thought I'd come by and offer my condolences.' He edged around her, keeping his back from view. 'How's the investigation going? Close to arresting someone?'

'Do you have information that might help with our inquiries?' She was still staring at his face. He wondered if he looked as wired as he felt.

'Me? No – I just want to feel safe again, coming to the store, you know?'

The cop shifted so that her weight was evenly distributed on both feet, and rested her hands on her belt.

A second cop slowly climbed out of the passenger seat of the patrol car parked right opposite the store. 'Everything OK here?' he said, as he got closer.

Linus angled his back away from both police officers.

'We're all doing just fine,' the woman cop said. 'Isn't that right, sir?'

'Sure. Good luck with your inquiries. I hope you catch the monsters responsible for this… atrocity soon.' He started to stroll away, his heart thumping so hard against his ribs he was convinced the cop would be able to hear it as he passed.

When he reached the corner and casually turned into the side street, he ran as fast as he could and didn't stop for two blocks. The adrenalin was pumping through him. He grabbed his cell from a pocket and dialled Richie's number.

'Hey Richie, my man!'

'I'm not you're man.'

'Sure, sure, whatever.'

'You still have the gun?'

'Don't stress.'

'You knocked off the old lady?'

'I'm getting real close.'

'So why are you calling?'

'We need another motorcycle.'

'We do?'

'I'm seriously stoked, man. I feel like doing some more grocery shopping.'

# 16

Jimmy Kapowski almost got to the end of his train of thought before he ran out of track and sank back into unconsciousness. He'd been speaking in half sentences ever since Jean and Stanley had arrived at his bedside. When he first laid his unfocused and watery eyes on Jean, his face broke into the widest of grins, displaying a set of nicotine-stained teeth.

'Hey – I remember you – the lady on the roof.' Jimmy had slowly turned his head toward Stanley. 'She's a sight for sore eyes. About what I said before…' And off he went again.

Half an hour later and Jean was beginning to think they might not get a cogent thought from him at all.

'Hey, Jimmy.' Stanley nudged his friend's arm and lowered his face closer to the bed. 'They keep asking me about your insurance.'

Jimmy's eyes flickered open.

'Health insurance, buddy. You got any?'

A tear worked its way out of Jimmy's left eye. 'Not since I left the department. Kind of job I get, employee benefits don't really come into…' He drifted again.

Stanley stiffened.

'It's OK,' Jean said. 'I don't think anyone overheard.' She grabbed a Kleenex from the locker next to the bed and blotted away the tear that had reached Jimmy's earlobe.

'Where's the goddamn doctor? They make it sound like life and death on the phone then they ignore you when you get here.'

'I'm sure someone will be along soon.'

Jean took a breath. In the cab on the ride over from the morgue she couldn't shake the image of Malcolm Oliver's beaten and bruised face from her mind. She'd tried phoning Simon and Cindy and yet again was shunted straight to voicemail on both calls. She couldn't bear the thought of Simon out there somewhere on his own, hunted down like an animal. She had to find some way to pay off his debt. He wouldn't be safe otherwise.

Jimmy stirred in his sleep, a smile on his face. What did she think she was doing sitting next to the hospital bed of a complete stranger? It wasn't as if she knew Stanley Rozello much better. She should be doing something to help get Simon back.

'He certainly seems happier than he did on the roof,' she said, trying to sound upbeat. But then the doctors had probably pumped Jimmy with so much morphine it was likely he'd forgotten he even owned a house, so the threat of imminent foreclosure must have been no more than a distant memory.

The curtains around Jimmy's bed suddenly opened. Jean turned to see a bearded man in white scrubs standing at the foot of the narrow cot.

'Mrs Kapowski?'

She stepped toward him.

'It's OK.' Stanley raised his hand. 'Jimmy's wife left town a long time ago.'

The man in scrubs looked down at paperwork attached to a clipboard. 'But I thought—'

'Crossed wires,' Jean said.

'So you are?'

'A friend.'

'And I'm the nearest thing to family Jimmy's got,' Stanley said. He moved around the bed and pressed a hand against the doctor's back, guiding him toward the door. Jean followed them into the corridor.

'How is he, doc?'

'Doctor Milligan by the way.' The doctor thrust his hand toward Stanley. They shook for a few moments, Stanley introducing himself, clasping the doctor's hand in both of his, apparently reluctant to let go. 'Give it to me straight. How bad is he?' Finally he released his grip. 'I'm guessing there's some brain damage – he wasn't making a lot sense in there. Kept losing it – like he doesn't even know his own name.'

'We'll need to do more tests before we can know if he's sustained any permanent damage. But it's looking good at the moment.'

'It is?' Some of the tension melted from Stanley's face, his eyes and mouth relaxed into a smile. He grabbed the doctor's hand again. 'Thank you. Thank you so much. You saved his life.'

'He should be out of danger by the morning. That's when we'll transfer him to an ordinary ward.'

'That's fantastic news,' Jean said and gave Stanley's arm a little squeeze.

'You do know what that means?' The doctor had lowered his voice.

'Out of danger – it's good news, isn't it?'

'According to Mr Kapowski's notes, we haven't yet received details of his insurance coverage.'

Both of Stanley's cheeks twitched upward so violently it looked as if a high voltage had passed through his face. 'As a matter of fact, I'm still trying to run down all the details. I'm sure I can get—'

'Only, I should warn you, up until now we've treated him under the EMTALA provisions.'

'The what?' Jean said.

'He was an emergency patient – his life was in danger. We treated him. As soon as he moves to an ordinary ward… well… then the meter starts running.'

'So you're telling us it's bad news he's out of danger?' Jean said.

'Only in that one respect, obviously.'

'Obviously.' Jean shook her head and sent up a silent prayer of thanks for the National Health Service. 'So what happens now? Do we have to bundle him into a taxi and take him home whether he's ready to go or not?'

'I have to explain the situation as it stands.' The doctor turned to Stanley. 'I'm sure you understand.'

'I've had great medical cover all my life. NYPD,' Stanley said. 'Never had to concern myself with any of this stuff. Never been sick a day in my life either.' He reached back toward the door and knocked twice on the wooden frame, looking more guilty than relieved. 'If we don't get him out of here tomorrow, what kind of bills are we looking at?'

'You'd have to speak to the administration department about that. I don't have those kind of numbers in my head.'

'Ballpark?'

'Certainly by the end of the week you're looking at many thousands of dollars.'

Stanley rocked backward as if he'd been punched hard in the stomach. 'That's some meter you got running.'

The doctor shrugged and pulled his face into a sympathetic grimace. 'Maybe we should sit down for a moment?'

'It's OK – I think I can manage on my own two feet.' Stanley opened his eyes wide and rubbed a hand up and down his cheek.

'Even so, if we just move along to the waiting area, sit down, get our breath back.' The doctor glanced toward a clock attached to the wall.

'It's OK, doc. I got the picture. If you've got somewhere else to be…' Stanley shot Jean a glance.

'Not the whole picture, I'm afraid.' Dr Milligan started down the corridor. 'Maybe a coffee for you both? There's a machine just down here.'

Stanley hurried after him and put a big hand on his shoulder. 'What the hell are you saying?'

The doctor let out a long sigh. 'Your friend has some other underlying medical problems.' He started tugging at his whisker-covered chin. 'Please – come and sit down.'

It took Dr Milligan a full ten minutes to describe and explain everything that was wrong with Jimmy. He told them if Jimmy recovered fully from his head injury, he then had to survive his acute hernia, cirrhosis of the liver and type 1 diabetes.

'He's not been keeping up-to-date with his medication for the diabetes,' the doctor said, having delivered one medical bombshell after another. 'It's obvious from the condition of his feet.'

'His feet?'

'I presume Mr Kapowski smokes?'

'Two packs a day. Maybe less now… now he doesn't have money to—'

'You have to stop him. And ensure he takes his meds. His circulation will continue to deteriorate until his lower limbs…' He glanced toward Jean. 'I don't want to go into graphic detail.'

'How's he going to pay for meds?'

'Mr Kapowski doesn't have insurance, does he, sir?'

'He doesn't seem to think so. I guess it's one of the luxuries he's given up.'

'After the head injury, my most immediate concern is the hernia. It could rupture at any time.'

'And what does that mean?' Stanley's face had gone white.

'It's not always possible to come back from that… depending on the severity of the case. Septicaemia could set in. Complications.' The doctor slumped back in his chair. 'It would seem Mr Kapowski has been neglecting his wellbeing for some time. Does he have any money at all?'

'I doubt it.'

'A hernia op may cost as little as ten thousand dollars. If we could just get that treated…'

'Then what? We can think about all the other problems we can't afford to solve?'

'I'm so sorry to have to bring you this news.' The doctor attempted a smile but failed. 'What the patient needs in the short term is some personal care. Is there anyone – a family member, a friend who might be able to help?'

'There's just me. And I ain't no Mother Theresa,' Stanley said.

Jean squeezed Stanley's hand. 'Don't worry, love.' She gave him her most fulsome smile. 'I'm sure you'll think of something.'

# 17

The call came through just as Luisa was sitting down to eat a rubbery omelette she'd forced herself to cook. Was there anything more depressing than eggs for dinner? Relieved to have an excuse to scrape the pale yellow mess into the trash, she left the dirty dishes on the drainer, ran into her bedroom and quickly gathered her gun, shield and hand restraints from the locked drawer in her closet.

She arrived at the grocery store on the corner of Prince and Mulberry to find Lieutenant Riley's favourite pet detective sitting on the hood of an unmarked Ford Crown stuffing a sandwich into his mouth.

'You drove here?' she said, shaking her head. 'We're only two blocks from the station house.'

His lip curled into a snarl. 'Audacious, wasn't it?'

'Your driving here or the robbery?'

He crammed the remainder of the sandwich into his mouth. 'Both,' he said through a mush of rye bread and chicken salad. Then he belched. 'Shall we?' He gestured for her to lead the way into the store. 'Riley said you'd come in – nothing better to do on your night off.'

'He said that, huh?'

Sanchez wiped the mayo from his moustache with a paper napkin then threw it on the ground. The CSIs would probably collect it later and add it to the haul of evidence.

'Nice of him to take such an interest in my social life,' Luisa said.

'Yeah – that's what I thought.'

They both pulled on overshoes and gloves at the door and made straight for the crime scene manager crouching behind the counter.

'Where is everyone?' Luisa said, looking round the empty store.

'Multiple homicide on Orchard.'

'*Multiple*?' Luisa had thought it was strange for Lieutenant Riley to assign her to an actual shooting. Seems she actually got the short straw again: this wasn't the main event. At least there was one consolation; Sanchez must have temporarily fallen out of favour to be partnered with her on the case.

'Looks like a family annihilation, but it's too early to tell. They haven't found the boyfriend's body yet. Should keep the team busy until tomorrow morning,' the crime scene manager told her. 'And I'm only here because I was stupid enough to pick up the damn phone. Middle of dinner.' He sighed. 'Thirty-day matured steak. Nice bottle of claret. Wasted.'

'What's the latest on the victim?' Luisa asked.

He got up slowly. 'Latest I don't know. But the paramedics said he might not make it through the night. Head's caved in on one side, brain coming right out of his skull.' He waved a screw-topped plastic jar at her. 'Looks like I scraped some of it from the floor.'

'Jesus.' She turned her face away. 'What's that smell?' She peered around the counter and saw a bloody pink pool of urine on the floor. 'Victim's or perp's?' she asked.

'Hard to tell. According to the uniforms on the scene first, victim was covered in piss. Might all belong to him. Might belong to the perp. Maybe he got scared and wet his pants.'

'Or maybe he's some twisted freak who wanted to mark out his territory.' Sanchez held a sleeve across his mouth and nose. 'It really does stink.'

Luisa pointed to a TV fixed to the wall behind the counter, the screen split into four images showing different locations within the store. 'Anyone looked at the security camera footage yet?'

'Waiting for the owner to arrive,' the crime scene manager said.

'He's on his way?'

'I guess.'

'OK,' she spun round and scanned the store. 'Any witnesses?'

'Guy sitting in the back of the patrol car. You must have passed him on your way in.'

'I'll go speak to him,' Sanchez said.

'What's the matter, Sanchez? Stomach getting a little weak after all these years?' Luisa said. 'Maybe the sandwich was a bad idea, huh?' She looked back up at the TV monitor attached to the wall. In the bottom left hand corner she saw her own tired face staring back at her. She should get more sleep. And exercise. And proper food. Tomorrow maybe. She tucked her hair behind her ears and straightened her jacket. 'Where's that goddamn storeowner?' she said, more to herself than anyone else.

'Right here.'

She pivoted on her heels. A sweating bald man hesitated at the entrance to the store.

'Where's Mikey?' he said.

'The clerk?' Luisa said. The bald man nodded. 'They've taken him to the hospital.'

'Nobody even told me he was hurt. I thought this was just a robbery. How bad is he?'

Luisa walked over to him, quickly guided him past the counter and onto a chair on the opposite side of the store.

'He only started last week.' Sudden tears filled his eyes. 'Is he going to be OK?'

'We don't have any details at the moment – I'm sorry, sir. He's in good hands.'

'I got to get down to the hospital. Where'd they take him?' He struggled to stand, but his legs failed him and he slumped back onto the chair. 'My wife's going to kill me. So long she's been badgering me to give him a job.' He wiped a sleeve across his nose. 'And this happens.' He tried to stand again.

Luisa gently pushed him back down. 'If you wouldn't mind answering a few questions, first, Mr…?'

'Waxman.'

'Is Mikey a friend of your wife's?'

'Her nephew. Her only nephew. She's definitely going to kill me. I'm supposed to be taking care of him.' He looked toward the door. 'Did the ambulance guys say anything before they took him to the hospital?'

Luisa glanced at the crime scene manager, whose face remained completely blank. How did he manage to do that? She made a mental note never to play poker with him.

After five minutes of gently coaxing the clerk's details from the storeowner, accommodating each of his sudden teary outbursts and stretches of mournful silence, Luisa finally managed to steer the conversation where she wanted it.

'You say you've got five cameras?' she asked, and looked up at the ceiling. She spotted one above the cash register, pointed toward the customer side of the counter, another just to the left of the door, and two more at the back of the store. 'I can only see four. Where's the last one, sir?'

The man let out a blubbing sob. 'It's not that I don't trust him… honest to God.' He sniffed back a nose full of mucus and swallowed. 'You've got to promise not to tell my wife.'

'I'm sorry, sir. I don't understand.'

'She says he's a good kid, but you don't know what really happens to them in juvie, do you?'

'Are you telling me your nephew—?'

'My wife's nephew,' he corrected her.

'He's spent time in a juvenile detention centre?'

The man nodded.

'How old is he?'

'Twenty-four.'

'So we're talking what, four, five years ago?'

'Seven.'

Luisa couldn't help but raise her eyebrows.

'Something like that you don't shake off too easy.'

She sucked in a deep breath. When she'd knocked off at six, it had already felt like a very long day, now, as she stared at the store owner's bald, sweating head, it seemed as if it was never going to end.

'He paid his debt, sir. That's the way it works. Everyone deserves a second chance.'

'I gave him a goddamn job, didn't I?'

'You haven't answered my question.'

'What was it again?'

'The location of the fifth camera?'

He lifted a shaking hand toward the cash register. 'On the other side of the counter.'

'Pointed toward the clerk?'

The sweating man nodded.

*God bless your mistrusting ass.*

'I just had it installed. It's state-of-the-art. That's what the guy who sold it to me said.'

'Digital?'

He nodded again.

'I need to see the footage. Now.'

Mr Waxman led her to a back room office and unlocked a large cupboard behind the desk. Inside were two TV monitors, two hard disk recorders and a large square safe. He turned on the monitors. The left hand monitor featured the same split-screen black and white images as the one above the counter in the store; the other displayed the messy pool of blood and urine in full colour. Waxman stared at the screen.

'What is that?' he said.

Luisa grimaced. 'We think something got spilled. A bottle of soda smashed on the floor, most probably.'

'It doesn't look like soda.' He sank heavily onto the side of the desk.

'Can you bring up the footage for the last two hours?'

He nodded slowly, his pale face turning greyer by the second.

'Tell you what, Mr Waxman, why don't you show me how it works and I'll take it from there?'

The storeowner fumbled with the remote, hitting two buttons at once with his thick fingers. He cursed freely without apologising until finally the image on the screen changed. A slim, long-haired man stood behind the counter, serving a customer. Waxman handed the remote to Luisa without taking his eyes off the screen.

'She's going to kill me.'

'Sir? If you wouldn't mind?' She jabbed the pause button.

He pulled a puzzled face.

'It's probably better if you don't see this.'

Waxman slowly levered his bulk from the desk and swallowed hard. 'There's no need for my wife to find out about the new camera, is there?'

'If there is, I promise I'll take care of it.'

'You don't know what she's like.'

'I can tell her you installed it following advice from the police department.'

'You'd do that for me?'

'Don't worry about it, Mr Waxman.' She handed him one of her cards. 'Any problems – you just tell her to call me.'

'Thank you.' He stared down at the card. 'Should I wait outside until you're done?'

'My colleague will want to speak to you. Why don't you go find him?'

She waited until he'd left the room and closed the door before she pressed *Play* on the remote. She kept her finger on the fast forward button to skip the part leading up to the robbery. Then, as soon as she saw the clerk suddenly back into the racks behind the counter she played it at normal speed. A moment later the moulded edge of a rubber mask appeared at the bottom of the screen. Then she saw the whole thing as the figure wearing it glanced around the store.

Obama.

She hit *Pause* and stared at the mask. Two stores in two days. These punks had a serious work ethic. She pressed the play button again and watched the drama unfold. The clerk flung his hands in the air and froze. The figure in the mask started waving his gun, but still the clerk didn't move. Then the perp thumped a fist into the cash register. Luisa stopped the recording again, and peered closely at the fist. The perp was wearing gloves. Thin blue latex ones just like she had on. She continued to watch as the fist hit the register twice more. Was Mikey the clerk refusing to open it? Maybe she should share that fact with Mr Waxman. The perp raised the gun high in the air and brought it down with such speed and force that when it hit the clerk's cheek, he jerked sideways, his hand reaching out to stop himself falling. His hand hit the cash register. Immediately the drawer sprang open. The clerk threw his body over it.

'What are you doing for Chrissakes?' Luisa said and continued to stare at the footage wide-eyed as more blows rained down on the clerk's head. 'That's not heroic – it's just plain dumb.' Then she spotted the clerk's hand slip inside the drawer and pull out a stack of bills that he shoved under his shirt. Her heart sank. Another ferocious blow hit the clerk on the temple and his legs buckled.

What Luisa saw next sent a chill through her whole body. Very calmly, after removing the remaining cash from the register, the man with the gun took a phone from his pocket and pointed it at the victim. Then he looked up, turning his head from side to side as if he was searching for something. He lifted his phone to the security camera, proudly displaying an image of the beaten man. Then, still staring directly into the camera, he raised a hand to his mouth and blew a kiss.

# 18

The heat in the apartment was unbearable. Jean had forced open the bedroom window a crack, but the air outside was no cooler. The air conditioning unit seemed to blow hot air rather than cold and made the sound of a jumbo jet taking off whenever she turned it on.

After three hours lying awake, worrying about Simon, she got up in search of an electric fan. Surely living somewhere that got this hot every summer they'd have a fan tucked away somewhere. Especially with Cindy expecting.

That thought stopped Jean in her tracks. She stood motionless in the middle of her son's bedroom and puffed out her cheeks. If she started crying now, in the deathly hour between three and four, she might never stop. And what good would it do? She'd just get a headache and a blotchy rash across her face. She took a couple of good deep breaths and headed for the kitchen.

She had poked around all the kitchen cabinets and the small bureau in the living room in under ten minutes. Still no sign of a fan. Back in the bedroom there was only the closet left to search. Shoved right at the far end, on Simon's side of the narrow space, Jean discovered a large cardboard box. She peered in, but the light from the overhead bulb wasn't bright enough to see what was inside.

Summoning all her strength, she grabbed a cardboard flap in each hand and hauled the box out into the bedroom, pulling it close to the bedside lamp. Using the lamp like a lantern she shoved a hand inside the box.

Balancing on top of a pile of magazines was an old computer game console. Jean dropped it on the floor beside her. She returned the lamp to the bedside table and grabbed the handful of magazines, not looking too closely at them for fear of what she might discover about Simon's reading habits. The only thing that remained was a brightly printed box, too small to contain the electric fan she was searching for. Curious to see what Simon had buried at the back of his closet, she lifted out the cardboard cube and held it under the light. Her heart thudded uncertainly for a few beats, feeling as if it might escape her chest. She lost her grip and the box dropped from her hands, splitting as soon as it hit the floor, sending bronze-coloured lozenges spinning across the floorboards. Tentatively, between trembling thumb and forefinger, Jean picked up the nearest lozenge. About an inch and a half long, the metal felt very cold against her skin. Cold and slippery smooth. She let it roll into her palm, grabbed her reading glasses from the bedside table and inspected it more closely. There was a word stamped into the metal at its base, a manufacturer's brand name, she supposed.

She'd never been this close to a bullet before in her life. Thank God.

She gulped a steadying breath and peered beneath the bed. She reached under and collected all the bullets that had escaped the box, then placed them carefully, one at a time, onto the bedside cabinet. Fourteen bullets from a box that held forty-eight. A chill crept across her shoulders and up her neck as she considered where the others might be.

She hurried from the room and into the kitchen, to start her search over. She turned every cupboard and cabinet, every drawer and closet upside down looking for the gun, praying Simon hadn't taken it with him. She fought to control the wave of fear that threatened to engulf her, swallowing hard against the constriction in her throat, snatching laboured breaths as her chest tightened.

When there was nowhere left to search she collapsed onto the couch in the living room and shoved her hands between her knees to stop them trembling.

She considered calling her daughter in London, just to hear a familiar voice. But Caroline would guess in an instant that something was wrong. For a moment Jean thought of dialling Stanley's number, but telling an ex-policeman her son was most likely carrying a loaded weapon would only get Simon into more trouble. What if the police did manage to track him down? Her four-o'clock-in-the-morning brain conjured grisly images of a bloody shoot out, Simon outnumbered by a balaclava-wearing SWAT team of marksmen. She rubbed her tired eyes and exhaled, trying to steady her breathing, to calm her racing mind.

She would just have to find Simon herself. Getting the police more closely involved might cause more problems that it would solve. Simon needed saving and it was down to her to save him.

She jumped to her feet and headed for the bathroom.

Showered and dressed, she switched on the television and busied herself in the kitchen making breakfast. The low burble of voices on the news report coming from the other room was somehow reassuring. After forcing down two slices of toast she fired up Simon's laptop and checked for new emails, in the faint hope one or two had arrived during the night. It was possible one of Simon's friends was sheltering him. Jean just had to keep trying his contacts until she managed to press the right button. She had to find a way of jolting someone's conscience into getting in touch.

There was just one new email. From an old friend of Simon's in the UK. Jean's heart sank as she read the message. No one at home would know where he was. But the school friend had suggested something Jean could try. She couldn't believe she hadn't thought of it herself. She opened up a browser window and starting typing, after a couple of letters the address filled automatically. She hit return and Simon's timeline appeared. There was a message on his wall from the same friend who had emailed. Jean typed in a request for help in locating her son and hit the enter button. It seemed Simon had well over five hundred Facebook friends. Hopefully one of them knew where he was.

She scrolled through his photographs. The most recent had been uploaded over two weeks ago. It was a close-up of a pregnant belly, the latest in a series of similar snapshots that had been added at weekly intervals. More photos of a smiling Cindy appeared, the trademark thick eyeliner and black lipstick not quite matching her happy expression. Jean navigated to Cindy's page and left a message begging her to get in touch.

She returned to Simon's pictures and studied his friend's faces, wondering if she should contact each one individually. She moved onto the next album. The first photograph to appear was a headshot of Malcolm Oliver, his unblemished face innocently smiling back at her. A completely different Malcolm Oliver from the one she'd met the day before. She pictured his pale body shrouded in a green sheet on the metal table in the morgue. He looked so young. Images of a battered and beaten Simon crowded her mind.

She slammed the lid of the laptop shut and grabbed her handbag from the couch.

Finally she'd thought of something she could do.

# 19

By the time the first glimmer of daylight started to brighten the Manhattan sky, Jean was already halfway to the subway station at Bowery and Delancey to catch a train to the Financial District.

Although she emerged at the stop at the end of the line a little ruffled and sweaty, her first foray onto the New York subway system had been a success. No one hassled her for spare change, no one mugged her at knifepoint and no one flashed their genitalia at her. She'd had all three happen to her on the London Underground over the years.

She walked the two blocks north to the headquarters of Fisher Krupps and stood at the long desk in the main foyer a full minute before one of the busy team of receptionists asked her 'how they could help her today'.

'Simon Henderson,' Jean said. 'I need to speak to his line manager. It's a matter of life and death.'

The blindingly white smile of the orange-faced woman behind the desk faded momentarily. 'I'm sorry, ma'am – speak to his what?'

'His boss – the person he reports to.'

'And you are?'

'Mrs Henderson. His mother.' Jean stood on her toes in an attempt to endow herself with a little more authority. The addition of two more inches failed to make an impression. 'Life and death,' she repeated.

She was directed to a very expensive row of leather seats with the promise that someone would be right with her. After a good ten minutes of checking her watch, she was finally whisked up to the eleventh floor in a vertigo-inducing glass elevator. She stepped out into a silent lobby decorated with maple wall panels and pale green carpet. An energetic young man shook her hand. His face was the same shade of orange as the woman on the reception desk.

'If you'd care to follow me, ma'am?' he said, a southern twang to his accent.

Jean couldn't help thinking that everyone in the building was acting as if they were auditioning for a role in *Fisher Krupps – The Movie*. How had Simon managed to work in a place like this for nearly three years?

She was ushered down a long corridor and into a small room at the other end. A man in a dark grey pinstripe suit jumped up from behind a desk and gestured toward another two expensive leather chairs arranged around a low glass-topped table.

'Please, ma'am, take a seat,' he said. Another southern drawl. Without looking at the orange boy who'd brought her there he barked, 'That will be all, thank you.' Jean suspected the slick-haired executive didn't know the name of his employee. 'Now,' he said, after Jean had awkwardly lowered herself onto one of the chairs. 'I gather you have something very important you wish to speak with me about.' He flashed her an insincere toothy smile. 'Life and death, they tell me.'

Jean cleared her throat.

'I do hope everything is well with your son and his new baby. I was rather expecting an announcement.'

'I'm afraid I don't know.' She heaved herself forward in the seat. 'I was hoping you might be able to help me in that department.'

'Me?' He jerked back his head and frowned at her. 'How can I possibly help?'

'Has he been in touch with you since Wednesday?'

'No. He has not. We rather assumed he would be back by now.'

'And Malcolm didn't say anything to you? Before he—'

'Malcolm?'

'Malcolm Oliver.'

'Oliver hasn't arrived yet today.' He pinched his lips and sighed, as if he was irritated by the tardiness of his employee.

'You don't know?' Jean let out a breath and gripped the edge of the chair.

'Know what?'

'Malcolm Oliver's body was found in a park by the East River yesterday afternoon.'

The man in the expensive suit shook his head. 'I don't understand.'

'I identified his body at the morgue myself.'

'You know Oliver?'

'I only met him for the first time yesterday.'

He hadn't stopped shaking his head. 'He's dead?'

Jean nodded.

'Dear God. I knew he was under a great deal of stress lately… but I never imagined he would do something like that.'

Jean shuffled further forward on the slippery leather. 'What makes you assume it was suicide?'

'I just… the stress… I don't really… I mean, was it an accident?'

'He was murdered.'

The executive sank back into his chair and ran a hand through his pomaded hair.

'I'm surprised the police haven't been in to speak to you about it.'

'Why would they want to speak to me?' He sat up very straight. 'What have I got to do with his death?'

'Eliminate you from their inquiries?' Jean offered. 'Isn't that what they call it?'

He jumped up and paced across the room. 'You're absolutely sure about this?'

'Do you think I'd be telling you if I wasn't?'

'Murdered? Not an accident?'

'I think the police are smart enough to know the difference.'

'Do they know who might do such a thing?'

Jean shifted her weight from one thigh to the other. She wasn't about to tell Simon's boss about the dodgy moneylender. 'I think they're keeping all lines of inquiry open.'

'But this is terrible news. I assume it hasn't yet been reported in the media?'

Jean shrugged.

'Has anyone linked Oliver to the company?' He stood over her accusingly.

'That's not really what's important here, is it?'

'Of course it is.' He pulled a phone from his pocket and started to tap at the keypad.

Jean reached up and put a hand over the phone. 'Malcolm Oliver is dead and my son is missing.'

'Missing?'

'That's why I'm here. That's what I've been trying to tell you.'

'But what does that have to do with me?' He dragged his phone away from Jean's hand. 'Or the company?'

'They both worked directly under you. I was hoping you could help me piece together Simon's final movements before he…' He voice wavered. She coughed. 'Before he disappeared.'

'I'm sorry – I can't help.' He pressed a button on his phone. 'I'll get someone to escort you back down to reception.'

'But you haven't told me anything about Simon.'

'Simon?' He'd already seemed to have forgotten why she was there.

'What was he working on recently?'

'I… uh… I have no idea. As you can appreciate, I have a very full schedule.' He mumbled something into the phone and a few moments later the orange-faced boy appeared at the other side of the glass door.

'Can you at least tell me what Simon does here?'

'You don't know?'

'Do you?'

He stiffened. 'He's a commodities trader. Emerging economies.'

'What does that mean?'

'I'm afraid I don't have time to give you a lesson in macroeconomics, Mrs…'

'Henderson,' Jean said through gritted teeth, her patience long gone. 'Was it the same job as Malcolm Oliver?'

'How is that relevant?'

Jean couldn't answer, she was clutching at straws and probably had been ever since she'd come up with the notion that someone at Fisher Krupps would be able to help.

The orange boy pulled on the heavy door and held it open.

'I'm sorry you've had a wasted journey, Mrs… ma'am. Please give my regards to your son and his good lady when you do finally catch up with him.'

*Catch up*? He made it sound as if she might meet Simon for tea and cucumber sandwiches. What was wrong with the man?

He shooed her out of the room and her orange-skinned usher gently guided her all the way to the elevator.

'Do you know Simon?' she asked him as they waited for the elevator to arrive.

'Not really, ma'am. We don't tend to… uh… fraternise with the traders.'

'You're not a trader?'

'Not yet – but I'm working on it.'

Jean was right – he *was* auditioning for a part.

Back in the main reception, her visitor's badge safely deposited in a giant glass bowl on the desk, Jean wandered out of the building, wishing she'd asked more pertinent questions while she had the chance. Though she still hadn't worked out what they might have been.

'Ma'am? Are you all right?'

Jean turned to see a tall doorman staring down at her. He wouldn't have looked out of place standing by the entrance of The Ritz in Piccadilly, for all the gold braiding on his uniform. What part was he auditioning for?

'You don't look so good.' He gently fixed a wrinkled hand onto her arm and guided her away from the entrance, toward a wooden bench on the sidewalk.

'Thank you – you're very kind.' She closed her eyes and took a steadying breath.

'You English?' the doorman asked after a few moments.

Jean nodded and rubbed her eyes.

'First time in New York City?' he said and stood a little taller, clearly proud of his hometown.

Jean nodded and to her dismay stinging hot tears filled her eyes. A large white handkerchief appeared under her nose.

'You want me to call someone for you? Did you get lost from your tour party?'

Jean sniffed and dabbed her eyes, concentrating hard on keeping any further tears at bay. 'I'm in the city visiting my son. He works here.' She nodded at the glass and marble façade of the thirty-storey building.

'He does? What's his name?'

'Oh I don't expect you'd know him. There must be hundreds of people coming and going all day long.'

'Try me.'

She forced a smile. 'Simon Henderson. Light brown hair, permanent confused expression on his face, remarkably thin, even though he never exercises. Young looking for his age.'

'I know him. Sure I do.'

'Really?'

'Always says good morning and goodnight to me. A real gentleman. An English gentleman.'

Jean smiled again. It must have been the first time anyone had referred to Simon as a gentleman. An English accent obviously went a long way in New York. 'Do you happen to remember the last time you saw him?'

'Come to think of it – I haven't seen him for a while.' He beamed at her. 'Hey – does that mean his baby's born?'

Jean felt her nose tingling again. She leaned her head back to keep the moisture in her eyes exactly where it was.

'There's nothing wrong with the little one, is there?'

'No!' Jean snatched a breath. 'At least, I hope not. I don't know. Both my son and his girlfriend have gone away. I can't reach either of them.' Jean blew her nose on the doorman's handkerchief. 'When did you last speak to him?'

He thought for a moment, his cloudy eyes gazing into the distance. 'Must have been a few days ago.' He thought again and nodded to himself. 'Yep, Tuesday evening, late.'

'This week?' Jean quickly worked out she must have been somewhere over the Atlantic on Tuesday night.

He nodded. 'I was here way after eleven. I stay around if the board are still meeting inside.'

'Does he normally leave that late?'

'Oh he wasn't leaving. He was arriving… Just a moment, ma'am.' He tipped his hat to her and hurried away to open the door of a long limousine that had pulled into the kerb. By the time he'd escorted the occupants safely into the building and returned to Jean, he seemed to have forgotten what they'd been speaking about. He frowned at her and tugged on the visor of his cap.

'Did Simon mention going away at all?' Jean asked.

'Didn't say much of anything. I asked him about the baby, but he just said there was no news. Seemed he didn't want to speak, you know?'

'Did you notice anything different about him?'

'Oh yes.'

Jean tensed.

'Looked like he was carrying the weight of the world on his shoulders.'

# 20

Jean wrote her phone number on a scrap of paper for the doorman and entered his into her phone. He promised he would contact her if he heard anything at all about Simon, told her to keep the handkerchief, and tipped his hat to her as she left.

Despite feeling unsteady on her feet, she started to walk, not sure where she was going, but knowing she had to keep moving to stop herself sinking.

Her trip to Fisher Krupps had yielded no new information about Simon. She wasn't sure what she'd been hoping for, but she felt thwarted. And helpless. She was no closer to finding her son, or discovering why he owed so much money. Now that Malcolm Oliver was dead, the loan sharks would no doubt come after Simon for the whole debt. A vision of her son in a *High Noon* style showdown with the ruthless moneylenders pushed its way into her mind. With some effort she managed to push it away again, only for another image to appear, this one featuring Simon dressed in an orange jumpsuit, his wrists and ankles shackled. She shook her head in an attempt to clear it.

She walked another three blocks and stopped counting. She crossed a busy intersection and carried on, one foot in front of the other. Perhaps it was better for Simon to remain hidden. Just until she could raise the money to pay off his debt. It was the only thing she could do to get him back. But she had no idea how she would manage it. One hundred thousand dollars? It made Jimmy Kapowski's mortgage default seem like small change in comparison.

She slowed to a halt, the heat and humidity suddenly adding to her distress. She retrieved the doorman's handkerchief from her bag and delicately blotted her cheeks, trying to leave her foundation in place. The handkerchief came away beige. Scanning the street she realised she hadn't a clue where she was. Half a block away she spotted the wide plate glass windows of a department store and headed straight for it. At least it would be cooler in there.

Once inside she discovered it was less department store and more outsized garage sale. Piles of disposable barbeque trays were stacked up next to jumbo packs of incontinence pads; enormous jars of pickles jostled for space on shelves otherwise occupied by bright pink plastic watering cans. It occurred to Jean as she stood beneath the column of cold air blowing down from the ceiling by the entrance that she might find an electric fan to take back to the apartment.

Relieved to have something practical to occupy her, she wandered down the first aisle, which seemed to be exclusively dedicated to tortilla chips of various shapes and flavours. Near the end she saw a woman moving determinedly toward a display of unbranded electronic equipment. The woman was wearing a long woollen overcoat, even though the temperature outside had to be close to eighty-five in the shade. She must have been Jean's age, but shuffled along like a much older woman. Her curiosity peaked, Jean kept her eyes trained on the strange figure and watched in disbelief as the woman slipped two phones and a portable DVD machine beneath her ankle-length coat.

Jean edged a little closer. The woman secreted three MP3 players and a bumper-sized packet of batteries inside the coat. Jean gasped and the light-fingered customer glanced in her direction, defiantly holding Jean's gaze for longer than was comfortable.

Jean looked away first and ducked down the next aisle, wondering what else the woman was concealing under her coat. A member of staff appeared at the other end and, feeling as if she was the guilty party, Jean took a sudden and intense interest in a display of stainless steel kitchen utensils. She picked up an egg whisk to occupy her hands. The store assistant passed and Jean nipped back toward the main doors, not wanting to be around for the confrontation between shoplifter and indignant member of staff.

When she reached the entrance she saw the woman again, gliding slowly toward the automatic doors, her long coat skimming the floor. To Jean's horror the woman passed through the security barriers and immediately triggered a shrieking alarm. But she carried on walking without so much as a twitch. The guard on duty, meanwhile, stopped a young African American woman pushing an enormous stroller into the store.

Jean considered telling him he had the wrong woman – that the real culprit was making good her escape. But she couldn't help admiring the jaw-dropping nerve of the thief and hurried after her. She caught up at the next intersection, the stream of traffic thwarting a clean getaway. When she drew alongside, Jean reached out a hand and managed to grab the woman's arm. She turned, her blank expression a picture of rosy-cheeked innocence. Then she narrowed her eyes.

'Don't tell me – they're recruiting old broads as store detectives now,' she said. 'What they do – bring you out of retirement especially?'

'I'm not a detective.'

The woman took a step back, Jean still holding on tight to her arm. 'Sure – that's what they all say – until they cuff you.'

'How did you do that?'

'Don't know what you're talking about.'

'I saw it all – how did you get away with it?'

'Same way you did.'

'What?'

The woman pointed to the egg whisk Jean was still clutching in her hand. 'Was that the best you could do?'

Jean froze for a moment then shoved the whisk into her bag. 'How often do you do it?'

'You think I'm going to tell you anything?'

'Please – what if…' A nebulous thought was forming in Jean's mind, so unexpected she couldn't quite bring herself to pay it proper attention.

The lights changed, but still Jean held on firmly to the woman's sleeve.

'Let go of me!'

'What are you going to do?' Jean said. 'Call a cop?'

'What do you want?'

'Tell me how you do it.'

'You saw how.'

'But you got clean away.'

'They don't notice someone like me. I might as well be invisible.'

'The alarms still went off.'

The woman shrugged. 'So?'

'But the security man didn't even say anything to you.'

'It's all about timing. Wait for some other sucker to walk into the frame. It's not complicated.'

'What are you going to do with all that stuff?'

'What stuff? Don't know what you're talking about.'

Jean couldn't help but smile at the woman's front. Since she'd arrived in New York, Jean had used her ability to remain unremarkable and unnoticed to steal a pack of cigarettes and a bottle of beer, so what? This woman was seriously exploiting the insignificance that came with old age and using it to her own advantage. Jean looked her up and down. 'But what about the coat?' she said.

'What about it?'

'Doesn't it draw attention to you?'

'Maybe. People just think I'm a crazy old lady who feels the cold. Then they go back to ignoring me.'

'You've never been caught?'

'Why don't you prove it for yourself?' The woman started walking back to the store, dragging Jean along with her. 'Be better if you had on a coat like me or a jacket or something. But I guess that purse of yours is big enough to fit a refrigerator inside.' She scrutinised Jean's bag. 'You got a hat in there? So the security cameras don't get any good pictures.'

'Security cameras?' Jean peered through the doors into the store. The woman with the stroller was now wagging her finger at the guard and shouting.

'Trust me – no one will notice you. You're just another crazy old lady.'

Jean finally let go of the woman's coat, expecting her to turn on her heels and race away up the street. Instead she pushed Jean toward the door and waved her in, clenching both fists in a show of support, like some geriatric cheerleader.

Jean hesitated for a moment near the entrance, then took a deep breath and strode purposefully to the high-value electronic items, grabbing her sun hat from her bag and jamming it on her head as she went. She snatched a couple of packets hanging from a display, not even registering what she was taking as she stuffed them into her bag. Head held high, her eyes fixed on the doors to the street; she walked as nonchalantly as she could back to the entrance. She then spent a minute or so browsing through a gardening catalogue while she waited for her moment. Her palms were moist and her heart was beating out an unsustainable rhythm.

Finally a scruffy girl in a short skirt and cropped tee shirt approached the entrance from the street. Jean took her chance and marched out, practically bumping into the guard as she went. The doors slid open and she was almost through as the alarm sounded.

Then she felt a heavy hand on her shoulder. She froze.

'Ma'am?' the guard said.

She inhaled and turned slowly to see him waving a white handkerchief at her.

'You dropped something.'

# 21

Luisa Rodriguez hesitated for a moment outside Lieutenant Riley's office. She inhaled deeply and tapped on the frosted glass, pushing the door open as soon as she heard him grunt at her to come in. The overpowering stench of stale tobacco hit her before she'd taken a step inside. The space was more smoking den than office. She knew for a fact Riley hosted the squad's monthly poker sessions in there.

She was still waiting for an invite to her first game.

Since he'd arrived at the precinct, Riley had run the detective squad like a private club, if your face didn't fit you were definitely left outside in the cold, looking in. For three years now Luisa felt as if she'd been pressing her nose against the glass. Meanwhile her male poker-playing colleagues were assigned the most interesting investigations. They received encouragement from the boss when they were successful and support when things didn't quite work out as planned. But no matter how well Luisa did, she was always made to feel she could have done better. Now Stanley was gone there was a real danger she might start to believe Riley when he told her how crap she was.

'Well?' he barked at her. 'I don't have all day.'

'No, sir.' She entered the room and left the door open a crack behind her, to let in a little air. Compared to this stagnant office, the squad room mix of sweat and over-brewed coffee seemed positively fragrant.

'Close the door,' Riley said.

She sighed and pulled it shut. 'I just wanted to update you on the Obama robberies.'

'You think that's an appropriate term to use?'

'I…' The whole squad was calling them that. Riley's lapdog Sanchez had come up with the name himself.

'I'm sure I don't need to remind you that two men are lying in refrigerated drawers down at the morgue.'

'No, sir. That's why I wanted to speak to you. I think maybe we're not looking at straightforward robberies here. It's feeling to me like something else is going on.'

'Something else?'

'I don't think the shooter is that interested in the money.'

'That's your *feeling* is it, Rodriguez?'

Why did he have to make it sound so stupid? There was nothing wrong with trusting your cop instinct. Hadn't Stanley told her that again and again?

'It is, sir. Seems to me the shooter's got a taste for killing. I think he may strike again. Maybe not in the same area. But I think it's going to happen soon. Two in two days. That's quite some standard they've set themselves.'

'And you think they'll *strike again* today? Make it three out of three?'

'It's possible.'

'And what do you suggest we do about it? Put a police guard on every grocery store in the city?'

'I thought maybe we should get the forensic psychologist involved – start on building a profile of the two perps. Get a handle on any pattern that might be developing that we're too close to see.'

'I don't have the budget for a shrink telling me how the poor perp's mom didn't love him when he was a baby.'

'But sir, if we can just get a little help in working out where or what they'll target next, we have a better chance of catching them.'

'That's your considered, expert opinion is it?' Riley pushed himself from his chair and walked around the desk, and sat down on the edge. 'As a matter of fact Sanchez beat you to it. He's already updated me on the case. Funny – he didn't mention anything about a pattern.'

'Did he tell you about the perp taking a picture of the victim with his phone and then blowing a kiss to the security camera? Why would he waste time doing that if he wasn't getting some kick out of it?'

'Is that all you're basing your *feeling* on?'

'Isn't that enough?'

'So the perp is a twisted little scumbag speeding on meth, enjoying his fifteen minutes. It means nothing.'

'But Lieutenant, if we just keep mopping up the mess after the event we'll never come close to catching them.'

'Sanchez is leading on this case. You take direction from him.'

Luisa bit her lip.

'Have I made myself understood?'

'Yes, sir, Lieutenant.'

'Get out of here.'

Luisa wandered back into the squad room looking for Sanchez but there was no sign of him. He knew when to keep his head down. She reached her desk to discover a Post-It note stuck to her computer.

*Int rm 3 – requesting lady cop*

It was Sanchez's handwriting. She had hours of video footage from the second shooting to plough through. She didn't have time to interview some over-sensitive crime victim.

Luisa made her way down to the second floor, cursing Sanchez all the way. When she reluctantly shoved open the door of interview room three, she found an immaculately dressed woman perched on the edge of the couch, an untouched cup of coffee sitting on the table in front of her. The woman stood quickly.

'Thank God. I was beginning to think you'd forgotten me completely.' She smoothed non-existent wrinkles from her designer skirt. 'Have you any idea how long I've been waiting?'

'Let's see if we can get you out of here just as quickly as possible then, shall we?' Luisa sat down and waited for the woman to do the same.

'I'd rather stand, if it's all the same to you.' She started to pace the width of the small room, stopping after only a few steps when she reached a wall. She turned and paced the four steps to the other side. 'I don't suppose I can smoke in here? Is there special dispensation for victims?'

'I'm sorry, ma'am. The rules apply all over the station house. Just like they do every other place.' Except Riley's office, of course. 'It would really help me if you could sit down. I'm getting a little dizzy, all the walking up and down.'

The woman rejected the couch and lowered herself gingerly onto the wooden chair facing it. Luisa wrote down the woman's name and address – a co-op on the Upper West Side – and her cell number and then asked her for an account of the crime exactly as it happened.

'Well… I don't really know where to start. You see, I'm not sure exactly where the robbery took place.'

'How about you back right up to the beginning?' Luisa only just managed to stifle a sigh.

'Well I started my day downtown – the Financial District. I met my husband for an early lunch. It's something we're in the habit of doing. Otherwise I never see him from one day to the next.'

Luisa had opened her notepad but her pen remained on the arm of the couch. 'When I said the beginning, ma'am, I was referring to the crime itself.'

'But that's just it.'

'Ma'am?'

'After lunch I met up with some girlfriends in SoHo to do a little shopping for an hour or so. We said our goodbyes at that new boutique on Prince Street – you know the one?' She immediately looked down at Luisa's feet then traced upward to her blank face. 'Well, anyway… I wandered for a while on my own. I'd had a little too much wine at lunch and needed to clear my head.' She uncrossed and recrossed her legs. 'Stupid of me – I don't know what I was thinking. I wasn't thinking, I suppose. Before too long I found myself somewhere on the Lower East Side, certainly much further south of Houston than I'd ever ventured on foot before, and felt quite lost and disoriented.'

'It must have been a terrible shock for you.' Luisa struggled to keep the sarcasm from her voice. 'I mean – in the middle of a strange neighbourhood like that.'

'It was. I went into a store to ask for directions – I didn't want to take out my cell on the street. You don't know who might be watching – waiting to come and snatch it.'

Luisa nodded expectantly.

'That's the only place I can think it could have happened. I must have put down my purse for the briefest of moments.'

'What was taken?'

The woman plucked her pocketbook from her purse and waved it under Luisa's nose. 'The cards are all still here. Only the cash has been removed.'

'All of it?'

'Yes – it's quite empty.'

'How much?'

'I'm sorry?'

'How much was taken?'

'All of it.'

Luisa let out a quiet sigh. 'And exactly how much is that?'

'Exactly? I have no idea. How would I know something like that?'

'You don't know how much money you carry around in your own purse?'

'Of course not – it's my tip money. I need bills to tip doormen and waiters and cab drivers and—'

'I think I know how it works.'

'It wasn't until I tried to tip the waitress at Balthazar's that I realised the money had gone.'

'On Spring Street?'

'That's right.'

'You walked to Spring Street from the Lower East Side?' Luisa glanced down at the woman's spotless strappy shoes.

'Of course not – I got a cab.'

'You didn't tip the driver?'

'I have an account with the cab company. Besides, he was very rude – he didn't deserve a tip.'

'So you don't know how much was taken, or where the crime happened?' For a moment Luisa wondered if maybe Sanchez had set the whole thing up just to yank her chain. But after studying the woman's clothes and demeanour a little more closely, she quickly dismissed the idea – Sanchez wouldn't know any women with this much class.

'That's right – but I know I've been robbed. Isn't it enough that I'm reporting it? Can't you send out some officers to patrol the area?'

'Looking for what exactly? I guess you can't give me a description of the perpetrator?'

'How can I do that?'

Luisa breathed another surreptitious sigh.

'There must be something you can do. I feel so… so violated. Someone has had their filthy hands all over my purse and pocketbook. I doubt I'll be able to go on using either.' She looked down at the legal pad on Luisa's lap. 'You haven't made any notes. Shouldn't you record every little detail – just in case it proves to be of use later?'

'Due respect, ma'am. You haven't given me an awful lot of detail to record.'

'But you must be able to do something. What do we pay our taxes—'

Luisa's cell started to buzz in her pocket. 'Excuse me, ma'am – I'm expecting a very important call.'

'Where are you going?'

'I really have to take this.'

'You can't just leave me.'

Luisa ducked out of the room and exhaled gratefully before hitting the call answer button. 'Detective Rodriguez, how may I—'

'Are you working on the First Avenue shooting?' The voice was harsh and clipped.

'I'm one of the detectives investigating the case. How may I—'

'I'm the owner of the store.'

No wonder she sounded so pissed.

'I'm so sorry for your—'

'Oh please, spare me the platitudes. My mother has been robbed. She had her purse taken. At gunpoint.'

'I'm sorry to hear that, ma'am. Is she OK?'

'What do you think? She had a gun pointed at her head. If I hadn't disturbed him, God knows what would have happened.'

'Have you called nine-one-one?'

'Do you think I'd be speaking to you if I had?'

'It's OK – I can call out the patrol officers for you. We'll get someone there just as soon as possible.'

'I want a detective to come here. I think that's best, given the circumstances.'

'I'm sorry – I don't understand.'

'That's because you haven't been listening to me.'

'What circumstances?'

'The boy who attacked my mother was wearing a rubber Obama mask.'

# 22

After exiting the department store, her shoplifting expedition safely behind her, a sudden rush of adrenalin had lifted Jean's spirits. She'd been expecting to feel at least some guilt, or remorse, instead she'd felt emboldened, invincible even, as if anything was possible.

She spent the next ninety or so minutes back in the Financial District putting her new-found skills to the test.

By the time she made her way to the diner opposite All Saints Hospital she was starting to work out a way to save Jimmy's house and rescue Simon. All she had to do now was get Stanley on board.

He was already sitting at a table by the window when she arrived. She shuffled toward him, the burning pain in her left leg making her limp. She gave his arm an affectionate squeeze. When he didn't react she wondered if she'd been too forward.

'What's the matter with your leg?' he said.

'Oh it's nothing – just my gammy knee playing up. Been on my feet too long today. How's Jimmy?'

'He's waiting for the final exam by the doc before they'll discharge him. Should be out real soon. Couple hours maybe.'

'Is he on the clock?'

'Not yet. They said they'll start the meter running if he sets foot in the recovery ward.' He looked at his watch. 'I should be getting back over there. Sit with him while he's waiting.'

Jean smiled and stared into his face. The lines around his eyes and mouth were etched a little deeper. He looked as if he needed a spell on the recovery ward himself. 'Are you sleeping?' she said.

'As well as I need to.' He rubbed his face, disappearing for a moment behind his hands. 'I'm still keeping NYPD hours.'

'What's going to happen after they discharge him?'

'I'll drive Jimmy home and take care of him for a few days.' He re-emerged from his hands. 'Until I start work on Monday.'

'You've still not told me what your new job is. Can't you work from home?'

'You've got to be kidding. I'm head of security for Dunlow Murphy and Sons.'

Jean looked at him blankly.

'They take care of security for banks and armoured vehicles right across the city.'

Jean let the new information sink in and said nothing for a few moments. 'What happens to Jimmy on Monday?'

'I don't have it all figured out yet.'

'Is there no one else who can help? What about Jimmy's family. He must have someone.'

'No one alive.'

He looked so forlorn, Jean wanted to reach out and hold his hands in hers, but she resisted, not wanting to overstep the mark.

'It's a long story,' he said, 'I don't have time to explain right now.' He started to get up. 'You coming?'

'Can we just sit for a moment? I've something I want to give you.' She surreptitiously slipped a plastic grocery bag under the table and onto his lap.

'What's this?' Stanley looked at her rather than the bag.

'Promise me you won't get angry.'

'Angry?'

'Or make a scene.' Jean glanced around the diner. As ever, no one was paying them any attention. 'You must promise me!'

'What are you talking about?' Slowly, he untied the long handles of the bag, keeping his eyes on Jean's face, one eyebrow raised, his bottom lip clamped between his teeth. He leaned back and finally lowered his gaze to his lap. 'Sweet Jesus!' He quickly scrunched the bag in his fists. 'What the hell is this?'

'Sshhh!'

'What do you mean "sshhh"? What *is* this?'

'An acorn.'

'What are you talking about?' He shoved a hand in the bag. 'How much money is in here?'

'I haven't counted. This is just a small beginning. Hopefully, with a concerted effort and a following wind, it'll grow into the Jimmy Kapowski Benevolent Fund.' Jean picked up a glass from the table and took a sip of iced water. 'Though at this rate, we might just have enough to buy Jimmy a winter coat and a new pair of shoes in time for Christmas.'

'Where did you get this?'

'Oh – you know, here and there.'

'How did you get it?'

'You don't need to know the details. Let's just say it came from generous donations from the good people of the Financial District. A trickle-down, if you like, from Fisher Krupps. And their ilk.'

'*Donations*?'

Jean pursed her lips. 'A figure of speech. I just… encouraged them to part with their money. But like I say – it's just a start – an illustration of what's possible.'

He stared at Jean, his eyes bulging. 'Did you steal this money?' He was speaking through clenched teeth, clearly trying not to raise his voice.

'Everything all right here?' A waitress appeared at the table, pen poised over notepad. 'Ready to order?' she said.

'Does it look like it?' Stanley hadn't taken his eyes off Jean.

'Take as long as you like. We're not busy.'

Jean looked at the woman's name badge. 'Thank you, Glenda – we'll let you know when we're ready.' She smiled up into the waitress's weary face. She looked too old to be waiting tables all day long. Jean glanced at her feet as she walked away. They were badly swollen and crammed into a pinching pair of pumps. 'Wasn't that just a bit rude?' she said, leaning toward Stanley.

'And wasn't this…' He shook the bag on his lap, his knuckles banging the underside of the table. 'Just a bit criminal? For crying out loud, what did you think you were doing?'

'I told you – making a start.'

'You have to return it.'

'How can I? I don't know who those people were.'

'What about their credit cards?'

'Oh I only take cash. I return the wallets as soon as I've taken the money. Why would I take their cards? I don't want to inconvenience them.'

'You don't want to… Jesus Christ.'

'None of them will even miss it. Trust me. It's just chicken feed to them – play money. They made it so easy for me.'

'What happened to your conscience? You're telling me you're all right with this?'

Jean hadn't stopped to consider it. She'd finally found a way, albeit a token one, to help bring Simon back. Conscience didn't come into. All she was feeling was overwhelming relief.

At that moment two uniformed cops strode into the diner. Stanley nodded toward them, a nervous twitch starting high up in his left cheek.

'Hey Brenda!' one of the cops shouted to the room in general. 'Two cups of coffee when you got a minute.'

The waitress called back, 'Got all the minutes in the day for you, honey. I'll be right over.'

Stanley shifted in his seat, the vinyl upholstery squeaking as he moved.

'It's all right,' Jean said. 'You don't work for them anymore – it's not as if they can sack you now.'

'No – but they can damn sure arrest me.' He glanced down at the bag again. 'Accessory to grand larceny. That's a great way to end my illustrious career.' He shook his head. 'As if I don't have enough to deal with right now.'

'But this is for Jimmy.' She decided it wise to leave Simon out of the equation for the time being.

'You got to hand yourself in.'

'Don't be ridiculous – they'll deport me, or worse. How am I going to help anyone then?'

'Maybe you should have thought of that before you committed the crime. Before you decided—'

He was cut short by the return of the waitress, who took one look at his face and swiftly turned on her heels and went back the way she came.

'Give me the bag,' Jean said.

He clutched it tighter. 'I'll take you down to the station house myself.'

'I did this for *your* friend.'

Stanley's face had flushed, the tips of his ears glowing bright crimson. 'You're out of your mind.'

'Actually I feel like I've only just started thinking clearly. It's quite simple really.'

The waitress returned. Jean could only admire her single-minded determination to serve them.

'For God's sake.' Stanley started to stand, remembered the bag, and swiftly sat back down again. 'Coffee. To go.'

'Two coffees?'

'That would be lovely – could I get a slice of pie too?'

'Cherry? Apple?'

'Apple.'

'With cream, ice cream?'

'How can you eat at a time like this?' Stanley blurted. 'Just the coffee. And the check.' He waited for the waitress to walk away before he spoke again. 'Why don't I have a quiet word with these cops? You can be their problem.'

'Go on then.'

'What?'

'Do your worst.'

Stanley bit his lip.

'You know what I think? I think you have no intention of turning me in. Because you know I'm right.'

Stanley let out a sigh and stared up at the ceiling. 'I can't deal with this. With you. I gotta get out of here.'

The words stung so sharply, sudden tears sprang into her eyes. She blinked and sniffed them back.

'Here we are.' The waitress planted the paper cups of coffee on the table. 'I added cream to them both. You seem like the kind of folks who know how to enjoy their coffee, huh? Am I right?' She pushed a paper bag next to Jean's cup. 'Nice slice of good ol' American pie.'

Stanley reached into his pocket and shoved some bills at her. 'Keep the change.'

'I'm right,' Jean persisted, despite the voice in her head screaming at her to stop. She took a peek at the triangle of sugared pastry inside the paper bag and pushed it away. 'I haven't worked out how to scale it up. My efforts are too small and too slow to drag Jimmy from the hole he's in. We need to seriously ramp things up.'

'We?'

'You, me…' Jean nodded toward the waitress, who was leaning against a table, one shoe off, massaging the ball of her foot. 'And her.'

'What the hell has she got to do with it?'

'Nothing. Not really. She's just representational.'

'She's what?'

'I mean people *like* her. Like us.'

Stanley flared his nostrils, unable to speak. Unable to move.

'There must be hundreds, if not *thousands* of us in this city.' Jean continued. 'Just in Manhattan alone. All we need to do is rally the troops.'

Stanley sucked in a sharp breath and regained the power of speech. '*Us* all of a sudden? Who's *us*?'

'Seniors. People who don't count anymore. The forgotten. The insignificant.'

'You're out of your goddamn mind.'

'I bet there are plenty of seniors who lost their pensions and their homes because of Fisher Krupps and other companies like them. I reckon they'd jump at a chance to get even.'

'I can't listen to this anymore.' Stanley stood up, thrusting the bag onto the chair next to him.

'Sit down, please. Just hear me out.'

'I heard enough already.'

Jean's phone bleeped loudly in her bag.

'Please, Stanley. Let me say what I've got to, then decide what you want to do.'

'Say anymore and I walk out that door and you never see me again.'

'Please. Just sit down.'

'I got to get back to Jimmy. Right now he's making a damn sight more sense than you.'

Jean pulled the phone from her bag and opened the message. She blinked at it, held it at arms length and squinted, unable to make sense of what she was reading. 'I don't understand. How could he have my number?' She tried to swallow, her top lip stuck to her teeth.

'Who?'

With trembling hands, Jean turned the phone around and slid it across the table.

Stanley glanced down at the screen and read aloud. 'Bang bang, you're dead… *Barack Obama*?'

# 23

Detective Rodriguez weighed Jean's phone in her hand and stared down at the small screen. 'The caller withheld their number,' she said.

Jean was sitting at the side of the detective's desk, Stanley stood behind her chair, refusing to sit down, still clutching the plastic grocery bag full of money. Every time he shifted his weight from one foot to the other the bag rustled in Jean's ear.

'Given who we think sent the message, that's hardly surprising,' Jean said, leaning forward, trying to get away from the noisy bag, wishing Stanley would stop drawing attention to it. Part of her was convinced he was just preparing himself to hand over the booty to his colleague. She leaned forward a little more, desperate to obscure Rodriguez's view.

'We can find out,' Rodriguez said. 'Trace the number at the phone company.'

'So you can track him down?' She looked up at Stanley. 'Thank God.'

The detective shrugged. 'It's not as simple as that – it might be a burner he's using. A disposable cell that isn't registered.'

'So you can find the number but not the owner of the phone?'

'Depends how careless he's been. Or stupid.' She flipped Jean's phone over and over in her hand. 'If the perp did send the message, how did he get your number?'

'Don't you think I've been wrestling with that question ever since I received the text?'

'How many people have it?'

'Just friends and family.' She turned her head a few degrees toward Stanley. 'And both of you, of course.'

'I can't figure it out,' Stanley said, the first time he'd spoken since they arrived.

Jean sat on her hands in an effort to stop them shaking. If the boy with the gun had managed to get her number, did that mean he knew where she lived too? Her throat constricted. She started to speak but the words wouldn't come. Then she remembered.

'There was someone…' She pulled a face. 'Sorry, I forgot. But there's no way he could have sent the text.'

'Leave that for us to decide, OK?' The detective held a pen poised over a large yellow pad and Jean told her about the doorman at Fisher Krupps.

'But he knows nothing about the grocery store, about the shooting, the masks. Nothing.'

'I'd still like to contact him.' Rodriguez carefully underlined the number and circled the name. 'Clarence Ashe – you're sure about the spelling?'

'Certain.'

'And that's it? Nobody else has your cell number?'

Jean sucked in a shaky breath. 'It doesn't make any sense.'

'We need to think this through. Retrace your steps since you arrived.' Rodriguez started to tap her pad with a pen.

'I've not really been anywhere.'

'Where did you go after you left Fisher Krupps this morning?'

'Nowhere.' The word came out too forcefully. 'I mean – I just walked from there to the diner near the hospital.'

'Did you leave your number with anyone at All Saints? Or the morgue?'

Jean shook her head. 'The only other places I've been are here and the grocery store.' A sharp intake of breath rattled in Jean's throat. 'Oh – the store. I gave my number to the poor woman who lost her son.'

The detective looked at her blankly.

'The older lady at the store. She's Korean, I think.'

'The store on First Avenue?'

Jean nodded.

'The clerk wasn't her son,' Rodriguez said.

'He wasn't? She seemed dreadfully cut up about it.' Jean pulled her hands from under her thighs and clenched her fists on her lap. 'I wanted to do something for her. Help in some small way.'

'So you gave her your number?'

'Sometimes it's easier to talk to a stranger.'

'Did you tell Mrs Kim where you were staying? Did she take down your address?'

'No – I just told her I was living locally. Why?'

'She had her purse stolen today – her cell phone was inside.'

'On my God – that poor, poor soul. As if she hasn't been through enough already.'

'The perpetrator was wearing a rubber Obama mask.'

One side of Jean's face had started to tingle. Feeling herself falling forward she reached her hands out for the desk. 'But how would he know my name? How would he know she even had my number?'

'The point is, he has your number and your name. It may be just a matter of time before he finds you. You're sure you didn't give Mrs Kim your address?'

Jean nodded, but a chink of doubt crept in. She hadn't, had she?

'I think perhaps you should return to England.'

'I can't go home now. I need to find Simon.'

'It may not be safe at your son's apartment.'

The bag rustled behind Jean and Stanley put a hand on her shoulder. 'Come stay at my house.'

Jean was sure she saw Rodriguez flinch. A definite tensing of the detective's upper body. What was it to her where she stayed? Jean wasn't sure if she should read anything into Stanley's offer. She glanced at his hand resting casually on her shoulder. She reached up and let the tips of her fingers touch his. 'I have to stay in the apartment. What if Simon comes home? I need to be there for him.'

'I can't offer you any protection – we don't have that kind of manpower,' Rodriguez said.

'I'm not asking for any. I'm just telling you I can't leave. Not without knowing Simon is safe.'

Stanley pulled away his hand and immediately the plastic bag rustled again.

'Are you OK, Stan?' the detective said.

'Fine. I'm fine. Never better.'

'You look a little shook up.'

Stanley passed the plastic bag from one hand to the other, as if it had suddenly become too hot to handle.

'What's in the bag, Stan?' Rodriguez was still smiling at him.

Jean sucked down a breath and waited for his conscience to get the better of him.

Stanley looked at the bag, then shoved it behind his back. He cleared his throat as if he was going to make an important announcement.

'What have you done with that photo I gave you?' Jean jumped in, to stop Stanley confessing on her behalf. 'I expected it to be all over the news.' She sat up trying to force Rodriguez to look at her instead of the bag. 'I haven't even heard it mentioned.' She dragged her chair closer to the detective's. 'In fact—'

'Hey, Lu – I really gotta get going. Jimmy's waiting for me at the hospital.' Stanley backed toward the exit. 'I'll call you later. OK?' He ran the last few yards. Jean watched him disappear into the corridor, half relieved, half dismayed she'd been abandoned.

'Photograph?' Rodriguez said sharply.

'Why are they still saying on the news you're looking for two black men?'

'I'm sorry, ma'am. I can't discuss police—'

'You didn't believe me, did you?' Jean snatched her phone off the desk. 'I'm surprised you're even taking me seriously now.' She slipped the phone into her bag, eager to ensure she didn't mislay it again. 'That's assuming you are, of course.'

Before the detective had a chance to answer, a uniformed female officer marched toward the desk, a tall woman in an expensive suit trailing a few feet behind.

'Oh crap,' Rodriguez said under her breath.

'This lady says she's been waiting over three-quarters of an hour,' the policewoman said.

'I'm sorry, ma'am.' Rodriguez rose quickly from her seat. 'I was just on my way to finish up.'

'It looks like it.' The well-dressed woman folded her arms. 'Robbed and no one gives a damn.' She looked Jean up and down.

Jean automatically raised a hand to her unruly hair and lifted the damp rat's tails from her neck.

Then she froze.

She'd seen this woman before. Barely two hours ago. In a small café just off Wall Street. An unwitting contributor to the Jimmy Kapowski Fund. The woman stared into Jean's face and tilted her head sideways.

Jean held her breath.

For those few moments time seemed to stand still, the background buzz of the squad room fading as if someone had yanked down the volume control. The woman frowned, tilted her head the other way. Then, without the slightest glimmer of recognition, she turned away.

# 24

From the other end of the street, Linus saw Richie leaning against the latest stolen motorcycle. He was smoking a cigarette like he'd invented it. He looked so cool it made Linus's stomach knot.

'Hey,' Richie said when he spotted him.

'Hey,' Linus watched Richie take a last drag on his cigarette and flick away the butt.

'What you got planned?' Richie asked. 'Another store? I'm not going back downtown. Too many people know me down there.' He yawned and stretched his arms high above his head, lifting his tee shirt from his pants and exposing an inch of hard brown flesh. Linus looked away. 'You still got my gun?' Richie punched him playfully on the arm. 'Did you hear the clerk from the second store died? Brain damage or some crap. Two dead bodies in two days – you're a regular serial killer.'

Linus smiled at him.

'You love this,' Richie said.

'Why shouldn't I?'

'You're just twisted.' Richie scratched his stomach. 'Why'd you hit him like that?'

'Why not?' Linus opened his arms wide and shrugged his shoulders. He still didn't understand it himself. The gun had been coming down fast and smashing into the clerk's face before he'd even registered what he was doing. And once he'd started, he didn't feel like stopping.

'You coulda just shot him. Bam! Straight between the eyes.'

'I could have. But I didn't. So what?'

'You better clean the gun properly. And throw out whatever you were wearing. Half that loser's brains musta splattered all over you.'

'You think the NYPD are about to search my closet? It's not like they're coming after me.' He curled the corner of his mouth, half-smiling at Richie. 'I'm not going to get caught.'

'Oh yeah? You wasted the old lady yet?'

Linus considered lying. After another fruitless search he was beginning to wonder if he'd ever track her down. But if he lied Richie might ask for the gun back. And he was nowhere near finished with it.

'I'm on it.' Linus smiled broadly and punched Richie, harder than Richie had punched him. He rocked backward, against the bike.

'Easy man – don't damage the merchandise.' Richie stood to one side and swept an arm along the length of the bike. 'How do you like this?'

Linus nodded appreciatively and let out a whistle, but he didn't recognise one brand of motorcycle from another. They took you places. Fast. And got you away again even faster. 'Great job.'

'So – where we headed?'

'East, out of the city.'

'How far?'

'An hour, maybe.'

'We gotta get gas. You paying for it?'

'I don't have any money – what about the money from the last grocery store?'

'What – you think I put it in my savings account?'

Linus stuck a hand in his pocket, pulled out a few crumpled bills and shoved them at Richie.

'What's wrong with staying in the city, anyway?'

'I got a plan.'

Richie was forced to slow down twice as they made their way along the I-495 toward Bellmore on Long Island. Once because he spotted a traffic cop parked up, just waiting for someone to fall into his trap, and again when a patrol car cruised alongside them in the next lane.

Linus felt Richie's muscles tense as he clung onto him. If they gave the police any reason to call in the registration, they wouldn't get further than the next exit.

The car stayed with them for nearly five minutes, the cop who was riding shotgun staring at them like he'd never seen a motorcycle before. Sweat had soaked right through Richie's tee shirt by the time the cops eventually peeled away. Linus thumped him on the back and shoved his hand in front of Richie's face, giving him the thumbs up.

They got to Bellmore in under forty-five minutes. Linus had memorised the route from the highway, but it all looked very different on the ground. He wasn't even sure which way was north. Eventually, after a few false turns, Richie steered the bike into the little avenue Linus had been searching for. He shouted for Richie to stop and wrenched off his helmet as they pulled into the kerb.

'Where's the store? This place is just full of big old houses,' Richie said. 'We come all this way to steal a few bucks from somebody's house?'

'A few bucks?' Linus shook his head. 'That's not why we've come here.' He moistened his lips. His skin was tingling just like it had the night before. 'You stay here.'

'And let you keep the best stuff for yourself? No way. We got a deal.' Richie took his helmet off and pulled the rubber mask over his head as he dismounted. 'Which house?' He looked up and down the street.

Linus started to walk toward the smallest clapboard house in the tree-lined street, keeping his pace brisk but unhurried. Like a man who had important business to attend to. When he drew level with a bushy tree obscuring a portion of the front lawn, he slowed a fraction and peered through the leaves. He had expected to knock on the door and go into the house. But as things were, he wouldn't even need to.

'Hey!' he shouted and picked up his pace once again, breaking into a run, aware Richie was shadowing him.

'Where's your mask?' Richie hissed at him.

The crop-haired man turned from his rose bush, lowered a pair of pruning shears and looked directly at Linus. The anxious expression on his face melted the instant he recognised him.

'What on earth are you doing here?' The shears fell from his hands and he stumbled slightly. It took him a moment to recover his balance. And his manners, Linus thought. 'What a lovely surprise,' he said, eventually, and turned his head toward the open porch door. 'Howard, honey – we have a guest. You'll never guess who!'

Linus pulled out the gun and quickly pumped two bullets into the old man's chest. The force threw him backward and onto the ground. Linus stood over his motionless body and shot him again, squarely between the eyes.

'What are you doing?' Richie's voice had turned into a panicky squeal. 'What the…?'

Linus glanced up and watched Richie scramble and fall, crawl along the ground a few steps, pick himself up again and finally sprint toward the motorcycle.

Without rushing, Linus fished the rubber mask out of a pocket and stretched it over his head. Then he pulled out his cell phone and took a picture of the man lying on the ground. He sauntered to the bike, as if he was just out for an evening stroll, taking in the pleasant Long Island air.

# 25

'Riley said there's no budget for overtime.' Sanchez sat on the edge of a table in the audiovisual suite.

'So?' Luisa refused to look at him, concentrating hard on the security camera images on the monitor in front of her.

'So what do you think you're doing?'

'You wouldn't understand it – for some of us this job is a vocation. You know – righting wrongs? Putting away the bad guys? That kind of stuff.'

'Oh I get it – you got nothing better to do on a Friday night. Poor little Lulu – couldn't get a date.'

'Screw you.'

'I'd like to help you out, but you're not really my type. Besides, I'm spoken for.'

'What? Your second wife's finally letting you back into the apartment? Did you get house-trained suddenly?'

He jumped to his feet. 'You don't know anything about it.'

'Yeah that's right – I mind my own business.'

'Remember to turn off the lights when you go.' He waved at her, looking like a small child, his bottom lip sticking out. Then he disappeared into the corridor. She stretched out her arms wide and rolled her head first clockwise then counter; trying to release the tension she'd been carrying around all day. A satisfying clunk sounded from the very top of her spine.

Was Sanchez right? Had she become so wedded to the job that she really didn't have anything better to do on a Friday night? For a moment she considered calling Stanley. Since his wife died, Stanley had always been good for a couple of beers and a game of pool. But he was too busy with his sick buddy and this new woman in his life. Luisa scribbled a note the back of her hand as a reminder to investigate Mrs Henderson. With the second shooting coming so close after the first, she hadn't had a chance to probe into the woman's past, murky or otherwise. Right now Stanley had enough on his plate without some demanding English woman getting under his feet. Getting under his skin. Getting under God only knew what else. Luisa shuddered and pushed any thought of what Stanley might be doing with Mrs Henderson from her mind.

Though she hated to admit it, Sanchez's comment had been right on the money. Another Friday night without a date, or even the possibility of one. She did sometimes feel a little lonely when the weekend came around. She hated leaving the noisy confusion of the squad room just to go home to her silent and empty one-room apartment in a downmarket corner of Brooklyn. But the idea of lurking in some bar, picking up a stranger just to wake up next to someone in the morning was too depressing to contemplate.

She had her work. And this evening at least, work was enough.

The recordings from the security cameras at the second grocery store had so far yielded very little in the way additional evidence. They could be pretty sure the same perps were responsible for both robberies – the general descriptions were the same and so were the rubber masks. What was puzzling Luisa was the change in M.O.

A multiple-bullet shooting in the first store then the physical attack in the second. It was almost as if it was personal this time. Did the perp know the victim? She made a note to check the clerk's juvie record. Maybe he'd made himself some enemies inside. It was a long shot, but right now she didn't have much else. She froze the recording at the moment the perp blew a kiss at the camera. It didn't matter what Riley thought, this guy was seriously getting off on this stuff. Which meant he was likely to do it again.

She stared at the still image a while longer then ejected the DVD from the player and inserted another – this one showing the split screen footage from the other four cameras. She skipped through the endless minutes of regular customers going in and out of the store at high speed until the two masked men entered. There was a time lapse between the first and second making their way inside. The first came in waving his gun, looked around the store and made straight for the clerk behind the counter. The second perp followed almost a minute later. He hesitated at the door, frozen for a moment, looking in the direction of the counter but doing nothing. Then he ran further into the store and disappeared from view. Luisa stopped playback. Something wasn't right. What had she seen? She skipped back and watched him hover at the door again, studying his movements, or lack of them. She clicked the footage forward one frame at a time as he started to run. Then she realised what it was. Unlike his accomplice, perp number two wasn't wearing gloves. And he was black. She fast-forwarded again until he reappeared in the top left-hand image. He hurtled toward the door so fast he stumbled and lurched forward, his arms flailing. She stopped the DVD again.

Finally – a break.

As he stumbled, he reached a hand in front of him, groping for something to stop his fall and leaned heavily on the metal frame of the door, leaving a complete set of prints behind.

Hopefully.

Luisa hit the play button again and watched him shoulder open the door and disappear into the street.

Her first instinct was to call Stanley and share the good news, but she checked herself and ran to the lieutenant's office to discover Riley had already left for the evening. Someone else with better things to do on Friday night. She hurried to her desk, her excitement only slightly dented, and called the CSIs to let them know if they hadn't taken prints from the door already, they needed to get back in there right now. By the time she put down the phone the thump of her heart had calmed a little. All she could do now was wait. Probably she wouldn't hear anything until Monday morning. But how could she go home, a night of mindless TV stretching out in front of her? She reached over to her computer to reboot it and noticed the reminder she'd scribbled on her hand: *Mrs H??*

Luisa took a deep breath and opened up a browser window. She hesitated for a moment, her fingers poised over the keyboard. About to snoop on Stanley's new friend, she suddenly felt a little dirty. But then who else did Stanley have in his corner? She only had his best interests at heart. Without thinking too deeply about the consequences, Luisa quickly typed 'Jean Henderson' and 'UK' into the Google search box. Over a dozen pages of results were returned. She narrowed the search by adding the word 'London'. The top result linked to a newspaper website, she clicked on it, trying to ignore the uneasy feeling stirring in her stomach. What was Mrs Henderson doing in the newspaper?

Her desk phone started to ring. She ignored it. She was on her own time, after all. She stared at the flashing red light. What if it was a new lead? She lifted the handset.

'Detective Rodriguez, how may I—'

'By getting your ass over here right now.'

'Ma'am?'

'My mother, Mrs Kim, remember? You said you'd send a detective to speak to her. We're still waiting.'

'I'm sorry ma'am. It's been a little busy here.' Sanchez had promised Luisa he would take care of it personally. Lazy bastard. 'I'll be right over. Please apologise to your mother for me.'

'Why don't you do that yourself when you get here?' She hung up.

Luisa slammed down the phone and clicked the first link listed on Google. She quickly scanned the story from the *Evening News* while she shrugged on her jacket. The report gave details of a scuffle that had broken out between demonstrators and police during a political protest in some place named Catford, in south London. A sixty-four-year-old woman, Jean Henderson, was arrested for attacking a police officer. It went on to profile the 'grandmother of five', describing her as 'a determined and fearless campaigner for justice'.

The thump in Luisa's chest returned.

There was no way someone arrested for attacking a cop would be allowed to enter the US. Which could only mean that the woman who currently had her hooks in Stanley Rozello must have lied on her ESTA visa waiver application. No wonder she'd been so reluctant to hand over her passport. Luisa should have followed her gut sooner, before the woman had gotten so cosy with Stanley. If she'd lied to get into the country, what other stories might she be spinning?

Luisa reached for her phone. She had to speak to Stanley. Then she'd put in a call to Homeland Security.

# 26

Jean woke to the sound of breaking glass. She sat up, listening. Had the noise come from inside the apartment? She slipped her hand beneath a pillow and retrieved the bread knife she'd placed there before she went to bed. She pictured the pale-faced boy with the damp curly hair standing on the fire escape wielding a brick. Or creeping toward her down the hall, a gun in his shaking hand.

*Bang bang you're dead.*

She stopped breathing, straining to make out any incongruous sound.

Silence. Not even traffic noise drifting in from the street outside. She lay down again, still clutching the knife, but couldn't force her eyes shut. She exhaled and swung her legs over the edge of the bed. Gripping the knife firmly, she crept to the bedroom door and listened again for movement on the other side. By now it was virtually impossible to hear anything above the noisy pounding of blood in her ears, so she opened the door and made her way to the living room. After a quick glance around in the gloom, reassured the glass panes remained secure in their frames, she moved on to the kitchen and finally the small nursery.

Everything was as it should be.

Thank God.

Jean unlocked the apartment door, knowing if she didn't check outside, she would never get back to sleep. Slowly she turned the handle then thrust open the door.

She gasped. Standing right outside, holding a fearsome meat cleaver in both hands, was the woman from across the hall. She gasped back. Both women exhaled simultaneously.

'I didn't dream it, then?' the woman said. 'You heard it too?'

'Smashing glass?'

The woman nodded and slowly lowered her weapon. 'I guess it was outside, huh?'

Jean swallowed, her mouth suddenly very dry. Her top lip was stuck to her teeth.

'I just boiled the kettle,' the neighbour said. 'You want some tea?'

Jean glanced over her shoulder.

'You think you're going to sleep now?'

'I suppose not. Hang on.' Jean grabbed her keys, locked her door and followed the woman into the apartment across the hall, a smell of long-boiled chicken bones intensifying as they entered the kitchen.

'Take the weight off.'

Jean lowered herself onto a rickety wooden chair beside a large antique table.

'I'm sorry about before – when you arrived?' the woman said. 'I was feeling a little grouchy.'

'Happens to the best of us.'

She waved a china teapot at Jean. 'How do you take it?'

'The English way, I'm afraid. Strong as you like with plenty of milk.'

A few seconds later a milk jug appeared on the table, together with a pile of sesame seed bagels and a pot of cream cheese. 'Just in case we get a little peckish,' the neighbour explained.

'At three o'clock in the morning?'

'I don't sleep too good in the heat.' She held out a bony hand. 'Carmen Steinway – like the pianos.'

Jean got the impression she used that line a lot. 'Jean Hender— I suppose you know who I am.'

Tea was poured into china cups, Jean adding milk, Carmen Steinway a slice of lemon. 'How's the baby?'

Jean was just lifting the cup to her mouth. She returned it to the table and let out a sigh. 'I only wish I knew.'

The woman pulled a sympathetic face. 'That bad, huh? I guess it was on the cards.' She smeared a healthy portion of cream cheese onto the bottom half of a bagel.

'What was?'

'Cindy leaving like that.' The woman dropped her gaze and concentrated on her cheese spreading. 'Maybe I've spoken out of turn. Take no notice of me. What does a stupid old woman know about it?'

'Tell me what you do know.' Jean managed a sip of tea, just to moisten her lips.

'Nothing, not really.' She lifted the bagel to her mouth and put it down again without taking a bite. 'I heard a little shouting – coming through the wall now and then.'

'Shouting?' Simon never raised his voice. The silent treatment was more his style.

'I guess it was her hormones – making her a little… tetchy?'

'Cindy was shouting?'

'Sounded as if she was getting angry with your son. Probably just because she was in her third trimester – and it was so damn hot. Hotter than this even.' She used a napkin to dab her top lip and forehead, by way of demonstration.

Jean considered for a moment. Something didn't ring true. 'Wait a minute. If you knew Cindy had gone, why didn't you tell me as soon as I arrived?'

Carmen took a sip of tea. 'I thought you already knew. Besides, I try not to get involved in family dramas. I've managed to avoid them ever since I left home.'

'Do you know when Cindy left?'

'Early hours of Wednesday morning there was one almighty fight. Yelling, doors slamming. I think I even heard…' She pulled a face.

'What?'

'I think maybe your son was crying.'

'Are you saying Cindy left in the middle of the night? In her condition?'

Carmen nodded. 'I looked out the window and saw her getting into a car. Big long thing. Like a movie star's car.' She started to speak and checked herself.

'What is it?'

'Your son was on the street. Started tugging at the bags the chauffeur was loading into the trunk.'

'Chauffeur?' How many more surprises would Jean discover about Cindy?

'Well, he was wearing a light grey suit, like a uniform – even had on a cap with a visor. He must have been roasting. If he was a cab driver, he sure was an upmarket one, that's all I can say.'

'Did you speak to her? Or Simon?'

'Like I said before—'

'You don't get into other people's business.'

'I feel kinda bad about it now. Your son watched the car drive away and stayed on the sidewalk for twenty, maybe thirty minutes. I guess he thought she'd change her mind and ask the driver to turn around.' She topped up her cup to the brim and stirred a teaspoon of sugar into the black tea. 'I should have at least checked he was OK.' She shrugged an apology. 'How's he doing now? I suppose not knowing about the baby is driving him crazy. You too.'

Jean stared down at the criss-cross of old scratches and scars on the wooden table. She cleared her throat to subdue a sob and quickly lifted her cup to her lips. 'I've not spoken to Simon all the time I've been here,' she blurted. 'I don't even know where he is.'

'He's gone too?'

Jean caught her breath and nodded. 'I don't suppose he mentioned where he was going when he gave you the keys?'

'What keys?'

'In the envelope you gave me.'

'I found that in my mailbox downstairs. A note stuck to the outside telling me to give it to you when you arrived. I had no idea there were keys inside.'

'When was the last time you spoke to him?'

Carmen thought for a moment, pursing her lips so hard the colour drained from them. 'Maybe a couple of weeks ago. Just a little neighbourly small talk when we passed on the stairs – you know, the weather, the lousy landlord.'

'How did he seem?'

'Distracted I guess. But I figured he had a lot on his mind with the baby and all. Better things to do than gossip with the old lady from across the hall.'

A loud clanking noise sounded from the hallway just outside the kitchen. Carmen grabbed a wrench from the kitchen counter and hurried from the room. A metallic clang rang out and she returned. 'Radiators need fixing,' she said, by way of explanation. 'They bang and whine from time to time. I'm surprised you haven't been disturbed by them. The landlord's letting everything slide – doing anything he can to make it easier to get rid of me.' She slid the wrench back onto the counter. 'He doesn't have a chance. I'm going nowhere. Forty years I've lived here. He's only owned the building for fifteen. Fifteen years he's been working on ways to make me leave.' She added another spoonful of sugar to her tea. 'Protected rent has been driving him crazy all that time.' She carried on stirring the tea long after the sugar had dissolved. 'Listen to me – you don't need to hear about my fight with the landlord!' She reached out a hand and patted Jean gently on the arm. 'I'm sure Simon will show up soon – he's probably just trying to make up with Cindy. I expect he doesn't want to call you until he's worked it out with her.'

Jean forced a smile but didn't comment, wishing a domestic quarrel was the worst of Simon's troubles. She took a final sip of tea and pushed her chair from the table. 'I should be getting back – at least try to get some sleep.'

'There's plenty of tea in the pot. You sure you're OK to be alone?'

'Oh I'm fine.'

The two women said goodnight in the hallway and Jean heard a battery of locks and bolts slide across her neighbour's door. She did the same as soon as she was inside Simon's apartment. Just as she turned the final lock, she heard her phone bleep from the bedroom. She rushed to grab it from the nightstand and discovered a message from a number she didn't recognise.

*Baby girl – 5lbs 7oz – mother & daughter doing fine*

Jean clutched the phone to her chest and drew down a deep breath. She dialled the strange number and was greeted with an outgoing voicemail message. She didn't recognise the voice either – it certainly wasn't Cindy. There was a slight clip to it, refined and precise. If there was an upper class American accent, Jean imagined this was what it sounded like. She left a message wishing Cindy and the baby all the best and asked the mystery texter to call her back urgently. Then she lay on the bed, eyes wide open, wondering what her son was doing right now.

# 27

Jean rose before the sun, showered and dressed and tried to force down some breakfast. She found a box of cereal in a kitchen cabinet and spent ten minutes pushing Coco Pops around a bowl, watching television, waiting for the phone to ring. Hoping Cindy would respond to her message.

The news channels were still full of business and finance stories, even on a Saturday. Yet again she was confronted with the tanned face and white teeth of the boss of Fisher Krupps, still defending his multi-million dollar bonus.

'Change the record,' she shouted at the screen.

She channel-hopped for an hour or so until the waiting became unbearable. She picked up her phone, wondering if seven-thirty was too early to try Cindy again and found her fingers deciding for her. Diverted straight to voicemail, she listened to the same clipped voice as it urged her to leave a message, which she did. She tried Cindy's number and left a message pleading for her to get in touch.

After another thirty minutes she scrolled through her contacts list and found Stanley's number. She hadn't spoken to him since he'd left the police station. He hadn't called her, and given how angry he'd been, she didn't feel able to call him. Her finger hovered over the call button. She sucked down a deep breath and pressed it.

When he answered, Stanley sounded groggy but cheerful. Jean couldn't work out whether that meant he'd forgiven her, or that the anxiety about his friend's situation had receded a little after a good night's sleep.

'How's Jimmy?' she asked.

'Comfortable. I was gonna call you this morning.'

Jean was surprised how relieved she was to hear that.

'How are you?' Stanley said. 'You heard from that lowlife again? He hasn't sent anymore texts?'

'No… listen, I think we should speak.'

Stanley's cheerful tone proved to be short-lived. 'We're speaking now, aren't we? What is it?'

'Face to face.'

'If this is about your…'

'Fundraising activities?'

'Not how I would choose to describe it.'

'You've made that quite clear. It's about Jimmy. It's important.'

As soon as she'd wrangled Jimmy's address from Stanley she left the apartment, and, miraculously, the fourth cab driver she waved at not only acknowledged her, but agreed to take her all the way to Queens. As soon as she got a good look at his face she realised why. He had to be pushing seventy-five.

Less than an hour later she was pulling up outside Jimmy's house, deep in Forest Hills, counting so many bills into the driver's hand she was beginning to wish she'd never given Stanley the bag of money.

During the journey she'd passed through some fairly affluent neighbourhoods; freshly painted houses set in well-manicured lawns. But as soon as the cab turned into Jimmy's street, the overall tone changed. Almost every house had a 'For Sale' sign planted in its front yard. Rusting old cars sat in driveways or lined the kerb, some of them without tyres, some with shattered windows.

She made her way up a broken concrete path to Jimmy's front door, stepping over weeds growing between the cracks. As she reached the porch of the two-storey clapboard house, she rested a hand on the wooden rail, and a layer of flaking paint came loose and drifted to the ground. A dog started barking in a yard nearby, the bark turned into a howl and then faded back to a whine.

She knocked on the frame of the door, waited a few moments then banged a little harder. She heard Stanley through the screen.

'All right – take it easy.' He yanked at the door and stepped out onto the porch and looked up and down the street. 'Where's the taxi?'

'Long gone.'

'I was gonna pay your fare.'

*Now he tells me.*

Stanley scratched his unshaven face and stepped to one side. 'Third on the left,' he said.

The house smelled of tobacco and beer. And mould. The carpet beneath her feet was matted with animal hair. 'Who's been looking after the cat?'

'Dog,' Stanley corrected her as he closed the door. 'It died last fall. I think maybe vacuuming hasn't been real high on Jimmy's to-do list.'

Jean's stomach clenched as if someone had grabbed it in both hands and squeezed. She could taste chocolate milk at the back of her throat.

'Nothing a quick run round with the Hoover won't fix,' she said and reached into her bag for a peppermint. She pushed open the third door on the left, expecting to see Jimmy in his sickbed, but instead discovered an empty living room. 'Where is he?'

'Sleeping – he's too sick for visitors.' Stanley joined her in the gloomy little room.

'Have you had any sleep?' she asked him.

'Some.'

Jean looked at him properly for the first time. He seemed to have aged ten years overnight. 'Why don't you put your head down now? I'll take care of Jimmy if he needs anything.'

'You don't have to do that.'

Jean put her hands up to Stanley's face. It was damp and cold. 'If you don't look after yourself properly, you'll end up in the bloody hospital.'

He grabbed her wrists, but made no attempt to move her hands from his cheeks. He just stared into her eyes.

'How about we share the burden?' she said, after a prolonged and awkward silence. 'We can work in shifts – until we get some proper care organised.'

'Proper care?' Stanley shook his head. 'I made a few calls. That kinda thing would use up all the money I got put away in no time.' He puffed out his cheeks. 'I start my new job the day after tomorrow. What am I going to do about Jimmy then?'

'That's partly why I'm here – I've been giving it some thought.'

'Partly?'

Jean looked around the room and spotted a photograph sitting on a low bureau running along one wall. She wandered over to it to get a better look at the two couples grinning out of the silver frame. 'This is you,' she said. She pointed at the dark-haired version of Stanley clutching a hotdog high above his head.

'Coney Island,' Stanley said. 'Nineteen-sixty-something.'

'And this is your wife?'

He nodded. 'And Jimmy's fiancée – Marjorie.'

'He looks so happy.'

'Different Jimmy, back then.'

'Was he still working as a policeman?'

He took the photograph from her and set it down on the bureau.

'You still haven't told me why he left the department. I thought you both loved the job. Why did Jimmy give it all up?'

'I can't get into all that right now. He left because he had to. Let's just leave it like that – OK?'

Jean looked at the photograph. 'What happened to his wife?'

'She ran away with an aluminum siding salesmen.'

'A what?'

'Another long story – this isn't the time or the place.' He raised his eyes to the ceiling as if Jimmy could hear their conversation through the floorboards overhead.

Jean turned her gaze back to the photograph, wondering where Stanley's wife was now. Given his reaction to her previous questions, she knew better than to ask. He grabbed the picture frame and placed it photo-side down.

'Taking a trip down memory lane isn't going to help Jimmy, is it?' he said.

Jean took Stanley's hand in hers and guided him to a dining table in the corner of the room. They sat down on the hard wooden chairs, the only seating not covered in dog hair.

'Jimmy needs more help than you're in a position to give him, is that fair? Both in financial terms and personal care.'

'I'll do whatever it takes to get him through this.'

'Whatever it takes?'

He turned his head toward her and narrowed his eyes. 'Tell me you haven't come all this way to suggest grand larceny again.'

'You can't have spent decades in the police force without bending the rules. There must have been occasions when you were forced to do what was morally right, if not strictly legal.'

'You think I'm about to just forget what you did yesterday?'

Jean wondered what Stanley had done with the money, but decided now wasn't the time to bring it up.

'Not forget it, necessarily. Just forgive me. I was acting with the best intentions.'

'You kill me – you know that?'

'Just listen to what I've got to say. Can you do that much?'

Stanley folded his arms, the thick hairs rippling as he flexed his muscles.

'If we could organise – I'm not sure how many bodies it would take – let's just say a *number* of willing individuals to pull off a single large-scale…' She was struggling to find language that would offend Stanley's strict moral code the least. 'A big enough *event* – we could solve Jimmy's problems in a flash.'

'I can't listen to this.' He started to get to his feet. Jean held onto his shirt and tugged until he sat back down.

'With your contacts, in your new job… plus all the people you know in the police department, we could pull off something—'

'Sweet Jesus. You're serious, aren't you?'

'But don't you want to help your oldest friend? Don't you owe him that much?'

He stood up and snatched the hem of his shirt from Jean's grasp. 'Don't try to tell me what I owe Jimmy. What do you know?'

'Practically nothing – you won't tell me.'

He plucked his phone from a pocket and scrolled through the contacts list.

'What are you doing?'

'Calling you a cab.'

'Please, Stanley. I thought we could discuss this like two adults.'

'Adults!' Saliva flew from his mouth as he spoke. 'I'm not the one acting like a juvenile delinquent.'

Before he managed to find the number he was looking for, his phone started to play a Dean Martin tune. Stanley looked at Jean, his eyes on fire.

'Shouldn't you answer that?'

The chorus of *That's Amore* faded then started up again. Stanley shoved the phone onto the table. 'It's just Lu – I can't speak to her right now.'

'It could be important. She might have news about Simon.'

'You speak to her then.'

Jean reached for the phone just as it fell silent. 'I suppose she'd call me direct if there was news.' She retrieved her own phone from her handbag to check she hadn't missed any calls. 'Speaking of news. I haven't told you mine.' She looked up at Stanley's angry face and smiled. 'I have a new granddaughter.'

The scowl on his face melted away. 'You do? Congratulations.'

'Mother and daughter are both doing well. I got a text late last night.'

'From Cindy?'

'No – it was a number I didn't recognise. I'm guessing it was Cindy's mother. I haven't managed to speak to either of them. I keep leaving messages.' She smiled sadly at him. 'I was hoping you might be able to persuade Detective Rodriguez to put a trace on the number. I don't even know the baby's name.' An unexpected sob caught in her throat. 'I've got to do something.'

Stanley reached out a hand and was about to say something when a dull thud sounded from the floor above.

'Jesus!' He ran from the room. Jean followed him out.

She reached the top of the stairs to see Stanley pulling one of Jimmy's wasted arms across his broad shoulders.

'I got you, buddy. Take it easy now.'

'I just wanted to get to the bathroom.' Jimmy looked at Jean. 'Hey – I had no idea we had company. I woulda dressed a little less casual.' He dropped his gaze to a greying pair of pyjama bottoms.

'What are you doing out of bed?' Stanley shoved an arm across his friend's back.

'I needed a couple of Tylenol. This headache is a bitch.' He looked at Jean again. 'Sorry ma'am, no offence.'

'None taken.'

Jimmy turned away, wincing suddenly. He clutched his stomach.

Jean threw Stanley an imploring look. 'It's OK, Jimmy,' she said. 'Stanley's got everything under control.'

# 28

Luisa pulled over to answer her cell. She grabbed the phone from the passenger seat and stared at the screen for a moment. It was now or never.

'Hey, Stan! I almost gave up on you. I've been trying you since yesterday.' Her upbeat tone rang false in her ears. She could only hope Stanley hadn't picked up on it. She leaned back against the headrest and closed her eyes.

'My cell uh… ran out of juice – I only just picked up your messages.' He sounded wrecked.

'Is Mrs Henderson with you?'

'Do you have news about her son?'

'No – the guys at the seventh are looking for him. I've asked them to call me if they get anywhere.' Her fingers found some loose stitching in the upholstery of her seat. 'How's Jimmy?'

'Oh – you know… getting by. No thanks to me. I can manage to pick up chicken soup from the deli and help him when he needs to take a piss, but that's about it as far as my nursing skills go.'

'He's lucky to have you.' Luisa had never understood the bond between Stanley and his friend. Jimmy had always seemed like a waste of space. Thrown out of the force all those years ago and still Stanley stood by him. Always ready to get him out of trouble. 'What are you going to do tomorrow when you start your new job?'

'So far I've managed to put that question to the back of my mind. I made a few inquiries about getting a private nurse for him.' Luisa heard him exhale a shuddering breath. 'Do you have any idea how much they cost? We've been in the wrong business, I'm not kidding.'

'What about his neighbours? The local church?' Luisa started to pick at the loose thread.

'Jean – you know, Mrs Henderson, is taking care of him right now at his place, just so I could come home, pick up some fresh clothes.'

'She is?'

'She insisted.' He sniffed. Was he crying? 'But Jimmy won't go to the bathroom without me. I gotta get back.'

'So the English lady isn't with you right now?'

'I just said… Why are you so interested in her?'

'I uh…'

'What did you want to speak to me about anyways?'

This was Luisa's chance. Just the facts. No need to offer any opinion. He could make up his own mind. She yanked on the lengthening thread coming out of the seat, the stitching quickly unravelling.

Just like her resolve.

'Come on, Lu – I don't have a lot of time. You left me a half dozen messages, you must have something to say.'

She took another deep breath and prepared herself to break the news that Mrs Henderson wasn't the angel Stanley had mistaken her for.

'You OK?' Stanley sounded concerned and irritated at the same time.

Luisa exhaled. 'Sure I'm OK. I'm worried about you, is all. And your buddy.'

'Thanks, Lu – it's appreciated.' He hung up.

*I wasn't finished, goddamit.*

She threw the phone back on the seat and thumped the steering wheel with both fists, cursing her own cowardice. She snatched up the phone again, but instead of hitting the redial button, she sifted through her picture library and found the photograph of the English woman's grandson.

Her visit to the grocery store on First Avenue on Friday evening had been more worthwhile than she could have imagined. With a little coaxing, Mrs Kim told her about a teenage boy who had been behaving strangely at the store the day before she had her purse stolen. After the old lady described him, Luisa showed her the photo of Mrs Henderson's grandson.

'Maybe he looks a little like this, I guess,' she'd said.

Confirmation of the English woman's description, however hesitant, was all Luisa needed to join the dots. The mask-wearing purse stealer also held up the grocery store, and now she was one hundred per cent sure he was white. She was looking forward to seeing Riley and Sanchez's faces on Monday morning when she told them.

She shoved the phone into her bag and climbed out of her little red Toyota, stretching her back as she locked the doors. The house she was looking for was obvious enough. Yellow police tape circled a tree on one side of the front yard, looped through a picket fence at the front and ended in an untidy knot around the porch rail. There was no sign of movement coming from the house itself. It looked just as lifeless as it had two hours earlier when Luisa first saw the news report about the shooting.

Two assailants, the reporter had said, both wearing rubber masks. Though he didn't describe the masks themselves, after a determined half hour of phone calls, Luisa had confirmed they were of the Obama variety – an eyewitness saw two men wearing Obama masks riding away from the scene on a motorcycle. No one at the Nassau County Police Department had linked the shooting with the two grocery stores in the East Village, but right now they had no reason to.

Across the road a middle-aged woman was pretending to water her hanging flower baskets, her eyes fixed on Luisa.

'Ma'am?' Luisa ran across the wide street, lifting her jacket to display the shield attached to her belt. 'Do you have a moment?'

'You don't work out of the Ninth Precinct.'

'No, ma'am – you're completely correct.' Luisa smiled confidently at her, hoping to convey an air of authority. Even though she had no jurisdiction, and was working on her own time on a Sunday morning. 'Did you see any of what happened here on Friday evening?'

'I already spoke to Todd and Kenny.' She pinched a brown leaf from a geranium plant above her head. 'Told them everything I saw.'

'Sure.' Luisa smiled again. 'I'm from a different division. We just need to corroborate every report, on the ground – you know – face-to-face with witnesses.'

The woman set her pink aluminum watering can on the porch. 'I wouldn't say I was a witness exactly.'

Luisa pulled a notebook from her pocket, nodding all the time. 'But if you could go through what you did see for me, I'd be most grateful.' Luisa was trying hard to knock off the hard edges of her Brooklyn drawl.

'I don't want to bring it up all over again.' The neighbour pulled a lace handkerchief from her sleeve and dabbed at her cheeks and forehead. 'Can't you speak to Todd?'

'Oh I will, ma'am – you can be sure of that.'

'I haven't slept a wink since it happened. Every little noise and I'm out of bed.'

'It must be difficult living on your own in such a big house.'

'Who said I live alone?'

Luisa peered around the woman through the open porch door and saw the rapid flicker of a TV screen bouncing off a wall.

'My husband would sleep through the third world war, even if it happened right outside the bedroom window.'

The woman blew out such a long sigh, Luisa decided she must have the lung capacity of a marathon runner.

'I only saw the side of his face, from this distance, in a bad light.'

'Ma'am?'

'The one who did the shooting.'

'So he wasn't wearing a mask?'

The woman shook her head adamantly. 'Not at first. Not until that poor man was sprawled across the ground.'

'Mr Redmond?'

'Why yes – who else would I be talking about?'

'But you saw the shooter's face?'

'Just a glance.'

'Can you describe him?'

'He had brown hair, a dark sweat top – far too heavy for this weather – blue jeans, sneakers.'

Luisa pulled out her phone and showed the woman the picture of Mrs Henderson's grandson. 'Something like this, maybe?'

The woman squinted at the image, snatched the phone from Luisa and took a closer look. 'I really can't say. It all happened so fast. Have you shown this to Mr Redmond's…' She pinched her face into an expression of mild disgust. 'His… *husband*?'

'He saw the boy without the mask too?' Luisa looked back at the house.

'I don't know – I doubt it – he was inside.'

'Then how would he—'

'Mr Redmond clearly knew the boy. Greeted him – I didn't hear what was said, but he seemed pleasantly surprised to see him.'

'Mr Redmond recognised his assailant?'

'I've just said, haven't I? I presumed he must be one of Mr Redmond's students.'

'Students? I thought he was a garden designer.' Luisa abandoned the pretence of a notebook and shoved it back in her pocket.

'Only since he retired.' The woman glanced forlornly across the street. 'He promised to take a look at my hydrangeas.'

'What was he doing before he retired?'

'Up until the beginning of last year he was a teacher – history and English. At Baxter High.'

'Is that a local high school?'

'You don't work with Todd and Kenny, do you?' She took a step back and lifted her watering can from the porch. She held it in front of her like a shield. 'Who are you?'

'Please ma'am – do you know where the school is situated?'

'It's in the city. Upper East Side, I think he said.'

# 29

When Stanley drove her back into Manhattan, Jean insisted he drop her at the grocery store on First Avenue. She'd been meaning to visit the Korean lady ever since she'd first heard about the mugging.

She waved Stanley away on his long drive back to Queens and stood on the corner of the street. The store had reopened and Jean watched from the sidewalk as customers came and went as if nothing had ever happened. She clutched her handbag under her arm and started for the entrance, just as the elderly Korean woman was coming out.

'Mrs Kim!'

The woman put the bundle she was carrying onto the pavement. She smiled at Jean and walked toward her, a small dog on a leash trotting behind. 'How are you?' Jean said. 'I've been thinking about you, after what happened here, then having your bag stolen…'

The woman hooked her thin arm through Jean's and guided her to the next cross street.

'Shouldn't you be resting? Going through something like that, it must have shaken you.' Jean looked at the dog, its nose grazing the pavement as they walked.

'I'm fine. This is my daughter's dog. I walk him every day.' She held her head high and smiled at Jean. 'Some punk is not going to stop me. I can look after myself.' She patted a pocket and gave a little nod. 'If he comes back, I'm ready.'

'You think he might?' Jean's knees weakened.

Mrs Kim shrugged and the dog barked. Jean bent down and patted his head as they waited at the intersection for the lights to change. 'Your daughter's dog, you say?'

'She's too busy with the other stores to walk him.'

'She runs them for you?'

'She *owns* them. I help her.'

The traffic stopped at the crossing and the little dog trotted ahead of them.

'It must be nice – having a family business.'

The woman grimaced. 'I'm too old to be working eighteen hours every day. I should be retired. Living by the sea, having a little fun.' She yanked on the leash and immediately the dog stopped pulling. 'Instead I'm living with my daughter and her husband.' She sighed. 'I should be in Florida with my friends.'

'Is that where you come from originally?' Jean only realised how odd that sounded when the words were left hanging in the air.

'It's where I should be now. But I lost everything when the banks went bad.'

'That's terrible.'

'Crap happens.'

There was no answer to that.

They walked another block in silence when Jean turned to Mrs Kim and held onto her arm a little tighter. 'It'd be nice to make them pay, don't you think?' she said.

'Who?'

'The banks. For what they did.'

'They're too big. Too powerful. There's nothing anyone can do.' Mrs Kim slowed down as they reached a large grocery store; fruit, vegetables and flowers neatly arranged in a long display on the sidewalk.

'Is this another of your daughter's shops?'

Mrs Kim shook her head and the dog let out a high-pitched howl. 'Competition.' She picked up an orange, sniffed it and put it down again. 'Sour,' she said and walked on.

They reached another intersection. On the other side was the entrance of a large park. 'Dog run,' Mrs Kim said, by way of explanation. 'Special treat for Yo-Yo.' The wiry white and grey dog yapped excitedly and tugged at the leash. He strained so hard Mrs Kim lost her hold on him and he bounded across the road, narrowly missing a delivery truck as it sped through the intersection. The elderly woman ran after him, her spindly little legs moving fast. Jean could only watch and admire. There was no way her knee would allow her to chase after them. She crossed when the lights changed, checking right then quickly left when she remembered which side of the road the traffic flowed.

That was when she saw him.

A figure stood completely still on the other side of the wide avenue, about twenty yards from the intersection, watching her. He was wearing clothes far too heavy for a hot August afternoon. The sidewalk was busy with people heading for the park. They dodged around him as he stood there.

Then he started to run.

Jean reached the other side of the road and hurried through the gates of the park, heading for the safety of the crowds enjoying a sunny Sunday afternoon. She glanced over her shoulder to see if the boy had followed her in. Through the mass of bodies, she could just make out someone in a dark blue sweat top passing through the gates.

She fumbled in her bag, her trembling hand groping desperately for her phone. She retrieved it and dialled nine-one-one. When she looked behind her again, he was gone.

'Nine-one-one?' the dispatcher barked in her ear.

'Oh my God!' Jean frantically scanned the entrance to the park, searching the faces of everyone coming in.

'Ma'am?'

'He's gone. Where did he go?'

'Do you need police assistance?'

'Yes, yes! Police.' Jean gulped down a breath. 'He was just across the street.'

'Who is this, ma'am? Are you reporting a crime in progress?'

Jean spun around in a circle. 'Not now – the crime happened before. I've just seen the boy with the gun.'

'Is someone threatening you, ma'am?'

'He just vanished – I looked and he was gone.'

'Can you give me your location?'

'A park – I don't know what it's called. We walked here from First Avenue.'

'Is someone with you?'

'No – not anymore.'

'Can you confirm you're located in Tomkin Square Park?'

'I don't… I know there's a dog run. Does that help at all?' She was walking backward, continuing to search the faces between her and the entrance.

Her heart shunted against her ribs.

There he was – barely forty feet away, the Obama mask over his head. She tried to speak, but no words came.

'Ma'am? Are you OK?'

Jean let out a faint squeak. He was walking toward her. Calmly, not taking his gaze from her face.

'Help me,' Jean whispered into the phone.

'It's OK, ma'am. Please stay on the line.'

'He's reaching under his top.'

It was too late. The police would get there in time to discover her body lying on the ground. She considered running. But how far could she get before he caught up with her? She raised her arm and pointed at him. 'He has a gun!' Her voice came out uneven and not much louder than a whisper. She tried again. 'Look! There! He has a gun.'

No one even slowed down or turned to look at her.

'He's wearing a mask,' she continued. Still he came toward her, unhindered. 'Stop him!' she hollered. 'He wants to kill me.'

A few heads turned toward the boy. But no one did anything.

'Someone stop him!' Jean shouted again.

The boy pulled the gun from his behind his back and levelled it at Jean's chest.

A tiny disembodied voice sounded from the loudspeaker of Jean's phone. 'Ma'am? Are you OK? Ma'am?'

The path between Jean and the shooter had cleared. He stopped, firmly planted his feet eighteen inches apart and cupped his gun hand in the other to brace it. He aimed.

Jean wanted to close her eyes, but they stayed stubbornly open. She saw the boy tilt his head to one side, as if he was mocking her. Then she saw a dog at his heels. Mrs Kim's dog. The boy looked down and shoved it with his foot. The dog yelped then came back and nipped his ankles. The boy kicked again and recovered his shooting stance.

Jean held her breath.

At the edge of her field of vision Mrs Kim appeared. The old woman lifted both her hands. She was holding something in each of them, Jean couldn't make out what. The piercing cry of an alarm sounded. The boy with the gun turned toward the noise. It was coming from Mrs Kim. He swung the gun in her direction and she started to run at him, screaming at the top of her voice, her left arm still held high. A few feet away she pointed the object in her hand at the boy's face, toward the eyeholes of his mask. The boy cried out, dropped to his knees and ripped the mask from his head. He lifted an arm to his eyes and shoved the gun under his top. Then he scrambled to his feet and started to run. Mrs Kim chased him as far as the park gates, the alarm in her hand still squealing.

# 30

The school bell sounded to mark the end of class and immediately a noisy stream of teenagers dressed in designer clothes drifted into the hallway. Luisa hadn't seen this much high-end attire outside of Saks window display. Boys and girls crashed into her with their bags and elbows as she tried to make her way against the tide to the other end of the corridor.

She hadn't expected to see any students at all at the school. Didn't they have better things to do during the summer vacation? Like playing polo, or sailing on their daddies' yachts?

Her appointment with the principal had been hastily arranged at eight o'clock that morning, the principal's personal secretary making it sound as if she was granting Luisa an audience with the Pope. Or the Queen of England. So precious was this man's time, Luisa wondered if she should curtsey when she entered his office.

The hallway eventually cleared and she made it safely to the other end. The desk outside the principal's room was empty, a chair tucked neatly underneath, the computer switched off.

Luisa tapped lightly on the door and waited until she heard a low mumble calling her in. For a moment, as she turned the cold metal handle, she was transported back to her own junior high, sent to see the principal for some minor misdemeanour or other. Every now and then a major one.

She pushed open the door and quickly closed it behind her. The man behind the desk straightened in his leather swivel chair, but made no attempt to get up.

'Oh,' he said. 'I was expecting someone else.'

Luisa strode to his desk and stuck out a hand. 'Detective Rodriguez. Your assistant arranged this meeting.'

'My assistant isn't here. She had to go home suddenly, she's had a terrible shock.'

Luisa thought about apologising to him for breaking the news about the murder of the former schoolteacher over the phone. But the way he was looking down his nose at her made her decide against it. She pulled out her notebook. 'What can you tell me about Mr Redmond?'

'Nothing.'

'I'm sorry?'

'I've only been here four semesters. Redmond was before my time.' He shook his head. 'It really is too bad. Jennifer might not return to her duties all week.' He let out a frustrated sigh.

Luisa slipped a hand into her bag and retrieved a colour print of the picture from Mrs Henderson's cell phone. She pushed it across the desk. 'Do you recognise this boy?' Suddenly she felt awkward, showing him a ten by eight of the English woman's grandson as if it were an actual picture of the perp. 'He was a student here. He looks a little older than this. Do you know him?'

'No.' He slid the photograph back to her, having given it only the most cursory of glances. Luisa slid it back again.

'Please, sir. Take a good look.'

He screwed up his eyes, turning his head one way then the other as if that might help his memory. 'No.' His tone was emphatic, but Luisa wasn't about to give up.

'I guess you can't know all of your students.'

'Of course I do – it's something I take great pride in.'

'But you don't know this one?'

'Because he's not a student here.'

'Maybe he's a former student.'

'If Jennifer were here you could ask her. She pre-dates me by some considerable margin.'

Reluctantly, Luisa returned the photograph to her bag. 'I guess there are other members of staff who were here at the same time as Mr Redmond?'

'Certainly.'

'May I speak to them?'

'Not now – you'll have to wait until after school. I don't want to worry the students during class. They haven't come in during the vacation only to have their learning interrupted.' He dusted down the sleeves of his jacket. No doubt to signal to his unwelcome guest that it was time to terminate the interview.

'You do realise how serious this is, sir? We're talking about first degree murder here.' Luisa walked around his desk and perched on the edge. 'I could have this whole building swarming with officers. It just takes one phone call.'

'And do you realise the kind of families who send their children here? I won't have you needlessly upsetting them. Do you understand?'

'Perfectly, sir. School roll down is it? Must have been tough these past few years. People making economies here and there. Maybe sending their precious sons and daughters to schools who charge just a little less for a good education?'

'I assure you, parents do not economise when it comes to the next generation's start in life.' His words sounded convincing enough, but the shift in his posture and the restless look in his eyes told Luisa she wasn't so far from the truth.

'OK – I'll come back later. But I will need to speak to students as well as staff.'

'You'll return alone?'

How discreet did this man need her to be?

'We'll see.' She rose from the desk. 'In the meantime you can show me the yearbooks for the last five years. Students aged fourteen years and up.'

Over an hour later, Luisa had ploughed through so many pages filled with photographs of perfectly coiffured hair, symmetrically arched eyebrows and dazzlingly white, straight teeth, that by the time she closed the final yearbook she felt as if she needed to check herself into a health spa for an emergency makeover.

There was no sign of the shooter in any of them.

She left the half dozen heavy books in an untidy heap on the secretary's desk and wandered back down the hallway, peering into classrooms through porthole windows set into the doors as she went. A few students stared back at her, more bored with their lessons than she had ever been. At the final door she stopped. Inside the teenage students were gathered in small groups, standing around tables rather than sitting rigidly behind rows of desks. It looked pretty informal. Informal enough for her to risk disturbing them.

Luisa knocked briskly on the door as she opened it. She entered the classroom without waiting to be asked, and strode toward the teacher sitting at a table at the far end. Luisa showed the woman her shield, briefly explained why she was there and handed her the colour photograph.

'I can't help you. I'm only here for the summer classes,' the teacher said, handing back the photograph. 'This is my first time teaching at Baxter.' She must have seen the disappointment show on Luisa's face, because she quickly called over a young girl from the nearest group of students. Luisa held up the photograph.

'Have you seen this boy before?'

'Who wants to know?' the girl said and screwed up her nose.

Luisa flashed her badge. 'NYPD. Do you recognise him?'

The girl shrugged.

'Does he look in any way familiar to you?' Luisa felt as if she was clutching at straws.

'Maybe. Is he, like, in trouble again?'

'Again?'

'It might not be him – the hair's like… *all wrong*. The nose is the same… maybe.'

'You know him?'

'I'm not sure.' She glanced over at the group of classmates she'd recently abandoned.

'It's OK – you can speak freely.' Luisa tried a reassuring smile. 'Don't worry about your friends.'

'Like – as if I'd worry!' She laughed and waved a middle finger at them.

'What's his name?'

'Why? What did he do? Was it like last time?'

'That depends on what happened last time.' Luisa tried to keep the urgency from her voice.

'It was like… you know… just a rumour. He got taken out of school just after we started. That *never* happens.'

'When was this?'

'My first year here.' She waved her finger at her friends again. 'Shut. Up!'

'And when was that?'

'I started fall of oh nine.'

'So he was a student here in 2009?'

'I guess. I was really young. The older guys never mix with the little kids. I mean – why would you?' She looked down at the photograph again. 'Maybe this isn't the same boy. He was way cuter than this.'

'How old was he, back then?'

The girl shrugged. 'Fourteen, I guess. Or fifteen maybe. We only like overlapped for a week or so.'

'But you remember him?'

'Some people thought he looked like Robert Pattinson – you know, from Twilight? I can't believe how many times I saw those movies. They are like, so lame.'

'So he made quite an impression on you and your friends?'

'I wouldn't say that exactly.'

'What was his name?' Luisa's patience was nearing the end of its natural life.

'We called him "Teddy" – you know, the vampire in the movie – Edward Cullen.'

'OK… but what was his real name?'

'I told you – he was only here for a week or so after I started. I don't know his name.'

Luisa's heart dropped into her shoes. 'You don't?'

'We tried to find out, after, you know, because of what he did. But no one would tell us *anything*.'

'And what did he do?'

'It was a rumour, like I said, but he was supposed to have attacked some girl in the sixth grade. Like, in the gym, after school?'

'Attacked?'

'He like,' she whispered, 'raped her.'

The classroom door flew open and two burly uniformed guards hurried in, the principal following on their heels.

'Who gave you permission to speak to this class?'

Luisa avoided looking over at the teacher.

'Get out!' the principal shouted, as if she was one of his students.

'I'm interviewing a potential witness.'

The principal turned to the girl and glowered at her. 'I do hope you haven't been exercising your overactive imagination again, Quinn.'

The girl looked down at her expensive shoes and said nothing.

'You know how much trouble that gets you in. And how much it disappoints your parents. Now I know for a fact you don't want to do that.'

The girl shuffled back to her friends, her head hanging low.

'Can I remind you, sir, we are investigating a very serious—'

'*We*? I just got off the phone from the Nassau County Police Department. They're sending over a couple of men later this morning to talk to me about the circumstances surrounding Mr Redmond's…' He lowered his voice. 'Untimely death. I mentioned your name to them.' His top lip curled into a snarl. 'They've never heard of you.'

# 31

The chairs must have been designed for three to four-year-olds, Jean decided, as she scanned the classroom. Two-hundred-pound men were perched on them, balancing a single buttock on the little plastic seats, their long legs splayed out either side to stop them sliding to the floor. The elementary class schoolroom was the best venue they could come up with at short notice. It wasn't ideal, but it would have to do.

The whole room was buzzing with individual conversations, old friends catching up on the births of new grandchildren, small groups gossiping about unexpected divorces or sudden illnesses. Jean should have been buoyed by the impressive turnout, instead all she could think about was how on earth she'd control such a rowdy bunch of seniors.

She'd organised protest groups in the UK, but they were generally a mild-mannered crowd, more than happy to be given instructions. Not easily led exactly, but certainly malleable enough to bend to Jean's will. This lot looked as though they might instigate a coup at the slightest provocation. She sat on the edge of the desk at the front of the class, wondering what she'd gotten herself into and whether or not it was too late to pull out. Most of these people were only vaguely related to her core group of

Jimmy Kapowski supporters, friends of friends at best. Could she actually rely on any of them?

While she waited for latecomers to arrive, Jean picked up her bottle of water from the desk, her hand trembling. She hadn't been able to stop shaking since the incident in the park the day before. She and Mrs Kim had been taken to the 4th Precinct station house to make a statement. She had been interviewed by the same detective she'd spoken to about Simon's disappearance and wasn't entirely sure he'd taken her any more seriously this time. At least Mrs Kim had been there to corroborate her story.

The door behind Jean opened with a creak. She turned to see Mrs Kim and two of her elderly friends hesitating in the doorway. Glenda, the waitress from the diner, and Carmen Steinway were bringing up the rear.

'You OK?' Mrs Kim asked her, a worried look on her face.

'Me? I'm fine. Tough as old boots,' Jean said and shoved her trembling hands into her pockets.

Carmen closed the classroom door and gently lowered herself onto the nearest table.

Time to call for order.

Jean shoved one of the dinky plastic chairs next to the desk. She stepped onto the chair, climbed up onto the desk and cleared her throat. Mrs Kim and Glenda stood either side of the desk and folded their arms, staring sternly at the noisy audience.

'Right,' Jean shouted. 'Can we have a little hush please?'

The general chatter didn't subside.

'Leave it to me,' Mrs Kim said and retrieved the rape alarm she'd used so effectively in the park the day before. She squeezed a button and released the unearthly howl. Immediately all faces turned toward Jean, conversations brought to an abrupt end.

'Thank you.' Jean took a breath. 'Now if we can call this meeting to order…'

A man leaning on a Zimmer frame in the front row thrust his hand in the air. 'I got a question,' he said.

'I'll take questions afterwards.'

'This is a point of order.'

Suddenly Jean was back in a crowded working men's club in the early seventies, watching her husband attempt to placate a room full of angry railway employees.

'Go on then,' she said.

'Who put you in charge?'

'I'm sorry?'

'How come you're running the show?'

'I organised the event.'

'What are you – English or something? How much money did *you* lose with Fisher Krupps?'

A disapproving mumble travelled through the room.

'I don't see what that's got to do with anyth—'

'He's right,' a woman dressed all in black piped up. 'I think we should have a vote.'

'Wait a minute!' Glenda scrambled onto the desk beside Jean. 'If it weren't for this lady, none of you would even be here.' She squeezed Jean's hand. 'Maybe it takes an outsider to see things clearly. Besides – a dear friend of hers landed up in the hospital because of Fisher Krupps.' She planted her hands on her hips. 'He was fighting for his life, goddamit.'

The man with the Zimmer frame raised his hand again. 'I just think we should take a moment—' A collective shushing, crackling through the room like radio static, cut him off.

'Let the lady speak,' the woman in black said.

'Thank you.' Jean scanned the crowd, all of them now waiting for a rousing Churchillian speech. 'Thank you all for coming.' She looked at their expectant faces, worried she was only moments away from disappointing them. 'First of all, I'd like to see a show of hands.' She sucked down a breath. 'How many of you feel ignored? Unimportant?'

People glanced at their neighbours, a few of them shrugged.

'Let me put it another way.' Jean struggled to identify an alternate approach, wishing she'd made some notes beforehand. 'How many of you caught the bus here today?'

A few hands went up.

'And the subway?'

A few more were raised.

'Did anyone give up their seat for you?'

A voice called out from the back of the room. 'What's that got to do with Fisher Krupps?'

'I'm coming to that.' Jean sighed. 'How many of you were jostled and bumped on the sidewalk outside this building?'

'That happens all the time – why are you asking?' the woman in black said.

'Can any of you remember the last time you were listened to, taken seriously, by a person in authority? When was someone last interested in what you had to say?'

Jean was rewarded with blank stares and confused expressions. She hadn't meant to over-complicate her point. A few mumbled conversations broke out amongst the crowd.

She was losing them.

'When was the last time you felt as if you counted? Like you made a difference?' she said.

'My daughter is always asking for my advice,' a woman at the back offered.

'What about people outside your immediate family?'

'Why would they care?' the woman said.

'Why shouldn't they?' Jean fired back.

'Last time anyone took any notice what I thought was when they wanted my vote,' the man with the Zimmer frame said. 'Or they were trying to sell me some useless piece of crap.'

Some people murmured in agreement.

'Doesn't that make you angry?' Glenda joined in.

'It's just the way it is. No point getting mad about it,' the man replied, leaning his elbow on the Zimmer frame and cupping his chin in his hand.

'How about getting even?' Jean said. 'Let's try another show of hands,' she said, praying it would be more successful than her first attempt. 'How many of you lost your pensions when the crash happened in 2008?'

A few people nudged one another. Others looked around the room. Glenda shoved her hand high in the air. 'Come on, folks!' she said. 'It's nothing to be ashamed of.'

A couple of hands rose at the back, then a cluster in the middle and a few more at the front.

'And how many lost your homes?'

This time Mrs Kim and one of her friends raised their hands, encouraging a dozen or so other people to do the same. Some of them had already admitted losing their pension.

'And what about other investments? How many of you lost a big chunk of your savings?'

The remaining arms went up, some of them halfway; Jean put that down to arthritis rather than reticence.

'And how many of you want to do something about it?'

A sea of white, black and brown wrinkled hands waved back at her.

'OK – now we're getting somewhere.' Jean gestured for Glenda to get off the desk then climbed down herself and took up her previous position perching on the edge. 'I've been thinking how we might get even with the banks, a way we can use the fact nobody gives a flying you-know-what about us and work it for all it's worth.' Now she had everyone's attention. 'What I'm about to walk you through isn't entirely legal. Actually, I may as well be honest…' She searched their eager faces. 'It'd be fair to say what I'm suggesting is downright criminal. If you have any objections to bending rules, or breaking laws, you should leave the room now.'

No one so much as fidgeted on the uncomfortable chairs.

'The banks bent so many rules it's like they were made of rubber,' a woman shouted from somewhere in the middle of the room. 'Don't see what's wrong with us doing the same.'

'Hey – and we might even have a little fun while we're doing it,' Glenda added.

A tentative cheer went up.

'Now,' Jean said, 'if this is going to be even halfway successful, I'll need each of you to recruit at least four of your friends. You'll need to be discreet, and they must possess two attributes that are absolutely non-negotiable.'

The audience nodded back at her enthusiastically.

She waved a thumb in the air. 'Number one, they have to be completely trustworthy.'

More nodding.

Jean stuck up a finger. 'And number two…' She scanned the room. 'They've got to be at least sixty years old.'

# 32

Jean tidied her hair in the reflection of the glass panel in Stanley's front door before reaching for the knocker.

'You look terrific,' Glenda said. 'He'd be blind not to see it.'

Jean turned to her and smiled. 'I don't know what you're talking about. Mr Rozello and I are just good friends.' She wasn't about to tell Glenda how she really felt.

'That's why you've got on so much make-up?' Mrs Kim was balancing daintily on the next step down.

'Don't be ridiculous.' Jean drew in a long breath. 'Are we all up for this?' She looked from Glenda to Mrs Kim and Carmen, then down at Clarence, the Fisher Krupps doorman, who seemed smaller somehow, out of his uniform.

'It's an adventure, isn't it?' Glenda said. 'I need a little more of that in my life.' Jean thought she noticed the weary waitress flash Clarence the briefest of smiles. Mrs Kim confirmed her agreement with curt nod of the head. Carmen gave her the thumbs up.

'And what about you, Clarence? Are you completely sure about this?'

'I'll feel just fine when I have a little more information. I want to get it all clear in my mind.'

'OK. Good.' Jean stared into the doorman's eyes. Was he really on board? Could she trust him? Could she trust any of them, when it came down to it? They weren't much more than strangers. Without giving herself time to dwell on that unhelpful fact, she turned back to the door and knocked loudly.

Through the glass Jean could hear Stanley humming as he hurried down the hall. The humming stopped as soon as he opened the door. He took a step back.

'What the hell is this?' He narrowed his eyes and scrutinised the face of the waitress. 'Wait a minute – I know you, don't I?' He peered behind her and looked the others up and down. 'You never said anything about bringing people with you. You gonna tell me what's going on here, Jean?'

'Why don't we speak inside?' Jean pushed gently against his chest with the flats of her hands.

'You know how long it took me to persuade Jimmy to stay here with me?' Stanley wouldn't budge. 'I can't be entertaining visitors.'

'Jimmy's the reason we're all here.' Jean lowered her voice. 'How is he?'

'A little better. I had a neighbour look in on him today while I was working.' He rubbed his eyes. 'I don't think they got along too well.'

'You need a more permanent solution,' Jean said. 'And these good people are here to help you find one.'

'They're what?'

'Let me explain.' Jean led the little gang of seniors through the door and into the hallway. 'Don't worry,' she whispered to Stanley. 'We'll be very quiet. Jimmy won't even know we're here.'

Stanley surrendered and directed the group into a kitchen at the back of the house. When everyone was introduced, they settled down around a big wooden table in the middle of the room and looked up at Jean.

'Any chance of some liquid refreshments?' she asked, deciding to stick to safe domestic matters while she was still working out how to the broach the subject she had come to discuss.

Once the cans of beer had been opened and a pot of coffee brewed, she couldn't put off the evil deed any longer.

'Sit down, Stanley,' she said.

'I'm OK on my feet.'

'Please?'

'It's my house, for crying out loud. I want to stand.'

Jean pursed her lips. 'As I said, we're all here because of Jimmy.' She smiled at the assembled seniors around the table. They nodded back at her and made encouraging noises. 'What's happened to him has been a bit of a wake-up call for all of us. We've been taking abuse from the likes of Fisher Krupps too, haven't we?'

More noises in agreement.

'And up 'til now, we've been taking it lying down. It's time for us to defend our rights and make a stand.' She paused, aware suddenly she'd lurched into full speech-making mode.

'Are you going somewhere with this?' Stanley took a glug of beer straight from the can and folded his arms across his chest.

'No one's been getting nearly angry enough,' Jean said.

'You're angry with the banks? Is that it?'

'Look what they've done to Jimmy – what a misery they've made his life. Isn't he sick enough without the added worry of losing his home?'

'Jimmy missed his payments.'

'You're not taking sides with the banks against him?'

Stanley slammed down his beer on the kitchen counter. 'Goddammit – you know nothing about it. Of course I'm not.'

'Jimmy made a stand – he was prepared to show them how angry he is.'

'And it got him just as far as the emergency room.'

'That doesn't mean we should sit back and do nothing. We can make some noise about it… take our grievances to the banks. We can take to the streets.'

Stanley was shaking his head, looking at the group of people sitting around his kitchen table. 'You came all the way here to tell me that? That a bunch of… old folk… no offence, is thinking of marching on Wall Street? Is that your answer to Jimmy's problems?'

'Hey, I'm sixty-three – that ain't even halfway old,' Glenda said. 'It's just nobody bothered to tell my feet… or my knees.' She uncrossed her legs and straightened her shoulders with a wince. 'Or my back.'

'But it's not just about getting angry at Fisher Krupps and all the other greedy banks like them.' Jean was determined not to be sidetracked.

'It isn't?' Stanley picked up his beer again and took a slug.

'For any of this to help Jimmy…' Jean glanced at Mrs Kim and Clarence. 'We need to get *even*.'

Stanley sank half his beer and didn't respond.

'Tell him how Fisher Krupps have treated you, Clarence.' Jean pulled out a chair and collapsed onto it.

The doorman looked down at his beer. 'I'm not sure it's that interesting.'

'Tell him.'

Clarence shrugged. 'I've been working for them for the past twenty years, come this November,' he said and rested his hands awkwardly on the tabletop. 'All that time I never got any vacation. And they paid me the minimum wage. And on Friday I found a note stuck to my locker telling me I didn't need to come back after the weekend.'

Stanley's expression tightened, he shrugged. 'So? Maybe you're better off out of there.'

'You know how hard it is for a man like me to get another job?'

'It's OK – I get it. Fisher Krupps are heartless bastards who only care about the bottom line. That's the business they're in.'

Jean was shocked at the bitterness in his voice. She'd never heard him speak this way before. 'And shouldn't they pay for that heartlessness?' she said. 'Shouldn't we demand a little compensation for everything the banks have forced us to endure?'

'What are you suggesting?' Stanley looked at each of them in turn. They all stared at Jean. 'Demand compensation how? You think if we sign a petition they'll hand over some cash?'

'I was thinking of something a little more… direct than that. More assertive.'

Stanley snorted. 'What? You think maybe we should rob a bank?'

There was a collective intake of breath around the table. None of them had put it into so many words before. When Jean had spoken to them earlier today, individually then as a group, the Big Thing they were contemplating had only been hinted at, suggested, skirted around. Here was Stanley using words like 'rob' and 'bank' in the same sentence, as bold as anything.

Stanley's mouth fell open when she didn't answer straightaway. The beer almost slipped from his hand. 'Oh come on. You can't be serious. What the f—'

Jean held up a finger to silence him and steered Stanley out of the kitchen. She closed the door behind them. 'These people are here because they genuinely want to help Jimmy. Just like we do.'

'You're out of your mind. You and that bunch of misguided cronies you've brainwashed.'

She raised her voice. 'Can't you just listen to what we've got to say?'

'Keep it down – you'll wake up Jimmy.'

'I was hoping that Jimmy might be able to help with the planning – he did use to be a policeman after all. Give him something to focus on.'

'Jimmy? You've got that all wrong. Jimmy's never even violated a parking restriction. I doubt he's ever had an overdue library book. I will not let you so much as *mention* this crazy idea to him.'

'It was just a thought.'

'You'd do better keeping your thoughts to yourself.'

'Just give me a chance to explain.'

'Forget it.'

'Don't you want to help?'

'This is no way to help Jimmy. You think you could pull something like that off?'

Jean held her tongue.

'Oh come on – have you lost all grip on reality?'

'You're refusing to help?'

He laughed and shook his head. 'With your crazy ideas? Damn right I am.'

'Then we'll just have to do it without you.'

'I can't let that happen.'

'You can't stop us.'

'No?'

'You'd turn me in?'

'I wouldn't have a choice.' He breathed out an angry sigh.

'It's too late now.' She struggled to disguise the tremor in her voice. 'You had plenty of opportunity before. You missed your chance.'

'I can't let you drag those wide-eyed dopes down with you.'

'You don't even know them.'

'Do you?'

'They can make their own decisions.'

'Make their own mistakes, you mean.'

There was a bang on the door.

'Who the hell is that? Another one of your geriatric 'merry men'?' He stomped down the hall and wrenched open the door.

'They're not geri—' Jean was interrupted by the sight of a redheaded woman standing at the top of the stoop. The same one she'd met outside the Italian restaurant.

'What the hell are you doing here?'

'That's a charming welcome – thanks, Stan.'

'Now's not a good time, Dolores.'

'When is it ever?' She pushed past him and stopped halfway down the hall when she spotted Jean. 'And what the hell is *she* doing here?'

'It's a long story,' Stanley said, rubbing his eyes with thumb and forefinger as he closed the door.

'Oh I got time.' Dolores carried on down the hall, sidestepped Jean without looking at her, and flung open the kitchen door. She took a step back. 'What's this? Have I wandered into an old folks' home? Or an outtake from *The Golden Girls*?'

'Don't worry. You haven't missed much,' Clarence pulled out a chair. 'We've only just started to discuss the actual plan.'

'Actual what?'

Stanley joined Dolores in the kitchen and Jean followed behind.

'What's going on here, Stan?'

'Never mind about that,' Stanley said. 'You still haven't told me why you're here.'

'I came to celebrate your first day in the new job.' She dug a hand into the bag slung over her shoulder, retrieved a bottle of red wine and put it on the kitchen table. Then she dug in again and brought out a box of chocolates. 'And I got these for Jimmy. Is he upstairs?'

'He's a diabetic, Dee.' Stanley snatched the box from her. 'Don't you ever listen?'

She snatched it back. 'For your information, these are low-sugar candies. I had to go to three drugstores before I found them.'

'Sorry,' Stanley hung his head like a scolded dog. 'I'll be sure to give them to him. Later.'

'Are you joining us?' Clarence asked her, his hand still resting on the back of the chair.

'No she isn't. She's just leaving,' Jean said, unable to put up with the woman for a moment longer.

'Are you going to let her speak to me like that?'

'We are kinda in the middle of something.' Stanley put an arm around her waist and attempted to steer her back toward the hall. Dolores didn't move.

'Tell me what's going on.'

'Nothing – believe me.' He pressed forward again and they edged closer to the door. 'Why don't you call me later, we can speak then.'

'Shall I meet you for lunch tomorrow maybe? Or we could get together after you've finished work some day this week, like we used to?'

'Sure, sure, whatever you want.' He guided her into the hall.

'Can I at least say hello to Jimmy before you throw me out?'

'He's sleeping right now. Maybe another time.'

Jean watched as Stanley coaxed and cajoled the mouthy redhead all the way to the front door.

'She not stopping?' Clarence seemed genuinely bewildered. Glenda nudged him with her elbow.

'She's not part of our… enterprise,' Jean said and began to think perhaps her fledgling plan was doomed to fail before she'd properly worked out the details.

Stanley returned to the kitchen and opened another can of beer without saying a word.

'Before we start,' Clarence said, lifting his glass in the air as if he was about to make a toast. 'I'd just like to say something to you, Mr Rozello.'

Stanley frowned at him.

'This thing you're doing for your friend, Jimmy… I think it's real brave, the way you're sticking your neck out for him. Considering you were a cop and all.'

Stanley continued to glare at him.

Clarence looked at his glass and lowered his arm. 'I mean, that's true friendship, ain't it? Makes me wish I had a buddy as good as you.'

Without changing his expression, Stanley turned to Jean. 'Did you put him up to making that little speech?'

Before Jean could answer, her phone bleeped. She rooted around for it in her bag, grateful for the interruption. She found the phone and took her time reading the new text message.

*Hey Mrs H. We need to talk about Simon – Cindy x*

# 33

Linus crept into his mother's bedroom. He could hear her in the shower. She was singing, which usually meant she'd been drinking. He stood for a moment, listening to the sound of the water and the low rumble of his mother's voice coming through the bathroom door. Then he made his move. Her purse was on the bottom of the bed, along with the clothes she'd discarded when she'd undressed. He opened the brass clasp on the bag and pulled out her fat wallet. Inside there were six credit cards and at least as many store cards. He wondered which piece of plastic he should take. Which one would she miss the least? He plumped for the AmEx and slipped a store card the same colour in its place. He returned the wallet to the bag and noticed a small brown plastic bottle. He popped the childproof cap, shook out a handful of red diet pills and shoved them in a pocket. He put back the bottle, closed the bag and left the room as quietly as he'd come in.

Safely inside his own room, he sat down at his laptop and found the website he'd visited the day before. He selected the product he needed and clicked the checkout button. Then he entered a fake email address and hit 'continue'. A page appeared requesting his full postal address. His fingers hovered over the keys for a moment, then he entered his real address and clicked the confirm button. And waited. Eventually the page reloaded. A warning alert filled most of the screen. Linus read the message in disbelief.

*Your city law prohibits sending ammunition to your shipping address*

It then gave him the option of entering an alternate address, or removing the offending item from his cart.

'Piece of crap!'

He slammed the laptop shut and shoved it across his desk.

Seven bullets were all he had left. No way was that enough for him to do everything he had planned. He retrieved the gun from a drawer and pulled a single bullet from his pocket and threw both on the bed. The gun bounced once then sank into the quilt.

He had to find another way. He grabbed his cell from the desk and dialled Richie's number. Richie answered straightaway.

'Hi Rich. How are you?'

'Like you care.'

'Come on, man.'

'Unless you're calling to grovel for forgiveness, I'm not interested.'

'What did I do?'

'Are you gonna tell me why you wasted that old guy?'

'I told you already – it's not important.'

'Important enough to pump three bullets into him.'

'I just had some unfinished business with him, is all.'

'What kind of business?'

'Personal. You don't need to know.' There was no way he'd ever tell Richie about Redmond.

'You promised me I could have all the money from every job. I never got a cent.'

'Neither did I.' This wasn't going the way Linus needed it to. He could hear Richie exhaling, his breath echoing from the cell phone.

'Two hours on the interstate and not a single cent.'

'I'm sorry – you're right, it was your business too. I should have explained before we got all the way over there.' He pushed his fingernails into the palm of his hand. 'I was afraid you might not agree to take me.'

'Yeah – too scared to do it all alone.'

The nails went in harder. Linus imagined them breaking his skin, pushing through into the flesh, and the pleasure he would feel as the blood flowed from his hand. Any amount of crap Richie gave him now about wasting Redmond was worth it. Disgusting old homo. Thinking he knew anything about Linus. He was nothing like Redmond. Never was and never would be.

'You still there?'

'Let me make it up to you,' Linus said. 'We can do another store tonight – anywhere you want. You keep all the money.'

'That's for damn sure.'

'I will need some more ammunition though.'

'Is that so?'

'Do you have any?'

'You knocked off the old lady yet?'

'Sure… sure I did – that's why I'm calling. I wanted to give you the good news.'

'You did?'

'I said, didn't I? But I used more bullets than I should. That's why I need more.'

'Forget it. I'll take back the gun. I don't need you.'

Just as Linus had feared. He couldn't give up the gun. Not now. He had to think fast. He started to pace. He wanted to run. 'Hey, Rich, thanks. That's really good of you.'

'What are you talking about?'

'Offering to take a murder weapon off my hands.'

'What?'

'You might have a little trouble cleaning all the clerk's brains off the handle. I did my best, but you can never tell how much DNA gets all caught up in the grooves.'

'You can't just—'

'Suits me just fine – you can take the blame for the other kills too. *You* can be a famous serial killer.' Linus stopped pacing and stared out of the window at a middle-aged couple eating dinner in an apartment across the street. The man was studying his plate and the woman was just watching him. It didn't look like either of them was speaking. They looked a lot like his parents did before his dad moved out.

*Piece of crap.*

He stood and stared a little longer, listening again to Richie breathing into the phone. 'So, should I bring you the gun right now? Where are you? Or you think maybe I should dump it some place instead?'

'Yeah – you better dump it before I call the cops and tell them all about you.'

Like there was anything to tell. All Richie had was the number of a disposable cell phone.

'Fine – and when they arrest me I can tell them all about you.'

'Screw you.'

The line went dead. He stuck the phone back in his pocket. He didn't need Richie. There was another way to get more bullets. And maybe a little cash at the same time.

He reached over and snatched the gun from the bed and aimed it at the couple in the apartment across the street. The woman turned her head toward the window. Linus could see her face tighten as she tried to work out what was in his hand. He threw the gun back onto the bed and waved at her, gave her the thumbs up. She continued to stare at him, unable to look away. Just like the old lady in the park yesterday. He spent too long watching her, left himself vulnerable, and look what happened. He wouldn't be making any more mistakes like that. No way.

He retrieved an unused throwaway cell phone from a drawer in the desk, switched it on and started to type another text to the old lady. Spook her again. He got halfway through the message and stopped. This was boring. She didn't reply last time. She might even have handed her phone over to the cops. He hit the speed dial button. The phone rang for so long he almost hung up.

'Hello? Who is this? Is that you Cindy, love?' An English accent – the old lady still had the phone. His mind went blank – what should he say?

'Who's there?' she said. 'Stop playing silly buggers. Simon? Is it you?'

Linus swallowed and tried to make his voice as deep as possible. 'Ma'am – I'm calling from uh… Homeland Security. I have a query about your…'

*Think!*

'…your immigration status.'

'My what?'

'Are you visiting the US for business or pleasure?'

There was a pause followed by a sharp intake of breath.

'I'm on holiday – it's all on the form I filled in. Is there a problem?' Her voice was shaky, he could hear her breathing fast at the other end of the line. She was nervous. Maybe even a little afraid.

This could be fun.

'We've discovered a few… anomalies with the application. You're certain you filled out everything correctly?' He started pacing again.

'I think so.'

'When are you leaving the country?'

'I… I don't know.'

'I thought you said you were on vacation.'

'That's right, I am.'

'So when does your vacation end?'

'I can't tell you that at the moment. It's complicated.'

'Maybe you could explain?'

'I'm waiting for my son... I mean... Have you been speaking to the police?'

'The NYPD?' Uncontrollably his voice got a little louder and a little higher. He coughed. 'Can you give me an estimated date of departure?'

'Why do you need to know?'

Linus reached his bedroom door and kicked it, leaving a rubbery scuffmark on the paintwork. Why was she acting so suspicious? He tried again to control the urgency in his voice.

'It appears our records are incomplete.'

He heard her gulp noisily. 'In what way?'

'We don't have your address here in the US on our computer system – can you confirm it for me now?'

'I put my address on the form when I completed it.'

'We don't have it on the system.'

'But it was an online form. How could you not have it? Shouldn't it be automatic?'

'Ma'am, if you'd just give me the details again.'

'Wait a minute... How did you get this number? I didn't put it on the form. Where are you calling from?'

'Homeland Sec—'

'What's your name? I'd like to speak to your supervisor. In fact, give me the number, I'll call you back.' The tremor in her voice had gone completely.

He hung up.

The room suddenly seemed much smaller. And airless. His legs twitched with too much energy. He needed to get out. But he was tired of endlessly stalking the streets downtown. He needed a little fun. To maybe see some people.

He dropped the phone on the bed and plucked his regular cell from a pocket and scrolled through his contacts. One by one he rejected each name as it appeared. He had nothing in common with these people. Dumb friends from Baxter High. Why did he still have their numbers? He should delete them all. He glanced down at the gun. Maybe he should delete them permanently. He continued to flick through the names and saw one he really wasn't expecting: Redmond. If he had Redmond's cell number programmed into his phone, did that mean Redmond still had his? What if the police contacted everyone in Redmond's address book? He hit the delete option.

Time was running out. Maybe he should make a start tonight.

He went back to the beginning of the list, looking for another name he should have deleted a long time ago.

There it was: *Anna Lundstrom.*

He stared at the two words so long he could still see them when he blinked. Was it possible she was still screwing his dad? She was probably too old now for his father to be interested. Linus shuddered at the thought of his dad's hands all over her.

He hit the call button. Then quickly cancelled the call. Instead, he punched the number into the disposable cell that he'd been using with Richie, relieved he'd thought of it in time. After a couple of rings she picked up. She sounded just the same.

'Just a minute…' she said.

The line seemed to go dead.

'Sorry about that.' Her voice sounded a little breathless. 'Who is this?'

'Hey Anna. How are you? It's been a long time.' He waited.

'Who are you?'

'Don't tell me you've forgotten.'

He could almost hear her stupid brain clunking through the possibilities. *Whore.*

'After you taught me to ice skate, and everything. You must remember.'

He heard a muffled voice, as if she had put a hand over the phone and was speaking to someone else.

'Is that Linus?'

Finally.

'Hey – yeah – it's me.'

'You sound so… grown up.'

'Like I say – it's been a long time.'

'Wow – so how come you're calling me now? It's great to hear from you, but is everything OK?'

'I'm good.'

'Good – that's good news.'

She sounded unsure.

'And the… family… how is everyone?'

'Everyone?'

'You know, your mom, your sister…'

'They're good too.'

'I'm really pleased to hear that. After what happened with me and your dad, I felt so—'

'No point in thinking about all that stuff now.'

'But I mean… I never really got the chance to apologise. I haven't stopped feeling bad about it, you know. I am truly sorry.'

*Why are you telling me this? I'm not your priest.*

'Hey, it's OK – we're better off without him. Like I say – let's not rake over all that crap – it's history.'

'You're right, of course you are – water under the bridge, huh?' She let out a squeaky unconvincing laugh. 'So, why are you calling?'

'I've been thinking about you a lot lately.'

'You have?'

'Decided maybe I should do something about it.'

'Oh – that's so sweet of you.'

*Sweet? Patronising bitch.*

'So – you wanna meet up – for a drink or something?'

'A drink? Now I know for a fact you're still underage.'

'I meant coffee.'

'Of course you did.' The line went very quiet again. She was definitely with someone. Linus imagined her pulling faces at the phone. For a moment he thought he heard laughter.

He wrapped his free hand around the butt of the gun. It felt cold and solid. Reliable.

'Sure,' she said, eventually. 'Why not?'

He squeezed the gun harder. *Why not?* He could think of so many reasons.

# 34

Three emails popped into Luisa's mailbox in quick succession. The first one was from the tech guys.

As she'd suspected, the phone used to send the text message to Mrs Henderson wasn't registered. They could tell her which store it had been sold in – or stolen from – but that was as far as it went. It seemed the perp was neither careless nor stupid.

The second two emails were from a detective she knew at the 7th Precinct, informing her the team investigating Malcolm Oliver's murder had checked Simon Henderson's credit card and cell phone use. For the last five days, Henderson hadn't used his credit card in a single transaction, and his cell phone had made no outgoing calls in that time. If he had registered as a blip on the electronic radar, she could have homed in on him, been instrumental in engineering a touching mother and son reunion, and happily escorted Jean Henderson onto her plane at JFK. At least that way Luisa would be spared the task she'd been avoiding so successfully all weekend. Mrs Henderson would return to the bosom of her family in England and Stanley would have been safely removed from her clutches. But the way things were, Mrs Henderson might be clinging to Stanley until her visa expired. Luisa had to tell him – the woman was a known felon. She reached for the phone.

'Working right through your lunch break now?' Sanchez appeared at her shoulder. 'And don't give me any insulting crap about wanting to "put away the bad guys". We all signed up for that the day we entered the Police Academy.'

'I'm not hungry.'

'Hey – and here he is,' he said.

Luisa followed Sanchez's gaze to see a uniformed officer stagger toward her desk balancing a huge stack of files in his arms. He dumped them right in front of her.

'What the hell is this?'

The cop shrugged and pointed to Sanchez. 'He said you wanted them.'

'Sanchez?'

'It's an epidemic,' Sanchez said when the uniform had walked away. 'Needs your forensic brain to piece it all together.'

'What game are you playing?'

'Me?' He patted a hairy-knuckled hand against his chest. 'You think I work that way? I'm hurt.'

Luisa decided it was best to hold her tongue. Any complaint would go straight back to Lieutenant Riley.

'Minor misdemeanours – a rash of them – all over the Lower East Side, stretching up to 14th Street in the north, west to Broadway and east to Avenue A.'

Luisa flipped open the uppermost file. 'What kind of misdemeanours?'

'Minor theft – a pot plant from a Chinese restaurant off Bowery, a bicycle from outside a store on Houston. Whole crate of lemons from a grocery store on Orchard… A lot of that kind of thing.'

'Why are you even connecting them? Stuff like that must happen every day – most store owners don't bother reporting it.'

'*Exactly.*' He folded his arms and nodded at her. 'Why all of a sudden do they start reporting this small fry stuff?'

'That's all you got linking the incidents together?'

'Plus the fact that no one saw *anything*. One minute the thing is there – the pot plant, the bicycle, whatever, then a second later it's gone. Right across the precinct.'

'The whole precinct?' She opened the first file.

'Weird, huh? Like they're targeting the fourth or something.'

'Did it occur to you that if it's all over the fourth it could well be all over the fifth, and the seventh? And God knows where else?'

He made a big show of scratching his head. 'See?' He tapped a finger against his own temple then pointed at hers. 'Forensic brain. Now why hadn't I thought of that?'

Very smart. Luisa decided not to underestimate Sanchez ever again. Sure he was getting sloppy and lazy as he got older, but he was still a manipulative sonofabitch.

'I don't have time for this – I'm chasing leads on the Obama grocery store case. I'm still waiting for the print lab to get back to me about the store on Prince Street.'

Sanchez pulled his expression into a tortured grimace. 'I got to talk to you about that. It's why I'm here.'

'You heard back about the prints?'

'No – nothing like that – you know how long it can take those guys sometimes.'

'So?'

'We do have a match on the bullets used at the first store and the shooting on Long Island.'

'Same gun?'

'Looking like it.'

'I *told* you it was the same perps. But you didn't listen.' Luisa allowed herself the faintest of smiles. Had Sanchez come here to apologise? No wonder he was stalling.

'Yeah… well…'

'We should have our guys all over that crime scene,' she said.

'You mean like you were?' He slammed a hand onto her desk so hard he sent a pencil rolling off the edge and onto the floor; a move she'd seen the lieutenant make many times before. Had Riley been coaching him?

'I don't know what you're—'

'Don't bother with the innocent crap. The neighbour told the Nassau County boys about you. They did some digging.' He leaned closer, resting his hairy knuckles on the desk.

'Turns out I was right – so what's the problem?'

'Riley is pissed with you.'

'So pissed he can't even tell me about it himself?'

'Pretty much.'

'Oh come on!'

'We had a complaint.'

'From the nosy old neighbour?'

'From the principal at Baxter High.'

'He's got a nerve – I'm investigating a triple murder and he was totally obstructive. Just to protect his lousy school's reputation.' Luisa poked the files on her desk with a pencil. 'Triple murder trumps this pile of crap – wouldn't you say?'

Sanchez backed away. 'You're not listening to me.'

'Maybe you should say something worth listening to?'

'You're not investigating a triple murder. Riley won't have…' He looked down at his feet and a smile played across his mouth. 'Uh… let me get this right… I wouldn't want to misquote the boss… "unstable hysterical cops roaming round the city upsetting school children".'

'This is bull. I didn't upset anyone – except maybe the prissy little principal.'

'That's just the attitude we're talking about.'

'We?'

'Riley and me.'

'Been having cosy little chats about me behind my back?'

'It's an operational thing. I'm in charge here. I've got to trust my men… my… people, to follow orders.'

'You're so full of crap I can see it coming out your ears.'

'Ask the lieutenant yourself if you don't believe me. He's been standing right behind you for the last two minutes.'

# 35

The continuing heat and humidity had sabotaged Jean's attempt to do something with her hair. Her scalp had started sweating even before she ventured outside. Though she wasn't entirely sure why she'd even bothered. Cindy wasn't the sort of woman to give a damn how bad Jean's hair was. But still. She planned to take pictures of Cindy and the baby, and she had to look at least half human in any photo she sent back home. Otherwise Caroline would be straight on the phone. She didn't need to give her daughter an excuse to meddle.

She waved down a cab on Houston and tried to make small talk with the chirpy taxi driver on the way to Central Park. Her mind really wasn't focusing properly and the poor man had to repeat everything he said. By the time she disembarked on 72$^{nd}$ Street, he'd lost the will to speak, his cheery outlook on life all but destroyed. Jean gave him a healthy tip to make amends and made her way into the park, preferring to walk the final few hundred yards to clear her head.

Cindy had refused to tell her anything during their brief conversation on the phone, promising to 'spill the beans' when she saw her. Were there beans to spill? And what kind? Cindy wouldn't be drawn and simply rang off, texting Jean the location of their meeting place a few moments later. Every time Jean had tried her since, she got diverted straight to voicemail.

She reached the Bethesda Fountain in the middle of the park, and searched the crowds for a woman she'd met only once before in the flesh, trying hard to remember what Cindy had looked like in the photograph she'd seen on Simon's Facebook page. Not that it would help much. Cindy changed hair colour more often than Jean changed bed linen.

She wandered down the steps toward the fountain and circumnavigated it twice, going over all the things she wanted to say, all the questions she needed answers to. She stopped on the third go round and waited by the low stone bench that edged the boating lake. She wondered if she should have bought a copy of the *New York Times* to shove under an arm. Perhaps she could have pinned a red carnation to her blouse. But then she really hadn't changed that much in the last two years – just a few more wrinkles here and there and a couple of extra pounds. She stared out over the water and breathed a long sigh. A tiny part of her was harbouring the unjustifiable hope that Cindy would bring Simon along to the meeting. That the pair of them had enjoyed a spontaneous and moving reconciliation and wanted to surprise her with the good news.

*Hope springs eternal.*

'Jean?'

Jean spun round to see a tall woman with a blonde bob smiling at her.

'Mrs H – how are you?' The woman threw her arms around Jean's neck and rocked her from side to side for a moment longer than Jean found comfortable. When she pulled away Cindy was still smiling. A plastered on, rictus grin. It looked as if Cindy was worried what might happen to her expression if she relaxed her face for more than a moment. Her eyes were puffed and lined. The baby must have been keeping her up.

'Where's the baby?' Jean said and stepped back, expecting to see a stroller parked nearby.

'I thought we should speak without being interrupted.' Cindy's smile faded and her eyes started to fill. She dabbed at them with the flimsy cuff of her linen shirt.

Jean reached into her bag for a clean handkerchief and folded it into Cindy's hands.

'It's ridiculous, I know. I've been weeping like this ever since Sookie was born.'

*Sookie*? Jean tried hard to keep her face neutral. *Sookie*?

'Should you even be out and about? It's only been a couple of days. You're body's been through the wringer.'

Cindy frowned, blew her nose and tucked the handkerchief into a pocket. She slipped her arm through Jean's. 'Shall we walk and talk?'

'If you think you're up to it. It was a short labour, was it? Easy delivery?'

They started strolling around the lake.

'It was almost a week ago,' Cindy said.

Jean pulled up. 'A week?'

'Sookie came just after I left Si… after I moved out of the apartment.'

'But I only received the text last weekend.'

'Mom said I couldn't ignore all the messages you left. We just left out the part about when Sookie was born.'

'Does Simon know about his daughter?'

'Of course he does – I called him…' She wouldn't take her eyes from the ground.

'How did he sound?' Jean grabbed Cindy's hands.

'Tired. A little lost maybe. We arranged for him to come by.' Finally she looked up and stared out across the lake.

'And?'

'He didn't show.' A little sob escaped from her mouth and she pulled the handkerchief from her pocket. 'I'm sorry about this – hormones, I guess. I'm just so emotional about every little thing.'

'Little thing? I'd hardly describe Simon's disappearance as—'

'I didn't mean… what I'm trying to say…'

'Did he tell you where he was when you spoke to him?'

'Not exactly – he said the less I knew the better. I got the impression he was out of town.'

'In the country?'

'Maybe another city. I don't know.' A tear dribbled down her cheek.

'And you haven't heard from him since?'

'When he didn't come to my mom's I thought the worst. That maybe something bad had happened.' She dabbed at her face. 'But I got a message from him saying sorry – he couldn't risk coming into the city. Even though he was desperate to see little Sookie.'

'Where's the baby right now?'

'She's with my mom.'

'And that's all right is it? I didn't even know your mother was still alive.'

'We never used to get along. That was all my fault – rebellious teenager right into my late twenties. I think getting pregnant mellowed me a little – you know?'

Jean looked at Cindy's perfectly coiffured blonde bob, her well cut linen trouser suit and her expensive shoes, and decided she liked her much better the way she was before. Where was the thick eyeliner? What had happened to the nose piercing? This new version of Cindy was more like a Stepford Wife than a flesh and blood woman. The old Cindy would have ridiculed this one for playing safe and selling out. She could hear her saying exactly that. What had happened to her spark? Where had the fight gone?

'I'd really like to see her – Sookie. Is she somewhere close by?'

'She's not far – I guess I could call mom.'

'Would you?'

Jean watched the pallid replica of Cindy make the call and speak in apologetic tones to her mother. She had to resist a very strong urge to shake some life into her.

'You know Simon needs you right now more than he ever has?' Jean said when Cindy slipped the phone back into her bag. 'He needs the love and support of his family – his new family I mean. You should all be together.'

Cindy sucked in a faltering breath. 'You know about the money he owes?'

'I know all about the loan shark. I know how frightened he must be.' She laid a hand gently on Cindy's arm. 'Promise me you'll call him again and try to persuade him to come back? He needs help – I can't bear to think of him out there on his own – terrified of those… gangsters.'

'It's not that simple.' Cindy's voice had dropped to a whisper.

'Tell him to call me, then – maybe I can convince him he needs to come home and sort things out. I can help. I really can.' She squeezed Cindy's arm, a bit harder than she'd intended. Cindy's face crumpled. 'Give me his number,' Jean said, 'I'll call him right now.'

'He's using a throwaway phone now – he wouldn't give me his new number.' She pulled her arm away from Jean's grasp. 'Besides, I'm not sure I want him to come back.'

'What?'

'It's not safe. Not just the loan sharks. It's bigger than that. More serious.'

'What do you mean?'

'I don't know for sure – he would never tell me anything when I asked. Even the night I left. He came back late from work. He looked… broken somehow. We had a big fight.' She spread her arms wide. 'I guess you know the rest.'

It seemed to Jean she knew less and less with each day that passed.

'The best thing for Si right now is to stay away from New York.' Cindy blew her nose again. 'He needs to run as fast as he can.' She wrung the handkerchief in her hands. 'And to keep on running.'

# 36

A fresh stack of files landed on Luisa's desk.

'You've got to be kidding me – more? I haven't even finished with the ones you gave me this morning.'

'It's an epidemic – spreading like a virus.'

'You've been listening to Sanchez too long – you want to watch out. Start talking like him, you might start looking like him too.'

The uniformed officer sucked his stomach in so that it barely overhung the waistband of his pants.

'See?' Luisa pointed at him. 'It's happening already.' She peered at the files on her desk and did a quick count. At least a dozen more crimes reported. 'Are these as trivial as the first batch you brought me – any more pot plants?'

'These are for later.'

'Why – what's happening now?'

'We got one of the perps downstairs waiting for you in an interview room.'

'I thought Sanchez said nobody saw anything – how did this one get caught?'

'The guy's over six feet tall. Besides, he ran straight into the owner of the store as soon as he grabbed the lamp.'

'You want me to interrogate somebody for stealing a lamp? What was it – made of solid gold?'

'It's not the value of the object; it's the principle of the thing. That's what the store owner said.'

'You've spoken to him?'

'Sure – we put him in the next interview room. You'd better hurry it up. He's been in there a half hour already. He's getting real antsy. Wants to get back to his store.'

Luisa glanced over at Sanchez – he was deep in conversation with the lieutenant. Probably hatching some other plan to make her life hell. She'd been processing paperwork all day. 'I'll interview the suspect before the storeowner. I don't care how impatient he is. Tell him we'll get to him just as soon as we can. OK?'

The policeman nodded, letting go of the hold he had on his abdomen. Soft flesh pushed back over his belt.

When Luisa opened the door of interview room five, the last along the gloomy hallway on the second floor, she took a step back, wondering if she was in the right room. The man slouching at the table certainly didn't look like an arch criminal. His eyes were watery and his nose moist. He was staring down at his long interlaced fingers, bony knuckles showing through the flesh. She stood in the doorway a few moments before he noticed her.

'There's been a terrible mistake,' he said, his voice shaky. 'I didn't mean to…' His shoulders slumped as the words trailed away.

'We all make mistakes, sir.' Luisa closed the door behind her and dragged the chair from the opposite side of the table to sit next to him. 'Things we regret afterwards. Why don't you tell me all about it?'

'Am I under arrest?'

Luisa checked the notes the uniformed officer had given her.

'No, sir.'

'Does that mean I can go?' He sat up a little straighter. It seemed to use up all his strength. 'She's gonna get so mad.'

'Who?'

'What?'

'Who's getting mad?'

'Nobody.' He looked away from her and licked his parched lips. 'I need a glass of water. Can you get me a glass of water, miss?'

'In a minute. First of all, why don't you tell me about the lamp?'

'I don't know what you're talking about. I don't know nothing about no lamp.'

Luisa took a deep breath and remembered the cosy little chat Sanchez was having with Lieutenant Riley in the squad room. Was this a set up? She stared deep into the network of creases in the suspect's moist face. Could Sanchez be behind this?

'Why don't we take this slowly?' She glanced down at the file she was still clutching and quickly checked his details. His name rang a bell. She thought about it for a moment, but the harder she tried to find some memory connected to it, the more her recollection failed. 'So – you were in the store on Bowery, right?' She carried on reading the file. 'Light Fantastic – that's the name of the store. Why did you go in?'

'I've never been in there.'

'We have the storeowner in the next room, sir. We can ask him for the security camera video.'

'Whatever's on the camera, it isn't me. I swear.'

*Give me a break, come on.*

'Who's going to get mad?'

'What are you saying?' He cupped a hand around his ear, but he seemed to be hearing her just fine.

'"She's gonna get so mad." That's what you said when I first came in.'

'Is she? Who?' He wriggled in his seat and clenched his hands together even tighter. 'I could really use that glass of water.'

'Do you have any idea how much trouble you're in, sir?'

'I never been in trouble my whole life.'

'Then why did you start now?'

He shook his head. 'I didn't start anything, miss. Can I go home now?'

There was a sharp knock on the door. Luisa jumped up and reached for the handle just as it opened. The uniform was standing the other side, looking pissed.

'What is it?' Luisa's day was getting worse by the minute.

'Storeowner just took off. Said he was losing business sitting in here. He's decided to drop the charges.'

'Why didn't you stop him and come get me?'

'Hey – I tried. He seemed real determined to go.'

'You tried, huh?'

He nodded unconvincingly. 'Wanna give me that?' He pointed to the file she was holding.

'No – I'll hang on to it.' She was still hoping she would remember where she'd heard the suspect's name before. 'Get him a glass of water before you let him go. I'm worried the old guy'll die of thirst before he makes it one block up the street.'

She took the stairs back up to the fourth floor three at a time and flung open the squad room door, not taking her eyes off Sanchez as she marched to his desk.

'Is it just him, or did you set up every goddamn case?'

Sanchez turned away from her, the handset of his desk phone pressed hard against his ear. After a few moments he slammed it back onto the cradle and jumped up. 'Whatever it is, Rodriguez, it'll have to wait.' He yanked open a drawer and pulled out a Kevlar vest.

'What's going on?'

'Tell you later.'

Luisa grabbed his arm as he looped the vest over his head. 'What's the rush?'

'We got a match on that print from the second grocery store.'

'We did?'

Sanchez narrowed his eyes.

'Who is it?'

'Kid from one of the projects down by the river. In and out of juvie since he was out of diapers – stealing, assault, possession… I could go on.' He Velcroed the sides of the vest tight around his thick stomach. 'If I had the time.' He smiled at her. 'Or the inclination.'

Luisa reached for the drawer and another bulletproof vest.

'What do you think you're doing?' Sanchez snapped at her.

'I found the print. This is my arrest.'

'Shouldn't have gotten yourself thrown off the case, then.'

'It's not right.'

'Whining again, Rodriguez?' Riley appeared behind her. It was getting to be a habit. 'Does it matter who arrests him? We're taking a cold-blooded killer off the street – isn't that what you want?'

'The white perp did the shooting. The killer is still out there.' Even Riley couldn't argue with that. Luisa stuck out her chin in defiance. 'I was getting close to him. If you just let me go back to the school, I can—'

'Read my lips. You. Are. Off. The. Case.' He turned away.

Luisa watched as Sanchez hurried out of the room with two more of Riley's poker buddies. She slumped onto her chair and threw the file she'd brought from the interview room on the desk. She looked at the name on the front, frustrated at not remembering why it was so familiar. She pulled a legal pad from a drawer and wrote down the name, hoping it would trigger some memory. She traced over it a few times, trying to make her mind go blank. It wasn't until she'd looped her pen around the final 'E' for the third time that she realised she'd written the name before.

*Clarence Ashe.* The other person Mrs Henderson had given her cell phone number to. Luisa stared at the messy scrawl of letters, trying to make sense of the unlikely connection. The English woman had some serious explaining to do.

# 37

Jean stood on Jimmy's rickety little porch and waved Stanley off. She waited until his car got to the very end of the street and turned into the main road before she felt happy going back inside. Stanley had promised to be gone no more than half an hour. It was a shame the store wasn't further away. As it was, Jean might run out of time.

When Stanley had dropped by Simon's apartment on his way home from work to ask her to sit with Jimmy for a while, Jean couldn't believe her luck. She'd planned to get a taxi all the way over to Forest Hills to speak to Jimmy anyway. Now at least she'd saved herself the hefty cab fare.

Jimmy was back in his own home after complaining he couldn't sleep in Stanley's spare room, so Stanley had arranged for a very expensive agency nurse to spend the day with him. The nurse had been gone nearly an hour by the time Jean and Stanley arrived and Jimmy had fallen badly in the bathroom. They discovered him sprawled across the floor clutching his stomach.

'I had to go,' he'd said. 'Sorry, Stan.'

The poor man seemed to be getting worse rather than better.

Jean was just deciding to wait a few moments longer on the porch, in case Stanley returned, having forgotten something, when she heard a faint cry from inside the house. She slammed the door and rushed up the stairs into

Jimmy's bedroom to discover he had spilled a glass of water over the bedclothes.

'Look at me,' he said. 'Can't even get myself something to drink without making a goddamn mess.'

Jean blotted the worst of the liquid with a towel and fetched Jimmy another glass. 'No harm done. It'll soon be dry in this heat.'

'Thanks, Jean. Can I call you Jean?'

'It *is* my name. I think we've gone beyond the "ma'am" stage – don't you?'

He nodded at her meekly. 'You've seen more of me than my ex-wife.'

'Well that's not saying much for your marriage is it?'

He looked at her with his mouth open, his eyes wide. Then he started laughing. 'I thought English ladies were meant to be polite.'

'I may be English… but I'm no—'

'Now that I don't believe. My old buddy wouldn't be feeling the way he does about you, if you weren't.'

Jean's eyebrows flew up.

'Come on,' Jimmy said. 'Don't tell me you haven't noticed the way he looks at you.'

'I can't really be sure what to think.'

'Stan's not good at expressing his feelings, that's all. Take it from me – he likes you.'

'Really?'

'Said he couldn't believe how quickly…' Jimmy trailed off and took a sudden interest in the damp bed sheet covering his wasted body.

'What is it?'

'He told me things in private, you know?'

'A few words of encouragement really wouldn't go amiss. I promise I won't let on you've said anything.'

'So, you feel the same way about Stan, huh?'

It was Jean's turn to look away. She hadn't blushed so much since she was a teenager.

'Hey, I'm getting to feel like Cupid here.'

'Should I broach the subject with him?'

'Hell no! Stan'd run a mile. You gotta go gentle with the fella.' Jimmy took a sip of water. 'What you gotta understand about Stan, he don't take to people too easy. He has to get used to them, kinda feeling his way.' He blew a breathy whistle. 'But he sure has taken to you – trust me. We go back a long way – I know him better than anyone.' He stared into his glass. 'At least since Maria passed away.'

'His wife?'

Jimmy nodded.

'He hasn't spoken to me about her at all.'

'It was only a few years ago. Traffic accident. It's still raw, you know?'

Jean remembered how bereft she'd felt when her husband died. She realised, much to her shame, she hadn't really thought about him during her stay in New York.

'I think it makes it harder for Stan that Isabella lives so far away. He misses her more than he lets on.'

'Does his daughter visit often?'

'Not as much as Stan would like.'

Jean counted the number of times she'd seen Simon in the last few years. It didn't run to the fingers of one hand. She'd visited her youngest daughter in New Zealand only once in the last decade. A lump started to form in her throat. If she wasn't careful, the floodgates would open and there'd be no closing them. She sniffed in a breath and puffed it out. She needed to change the subject. Fast.

'So... tell me about how you first met Stanley.'

'How much has he told you?'

'I know you're from the same neighbourhood. Same school.'

Jimmy's face brightened a little. 'The priests taught us everything we know.'

'Not everything, I'm sure.'

'True. But the fact we both got good enough grades to make it all the way to the police academy was down to the dedication of those guys. They kept us on the straight and narrow. Not easy in our neighbourhood.'

'What made you both choose the police?'

'It was my idea.'

'It was? I got the impression Stanley persuaded you to join.'

'He said that?'

'Not in so many words.' He'd said nothing of the sort. The more she thought about it, the more she realised Stanley had resolutely refused to say anything at all. But Jean was running out of time before Stanley's return. A white lie here and there wouldn't hurt anyone. 'It's clear to anyone he loves the department so much he never wanted to retire.'

'Oh, he took to it soon enough. Everything about the department he loved. Maybe a little too much.' Jean thought she detected a hint of bitterness in his tone.

'But not you? Didn't it live up to your expectations?'

'What's he said?'

'Nothing, not really.' She looked away, wondering how much she could invent without being found out. 'Just that Stanley had to be forced out because of his age, yet you left with years of service still ahead of you.'

Jimmy winced.

'What is it? Do you need more painkillers?'

'I've taken enough of those goddamn things.'

'I could just nip to the bathroom.' She started to get up. Jimmy gripped her hand.

'The pills the hospital gave me make my head spin when I take too many. I like to be able to think straight.' He sighed and looked toward the window. Jean followed his gaze. The sky was as blue as it had been every day since she'd arrived. 'I guess Stanley never told you why I left, huh?'

'I have asked him. He just changes the subject.'

'That doesn't surprise me. Apart from Maria, I don't think he's told anyone outside the department. Not the real reason, anyhow.'

'What was it?'

'You just need to know it had nothing to do with Stan. Not really, not when you boil it right down. It was my decision. I did the only thing I could.' He shifted and wriggled awkwardly in the bed. Jean reached forward and plumped his pillows. 'I guess the priests taught me a little too well.'

'What happened?'

'I'm feeling a little tired now – maybe we could talk later. When Stan gets back with the groceries, huh?'

Jimmy's face seemed to have closed in on itself. It was quite clear he wasn't about to divulge any more information, not now and especially not when Stanley returned.

A loud thump downstairs on the front door made Jean jump. Stanley had made it back with Jimmy's groceries much sooner than she'd anticipated. 'Doesn't Stanley have a key?' she asked Jimmy. But Jimmy had closed his eyes.

There was another thump outside on the porch.

'All right, all right. I'm coming,' Jean muttered. 'There's no need to tear the house down.'

When she reached the downstairs hall, something told her to stop. The silhouette on the other side of the screen door didn't look right. It was too short and too wide to be Stanley. She watched as a fist rose and came crashing down on the flimsy wooden doorframe.

'I know you're in there,' the voice shouted through the door. 'I seen you walking down the hall.' The man banged his fist against the wood a fourth time. 'Come on. We can do this the easy way, or the hard way. Makes no difference to me. I still get paid.'

Jean pressed herself against a wall and waited.

'It's no use hiding.' He banged again. 'Any damage I do is down to you – it's your responsibility. Understand?'

*Damage?*

He said something under his breath and moments later printed sheets appeared beneath the door. 'That's your paperwork – it's all in order, what I'm about to do is perfectly legal.' He didn't sound convinced. 'So no calling the cops.'

'Who is that?' Jimmy called faintly from his bedroom at the top of the stairs.

'Don't worry about it,' Jean hollered back and yanked open the door. The figure just about to step off the porch swung around and stared into the house for long moments, before he said anything. 'You Mrs Kapowski?'

'Who are you?' Jean took in his greasy overalls and the grimy white vest underneath.

'I'm the repo man – congratulations – you're my last visit of the day.'

'You'll have to come back another time – Mr Kapowski is indisposed.'

'He's *what*?'

'He's poorly.'

Still the grubby man stared at her, none the wiser.

'He's ill, unwell… sick.'

'And I should care about his health, because…?'

'He's really very sick – this is going to make him worse. I'm sure we can arrange to make some form of payment. How much does he owe?'

'We got past that stage a long time ago. Either you give me the car key, and I drive away nice and civilized, or we dump the car on the back of the truck. Like I say – I can't promise we won't scratch a few other vehicles in the process.'

Jean looked out at the battered cars parked on the street. She doubted a few more dents and scratches would make much difference to the owners. 'Twenty-four hours and I can get you whatever he owes.'

'What are you? The Queen of England?'

'Please – I swear – I'll make it worth your while.'

'Are you trying to bribe me, lady?'

'With a small gratuity? Hardly.'

'What's going on down there?' Jimmy's weak voice came floating down the stairs.

Jean wasn't sure why she was trying to save his car from repossession. God only knew when he'd be well enough to drive it again. Perhaps she just wanted to do something real, a sign that she was looking out for him. A sign that he wasn't beaten. One little victory might lift Jimmy's spirits. Save his car today. Perhaps his house tomorrow.

The man in the overalls seemed to hesitate, considering her offer. 'Nah – can't do it. Gotta make my targets. Whatever figure you have in mind won't get close to the bonus I got coming to me.'

'Five hundred dollars,' Jean blurted, plucking a random figure from the air.

He sniffed.

'A thousand – but that's my final offer and you have to give me forty-eight hours to raise it.'

'Is that right?'

'You'll still get your bonus, presumably, if you collect all the outstanding payments before the end of the week?'

He shifted from one foot to the other. 'I guess.' Something caught his attention behind her. 'Jesus Christ.'

Jean turned to see Jimmy propped up against the wall at the bottom of the stairs.

'I'll be back here seven o'clock Thursday evening – you just make sure you got all the money.' He kicked at the sheets of paper still lying on the floor. 'Amount owing is right there, last page.' He turned and ran across the front yard to a waiting recovery truck.

'You shoulda let him take the car.' A key on a fob dropped from Jimmy's hand and landed heavily on the floor. 'Uses too much gas anyway.'

Jean rushed to Jimmy and helped him along the hall and onto a couch in the living room. He weighed practically nothing. 'What did you think you were doing?' she said. 'Getting up like that. You could have really hurt yourself.'

'I had to see what was going on. I thought they'd come for the house.' Tears filled his eyes. He rubbed a hand across his face. 'I'm sorry. It's just… I've lived here a lot of years.'

Jean plumped a cushion and tucked it behind Jimmy's head. 'It is hard. I know exactly what you mean. I sold my house to help out my daughter and her husband. It very difficult to leave it – so many memories.'

'Where are you living now?'

'With Caroline, my daughter.'

'And how's that working out?'

'We have our ups and downs.'

'You got grandkids?'

Jean opened her eyes wide and thought about her brief introduction that morning to the newest member of the family. Little Sookie had Simon's eyes, and quite possibly his nose, the poor little mite. She fished her phone out of her bag and showed Jimmy the pictures she'd taken of her granddaughter.

'Sookie,' she said, trying not to make her tone apologetic. 'Almost a week old.'

'She's a beauty – just like her grandma.'

Jean felt a breath catch in her throat, threatening to develop into a pitiful sob if she wasn't careful. 'My son is yet to meet her.'

'Stan was telling me about him, I hope you don't mind.'

'Not at all. If you have any bright ideas about where he might have taken himself off to – do let me know.'

'Seems he owes even more money than me, huh?'

Jean couldn't run the risk of answering, not without a sob escaping from her mouth.

'At least he's a fit young guy – he can find a way to fix it. Soon as he does, I'm sure he'll come home.'

'I think you're overestimating my son's abilities.' She let out a sigh. 'Simon isn't known for having a cool head in a crisis. Why do you think he's run away?'

'I would if I could.'

'But you didn't – you made a stand.'

'And look where it got me.' He glanced down at his spindly little legs in his pyjamas. 'Laid up like some kinda invalid.'

Jean glanced surreptitiously at her watch. Stanley had been gone over twenty minutes. He could return at any moment.

'I've been thinking of a way I can help Simon,' she said. 'So he could come home. It would have the knock-on effect of helping you too – save your house, get you the right medical care. And stick two fingers up to Fisher Krupps.'

'Hey sticking anything to Fisher Krupps is OK by me.'

'The only problem is… well…'

'Jeez – what is it?'

There was no option – she just had to plunge straight in.

'I can't really pull it off without a lot of help from Stanley.'

'I'm sure he'd do anything for you – you just gotta ask him. You shouldn't be bashful.'

'Oh, I've asked him. He turned me down flat.'

'Maybe you didn't ask the right way. You gotta handle him careful. Why don't you tell me what you got in mind and I can ask Stanley on your behalf?'

'It's not quite as simple as that.'

'Why don't you try me?'

'The plan I'm working on isn't exactly…' Jean remembered what Stanley had told her about Jimmy's blameless character. His high moral standards. She looked into his eager face. He was the most animated she'd seen him. 'It's not exactly *legal*.'

Jimmy frowned at her and tilted his head to one side.

'And you know what a stickler Stanley is for playing by the rules. Doing the right thing. Just like you are.'

He looked away and swallowed hard, his Adam's apple bobbing in his scrawny throat. 'Playing by the rules, huh?'

'I know how important that is to both of you.'

He sank further into the cushion behind his head, as if he'd deflated somehow. 'Depends whose rules you're playing by.' He gripped the side of the couch. 'He hasn't always been that way. I guess the guilt crept up on him over the years.'

'Guilt?'

'Never mind.' He glanced back at her. 'How illegal we talking, anyway?'

'I like to think of it as taking from the rich to give to the poor.'

'The rich being Fisher Krupps?'

Jean nodded so enthusiastically, she felt her head might detach from her shoulders.

'And the poor being me?'

'And Simon.' Jean wrinkled her nose. 'I suppose that's where the Robin Hood analogy falls down. I'm prepared to help Simon any way I can.' She heard a car door slam outside. 'Of course, if it's possible, I'd like to distribute to other needy causes.'

'Is that what I am? A charity case?'

'That's not what I meant. I'm just trying to—'

'It's OK – I don't offend that easy.' He winked a watery eye at her. 'And Stanley's high principles are getting in the way?'

'He won't even listen to me. I've explained how I want to help you. He still won't budge.'

A key scraped against the lock at the front door.

'You leave Stanley Rozello to me.'

# 38

The sidewalk fell away as a muscled arm clamped around Linus's throat and lifted him off his feet. He was dragged backward for almost half a block from the entrance to his apartment building, finally stopping at the next corner. Linus didn't put up a fight. He recognised the telltale odour of Johnson's Baby Powder.

When the grip loosened he managed to gasp a painful breath. 'Jesus, man. What the hell has gotten into you?' Linus rubbed his throat when Richie's arm finally disengaged.

'Needed to get your attention.' He started bouncing from one foot to the other. 'Got it, didn't I?'

'What's the matter with you?' Linus made a show of brushing down his crumpled clothes.

'I gotta get off the street.' Richie gestured to the building behind them. 'We should go inside.'

'I don't live in there.'

'No? Then how come I seen you go in and out like you do?'

'What? When?'

'I followed you.'

'Followed me?' Linus looked up and down the street. 'Why?'

'Wanted to know where I could find you in a hurry if I needed to.'

'You're not making any sense.' Linus spotted a neighbour from his floor crossing the street toward the building. He held up a hand to his face. There was an outside chance the neighbour would remember his name and call over.

Richie hugged his arms to his chest. 'I need a place to stay – just for a little while.'

'You want to stay with me?' Linus spat out the words. 'Why?'

'The cops are all over my mom's. I saw the cars outside. Unmarked, but you can tell a cop car from a mile away. I ran as fast as I could.'

'We've been careful – masks, gloves. I don't understand.'

'You weren't wearing a mask the other night – out on Long Island.'

'You're the one they're after. How did they find you?'

Richie closed his eyes and leaned back on his heels. 'Hundreds of people must go in and out of that store every day.'

'Which store?'

'Prince Street. The second store. Why would they even waste their time with that crap?'

Linus grabbed Richie's shoulders and shook him until he looked into his eyes. 'Who? What crap?' Although he didn't have the gun and Richie was at least six inches taller, Linus felt sure he could take him on if he had to.

'You gave me the money and I left the store. I didn't need to wear gloves. I didn't plan on touching anything.'

'What are you saying?'

'It's the only way they could have traced me. From the fingerprints.'

'You left fingerprints in the store?'

Richie looked away. 'I tripped over something near the door. I touched the doorframe on the way out.'

Linus shook him again then let go of Richie's shoulders. He balled his fists, stretched his fingers then balled them again, unable to quite understand the charge he felt rushing through his veins. Richie had just told him how close the cops were to tracking them down, but instead of feeling fear or panic, he somehow felt elated. Invincible. Untouchable. All he had to do was make sure the cops had no way of linking him to Richie.

'So I can stay, yeah? Just for a few days, until the heat is off – then I can get my stuff from my mom's and leave town for a little while.'

Linus stared at Richie as he bounced on his toes and shoved his hands into his armpits. He looked smaller than he ever had before, vulnerable. It was like he was seeing him for the first time, as if Richie were a stranger. And he was, wasn't he? How well did Linus really know him? Barely at all. He didn't owe him a thing. But he couldn't just cut him loose. Not now Richie was a marked man.

Linus licked his lips and blinked slowly. 'You can't stay with me. My mom would freak.'

'Come on, man – you gotta help me.'

'Sure – I'll take care of you – just not at my place – OK?' He rested a hand on Richie's shoulder and looked into his eyes.

'Where then?'

'Wait here for a second – I need to go get something from the apartment. Then I'll take you somewhere safe – you can stay there just as long as you like.'

Richie's shoulders dropped as he exhaled. He even smiled at Linus with the corner of his mouth. 'Where is it?'

'It's a place… uh…' A plan was forming in Linus's mind. 'It's on the other side of the park. We can walk there. My mom has a set of keys. I know where she keeps them.'

Richie's face brightened. 'Somewhere safe, yeah?'

'You don't need to worry about the cops finding you there. OK?'

'I guess.'

'Don't you trust me?'

Richie was sweating, his pupils just little dots, desperately searching Linus's face. 'Sure,' he said eventually. 'We're a team, yeah?'

Linus ran into his building. The elevator took forever to arrive in the lobby then seemed so slow getting up to the thirty-fifth floor he wished he'd taken the stairs. He didn't have time for this. He was supposed to be meeting Anna in less than an hour. He'd just have to deal with Richie as fast as he could.

He finally reached the apartment and flung open the door, running right into his mother.

'Honey! Where were you? I've been so worried. Your sister and the baby are here. Come say hi.'

Linus pushed past her and let out a non-committal grunt.

'Oh come on, honey. I see nothing of you these days. Why don't you have some supper with us?'

'I've got to go out.'

'You only just got in.'

'I have some business to attend to.' He ran into his bedroom and slammed the door. He could still hear her chattering on the other side.

'*Business*? Do you know how like your father you sound?'

She knew exactly which buttons to press.

*Bitch.*

He rushed into his closet and dug out a shoebox buried under a pile of clothes. He reached inside for the gun and immediately the sharp spike of anger in his chest started to subside. He raised the gun to his face and rested his cheek against the cool metal.

'Linus, honey!' His mother's muffled voice even managed to reach him deep inside the closet. 'Come and have a bite to eat before you go. It's your favourite.'

She could shove her supper up her ass. Or even better – she could choke on it. His sister too, and her bawling brat.

He checked the barrel, counting the bullets, even though he already knew how few he had left.

Only one of them had Richie's name on.

# 39

Jean arrived at the café early. It was located on the corner opposite Stanley's new workplace, just a few blocks north of the Financial District. She scrutinised her fellow diners and decided they were easy marks, too distracted by their coffee orders and phone conversations to notice a deft hand dipping into pockets and handbags. But she decided to forego the rich pickings; Stanley could turn up at any moment and she didn't want to go over the same argument they'd had before. Instead she settled herself into a seat next to the window and prepared for the long wait for table service.

Stanley arrived ten minutes later, out of breath and flushed in the face. 'Sorry I'm late.' He squeezed her shoulders then manoeuvred around the table in the jammed coffee shop. 'Something came up.'

'Has something happened with Jimmy?' As soon as he slid into the booth she grabbed his hand.

Stanley shook his head. 'I just spoke to him. He's doing OK. Friend of your neighbour's is sitting with him today.'

'I know – Carmen's organised a roster for the whole week.' Jean leaned over to an elderly busboy clearing the next table. 'Do you think you could let someone know we're ready to order?' The man nodded and heaved an over-laden tray onto his shoulder. As she watched him walk away Jean wondered whether he was a potential recruit for the cause. 'What did you want to meet me for?' she said to Stanley.

'Can't a guy share a little lunch with a friend?' He busied himself with a menu.

'That's all?'

Stanley let out a heavy sigh and shoved the menu back on the table. 'I've been doing some thinking.'

'You have?'

'Hardly slept last night going through it all in my mind.'

The busboy reappeared with an empty tray and pointed to a young waitress making her way slowly through the crowded café. The waitress hesitated for a moment and peered in Jean's general direction. The busboy gestured at their table. When she arrived Jean ordered quickly for them both and watched the waitress disappear through a swing door.

Probably never to return.

'After you left last night,' Stanley continued, 'Jimmy and me had a long talk.' He looked away.

Jean snatched a breath and fanned herself with Stanley's discarded menu. 'Did you? What about?' She braced herself, wondering if Stanley was about to finally declare his feelings.

'The past, I guess. He seemed real eager to talk about old times. About me and him. How long we'd known one another.'

Jean did her best to disguise her disappointment. 'What brought all that up?'

'I thought maybe you could tell me. What did you speak to him about while I was at the store?'

'Oh, you know… nothing really. The weather… this and that.'

'He didn't say anything about what happened when he was a cop?'

Jean strained to keep her expression blank. 'No, why would he?'

'Maybe it's the accident. Or the medication. He got real agitated.'

Jean glanced around the café, unable to look at Stanley. 'Where did that waitress get to?'

'Forget about that,' Stanley said and put his hand over hers. 'I'm trying to talk to you here.'

'Sorry.' Jean risked looking up into his eyes. They were bloodshot and slightly moist.

'Jimmy told me some stuff I never heard before. It shook me up. I've been going over and over it in my mind. All these years.' He shook his head. 'It's like I didn't really know the guy.'

'What did he say?' When Jean had asked Jimmy to work on changing Stanley's mind, she'd had no idea it would have this kind of effect on him. She was beginning to wish she'd never mentioned it.

'Jimmy told me he'd regretted leaving the department every single day since. I never knew that. He always made out it was what he wanted. I got into so many fights with him about it over the years. But now he's telling me I was right and he wished he'd listened to me from the beginning.'

'Why did he leave?'

'I don't want to get into that. That's not why I'm telling you.' He sniffed hard and rubbed his nose with a fist. 'Goddamn it, the guy started weeping, right there in my arms. Sobbing his heart out like a little kid. I never seen him so broke up about anything. Even when Marge left.'

Jean squeezed Stanley's hand, unsure whether she should speak or leave him to carry on.

'Then he started talking about his house. How he couldn't cope with the idea of moving out. Asked me to help him save it from the bank. He's never asked me for so much as a dime before. He's always been a stubborn sonofabitch.'

'Did he suggest a way of doing that?'

Stanley pulled his hands away from Jean's. He stared down at the table and shook his head. 'Are you sure you he didn't say anything to you?'

'Not a word.'

'And you didn't tell him about your crazy ideas?'

'You told me not to.'

'I just don't understand the change in him.'

'What are you going to do?'

'I've gotta help him. Jesus, I owe the guy.' He let out a breath and slumped back in his seat. He looked exhausted.

Jean looked around the café again, searching for the waitress. She couldn't risk making eye contact with Stanley. She was just about to wave the busboy back over when Stanley spoke again.

'How are we gonna do this?'

'What?'

'Tell me what you got planned.'

'You actually want to know the details?'

'I'm asking, ain't I?'

'Are you sure about this?'

'Do I look sure?'

'I don't have it all worked out. Maybe you could help me?'

Jean spent the next quarter of an hour sketching out the bare bones of a plan. Stanley listened without interrupting. When she'd finished he finally made a comment.

'That's never gonna work. Not in a million years. It's the stupidest plan I ever heard.'

Before she could argue with him, Jean's phone started chirping. She yanked it out of her bag, hoping Cindy had decided to reply to one of the dozen or so messages she'd left over the last twenty-four hours. She hurriedly tapped thc appropriate buttons and discovered someone had sent her a picture message. She held the phone at arm's length and tried to focus on the blurry image. When she eventually worked out what she was looking at, she felt a strange buzzing sensation in the base of her skull.

'Hey!' Stanley leapt from his seat. 'What's the matter?'

Jean tried to focus on his face as the room faded to black.

# 40

Luisa saw Stanley at the half-open squad room door, his drawn face poking through the gap. She jumped from her seat, shouting as she rushed toward him. 'What the hell happened to you?' She'd never seen him look so bad. All the things she wanted to tell him about Mrs Henderson crowded into her mind. She couldn't put it off any longer. 'Stan,' she said, trying to force her mouth into a smile. 'Come and sit down – I need to speak to you.'

It wasn't until she'd practically reached the door and Stanley pushed it wide open that she spotted the woman herself leaning heavily against him. 'Oh.' She couldn't help sounding disappointed. 'Mrs Henderson.'

Stanley pushed past her and guided the woman to a vacant seat next to Luisa's desk. He stood behind the chair and held on tightly to her shoulders as if she might topple sideways if he let go.

'Do you think I could have a glass of water?' the woman said, her lips trembling.

*Glaaas of wartaar.* Luisa was beginning to despise her. Why did she have such a hold over Stanley? 'Sure,' she said and found an unopened bottle of Poland Spring on the neighbouring desk. She shoved it toward the woman but Stanley intercepted it and carefully unscrewed the lid, gently handing it to his new best friend.

'What do you need to talk to me about?' he asked.

Luisa stared at Mrs Henderson as she glugged down half the bottle. 'What?'

'Just now – it sounded urgent.'

'Thank you, love,' the English woman said when she'd finally finished slurping the Poland Spring. 'You're a real life saver.'

'Well?' Stanley said, glaring at Luisa now.

'It can wait. It's private.'

'You can say anything you like in front of Jeanie.'

What was it with him and this woman? Luisa shoved her fists into her pants pockets and snatched a breath. How could she tell him now? There was no way of knowing how he'd react with the woman sitting right next to him. Or what other lies she might spin him to get herself off the hook. First the ESTA form, now the link with a sixty-eight-year-old lamp-stealing felon from the Bronx, Mrs Henderson was collecting black crosses like coupons.

'Well?' Stanley said.

'Like I say – later.'

Without another word, Stanley handed Luisa a cell phone she'd seen before. She glanced down at the image filling the small screen. 'What is this?' She peered at it more closely: a girl's face bloodied at the nose and top lip, blonde hair falling over one eye, the other eye starting to swell.

'That twisted bastard sent it to her.' Stanley prodded a finger toward the cell. 'Signed it the same as before.'

'No number?'

'Withheld,' Mrs Henderson said, the colour slowly returning to her face. 'I suppose he's using the same throwaway phone as before.'

'We've been tracking activity on the other phone. I doubt the perp has been dumb enough to hang on to it,' Luisa said. She read the message that came with the picture.

*You're next – Obama xoxo*

'When did you get this?'

'Just now – no more than half an hour ago. Do you think it's real?' Mrs Henderson laid a hand on Luisa's arm, almost knocking the phone from her grasp. 'Is it possible he's mocked it up, you know – got some silly girl to go along with a sick prank?'

Luisa glanced up at Stanley. He shot her a warning glance. But she wasn't about to protect the woman from the stark facts.

'We know what he's capable of. I think we have to assume this is genuine.'

The woman gulped and raised a hand to her mouth. 'Please tell me you are actually looking for a white boy now?' Her voice was shaky. 'I haven't seen anything on the news. Do you think he's attacked this poor girl? Killed her? Why haven't you caught him yet?' The words flew out of her mouth in a breathless rush.

Stanley made a gentle shushing noise and slipped one of the woman's hands into his, delicately, as if he might crush it.

'I can't discuss the ongoing case with you.' Luisa stared at their interlocking fingers.

'Of course you can't – just like before.' The woman sniffed loudly. 'But at least tell me you're getting closer to catching him.'

Stanley shot Luisa another penetrating look. This time she couldn't ignore it. 'We're making progress – that's all I can say.' She shifted her gaze back to the image on the cell phone. If it was a fake, the perpetrator had definitely broken the girl's nose for the sake of authenticity. Luisa looked around the room. No one working on the Obama investigation was in. Could she keep this new piece of evidence to herself? Maybe use it to get back on the case?

'I'll need to keep your cell phone,' she said.

'You can't – I need it. How else will Simon get in touch with me? And Cindy?' Mrs Henderson reached out a shaking hand and snatched at the phone. Luisa pulled it away just in time.

'I'm sorry, ma'am – I'm just following procedure.'

'Come on, Lu – give her a break,' Stanley said. 'You can bend procedure a little. The perp probably used a burner to send the message anyway.' He held out his hand for the phone. Luisa shoved it behind her back. 'Just take the photo,' he said. 'Leave us the phone.'

Stanley had taken sides with the English woman against her. How could he do that? 'Oh come on, give me a break.' Luisa jumped from her seat and pulled him to one side. She lowered her voice. 'I'm fighting hard to be taken seriously around here. I can't do anything that'll come back and bite me on the ass – Riley is looking for any excuse to shut me out.'

'But Jean needs her phone – it's the only way she feels connected to her son.'

'And when was the last time he called her on it?'

'I can still hear you, you know,' the English woman said.

Luisa pulled Stanley further away.

'But he might call,' he said. 'It's that little sliver of hope she's clinging to.'

'I'll get it back to her just as fast as I can.' Luisa laid a hand on his arm. 'We'll be monitoring incoming calls – I'll pass on any messages that come through. How about that?'

Stanley looked down at her hand. 'You've changed, Lu.'

Luisa wanted to scream at him: it's not me – it's you! And this woman who's cast some kind of spell on you.

The phone on Sanchez's desk started to ring. Luisa hurried over to it and lifted the receiver. She gave her name held up a hand to Stanley, letting him know she wasn't finished with him yet. The voice on the other end of the line grunted, then barked at her. 'Where's Sanchez?'

'No idea – you want to leave him a message?'

'Hell no. This can't wait.'

Luisa scrabbled for a notepad and pen on her desk.

'Transfer me to Lieutenant Riley.'

'He's out too.' Luisa glanced toward Riley's office. The last time she checked, the Lieutenant was busy filling the tiny room with a thick blue cloud of cigar smoke. One white lie. What harm could it do?

'We got a female, Caucasian, twenties, head injuries, broken nose, bullet wounds to the chest and head. You sure there's no one else can deal with this?'

No way was Luisa going to let this opportunity slip through her fingers. It was just the break she'd been hoping for. 'Where are you?' She was still clutching the English woman's cell phone in her fist. She looked at the image on the screen.

'Disused building on Orchard, south of Delancey.'

'How long before the paramedics get there?'

'It's too late for paramedics. She'd been dead a while.'

'How long?'

'She died last night, maybe. Less than twenty-four hours ago.'

'You're sure it didn't just happen?' Luisa stared at the image, trying to work out why the perp would wait to send the message.

'Hey… I'm not a medical examiner. But I know a fresh corpse when I see one.'

Luisa glanced up at Stanley as she spoke into the phone. 'The victim, does she have long blonde hair? Wearing a pink blouse?'

'What are you, psychic or was that a lucky guess?'

# 41

Linus peered through the metal grille into the store. Satisfied it was empty except for the fat bearded clerk leaning heavily on the far side of the counter, he pulled open the door. A loud clanging bell announced his arrival. The door snapped shut behind him and he hesitated just over the threshold.

'Be with you in a second.' The clerk raised a hunting rifle to his face and peered through the sight, the long barrel pointing directly at Linus. He swung the gun away in a sweeping arc, then swung it back again. Then he pulled the trigger with a clunking click.

Linus exhaled.

'You OK, son? You look a little pale.' The clerk started to chuckle. 'Needs some fine tuning.' He inspected the telescopic sight and shook his head. 'Been trying to fix it all morning.' He lovingly slipped the rifle under the counter and stood up straight, pulling back his meaty shoulders. He scrutinised Linus, beady eyes tracing a line from his face to his feet. 'You here window shopping, my friend?'

Linus looked up at the shuttered cabinets covering the wall from floor to ceiling behind the counter.

'Not much to see, is there?' The clerk was chewing with his mouth open. A stringy mess of purple gum stretched between his top and bottom teeth.

'I need some ammunition.'

The clerk raised his dandruff-speckled eyebrows and pulled down the corners of his mouth. 'That so?'

The noisy bell above the door clanged again as another customer stepped in off the street.

'Ryan, buddy. How you doing?' The clerk beamed at the heavily tattooed man ambling toward him. When he reached the counter the two men shook hands and hugged for a second, the clerk mumbling something in his friend's ear. The tattooed man turned and stared unashamedly at Linus and gave him a wry smile.

*Screw you.*

Linus looked away, grabbed a magazine from a nearby carousel and pretended to pore over its busy cover page. A bald man wearing glasses and dressed in camouflage gear holding some kind of semi-automatic weapon took up the bulk of the space. He looked like an accountant in fancy dress. Linus let out a snort. What did he know about shooting? Or killing. And the two men at the counter throwing him dirty looks? Had either of them shot anything more animated than a paper target at a firing range? He shifted his weight a little just to feel the gun press against the flesh at the small of his back. The only bullets he had left were the two inside the chamber.

He shouldn't have wasted so many on Anna.

But he hadn't been able to stop himself. When he'd first walked up to her on the street it had taken her a few seconds to recognise him. She'd smiled, hesitating before she reached out her hand.

'Linus? Is that really you?' She pecked him on both cheeks. Linus remembered her perfume from years before. She smelled of fresh laundry. 'You've grown so handsome. Just like your dad.' Immediately she said it, Linus could see she was sorry. She quickly changed the subject. 'Hey – how's school? Or have you already graduated? Are you at college now?'

'You don't know?'

'How could I?'

'Doesn't my dad ever mention how I'm doing?' Linus already knew the answer: his dad probably didn't think of him from one week to the next.

Anna's smile faded. 'I haven't seen your father for a while now.'

Linus grunted.

'Do you… I mean, I hope you've managed to forgive… You don't know how much I regret what happened… the consequences.'

Linus stared into her eyes and didn't look away until she did.

'You have to believe me,' she said. 'If I'd thought for a second that—'

'Maybe you didn't think, huh?'

Anna screwed up her eyes as she turned away. 'Maybe not.' She wrapped her arms around her ribs and hugged tightly, rocking for a moment from side to side then back on her heels. Linus noticed she was wearing sneakers, something she never did when she lived in the apartment with them. She looked back at him, reached out a hand and lightly touched his arm. Linus jerked away from her.

'You know I tried contacting your mom… after…'

'After she threw you out? Or after the divorce?'

'I just wanted to apologise. But she wouldn't listen.'

'Why didn't you apologise to me?'

'You were only thirteen years old. What could I have said?'

'Maybe you should have tried.'

'I was so young then, naïve, I suppose.'

'Not too young to know the difference between right and wrong. I did.'

'You've got to understand what kind of man your father is.'

Linus could feel his face burning up. He understood all right.

'He has such charisma. I was fresh out of college. New to the city. He treated me like—'

'Why are you telling me all this now?'

'I thought that's why you wanted to see me – for an explanation. I must admit, I've always expected to hear from you one day. You're almost a man now yourself, it's natural you'd want—'

'Almost?' He ground his teeth together and forced his arms to stay fixed to his sides.

'You know what I mean.' She looked away again. 'Look – maybe this was a bad idea. I should never have agreed to meeting you.'

'Don't say that. I'm sorry – I've just got a lot on my mind at the moment.' Linus could see a little moisture prickling Anna's hairline. He forced himself to smile at her. 'Don't go now. At least let me buy you a coffee.'

Anna looked up and down the street. It was busy with late evening commuters making their way home. 'OK.' She checked her cell phone. 'I can't stay out too late. I have an early start in the morning. Got to get the kids to kindergarten.'

'Still an au pair, huh?' Linus gently cupped a hand around her elbow and started to guide her along the sidewalk.

'A nanny,' she corrected him. 'I have more responsibility now.'

'Good for you.' He smiled again and picked up pace. He needed to get her somewhere quiet before she changed her mind. 'I know a great little place just around the corner.'

She started to resist as soon as he'd steered her into a narrow alley. She tried to claw at his face, but he grabbed her wrist and brought his fist down hard across her cheek. She must have had really delicate bones for them to break so easily. She passed right out.

He didn't use the gun until he'd dragged her from the alley and into a nearby derelict house. She was still unconscious. But he let his anger get the better of him. Three bullets when one would have done the job.

He shoved the stupid magazine back in the rack and watched as the clerk's buddy left the store. He shoved a hand into his pocket and pulled out the bills he'd taken from Anna's purse.

'Sorry to keep you waiting… sonny.' The clerk smiled broadly at him. 'So – I need ID, weapon license and a credit card.'

'What?'

'You said you wanted ammunition?'

Linus strode over to the counter, keeping his eyes fixed on the clerk all the while. He reached slowly behind his back. The clerk glanced up high above his head.

'Listen son – a word to the wise… not only can I see exactly what you're doing in the mirror on the far wall…' The man behind the counter paused for effect and shook his head. 'But so can the three cameras recording every move you've made since you came in.' He folded his arms. The bell above the door clanged again and the tattooed man came in carrying a six-pack of beer. 'Now if you don't have the necessary documents, and my finely-tuned perceptive skills are telling me you don't, I suggest you get the hell out of here.' He leaned his fat forearms on the counter. 'Before I call the cops.'

Linus pulled out the gun, pointed it first at the man with the beer, then swung it round to the clerk.

The clerk stopped smiling.

'What's up?' Linus said. 'You're looking a little pale.' He glanced at the gun in his hand. Two bullets.

Not enough to floor these losers and blow the locks off the sealed shutters behind the counter.

Linus ran at full speed toward the tattooed man, shoving him out the way as he passed. He turned when he reached the door and pointed the gun again.

'Screw you!'

# 42

Jean checked her watch. There was no sign of Stanley. She was sure they'd agreed on five-thirty. When he'd asked her to meet him after he finished work, she'd felt such relief it was all she could do not to beg him to stay with her all afternoon. The picture on her phone had shaken her more than she wanted to admit. She hated feeling so dependant, but right now the thought of having Stanley looking out for her was an enormous comfort.

She glanced up and down the street, checking for anything that looked out of the ordinary, anyone dressed in a dark hooded top. There was no reason to suppose the boy with the gun would be in the neighbourhood, but even so, she couldn't shake the feeling she was being watched.

A police car cruised past and turned into the next street. She checked her watch again, wondering if she should go into Stanley's workplace and wait inside for him. But that made her seem even more needy, so she decided instead to keep herself occupied by taking a brisk walk around the block.

Halfway along the adjoining cross street she spotted a woman lingering by the storefront of an exclusive boutique, apparently mesmerised by the window display of expensive bags and coordinating accessories.

Jean waited for a gap in the traffic and crossed the road, her eyes trained on the stationary pedestrian. The window-shopper's overfilled bag was slung loosely over one shoulder, the contents almost spilling out. A bright red wallet sat temptingly at the very top.

Jean felt herself being drawn inextricably toward the bag, like a small child to candy, an unmistakable thrill travelling up her spine and down her arms, making it all the way to her fingertips. When she was just a couple of feet from the woman she slowed her pace, savouring the moment. She checked over her shoulder. There was no sign of the patrol car that had cruised by earlier. She reached a hand into the bag. She wrapped her fingers lightly around the faux snakeskin wallet. She pulled it quickly toward her.

It snagged.

Jean tugged harder.

It's owner spun round.

Too late, Jean realised the wallet was tethered to the bag by a thick brass chain.

Recognition followed a moment later.

'You? What do you think you're doing?' the woman screamed at her.

Jean opened her mouth, but for once in her life, no words came. A claw-like hand clamped on to Jean's upper arm and squeezed tight. All Jean could do was stare at the blood red painted fingernails as they dug deeper into her flesh.

Dolores.

What was she doing here? Remarkably strong for a stick thin woman in her sixties, Stanley's friend started to drag Jean along the street. 'I knew I was right telling Stan not to trust you.' The fingernails sank deeper. 'You are getting your fat English ass deported so fast you won't know what's hit you.'

Frantically, Jean looked up and down the street, trying to spot something she could hook her free arm around. She tugged on Dolores's fingers. They wouldn't budge. Jean pinched at the woman's fleshless forearm, but she didn't seem to feel a thing.

Dolores dragged Jean all the way back to Stanley's building. Stanley was just coming out of the door, checking his watch. He glanced in their direction and froze.

'Call the police, Stan!' Dolores hollered. 'Do you know what I caught her doing?'

Stanley looked at Jean. Jean shrugged her shoulders in apology.

'Stealing my goddamn pocket book, that's what. From right under my nose.'

A moment later Stanley finally managed to overcome his shock and moved toward them.

'Hey, Dee.' He smiled at Dolores, ignoring Jean. He reached for Dolores's arm, but she slapped his hand away. 'What's going on? Some kind of misunderstanding – am I right?' He looked at Jean. 'Am I right?' he said more forcefully.

But no matter how hard Jean tried to come up with something to say in her defence, nothing came. 'I… erm… I thought she was someone…' She quickly gave up.

If Dolores had been dressed like a woman in her sixties rather than a teenager, Jean wouldn't have considered trying to steal her wallet. A younger woman wouldn't have noticed her. A younger woman wouldn't have chained her wallet to her bag.

'For Christ's sake, Stan! Do I have to call the cops myself?'

Stanley held up both hands in a gesture of peacekeeping and mediation. It had the opposite effect. Dolores slapped him across the chest with her free hand. 'Are you actually going to help or should I just start screaming?'

The fingers of Jean's right hand were starting to go numb. Something had to be done and she couldn't wait for Stanley to do it. She swung up her leg from the hip and brought her foot down as hard as she could on Dolores's open-toed sandal. Dolores rocked sideways, shrieking, and

Jean managed to pull her arm free. She ducked out of swiping distance.

'Don't let her get away, Stan!' Dolores hopped on one foot, the other grasped in her hand.

'I'm going nowhere,' Jean said. 'Stanley and I have a prior engagement.'

'Oh yeah? I don't see how that's gonna work with you in a jail cell.' Dolores pulled a phone from her bag. It too was attached to the interior by a metal chain. She got as far as punching in the second digit before Stanley snatched the phone from her.

'Why don't we go some place?' he said, in a treacly tone Jean hadn't heard before. 'Just you and me? What do you say, Dee?' He was avoiding Jean's gaze.

'Well I did come here to see you.' Dolores smiled sickeningly, her front two teeth smeared with scarlet lipstick.

'You did?'

She nodded and drew her lips into pout.

'Then why don't you let me buy you dinner, huh? Forget this stupid… misunderstanding?'

'She's a thief. She needs to be punished.'

'It's like a sickness with some people.' He lowered his voice. 'I know – I seen it before. It's an age thing.'

Jean held her tongue, squeezing her hands together when she wanted to wrap them around Dolores's throat. She watched in silence as Stanley put an arm around the woman's waist and guided her away. When they reached the next corner Stanley glanced back over his shoulder. He wasn't smiling.

Rising anger sent a wave of heat up Jean's throat and into her face as she watched Stanley disappear. She stood there for a while, struggling to draw air into her lungs. It took her a moment to work out what was causing the pain that radiated across her chest.

Naked jealousy.

# 43

All three heavy-duty locks had been ripped from the wooden doorframe. The door hung askew by its hinges on the opposite side. Jean fell back against the wall.

'Dear God.'

She reached into her bag and fumbled for her phone, remembering after a few frantic moments of searching that she'd been forced to leave it at the police station. She hurried to Carmen's apartment and raised a fist to hammer on the door just as it opened.

'I've been listening out for you,' Carmen said. 'Come, come in.'

Jean hesitated. 'We have to call the police.' Her mouth was dry, her tongue sticking to the roof of her mouth. 'I need to use your phone.' She turned and looked into her son's apartment.

'I called the cops just now,' Carmen said.

'Someone might still be inside.'

Jean closed her eyes for a moment and took a deep breath, the rush of oxygen making her head spin. 'Did the police say how long they would be?'

'Not in so many words. I got the impression they weren't in a hurry.'

'Where's that vicious-looking meat cleaver of yours?'

'You suggesting going in there?'

'I can't just wait for them to arrive and do nothing.

Carmen disappeared inside her apartment and returned seconds later with the cleaver. Jean took it from her carefully and wrapped her fingers firmly around the smooth wooden handle. 'Were you here when it happened?' she whispered.

Carmen nodded. 'Racket like that is hard to ignore. Scared the crap out of me.'

'How long ago was this?'

'Half hour, maybe less.'

Jean stepped across the hall. Carmen grabbed her arm. 'They were looking for your son. I heard them mention his name a couple of times.' She tugged on Jean's arm. 'What kind of trouble is he in?'

'Did you see them leave?'

'You think I would open the door? I was too busy making like a mouse and pretending I wasn't home.' She sighed. 'I'm just relieved they didn't torch the whole damn building.'

Jean's legs weakened again. The smell of Carmen's chicken stock had permeated the hall and was making her gag. 'So they could still be in there?'

'I haven't heard a peep out of anyone for a while now. Some of them definitely left.'

'How many were there?'

'More than two, for sure. I heard at least three different voices.'

Jean firmed up her grip on the meat cleaver. 'Maybe you should get a weapon for yourself. Do you have a walking stick or something?'

'You want me to go in there with you?'

'You're prepared to let me go in alone?'

'I guess not.' Carmen reached behind her door and produced a long folded umbrella with a sharp metal tip. She held it like a rifle and straightened her back. 'Let's get it over with.'

Jean ventured closer to the door and pushed at it gingerly with the tips of her fingers. The door creaked on its hinges, long sharp splinters of wood tore away from the frame and dropped onto the floor by her feet. She felt Carmen's hand on her arm again.

'Maybe this isn't so smart. Maybe we should wait for the cops. Or how about we call your friend – Stanley? He'll know what to do.'

'He's otherwise engaged.' The image of the ginger witch tugging Stanley around the corner had stayed with her. *Be buggered if I'm calling him.*

'But I'm sure if you called he'd be over faster than anything.' Carmen couldn't look her in the eye. 'The way I've seen him look at you, I get the impression there's nothing he wouldn't do, if you know what I mean.'

'That's just not an option.'

'You want me to call him? Why don't I do that right now?'

'Leave it!' Jean pushed the door wider, freed her arm from Carmen's grip and stepped inside. Even from the other end of the hall she could see the devastation that had been wrought in the living room. Books and records lay scattered across the floor, cushions spilled their stuffing. She trod carefully to the door of the nursery and peered inside. The mobile had been ripped from the ceiling and the crib was reduced to fire wood in the middle of the room. She moved onto the bedroom and discovered bedclothes dragged to the floor, the mattress askew on its frame. She joined Carmen back in the hall and puffed out a breath.

'I checked the bathroom,' Carmen said. 'Nobody's hiding in the shower.'

'Just the kitchen and living room to go.'

A loud noise from just outside the apartment made them both jump. Carmen swung the umbrella toward the door, as if it might fire off a round of bullets. 'Holy crap, they're back!' she shrieked.

'Why the hell have you brought me to this dump? Jesus. What's that God awful smell?' It was a woman's voice.

'Who's there?' Carmen hollered.

Moments later, slightly out of breath, Stanley appeared at the broken door. He hurried toward Jean and slipped an arm around her shoulders. 'Are you OK?' He took the cleaver from her hand.

Jean wriggled free. 'I was fine before I heard *her* voice. What were you thinking bringing her here?'

'I can't shake her off,' he whispered.

'Stan? What's going on?' Dolores marched down the hallway in her high heels, her nostrils flaring as soon as she saw Jean. 'What the…?'

'What are you doing here, anyway?' Jean asked him.

Stanley glanced at Carmen.

'I'm sorry – I called him before you arrived. I tried to get a hold of you, but you weren't answering. I thought it's what you'd want.'

Stanley poked his nose into the kitchen and the living room and let out a whistle. 'You can't stay here.'

'Don't be ridiculous.'

'Would someone tell me what the hell is going—' Dolores marched a few steps down the hall when Carmen stopped her.

'I'm going nowhere.' Jean widened her stance.

'Let me book you into a hotel,' Stanley said.

'Are you even listening? I'm not leaving. Simon might call on the landline.'

'He can leave you a message.'

'I have to be here to speak to him.'

'Whoever did this might come back – did you think of that?'

'I'll have to take that risk. I can't just abandon Simon. This is where I should be.'

'Come on, Jeanie… you need to be sensible about this.'

'Jeanie? What is this?' Dolores tried to move forward but Carmen jabbed the umbrella at her.

'I've got to think of something to get Simon to come home. Then we can start sorting out the mess he's got himself into.'

'You think he's gonna come back with these animals after him?'

'Yes – as long as we give them what they're owed.'

'And how are you gonna raise that kind of money?'

'The same way we plan to help Jimmy. I was hoping we'd have a chance to discuss it earlier. Before she tipped up.'

'What she saying about me?' Dolores hollered. 'Stan?'

Jean grabbed Stanley's hand. 'Come on – you can make yourself useful while you're here.' She dragged him into the bedroom and told him to lift the heavy mattress off the bed. Much to her relief, the laptop she'd struggled to hide underneath was still duct-taped to the bed frame.

She opened the lid and fired it up. Dolores was hollering from the hall.

'For crying out loud, Stan. Let's get out of here.'

'Wait a minute, will you? Can't you see Jean is in trouble?'

Dolores appeared in the doorway and took a cursory glance around the room.

'So she doesn't keep house real well – why is that my problem?'

'Come on, Dee, where's your compassion?'

'I got plenty. But maybe it's running out – just like my patience.' She reached into her bag and retrieved the phone on its metal chain. 'Maybe I should call nine-one-one right now, tell the police exactly what happened earlier, huh?'

A groaning noise bubbled out of Stanley's throat.

'I mean it, Stan. Take me home. Right now.' She strode into the room. 'No need for tearful goodbyes. She looks like a tough old broad. Leave her be.' She hooked her arm through his and started for the door.

'I'll call you later, Jeanie. Make sure you're OK? We can maybe talk about what we're going to do for Jimmy?' Stanley said as he reached the other side of the room.

Jean looked up, but before she could reply, Dolores yanked him out into the hall. Jean stared back at the laptop. She needed to get the wording just right. Something compelling enough to force Simon to get in touch. Something he just couldn't ignore. She wondered how far she should stretch the truth. She started typing.

*Everything under control. $100k here waiting for you. Please call on landline (lost my mobile) to let me know you're all right and make arrangements to pick up the money.*
*Mum x*

# 44

'My office – now.' Lieutenant Riley thumped the back of Luisa's chair then turned away without another word.

Luisa abruptly ended her conversation, returned the phone to its cradle and followed Riley to the little cubicle office at the far end of the squad room. She closed the door quietly behind her. The smell of tobacco was overwhelming. Riley squeezed behind his desk but didn't sit down. Luisa waited for the explosion.

'What did you think you were doing?'

'Sir?'

'Come on, Rodriguez. I don't have time for this. The homicide on Orchard. You had no authority to take on that case.'

'Sanchez wasn't around. I thought you were out of the building… Somebody had to respond.'

'And when exactly did you discover the link with the grocery store killings?'

Luisa made a half turn and looked back at the door, wishing she'd left it open just a crack. She was struggling to breathe. 'I'm not sure.'

'Why didn't you inform Sanchez as soon as you made the connection?'

'I did.'

'You need to try a little harder. You're just not cut out for covering your own ass.'

'Check the records – receipt of Mrs Henderson's phone was logged as evidence at midnight yesterday. I left a message for Sanchez two minutes after twelve.'

'So you're telling me it wasn't the preliminary ballistics report that prompted you?'

Luisa managed to stifle a groan. Maybe Riley was right and she didn't have a talent for self-preservation. 'Yes – of course, that was it.' She snatched a breath. 'The ballistics report confirmed my suspicions – but that's all they were before that. I couldn't tell for sure the picture of the woman on the old lady's phone was the victim.'

'The "old lady" was signed into the station house at two-thirty in the afternoon. Why'd it take you ten hours to tell Sanchez about the phone message?'

Automatically, Luisa's shoulders shrugged before she could stop them. Riley's glare intensified. Was it such a crime to manoeuvre her way into a murder investigation any way she could? The lieutenant must have done the same thing when he was a third grade detective. 'Due respect sir, no one has taken my hunches seriously before.' Except Stanley. She decided to keep that thought to herself.

'When you've got nothing more solid than…' He raised both hands and made quote marks with his fingers. 'A *woman's intuition*, can you blame anybody for ignoring you?'

Luisa ground her teeth, refusing to rise to the bait. Riley didn't need any more reason to label her as a hysterical over-reacter. The perp was turning into a regular serial killer. First the two random store clerks, then he'd got personal with the retired teacher. She couldn't shake the thought that the latest victim must have known him too. But how could she tell Riley that without getting laughed out of his office? The perp could be choosing his next victim right now. She took a breath and tried to find the right words. She hesitated just a moment too long.

'Has the body been identified?' Finally Riley lowered himself onto a chair.

'No ID was found at the scene.' Instantly Luisa pictured the bloody mess of the woman's head and chest, and she was right back in the tenement building.

'That I knew already. What have you been doing all morning?'

'I just got off the phone to Missing Persons. A twenty-eight-year-old white female matching the victim's description was reported missing by her employers yesterday.'

'Her employers? Not her family? Husband? Boyfriend?'

'She works as a nanny on the Upper West Side. I don't think she has family in the city.'

'And is someone getting to the morgue to ID the body?'

'The family housekeeper is due in at lunchtime.' She took a breath. 'I was thinking, sir, when we do confirm the iden—'

There was a knock on the door and Sanchez poked his nose through the gap without waiting to be called in. He scowled at Luisa.

'Well? What is it?' Riley barked at him.

'Just got a very interesting call from the twenty-second,' Sanchez said without tearing his disgusted expression from Luisa. 'I thought you should be the first to know.' He glanced at Riley and clamped his mouth shut.

'I'm not finished with you, Rodriguez,' Riley said. 'In the meantime, I think you can safely assume we won't be needing any further assistance in this investigation.'

'But sir, surely—'

Sanchez slipped into the room and held the door open ready for Luisa's departure. 'I left a little gift on your desk,' he said, smiling for the first time. 'Have fun.'

She turned to look back at the lieutenant, but he was already dismissing her with a flick of his hand. Luisa backed out of the room and Sanchez slammed the door in her face, leaving her stranded on the wrong side, excluded from the action yet again.

Leaning against the wall, she took a deep breath to try to stifle the angry roar hurtling from the bottom of her lungs up into her throat. She blew out her cheeks a few times.

Just over a week since Stanley had retired and already she was wondering how bad things might get without him. Whenever Riley had been an asshole to her in the past, Stanley always seemed to be able to say the right thing to calm her down, get her focused back on the job. Maybe a quick pep talk with Stanley would do the trick right now. She reached into her pocket, but as her fingers wrapped around the slim cell phone she changed her mind. What was she thinking? She couldn't go running to Stanley every time the job was crappier than usual. What was so wrong with her that suddenly she needed counselling? Besides, she'd promised herself the next time she spoke to Stanley she would tell him all about Mrs Henderson's murky past.

Sanchez could go screw himself.

Her heart sank as soon as she spotted the 'little gift' on her desk. Balancing on top of her overloaded in tray was a stack of silver discs in clear plastic cases. The note attached to the uppermost disc confirmed what she suspected. The gleaming DVDs contained security footage from various locations within the two neighbouring precincts.

Luisa looked up at the door. If she left now she would arrive at the morgue for the formal identification and get a chance to question the Upper West Side housekeeper about the victim's background. She might find out about the woman's friends or previous employers. Something concrete to convince Riley he should let her back on the case. She glanced back toward the lieutenant's office. She couldn't risk making him any angrier. Viewing the first few DVDs in the pile at triple speed might get Riley off her back and still leave her enough time to get over to the morgue to catch the housekeeper before she left the building.

Luisa carried a half dozen discs in one hand and a rapidly cooling cup of coffee in the other and hurried to the audiovisual suite.

Two discs down and she was running out of time. It was taking much longer than she'd thought. She slipped a third disc into the player and found herself looking at a street somewhere in the Financial District. She stared at the mass of sombre suits weaving around each other on the grey sidewalk outside a coffee shop. A bright yellow taxi drew up to the kerb a few seconds into the recording, throwing its drab surroundings into sharp contrast. Just as she had for the other two discs, Luisa scanned the scene, searching for someone who was acting suspiciously. Or someone who looked out of place.

For minutes everyone moving in and out of shot seemed perfectly suited to their environment. She checked the counter in the corner of the picture as it ticked by in triple time. This was worse than watching paint dry. As her gaze shifted back up to the middle of the screen she noticed someone moving awkwardly against the main flow of foot traffic.

She hit the pause button and squinted at the shape. After a moment she decided the figure was definitely a woman, but the features were indistinct. She started the DVD again at normal speed and stared intently at the woman as she struggled against the tide of bodies heading in the opposite direction. There was a strange roll to the woman's stride, a limp, as if she'd hurt her leg. Finally she reached the entrance of the coffee shop, but instead of going in, she stopped just outside the door. She stayed there for ten, fifteen seconds. Luisa hit the pause button again and stared at her, unable to shake the feeling she'd seen that loping walk somewhere before. Then she advanced the play a frame at a time and watched as a line built up outside the coffee shop. Suddenly the woman came to life. She reached a hand into a large purse swinging from the shoulder of a customer in the line, pulled something out, held it in her hands for a moment, then returned it to the purse just before the woman stepped away.

Luisa rewound the footage and peered at the remote, eventually finding the zoom button, convinced enlarging the image would only result in a pixelated mess. She hit the button and was surprised how clearly she could see the hand dip into the purse and remove a wallet, count out some bills, then slip the wallet back. Luisa stared so hard at the woman's features her eyes began to water.

She knew that face.

But it couldn't be, could it?

She watched as the woman rolled back up the street the way she'd come, lifting a hand to her head to pull her hair from the back of her neck. Luisa had seen that gesture at least a half dozen times before.

She grabbed her cell phone from her pocket and selected Stanley's number from the short list of contacts. She couldn't put it off any longer. She had to let him know what kind of woman he'd hooked himself up with.

Before she arrested her.

Luisa's finger hovered over the call button as Sanchez appeared at the door of the viewing suite. 'You don't have time for phone calls, Rodriguez. How many discs have you looked at?'

'Have you just come here to gloat?' She shoved the phone back into her pocket.

'Actually, I wanted to tell you something about the grocery store perp.' He studied his nails. 'But hell – if you're not interested.' He turned to leave.

'What about him?'

'Friend of mine up at Central Park just called. Found a gunshot victim in the park early hours of yesterday morning.'

'Dead?'

Sanchez nodded.

'And they think our shooter did it?'

'Have to wait for ballistics.'

'So why are they even telling you about it?'

'Take it easy. I'm coming to that.'

He was enjoying making her wait. *Prick*. She folded her arms. Sanchez could go to hell if he wanted her to beg. 'Well?'

'Victim's prints match the ones we found at the second grocery store.'

'The perp's dead?'

'He better be – he's been lying in the morgue for the last twelve hours.'

# 45

The buzzing started just as Jean was closing her eyes. She struggled up from the armchair and hurried out of the living room and down the hall. She reached for the handset of the intercom and hesitated, trying to decide whether a return visit from Simon's creditors would be heralded by a polite pressing of the buzzer on the door downstairs.

The buzzing stopped, only to start up again across the hall. Moments later she heard laboured footsteps coming up the stairs. Then heavy breathing and a thump on the newly repaired door.

'Hey, Jeanie. It's me.'

Jean unfastened the safety chain and the first of the four new locks the carpenter had fitted to Simon's damaged door. She ran a finger down the unpainted wood of the replacement doorframe. The smell of fresh pine reminded her of her son-in-law's workshop in the back garden at home.

'What are you doing here?' she yelled through the door.

'What do you think?'

'Is that awful woman with you?'

'You think she'd want to come visit again?'

'Only to scratch my eyes out.'

'Come on, Jeanie. Carmen'll start thinking we've had a fight.'

'Haven't we?'

Jean hadn't seen Stanley since he'd turned up unannounced the previous evening with Dolores. She still hadn't forgiven Carmen for calling him.

'Last time I looked, you were in the clutches of a red-haired dragon.'

'Hey – I was doing that for you. She threatened to call the police another half dozen times after we left here.'

'But somehow you managed to persuade her not to.' Jean didn't want to imagine what securing Dolores's silence had cost him.

'I did what I had to.'

Jean closed her eyes and swallowed.

'Come on, Jean. How about you open the door? I feel kinda stupid out here. Let me in so I can apologise.'

Jean had been sitting by the phone all day hoping Simon would call, dozing occasionally, waking with a start at any loud noise. A bit of company would be more than welcome. Slowly she slipped across the remaining bolts and opened the door to find Stanley beaming at her, a bunch of wilting flowers in his hand.

'I think these may need a little water.'

Jean wandered back to the living room without taking the bouquet from him. 'So… how did you finally manage to get rid of her?' she shouted over her shoulder as Stanley carefully refastened all the locks.

'Haven't seen Dolores all day.'

'And she doesn't know you're here?'

Stanley laid the flowers on a table and looked at his feet. 'We've just got to handle her right.'

'I have no intention of handling her at all.'

'I couldn't bear the thought of you spending another night here all alone. I hardly slept last night worrying what might be happening.'

'Was she with you?'

'Oh come on. Give me a break!'

Jean brushed past him, scooped up the flowers and did her best to flounce out of the room.

Stanley joined her in the kitchen after a minute or so.

'Simon doesn't have a vase,' she said and turned to see Stanley standing hesitantly in the doorway. She held up an old orange juice carton, hastily arranged blooms spilling out.

'They look just beautiful.'

Jean set the makeshift vase on the kitchen counter. Suddenly Stanley's arms wrapped around her waist. 'Sorry,' he said.

She allowed herself to enjoy his embrace for a few moments before pulling away. 'Have you managed to find a suitable location?'

Stanley nodded, his eyes searching her face. 'Can't we talk about something else?'

'Where is it?'

He blew out a breath. 'There's a branch of Fisher Krupps on West Broadway, between Thomas and Worth. Not that the address would mean anything to you.'

'I'm perfectly capable of looking it up on a map.'

Stanley ran a hand over his head, his jaw muscles flexing.

'Is it in the Financial District?'

'No – it's around twenty blocks north-east of their HQ.'

'And the guards aren't armed?'

'I checked the records. Just two unarmed security guards and three tellers. The manager's on vacation for the next week.'

'So we need to strike soon?'

'Strike? Jesus. You make it sound like a military operation.'

'That's exactly how we should be treating it.'

He scratched the thin layer of stubble on his chin.

'You're not having second thoughts?' Jean said.

He didn't answer.

'Stanley? I thought we'd been through this.'

His phone started ringing in his pocket. He ignored it.

'Shouldn't you answer that? It might be important,' Jean said.

'It'll be Lu again, I expect. She's been leaving messages all day.'

'You could pick up and find out.'

'She can leave me another message – I can't deal with her right now. She says she wants to speak to me urgently about a "personal matter".'

'Personal? And you haven't called her back?'

'I know Lu – it'll be something to do with the department. Some investigation she wants to pick apart. I got too much on my plate.'

'What if she's found Simon? She could be calling you to contact me. You should get back to her.'

'Anything to do with your son and she would have said so in her messages. Besides, she has the number here.'

Jean reluctantly accepted he was right and returned to the living room. She stared at Simon's home phone sitting inert on the side table. Why hadn't he responded to her email about the money?

'I'm beat,' Stanley said.

She turned to see him checking his watch. 'Where can I find some pillows?' He pointed at the small couch in the middle of the room. 'I'd like to get some shuteye.'

Jean looked at the crumpled and sagging seat cushions of the leather couch that was to have been her bed during her stay. 'Don't be ridiculous. You won't last five minutes on that clapped out old thing.'

'What else do you suggest?'

'Go back home. Or to Jimmy's. He needs you more than I do.' She wasn't even convincing herself. 'I'm fine on my own.'

'Jimmy's OK at his place.'

'Who's looking after him?'

'Clarence is sitting with him for a while.'

'Honestly – I feel quite safe here.' Jean half-heartedly gestured toward the door, feeling anything but secure.

Stanley hurried over to her and lifted her hands to his chest. She could feel his heart pounding. 'If you think for one second that I'm leaving you here for another night, you're even crazier than I thought.'

'So you think I'm crazy, do you?'

'I sure do.'

He pressed her hands harder against his shirt. She looked up into his eyes, her heels lifting from the floor as she rose onto her toes. He lowered his face toward hers and their lips met. Jean pulled away first.

'I'm sorry,' Stanley said. 'Did I get it wrong?'

Jean took a breath, her own heart beating just as hard as his. 'I'm not sure you've got anything more right.' She slipped her hand into his and pulled him gently to the door. 'There's a phone in the bedroom. I can wait for Simon to call just as well in there.'

# 46

With her head resting on her hand, her elbow propped on a pillow, Jean traced Stanley's profile with a forefinger, sloping down his straight nose, bumping over his lips and dimpled chin and finally coming to rest on his wiry-haired chest.

'Everything OK with you?' he said.

'Why wouldn't it be?'

'It's been a while, is all. I'm a little out of practice.'

'Let's just say your muscle memory kicked in quite instinctively. You've no need to worry on that front. Or ask stupid questions and spoil the moment.'

'Sorry.'

'Or apologise needlessly.'

'Sorry.' He grinned at her.

Jean pulled the thin cotton sheet over her shoulder, suddenly self-conscious about her nakedness.

'You sure you're OK?'

'I'm fine. Let's just relax, shall we? I feel like it's the first time I've properly exhaled since I arrived.' She leaned closer and pecked his cheek. 'Who'd have thought I'd end up in bed with you eight days ago.'

'I had high hopes.'

'Really?'

'Since I first laid eyes on you.'

'In the police station?'

He nodded, his face reddening like an awkward teenager's.

Jean remembered the way Stanley had stared at her chest as she stood on a bench threatening to take her bra off. She tugged the sheet further over her shoulder. 'It's been quite a ride since then, hasn't it?' she said.

'And we're not finished yet.'

'I should hope not.'

'I was talking about your crazy plan.'

Jean swallowed. 'So was I.' She wriggled down the bed a few inches and turned onto her back, tucking the sheet firmly under her armpits. 'We are doing the right thing, you know.'

'I'm not sure you can call it that.'

'The right thing morally. Jimmy needs our help. And we have the means to help him.'

'It's OK – you don't have to give me the sales pitch again. I'm committed now, for better or worse.'

'I know how much you owe Jimmy. It's natural you'd want to pay him back.'

Stanley quickly sat up. 'What did he tell you?'

'Enough.' Jean wasn't sure now was the right time to fish for information, but she couldn't resist doing a little digging while Stanley was naked and vulnerable.

'Yeah, well, maybe Jimmy didn't tell you how it's eaten me up every day since,' he said.

'Oh he knows about your guilty conscience, believe me.'

'He's a better man than me, always was, always will be. It's as simple as that.'

'But I only know his version of the story. You've not told me yours.'

'I don't have a "version". There was a line and I was on the wrong side of it. I knew it then, just like I know it now. Trouble was, the rest of the precinct were on my side of the line.'

'The *whole* precinct?' Jean's imagination went into overdrive. What could it have been?

'More or less. I moved to the third a few months before Jimmy. I kinda got sucked in. A few dollars here, turning a blind eye there. Before I knew it I was just as crooked as the rest of them.'

Jean took a moment to let it sink in. Crooked?

'What happened when Jimmy arrived?'

'He couldn't believe I'd sunk so low. He threatened to blow the whistle. Made so many waves it couldn't be ignored. So they set him up, made it look like he was a dirty cop.'

'They?'

'OK – we. You gotta remember this was before the days of Internal Affairs, even before Frank Serpico. You seen that movie?'

'It rings a vague bell.'

'Jimmy thought he could clean up the whole department. One guy on his own!' He shook his head. 'Didn't matter what I said to convince him to roll with the punches.' He rubbed his nose with the back of a fist. 'Just to survive – you know? You survive long enough, things start to change – little by little. NYPD's gotta be the straightest department in the country these days. Probably the world.'

'You're helping Jimmy now – when he needs it most. That's the important thing.'

'I guess.' Stanley reached under the bedclothes and fidgeted for a few moments before swinging his legs onto the floor, his underpants safely back on, even though they were inside out and round the wrong way. 'I need the bathroom.'

Jean waited until she heard the bathroom door close then grabbed her pyjamas from under the pillow. She fastened the two buttons on the pyjama top and hopped into the bottoms as she crossed the room.

She'd got as far as the kitchen when she heard the noise.

She stood very still, listening. There it was again, a definite scrape of metal against metal. She quickly retrieved a bread knife from the wooden block on the kitchen counter, crept silently out of the room and steadily made her way down the hall, whispering Stanley's name as she passed the bathroom door.

The metal scraped again. She let out the breath she'd been holding and forced her parched tongue between her teeth to moisten her lips before she attempted to speak.

Something thumped hard against the door from the other side, shaking the wood on its hinges.

'The police are on their way,' she managed, wishing she'd thought to pick up the phone. 'And I'm armed.' She looked down at the large knife in her trembling hand. 'They'll be here any minute.'

Stanley thudded toward her, hurriedly wrapping a dressing gown around his half-naked body. 'What the hell do you think you're doing?' he said.

'Mum?' The voice was thin and reedy. 'Who have you got in there with you?'

Jean let out a breath and the knife clattered to the floor. She scrambled to unlock the door.

Simon was cowering in the hallway. She barely recognised him. His hair was shaved to his scalp, a ginger beard sprouted from his dirty face. His clothes smelled of soil and hung loose on his limbs. He straightened up as soon as he laid eyes on the strange man wearing his robe. Simon's gaze started at Stanley's bony feet and traced all the way up to his embarrassed expression. 'Mum? Who the—'

Jean grabbed her son by the wrists and hauled him inside the apartment. 'Oh don't worry about him.' She stared into his bloodshot eyes. 'Look at the state of you. When was the last time you ate?' They shuffled down the hall, both limping as they went. 'We need to get you washed and fed.'

Simon sniffed and dragged a dirty sleeve across his nose. 'I'm fine.'

'Have you been sleeping rough?' Jean stopped and clamped both hands on his face, forcing him to look her square in the eye. 'We'll talk when you've got some food inside you. But you've got to promise you'll tell me the truth. About everything. Do you understand?' She pressed her hands into his gaunt cheeks. 'No more lies. Promise?'

Despite her fierce grip, he managed to nod.

'Good.' She led him to the bathroom door. 'I'll bring you some fresh clothes.' Then she turned back to Stanley who had been keeping his distance. 'You might want to make yourself decent too.'

# 47

Fifteen minutes later Jean had rustled up ham and eggs, a stack of buttered pancakes and a big pot of coffee. At first her son pushed the food around his plate, staring intently at the trail of grease he'd smeared over its surface.

Jean slapped the back of his hand. 'Stop playing with it!'

Simon quickly complied, devouring everything she'd prepared and asking for more coffee when he'd drained the last cup. He let out a hearty belch, apologised and leaned back in his chair.

'Why don't I do the dishes?' Stanley was on his feet and collecting dirty chinaware before anyone could object. 'You two need to talk. In private.'

Jean led Simon to the living room. They sat quietly for a few moments on the uncomfortable couch, Jean unable to decide whether the silence was companionable or unbearably awkward. She couldn't remember the last time she'd actually spoken to him.

'Why don't you start at the beginning and work your way from there to here,' she said eventually, looking Simon up and down, her gaze lingering on the empty pockets of his hooded jacket. 'What have you done with the gun?'

'Gun? What are you talking about?' He shuffled forward to the edge of the couch, as if he was getting ready to flee.

'Don't play silly buggers. When have you ever known that to work with me?'

'I'm not.' A telltale whine had crept into his voice. The way it always did when he tried to wriggle out of blame for some childhood misdemeanour.

'I found a box of bullets in your closet.'

'Oh.' His nostrils flared and he raised a hand to his mouth. He started chewing a nail.

'For God's sake, Simon.'

'I shoved the gun under the bed when I was getting dressed.'

She shook her head and puffed out an exasperated breath. 'Do you know how serious it is to carry a concealed weapon without a licence?'

'I've got a licence.'

'You promised to tell me the truth. I know for a fact foreign nationals on temporary visas can't buy guns.' She sighed. 'Not legally.'

'Who told you that?'

'I've been doing some research.'

'Well it's wrong.'

'Shall we just get Stanley in here and ask him?'

'Why would he know what—'

'He's a policeman, Simon.'

Simon struggled to get to his feet but Jean clamped a hand on his knee.

'Don't panic – he's a *retired* policeman. And a very understanding one at that. I'll have to ask him to get rid of it for you.'

'You can't do that. That gun cost me a fortune.'

She sighed again.

'I need it for protection.'

'Do you even know how to use it?'

He shrugged. 'How hard can it be?'

'You have no idea.'

Simon looked down at her hand on his leg. 'I know what I'm doing. You have to let me get on with it. You shouldn't even be here. Why didn't you go straight back home – like I told you to?'

'You seriously expected me to take any notice of that silly note of yours? I can tell when you're lying. How could I get on a plane knowing you were in trouble?'

'It's my mess – I need to sort it out myself.'

'Well you've done a fine job so far. Besides, you need money and I'm your best hope of getting any.'

'How did you even find out about the money?'

'Your friend from work let the cat out of the bag.'

Simon grabbed her hand, lifting his head to finally look her in the eye. 'You've spoken to Malcolm? When was this? What did he want?'

'He was looking for you.'

'I told him to get out of town. How was he?'

Jean remembered Malcolm Oliver's body lying on the metal trolley in the morgue. A shudder crept across her shoulders. 'He was terrified. But that's a bit academic now, wouldn't you say?'

'I don't understand.'

'After what happened to him.'

'What?'

Jean levered herself off the sagging couch and limped into the kitchen. She came back out with a half bottle of bourbon and a single glass. She poured Simon a generous measure and thrust the tumbler into his hands. He looked down at the Jim Beam and back up at his mother.

'Drink it,' she said. 'All of it.'

He pulled a face as he knocked back the whiskey and Jean poured him another. She then explained exactly what had happened to Simon's colleague without sparing him any of the grisly details. When she was finished he poured himself another drink and downed it in one.

'Everything OK, Jeanie?'

Jean looked up to see Stanley standing in the doorway, a blue and white dishtowel slung over his arm. He was across the room and sitting on the arm of the couch before she had a chance to answer.

'We should be leaving,' he said, placing a hand on her shoulder and gently squeezing the tight muscles. 'Now your son's here, there's no need for you to stay in the firing line.'

'What's he talking about?' Simon frowned at his mother.

'He's right – we should pack a couple of bags and head for Stanley's place.'

'I'm not going anywhere.' Simon slumped back against the couch and gripped the arm tightly.

'It's OK – I'll throw a few things in a case for you – just a change of clothes and a toothbrush.'

'No!'

'For crying out loud – do you know how close your mother came to running into those *associates* of yours?'

'Leave it, Stan.'

'They were right here in this apartment and could be back anytime. I've been trying to persuade her to get out of here for the past twenty-four hours.'

# 48

It didn't take long to get everything they needed packed up and stowed in the trunk of Stanley's big station wagon. Simon sat next to his mother in the back as Stanley drove them to his house in Williamsburg.

They'd been on the road less than ten minutes when Simon broke the tense silence. 'I realise it's a stupid question, but you did remember to pack the money?'

It took Jean a moment to realise what he was talking about.

'I mean, I could just take it off your hands now. Swing by Cindy's to pick up her and the baby and leave tonight.' He was wringing his hands and had started to shiver. 'It's probably the best thing. Get a bit of distance between us and the city.'

Jean saw Stanley check his rear-view mirror. They locked eyes for a moment.

'There's no way we can stay in the country,' Simon continued. 'I was thinking Mexico. Or maybe somewhere further south. Melt away where nobody knows us. Or cares.'

'That money is for paying off your debts. It's not some… escape fund,' Jean said. 'We just need to contact the people who loaned it to you and arrange for them to collect it. From a neutral location. Somewhere anonymous. We don't even have to see them.'

Simon stiffened. 'You're not serious?'

'Why wouldn't I be?'

'You think they would just leave it there? They'd come after me.' He leaned forward. 'Tell her, will you? You used to be a cop. You know how it works.'

Stanley shrugged, his wide shoulders reaching up to his ears.

'You think what they did to Oliver was bad? I bet that's nothing compared to what they have planned for me.'

'But I thought that's why you came back – to settle things. Straighten everything out.'

'God no – I'm only interested in Cindy and the baby. And a new life somewhere. All of us together.'

Jean stared out of the window and watched the metal girders of Williamsburg Bridge blur past. 'Do you really think Cindy would want to live like that?' she said quietly. 'It's certainly not the impression she gave me when I saw her.'

He sat up. 'You've seen her?'

'And the baby.'

'How are they?'

'Thriving.' Without you, she thought.

'Cindy'll come round to the idea – I just need to explain everything to her.'

'I wouldn't bank on it.' Jean pictured Cindy's conservative clothes and her sensible hairdo. She remembered how scared the poor girl had seemed. 'When I saw her, Cindy spoke about the trouble you were in. She said it wasn't just the loan shark you were running from, but something more serious than that.' She fixed Simon with a look she knew he wouldn't be able to turn away from. 'What did she mean?'

'I've got no idea.'

'Why must you continue to lie to me when you're so bad at it?'

Simon sucked in an uneven breath, his cheeks started to dimple. 'Oh Christ.'

Even in the gloom of the car's interior, Jean saw several fat tears fall into her son's lap. She squeezed his hand. 'Is it drugs?' she said. 'Is that why you needed the money?'

Simon snorted as the tears continued to fall. 'If only it was that simple.'

Jean handed him a tissue from her bag and he dabbed his face. 'What, then?'

'I can't tell you.'

Jean sighed.

'You don't need to know. You'd be… an accessory or something.'

'For God's sake, Simon, what have you done?'

He put an arm across his eyes and started to sob, making a noise Jean hadn't heard since he was twelve years old. He rested his head against the back of the seat.

'Tell me!'

Mucus rattled in his nose. 'I screwed up at work.'

'Is that all?' She exhaled. 'Everyone makes a mistake now and then. It's just part of life. How bad can it be?'

'Worse than you can imagine, believe me.'

'Oh come on, I'm sure you're just getting things out of proportion.'

'You don't understand.'

'Why don't you try explaining?'

'It was the only way to keep my job. I couldn't risk losing it – not with the baby and everything.' He sobbed again. 'They push you so hard to take bigger and bigger risks. So I did. We both did, me and Malcolm. Only the gambles we made didn't pay off.'

Jean handed him another tissue. 'Is that why you needed to borrow the money? To balance the books?'

'We had much bigger losses than that. We borrowed the money to gamble some more. So we could make investments with higher returns.'

'And bigger risks?'

He nodded.

'And somehow you managed to keep this from your bosses?'

'They expected us to sail close to the wind. It's their strategy. We were doing exactly what they wanted.'

'But you said the gambles you were making weren't paying off,' Stanley said.

'We managed to disguise the losses. We hid all the unauthorised trades in a secret account.'

Jean turned away from her son and stared out of the window, taking a moment to absorb everything he'd just told her. After a long pause she turned back to him. 'How big?' she said.

'What?'

'The losses, how big are they?'

Simon sucked in a noisy breath through his mouth.

'Tell me!'

'Last time I checked, about nine hundred.'

'Nine hundred?' Stanley threw Simon a glance over his shoulder. The car swerved into the next lane. 'Doesn't sound so bad. That's chicken feed to an organisation the size of Fisher Krupps.'

Simon blew his nose. Jean handed him the packet of Kleenex. 'I tried to get into the office last Tuesday to see if I could cover my tracks.'

'Late at night?' Jean asked.

'How did you know that?'

'Never mind.'

Simon shredded the damp tissue he was clutching. 'Only I couldn't even get to my desk. All the board members had been called in for an emergency meeting. They must have found out.'

'About the losses?'

Simon swallowed. 'They must have discovered the hidden trading account.'

'So you ran?' Stanley swung the car right to leave the highway.

'But why would they call in the whole board for losses of less than a million dollars?'

'For God's sake, Mum! Don't you get it? We lost nine hundred *million*.'

Jean's heart fluttered in her chest. She gripped the door handle with one hand and held on tight to the seat with the other. 'Dear God.'

Stanley hung a left and they drove down the long wide avenue in silence. He turned right at the end and pulled in toward the kerb. 'This is it. Home.'

Simon peered out of the window and popped the door.

'How can they keep losses as big as that to themselves?' Jean's heart was still pounding hard against her ribs. She tried to take a deep breath. 'I don't understand why it hasn't been all over the news.'

'Me neither.' Simon swung a leg out of the car then stopped. 'All this week I thought it was going to hit the fan. The board must be better at covering up a crisis than I imagined. But someone is bound to leak it soon. It's got to come out any day now. Could be tomorrow. Might be over the weekend.'

Jean shot Stanley a look that Simon didn't notice. 'And what will happen then?'

'When the news gets out there'll be a run on the bank, most probably. Fisher Krupps will cease trading. All the remaining assets will be frozen.'

'And how quickly will that happen?'

'Fast – lose the confidence of the investors, of the customers, it all comes tumbling down.'

'Where does this leave you?' Jean said. 'Do they know you're responsible?'

'They must have a pretty good idea by now. I did go AWOL, after all.'

'When I spoke to your boss last week he assumed you were away on paternity leave.'

'You spoke to Fletcher?'

Jean thought for a moment. 'I don't think he actually introduced himself.'

'What were you doing there?'

'Looking for you.'

'So you told him, what? That I'd disappeared?' He thumped the car door with a fist. 'That's like putting a big flashing sign over my head.' He raised his voice. 'Why couldn't you just leave well alone?'

'Hey – don't speak to your mother that way. Show some respect. What was she supposed to do? Just shrug her shoulders and go back home? Goddamit, she was out of her mind worrying about you.'

Simon jumped out of the car and slammed the door. Jean watched him march up the street.

'Do you want me to go after him – make him apologise?' Stanley said.

'Leave him be. He didn't mean it. He'll calm down and apologise in his own good time.'

Stanley slumped over the steering wheel. 'What a mess. Jesus – a run on the bank. That screws everything.'

He sounded relieved.

'I mean – if there's no money, the show's cancelled. We should call people first thing, tell them the plan's off. No point in letting it drag on.'

'We'll do no such thing.'

'What?'

'We're not cancelling anything.'

'Wait a minute.' He swivelled in his seat to face her. 'You know how difficult this has been to set up. We can't just switch the whole plan to another bank, you only got everyone on board because Jimmy's beef is with Fisher Krupps.'

'Who said anything about switching banks?'

'Then I don't understand what you're saying.'

'That's because you've been so keen to admit defeat, you haven't given me the chance to say anything.' She opened her door. 'We'll both call a few people tonight and they can each call a few more. We've got a lot to organise before the morning. We'll just have to strike tomorrow, you heard what Simon said. The bank might have failed by Monday.'

'There's no way we can move that fast. It's too risky.'

'We have no choice. It's now or never.' She eased her legs out of the car. 'I can't just sit by and watch Simon go under.'

'You can't help him now. This is a whole new ball game. He might have been able to escape a bunch of low-level moneylenders, but he can't run away from the Feds.'

'The Feds?'

'F-B-I. It's a federal matter. Once the Feds start digging, they just don't stop.'

'It might not come to that.'

'Who's gonna stop it?'

'I'll think of something. I'm not giving up on Simon that easily.' She levered herself off the sticky vinyl upholstery, her left knee protesting as she shifted weight onto her feet. 'Anyway, we can't cancel the plan – we still need the money for Jimmy.' As she stood up, Stanley's phone bleeped. He looked at the illuminated screen.

'Is that your detective calling again?'

'A text message.' He shook his head as he read it. 'Jesus.'

'Has something happened?'

Stanley reached over and handed her the phone.

*Sorry Stan – can't sit on this any longer.*
*6 counts of larceny. And counting.*
*Riley is busting my ass. I have to bring in Mrs Henderson.*

# 49

Stanley glanced up at the clock attached to the wall above the stove in his kitchen. Something Jean noticed he was doing more and more frequently. 'Maybe he forgot the address,' he said.

'He's only fifteen minutes late. There's no need to panic just yet.'

'Who's panicking?' He stuck a finger between his collar and neck, then loosened his tie.

'Have a little faith. Clarence won't let us down.' She laid a reassuring hand on his arm. 'He won't let Jimmy down.'

'How many years did he work for Fisher Krupps?'

'Long enough to know just how unscrupulous they are.'

'You know we can't do this without him.'

'He'll be here.'

Stanley transferred a notebook, three unregistered cell phones and a bundle of latex gloves from the table to a small backpack. He then checked off each item from a list on a white board attached to the fridge. There was the hint of a tremor in his hands. He looked at the clock again then reached back into the bag and retrieved a phone. He flipped it over and over in his hand.

'I should call Lu. I need to explain she's made a terrible mistake.'

'That was a daft idea when you first suggested it last night and it's a bloody awful one this morning.'

'I've got to do something. I can't let her arrest you.'

'I don't see how you can stop her. I'll face up to the consequences just as soon as we've done what we have to. Let's just get through this morning.' She smoothed down her blouse and left a trail of perspiration on the pale linen. 'She won't be looking for me here.'

Stanley dropped to his knees and started fiddling with the zip on a large nylon sports holdall. 'I'm not sure we have enough bags.'

'Stop fussing. We have as many as we have. We can't do anything about it now.' She held out her hand and helped him to his feet. 'Why don't you sit down for five minutes, try to relax.'

'I'm fine.' He blew out his cheeks.

'You can't be having second thoughts now. We've come this far.'

Stanley rubbed the back of his hand across his mouth.

'All we're doing is liberating the money before the lawyers and the receivers get their hands on it,' Jean said.

'You make it sound like it's some public duty.'

'Maybe it is. Surely you can see—'

'I know, I know. We've been through it enough times already.'

A thump sounded from the second floor, then heavy footsteps clattered down the staircase. A few moments later Simon staggered into the kitchen, his cheeks a greyish green. 'Why didn't anyone wake me up?'

He disappeared into the living room and Jean followed him.

'Do you want some breakfast?'

He clutched his stomach. 'I couldn't keep anything down. You should never have forced me to drink that whiskey.' He hurried to the television and grabbed the remote, flicking through channels until he found a rolling news station. Then another and another. 'Nothing?' He turned back to Jean.

'Nothing yet.' Jean sighed. 'You sound disappointed. Wouldn't it be better for you if the bank didn't fail?'

Simon shrugged. 'Even if they don't, I still lost them almost a billion dollars. At least bringing them down would be some kind of achievement.'

'Don't talk daft,' she said, but couldn't help agreeing with him. Just as long as the bank didn't fall until later. 'Are you sure you don't want any breakfast?'

'I need to get going.' He was staring intently at the television, even though the news programme had been replaced by noisy commercials. 'About the money…' He half turned to Jean. If you can let me have it now…'

'That's not possible.'

'We've been through this. I only want to protect my family – honestly, leaving the country is the best option for us.'

'Have you even spoken to Cindy yet?'

'I thought I'd tip up unannounced and sweep her off her feet.'

'You need to think about this properly, before you do anything rash.'

'What do you think I've been doing for a week? I've driven myself mad thinking about it.'

'You should go back to the office, brazen it out.'

'What?'

'You can't stay away any longer without arousing suspicion. As it is, you're just a new dad returning to work, exhausted, but happy to be there.'

'Are you forgetting about the people I owe money to?'

'We're going to pay them off – with a little extra to sweeten the deal.'

'You've got no idea. Let's just say they agree to not breaking every bone in my body after they've taken the money. What happens when the FBI start sniffing around the bank?'

'Isn't it possible they'd discover Malcolm was behind the whole thing and leave the matter there?'

'You really think the Feds would do that?'

'They might. If you helped them.'

'Oh please. Get real. Why don't you ask your boyfriend what he thinks?'

'He's not my boyfriend.'

'That's not how it seemed last night.'

'It's none of your business.'

'Really? My apartment… my bed… For God's sake – he was wearing my *dressing gown*.'

Jean laid a hand on his arm. 'Will you at least think about what I've said. You can't just leave. You'll spend your whole life constantly looking over your shoulder.'

'Better than spending it locked away in a federal prison.' He stared into his mother's eyes. 'I know you only want what's best for me, but believe me, that does not involve staying in New York just waiting for the axe to fall.'

'At least phone Cindy before you spring it all on her.'

'I need to do it my way.' He raised a hand to his face and seemed surprised to find a beard there. 'Listen – I need to take the money with me now. Where is it? Have you put it somewhere safe?'

'Oh it's quite safe. For the time being at least.' Jean plucked the remote from her son's sweaty hand and changed channels, clicking through a couple before the arresting image on CBS News made her heart throw itself against her ribs.

Simon stared open-mouthed and pointed a finger toward the screen. 'What the…?'

Jean planted a hand on her chest and tried to take a breath. 'Stanley!' she hollered. 'You need to see this.'

'Mum! Why are they showing a picture of—'

'Shhh! I'm trying to listen.'

The image of a curly-haired teenager was replaced by another featuring the same sullen boy, standing next to a tall, tanned man who seemed to be forcing a smile.

'Has it happened?' Stanley said when he reached the doorway. 'Has Fisher Krupps gone down?'

Jean held up a hand to silence him and turned up the volume as the second photograph disappeared to be replaced by video footage of the tall man speaking directly into the camera, reporters jostling in front of him and shoving microphones under his nose.

'Please, if anyone knows where my son is, call the police immediately. He hasn't been home for over two days and his mother and I are out of our minds with worry.' He paused and took a deep breath. 'Please, son. If you're watching this, I'm begging you to contact me. Or the police.'

The scene cut to a reporter standing on a busy street. 'Chuck Conner's plea for information about his missing son, recorded just a few moments ago. The number for NYPD's Missing Persons Bureau should be on your screens now and will be repeated at the end of this bulletin. Please call if you know anything that might help.'

'The missing boy,' Jean told Stanley, 'he's the one from the grocery store.'

Simon turned to his mother. 'He looks just like—'

Stanley cut him off. 'You mean the perp? The kid who shot the clerk?'

Jean nodded, biting her lip.

'You're sure?'

'Positive.'

'What are you two going on about?' Simon looked from his mother to Stanley.

'That evil little bastard is Chuck Conner's son?' Stanley said.

'Wait a minute,' Simon said, 'I don't buy it. The bank is about to fail and suddenly its CEO announces his son's missing? Isn't that just a tad convenient? Seems like a smokescreen to me.'

Jean reached for the phone sitting next to the television.

'What are you doing?' Stanley moved swiftly across the room.

'I have to call the police.'

'What's gotten into you?' He lurched for the phone and managed to knock it out of her hands.

'He's not missing, is he? He's most probably on the run. They've got to stop him. He could be anywhere by now. Phone Luisa – tell *her* at least.'

'Would someone please explain what the hell is going—'

'Shut up!' Jean and Stanley roared at Simon.

'I can't call Lu – not after her message. You said so yourself. We can call all the people you want – but not until after.'

'After what?' Simon picked up the phone from the floor and laid it back in its cradle.

'Nothing – it doesn't matter.'

A loud bang echoed from the hallway. Jean started. Then opened her eyes wide. 'Clarence!' She pushed Stanley toward the door. 'I told you he wouldn't let us down.'

Stanley disappeared from the room. A moment later Jean heard a loud groan from the hallway. She hurried after him in time to see the door open and Dolores standing outside. 'Do you know what time it is?' he said and hauled her over the doorstep, then checked the street, left and right, before closing the door. 'Are you on your own?'

'I've come to see you, haven't I? Who would I bring with me?' She turned slowly and squinted down the hallway toward Jean. 'In the name of all that's holy, what is that woman doing here?' She stamped a high-heel onto Stanley's foot. 'Tell me she hasn't been here all night.' She pinched his arm. 'Stanley?' She marched toward Jean, shoved her out of the way and rushed into the kitchen. The sound of cabinet doors opening and closing carried down the hall, glassware clinked and clattered. 'And don't tell me it's too early in the morning – I need a drink.' More clinking. 'Stan!

Are you going to throw her out, or do I have to do it myself?'

Jean looked at Stanley. He shrugged back at her.

'Yes, I would like the police please… hold? This is a goddamn emergency,' Dolores shouted.

Stanley ran to the kitchen, Jean following close behind. He lunged at Dolores. Her phone flew out of her hand and somersaulted into the air. Jean leapt for it, swinging her arm, and batted it across the room.

Dolores pushed Stanley away. 'What kind of evil spell has she put on you?' She spun around and pointed at Jean, knocking a bottle of whisky with her elbow, sending it crashing onto the floor. 'Where's my goddamn phone?' She dropped to her knees. 'What is this?' She got back up, Stanley's backpack in her hands. She shook the contents onto the table. 'You opening a hardware store?' She waved a pair of pliers and a roll of duct tape in Stanley's face. When he didn't reply she sifted through the other items piled on the table. 'What are you doing with three cell phones?' She unrolled the floorplan of the Fisher Krupps branch on West Broadway.

The expression on Stanley's face changed so suddenly he looked as if he'd been slapped.

'Hey, Stan, what are you planning to do, rob a bank?' Her sarcastic laugh died in her throat as she looked up at his face.

Simon joined his mother in the doorway. 'Would someone please tell me what's going on?'

Jean grabbed the pair of pants and shirt hanging in a dry cleaners' bag on the back of the kitchen door. 'The legs might be a bit long, they're meant for a much taller man, but I don't have time to fix them.' She pushed the plastic bag at her son. 'You can put these on in the car. I'll explain on the way.'

# 50

Luisa took a deep breath at the bottom of the stoop and looked up at the house. The drapes were pulled across the downstairs window. Stanley never closed the drapes. She stood perfectly still, unsure suddenly what she was even doing there. She considered turning around and heading directly for the English woman's apartment in the East Village.

Sending Stanley the text message last night was enough to get Luisa into a crap ton of trouble. Coming to his house only made it worse.

But she couldn't deny that she was secretly hoping the message on its own would have been enough to persuade Mrs Henderson to get on the first plane out of the country. A nice neat solution. Lieutenant Riley need never know Luisa had identified her on the security camera footage. And more importantly, Stanley would be out of the woman's evil clutches. He'd thank her for it. Eventually.

She bounded up the steps and hesitated again before knocking on the door. If Mrs Henderson was inside, she'd give her one last chance to flee before arresting her. Luisa took another breath and pounded on Stanley's door with the flat of her hand, then eased down a step and waited.

No response.

This time she pounded harder, using her fist. She listened carefully for a few moments, but there was no sign of movement from inside. She bent down to the mail slot and pushed open the flap.

Nothing out of place in the hall.

'Hey!' she hollered through the gap. 'Stan – come on, buddy, open up!' She checked her watch – it was too early for him to have left for work. Besides, his car was still parked on the street. An underground parking lot was one of the perks of his new job – no way would he be using the subway. 'Come on, Stan – I need to talk to you. Maybe we can work this out, huh?' She turned her head toward the flap and listened again.

A sound this time, definitely. A low murmur, getting louder.

'Is somebody there?' She strained to listen again.

The murmur turned into a moan, the volume increasing and the pitch rising. A muffled scream, then, 'Help me!'

A voice she recognised.

'Who is that?' she shouted back.

'For Chrissakes – who'd you think it is?'

*Dolores?*

'Where's Stan?' Luisa hollered.

'Just help me will you?'

'Come to the door.'

'Don't you think I would if I could? You think I shut myself in here? Stanley and that English witch locked me in.'

'They did what?'

'You heard me.'

'Why?' Even as she asked, Luisa understood completely the desire to lock up Dolores, if only to get her to stop talking.

'I'll tell you why when you get me out of here.'

'Where are you?'

'In the closet at the end of the hall.' There was a moan, then, 'I'm in a lot of pain. You need to hurry.'

'Hang on, I'll be right there.'

Luisa stepped back, grabbed the stoop rail for balance, and aimed a heavy boot at the locks on the door. The force jarred her ankle, sending a shockwave all the way up to her knee, but the door barely moved. She tried again and again, stopping at regular intervals to flash her shield toward the neighbours' twitching drapes or the occasional curious passer-by.

The hunk of wood stayed firmly within its frame. She should have guessed a cop's door would be well protected. Too many locks to overcome through brute force alone. For a moment she considered shooting the locks off, but as she reached for her gun she thought better of it. Instead she bent down to the mail slot again.

'Dolores – can you hear me?'

'I'm not deaf.'

Luisa hissed out an irritated breath. 'I can't get in.'

'You've got to. I'm in trouble here. Call the fire service.'

'OK.' Luisa pulled her cell phone from a pocket then stopped. 'Tell me why they shut you in the closet.'

'So I couldn't stop Stanley making the biggest mistake of his whole goddamn life.'

Sudden cramp in Luisa's calves forced her to her feet. She shook one foot then the other. She crouched back down, lifted the metal flap and immediately heard Dolores cursing from the other end of the hallway.

'Dolores!'

'Jesus! I thought you'd gone.'

'Just tell me what you meant – what mistake?'

'Did you call the fire service – are they coming?'

Luisa stared at her cell phone. 'Sure, they'll be here real soon. What is it Stanley's going to do?' She couldn't shake an image of Stanley and Mrs Henderson standing at an altar somewhere exchanging vows.

'Something damn stupid with that evil English bitch.'

'What kind of stupid?'

'You've got to get me out of here.'

'I will, I promise. What are they planning to do?'

'Like you of all people would believe me.'

Luisa thudded the door with a fist. 'Where did they go?'

'I don't know for sure – I tried to hear what they were saying. Downtown some place, the Financial District, I think. Fisher Krupps – that much I know.'

'Fisher Krupps the bank?'

'I can't hear any sirens – did you tell them it was urgent?'

'Are they going to the company headquarters downtown or a local branch?'

'I don't know – a branch I guess.'

'Which one?'

'How many can there be?'

'Why are they going to Fisher Krupps?'

'You wouldn't believe me if I told you.'

Luisa banged the door again. 'For God's sake – just tell me!'

'You got to stop Stanley. Promise me you'll stop him – you can't let him go through with it.'

'Go through with what?'

'You gotta save him from that evil bitch.'

'What is he going to—?'

'Rob a bank.'

Luisa snatched a breath and shook her head. 'That's crazy – I never heard such a stupid—'

'I said you wouldn't believe me.' She was hollering hysterically now. 'You think they would lock me in a closet if they were just planning a trip to the mall? You've got to stop them. I can't see Stanley go to jail.'

With weak knees Luisa struggled to her feet. As the metal flap closed on the mail slot, she heard a plaintive cry from the other end of the hallway.

'Don't leave me! I need to pee!'

# 51

Jean climbed down carefully from the passenger side of the high vehicle and slammed the door. She waved Simon on his way and joined Stanley in the used Ford Crown he'd bought two days earlier.

'You OK?' he asked when she'd shut the door and buckled up.

She nodded and peeled the damp strands of hair from her neck. 'Couldn't have picked a nicer day for it.'

'And what about him? He knows what to do, right?'

'Despite what you might think, he's a lot smarter than he looks. Everything's under control.'

'I only wish I could believe that. Do you know how many opportunities there are for any one of us to screw up?'

'Of course I do – you never tire of telling me.' She reached over and squeezed his knee. 'You can stop worrying now. No one will let us down.'

'It's me I'm worried about.'

Jean leaned in closer and kissed his cheek. 'You, my love, will be perfect.'

Five minutes later they were parked up in the Financial District, a 'Police on call' notice shoved between the dash and the windshield.

'It's all right – I can do this bit on my own,' Jean said, knowing that one look at Stanley's face was liable to convince the latest recruits that the plan was destined for failure. 'I'll only be a minute.'

Stanley let out a complaining moan but made no attempt to follow her out of the car.

Jean turned the corner and spotted Carmen first, a pink and green crocheted blanket hanging over one arm. In her other hand she held a large grocery store bag. When she spotted Jean she waved the bag at her, smiling broadly.

'All set?' Jean said and glanced at the assembled crowd of seniors, all dressed in various shades of brown, bright yellow vests clutched in their hands and pillows shoved under their arms.

Carmen nodded enthusiastically and lifted her bag under Jean's nose. 'Want a cream cheese bagel? Or a pretzel?'

Jean politely declined.

'Rosemary over here has some ice tea – you thirsty?'

'I'm fine.' She surveyed the motley group of seventy and eighty-somethings again as they assembled at the crosswalk of the intersection of Pine and Nassau. With some difficulty, due to various arthritic wrists and shoulders, they began to slip the vests over their heads. Then each one linked arms with the person next to them, forming a wall of luminous yellow and beige.

'I suppose this is it,' Jean said and smiled at Carmen. 'Good luck. Hope you don't get too bored.'

'Between us we got about one hundred grandchildren to talk about and when we're done with that I got a few songs we can sing – we'll be fine.'

When the lights changed the gang of seniors marched slowly to the middle of the crossing and gingerly sat down, the more nimble individuals helping their neighbours lower themselves safely to the road. The lights changed again and immediately the car horns started blaring. Jean waved a triumphant fist at the protestors. It was a shame they hadn't had time to prepare banners and placards, but a few resourceful individuals had scrawled slogans across their vests in thick black marker pen: *SIT DOWN FOR WHAT'S RIGHT*, and *PEOPLE NOT PROFITS*. One particularly rotund man had even managed to write, *NEVER HAVE SO FEW TAKEN SO MUCH FROM SO MANY*.

By the time she returned to the car, Jean had checked in with another three locations by phone, each group confirming they'd brought traffic to a standstill in Little Italy, Chinatown and Tribeca.

Stanley drove for another ten minutes and parked up in a lot two blocks south of the Fisher Krupps branch on West Broadway. They continued the journey on foot, splitting up thirty or so yards from the entrance to the bank so Stanley could arrive alone. Jean nodded at the straggle of seniors already assembled on the sidewalk outside the bank and made her way to the head of the line. She took up her position just in time to see Stanley waving his company ID badge at the guard standing at the door.

'I got nothing in my schedule about a security check,' the guard said, peering carefully at the plastic rectangle hanging from a lanyard around Stanley's neck.

'That's the point of a spot check – it's meant to be a surprise.'

'Regular comedian, huh?'

'I've received a report about faulty surveillance equipment.'

'Don't know anything about that.' He narrowed his eyes and scrutinised Stanley's face. 'Why didn't you send an engineer?'

'I was in the neighbourhood. I'll send the technical guys once I've taken a look at it myself and know what I'm dealing with.'

The guard turned and shouted something to a colleague within the bank. As his hip swung toward her, Jean's breath caught in her throat. A holstered gun was attached to his belt.

'Wait a second.' The security man shut the door in Stanley's face.

'Did you see his gun?' Jean whispered to Stanley.

Before he got a chance to reply the door swung open again.

'Guess you'd better come in,' the guard mumbled.

Stanley stepped inside and the door clanged shut behind him.

# 52

Linus blinked hard at his reflection and straightened his tie. That small gesture reminded him so much of his dad he had to look away.

From somewhere at the other end of the apartment he heard the phone warble. It rang for long seconds before someone picked it up. Since he'd returned home just after sunrise, the house phone hadn't stopped ringing. He had ignored it, so had his mother. Assuming, of course she was conscious enough to hear it ring.

This time the housekeeper answered it. After speaking a few rushed words Linus couldn't make out, she clattered up the stairs and knocked on his mother's bedroom door.

'Mrs Conner? There's a phone call for you. They say it's urgent.'

Linus forced himself to look in the mirror again and pushed a hand through his hair, and tried to flatten it against his scalp. He pulled back his shoulders and puffed out his chest.

'Mrs Conner?' Rosaria said, shouting this time. She got no response. Then down the hallway came the clickety-click of her heels against the wooden floor. She was swearing under her breath in Spanish. Perhaps his mother was out, and had been all night. It didn't happen often, but it was possible. Rosaria hurried noisily down the stairs. A radio came on and she started to sing along in her deep raspy voice. The phone rang again, she cursed and turned off the radio.

Linus rotated his body in front of the mirror. It was impossible to conceal the gun wearing a suit. No matter where he tried to hide it, pants pocket, waistband, jacket pocket, it made an unmistakable bulge obvious to anyone who might happen to glance in his direction. He frantically searched his bedroom for a discreet bag, something dark and unobtrusive. Something he could shove under his arm and reach into unhindered when the time came. Eventually he located a leather satchel his mother had bought him for his last birthday. It was so gross he'd shoved it onto a shelf at the back of the closet almost as soon as he'd ripped off the gift wrap. The size and shape wasn't ideal, but it would get him downtown without arousing suspicion.

There was a knock on his bedroom door. Linus quickly scrambled for the gun and shoved it in the bag, hoping he'd remembered to lock the door.

'Linus?' It was Rosaria. 'A phone call for you.'

No one called him on the home phone. Linus pulled his cell from a pocket. It was switched off. When he didn't answer, Rosaria tried the door handle. He held his breath. The door rattled but didn't open. Rosaria cursed again, and walked away.

Linus crept out of the closet and listened. The tapping of her heels stopped at the other end of the hall. She shouted his mother's name and rapped on her door. She continued to bang and shout until the door creaked open.

'For God's sake, do you know what time it is?' he heard his mother say.

Rosaria had just woken angry mom. Linus needed to make his escape while he still could.

He eased open his door, the satchel slung over his shoulder.

'Are you sure? And this was just now?' His mother's nose sounded blocked, as if she had a cold or had been crying all night. Or drinking.

'I checked – the door is definitely locked from the inside.'

'I'll be right there.'

Linus crept into the hallway. Too late.

'Linus! Honey!'

He turned to see his mother wrapping a silk robe around her as she hurried toward him.

'Where are you going? I've been so worried about you. Why didn't you call?'

Linus gave her a non-committal shrug.

'Where have you been?'

'At a friend's house.'

'But I called all your friends.'

'Not all. Obviously.'

'You know how close I came to calling the police?' She held a finger and thumb close to a bloodshot eye. 'This close.'

'The police?' Linus squeezed the satchel a little tighter. 'Why'd you want to call them?'

'You haven't been home for two days. What else was I supposed to do?'

'But you didn't call them?'

'No, your father persuaded me to wait another twenty-four hours.'

'You spoke to dad?'

'Of course I did – he is your father. He does still love you, you know.'

'Sure he does.'

She laid a cold hand on his forehead. 'You're burning up. Are you sick? Should I call the doctor?'

He batted her hand away.

'Rosaria! Call Dr Evanovitch.'

'I'm not sick!' Linus edged back toward the staircase.

'OK! No doctor. But stay with me a little while. Rosaria will make us some breakfast. How about some huevos rancheros?'

'Not hungry.'

'Not even for your favourite? At least sit and talk to me.'

What did they have to talk about? 'I've got to go out.'

'But you just got back, didn't you?'

'I'm late already.'

His mother looked at his suit for the first time. 'You're dressed as if you're going to a funeral. Did someone die?'

*Someone? You have no idea.*

'At least stay while I call your father, tell him you're all right. He'll want to speak to you.'

'No!'

'But honey—'

'I'm going to see dad right now. I want to surprise him.'

'You do?'

'I've been doing a lot of thinking and I've decided it's time I started taking my life more seriously. I'm ready.'

She grabbed his hand. 'Look at my baby, all grown up.' Linus tried to pull away, but her grip held firm. 'I'm so proud of you.'

He tugged again and this time she reluctantly unclasped her fingers.

The door entry phone started buzzing downstairs. Rosaria hurried away.

'Who on earth could be visiting at this hour?' His mother tightened the sash around her waist, then held a hand up to Linus's face. 'Do you need money? I have a little cash. Or maybe Rosaria has some. Rosaria!'

'I don't need any.' He felt his face flushing. 'Not now.'

'You're right – I'm sure your father will reinstate your allowance. He'll probably put you straight on the payroll.'

'Whatever.'

'Why don't you take the car? Taylor is in the parking lot with nothing to do but polish it. Let him drop you downtown.'

# 53

At two minutes after eight the bank finally opened. Jean waited for the tall elderly man standing next to her in the line to don his yellow vest and hardhat.

'Now you know what you've got to do?' she asked him.

'I've got it.'

'And if anyone insists on coming in?'

'You think once I tell them about a gas leak they're going to insist?'

'If they do?'

'I know the drill – I get Tony and Miles here to back me up.'

'Good – that's great,' Jean said, hoping their powers of persuasion wouldn't be put to the test.

She went inside and surreptitiously glanced up at the camera trained on the entrance. Hopefully Stanley had already disabled the surveillance equipment front of house. She scanned the bank, trying to match it to the floorplan she'd studied the night before. The counter was set off to the right, about fifteen yards from where she was standing. She nodded politely to the three unsuspecting tellers sitting behind thick security glass. They didn't nod back. To the left of the counter was a closed inner door, an electronic swipe lock attached to the wall to one side. The security guard who had spoken to Stanley was standing in the middle of the bank, his feet wide apart, one hand on his belt, the other on his gun.

Behind Jean the first few seniors entered the bank and strode purposefully to the counter. The guard glanced over then quickly turned away. A handful more of Jean's gang drifted in and started to browse through information booklets mounted on a display to the left of the closed inner door. A few more came in, took one look at the line building at the counter, then eased themselves into soft chairs positioned around a low circular table. The remaining two dozen or so seniors waited outside on the sidewalk. The yellow-vested man on the door continued to let them in one or two at a time, regulating their entry like on over-zealous nightclub bouncer.

The plan was to seem as insignificant as usual, not attract any unwanted attention. A hoard of old people descending on the bank all at once might just look a tad suspicious.

The line at the counter had now swelled to a dozen or so. Jean scrutinised the tellers' reactions closely. The two women on the left glanced at one another, but their faces registered nothing more than mild annoyance.

Good.

She didn't want them panicked into calling for reinforcements.

The few customers who had already been served rejoined the end of the line, gearing up to accuse the tellers of short-changing them, demanding their withdrawals be recounted, bill by bill.

Jean's phone vibrated in her hand. She glanced down and read the message from Stanley.

*Weather lovely here beach is empty*

She slipped the phone into a pocket, stretched her arms above her head and yawned loudly. Right on cue, a seventy-eight-year-old named Hal, sporting owl-lensed glasses and a baseball cap pulled low over his forehead, pushed his way to the counter. He glanced over at Jean and she tipped her head toward him. He then slipped a note to the teller and stood back.

The young teller shook her head and said something to him.

'What do you mean, you don't have that kind of money?' Hal raised his voice. 'Is this a bank, or have I inadvertently wandered into a dry cleaners?'

The girl behind the glass screen leaned forward and said something else Jean couldn't hear. The teller looked flushed and nervous.

'It's my goddamn money, why can't I have it?' Hal thumped a hand on the counter. 'Why don't you go get some more?'

The people behind him in the line cheered and shouted words of encouragement. The girl left her station and disappeared through a security door buzzed open by her colleague. Jean quickly retrieved her phone and sent a text to Stanley.

*Expect some visitors*

The security guard, who up until now had barely given the proceedings more than a disinterested backward glance, worked his way to the head of the line.

'OK, sir,' he said, 'let's just take it easy. It's not like the bank is running out of money anytime soon. You'll get your cash – just be a little patient.'

'I demand to see the manager!' Hal cried at the top of his voice. 'Bring him out here now.' He slammed a hand against the glass.

A teller flinched, recovered quickly and grabbed a phone. She spoke urgently into the mouthpiece.

'I'm not talking to anyone through this goddamn goldfish bowl,' Hal said. 'Tell the manager I want him out here, where I can see the whites of his eyes. Then he can explain himself to the people who pay his wages. Right?' Hal turned to face his audience and they cheered again. Several liver-spotted hands slapped him on the back.

A few moments later Jean's phone buzzed with another message from Stanley.

*looks like rain. call before you leave*

She read the message twice to be sure she hadn't misunderstood. Then she called Stanley's throwaway phone. He answered, but said nothing. All she could hear was an indistinct woman's voice in the background. Jean presumed it was the young teller who had just left the counter.

'I'm sorry, miss. I don't understand…' It was Stanley speaking now. 'I've checked the schedule myself. The vault can be opened at eight-thirty every day. It's twenty-nine minutes after.'

'We don't need to open it.' The teller must have moved closer to Stanley. Jean could hear her quite clearly as she raised her voice.

'I thought you said you had a customer out there asking for thousands of dollars?' Stanley said.

'It's fine. We have a separate safe to cover that level of withdrawal.'

'Why do I know nothing about it?' The pitch of his voice was undulating alarmingly.

'It's something the manager introduced recently. Perhaps your predecessor forgot to pass on the details.'

Jean glanced back at Hal. He was still gesticulating and hollering at the tellers behind the counter, spraying saliva at the thick glass screen protecting them from him. She closed her eyes for a moment, concentrating on the conversation at the other end of the phone. If the teller was refusing to open the vault, did that mean the plan was off?

'How many customers you got out there?' Stanley said.

'A few.' The teller paused. 'More than we would normally have this time of the morning.'

'What if they all want to take out a lot of money?' Stanley sounded irritated now.

'We have plenty in the safe.'

'How can you know that for sure?'

'I gotta get out there.' A man's voice interrupted the conversation. 'Some old guy is getting antsy.'

'I should go back too,' the teller said.

Only a few seconds later a second security guard appeared at the inner door. He couldn't have been far out of his teens, both his cheeks were covered in acne.

'It's OK, miss.' It was Stanley again.

Jean pressed the phone closer to her ear.

'I'll bring the rest of the money out to you,' Stanley said.

'I don't know. I can't really leave the safe unattended.'

'I'm head of security for the southern district. Don't you think you can trust me?'

There was a long pause. 'I guess.'

The young security guard was still lingering in the doorway, staring at the crowd surrounding his colleague at the counter. He blew out a breath. In the corridor behind him Jean saw the teller rush past, a dark blue bag cradled in her arms. The guard finally stepped onto the floor of the bank and hurried toward the counter. He squeezed through the rabble of seniors and stood shoulder to shoulder with his colleague. Hal looked him up and down.

'Where's the goddamn manager?' Hal poked a finger into the young guard's chest. 'I said I wanted to see him.'

The guard reached for his gun. He unpopped the fastening of the holster. The older security man yanked back his arm.

'What the hell do you think you're doing?' He gestured to the crowd threatening to engulf them. 'It's just a bunch of old ladies. Don't let me see you go for your weapon again.'

Stanley appeared at the inner door and tugged his earlobe. Jean slipped her phone back into a pocket and frowned at him.

Without the money from the vault, was there any point in continuing?

Stanley tugged at his ear again and nodded at her. Jean shrugged, removed the headscarf from her neck and waved it extravagantly in the air.

In one orchestrated movement, the handful of seated seniors struggled out of their chairs. Unfortunately, Ethel Cryocek was having especial difficulty rising. The three-hundred-pound woman seemed to be wedged between the arms of the seat.

Why hadn't Jean insisted Ethel remain on her feet? Without Ethel taking up the correct position, the plan would definitely be scuppered. Jean silently willed the woman upward, clenching her fists, straining every sinew, rising on her toes, as Ethel valiantly tried to escape the chair.

Jean glanced across the bank at Stanley who was surreptitiously checking his watch, careful to avoid eye contact with her and the three seniors now wandering slowly toward him.

Jean looked again toward the counter. The three tellers were busy serving customers as the two guards did their best to subdue Hal and corral the other seniors into a more orderly line.

With a clatter of wooden chair legs banging the hard tiled floor, Ethel finally made it out of the chair. The woman staggered a few steps, struggling to control her forward momentum. Jean held her breath. After a moment Ethel righted herself and shuffled toward the inner door and a grim-faced Stanley. A yard away she let out a gurgling cry and clutched a hand to her chest. She lurched forward, drew level with the door and gracefully dropped to her knees then toppled sideways, finally resting on her back, wedging open the door with her bulk.

'OK, people – everything's under control – I'm calling nine-one-one.' Stanley shouted loud enough for the security guards to hear and held his phone high in the air. 'You stay where you are, guys. I have this covered.'

Ethel moaned and twitched a couple of times for good measure.

'Is there a doctor in here?' Stanley hollered.

As rehearsed, two seniors broke away from the line snaking in front of the counter and waved their hands at Stanley. One of them crouched low over Ethel's inert mass, and felt for a pulse.

'Cardiac arrest,' he announced loudly.

Jean retrieved her phone and sent two texts.

Moments later the remaining seniors from the sidewalk came into the bank. Mrs Kim, wearing dark glasses, tapping a white stick against the floor, and her two friends joined the small crowd standing near the doorway. They nimbly stepped over Ethel and into the corridor beyond. They turned right, toward the staff entrance to the counter. Three more of the group from the sidewalk slipped past Ethel and headed down the corridor in the opposite direction. Toward the safe.

Jean checked the bank staff again. All of them were too preoccupied to notice six elderly members of the public disappearing into the inner recesses of the bank.

'You can't treat me like this,' Hal shouted into the young security guard's face. 'I'm a veteran. Do you hear me?' Hal grabbed the sleeve of the guard's uniform and tugged. 'Two tours in Vietnam and I can't even get at my own money. What's this country coming to?'

The guard tried to shake Hal's hand free. When it didn't budge he reached for his gun again. This time, his colleague was too busy helping a woman who had fallen down to notice what he was doing.

Jean rushed forward.

'Please!' she shouted and waved at the young guard. 'We need your help over here.' She managed to grab his arm and started to pull him toward Ethel, who was still lying on her back in the doorway. 'We need to turn this lady onto her side. So she doesn't choke on her tongue.'

They reached the door and Stanley laid a fatherly hand on the young man's shoulder. 'Do you think you can help me do that?'

The guard hesitated for a moment, apparently unsure whether he should help save a woman's life, or assist his colleague at the counter.

'Goddamit! Put that gun away and help me!' Stanley grabbed the guard's other shoulder and shook him hard. 'What's the matter with you? She's turning blue.'

Behind her Jean heard the heavy entrance door clang open.

*Thank God.*

She turned quickly. Her premature smile faded on her lips as her brain first took in the Dunkin' Donuts bag and the large cardboard cup. A moment later she registered the significance of the uniformed cop holding them.

# 54

Luisa nosed the car a foot or so forward and stopped. Traffic travelling south on Bowery had snarled to a standstill. She slammed her fists against the steering wheel.

On her way downtown from Stanley's house, she had crossed Williamsburg Bridge with no problem and decided to drop by the station house to switch her own car for a department vehicle. Careful to avoid both the lieutenant and Sanchez, she managed to park up her fuel-efficient Toyota and sign out a gas-guzzling Ford Crown sedan with no difficult questions from the duty sergeant. She'd hoped the addition of a siren and lights would speed her journey to the Financial District, but each time she'd tried to use either, all she got was a symphony of honking horns from the neighbouring vehicles.

She was running out of time. If she'd been doing her job, she would have called in a suspected bank robbery as soon as Dolores told her about it. But how could she do that to Stanley? If she stopped him herself, before he'd actually done anything illegal, no one need ever know.

'All right already!' she hollered at the driver in a neighbouring car.

According to the information she'd found on her cell phone, Fisher Krupps only had one commercial branch within the Financial District, and that was just around the corner from their headquarters. The details Dolores had given her were sketchy at best, but Luisa had to head somewhere and Pine Street was as good a place as any.

After another few inches of forward motion, she stopped again. Her phone lit up on the passenger seat and started to vibrate its way toward her. It was Riley. No doubt calling to find out how the street robbery investigation was progressing. She didn't pick up to find out. A few stolen purses and pocket books were totally insignificant now, if what Dolores had told her was true.

She slammed the steering wheel again. Then snatched her phone from the seat and tried Stanley. She'd lost count of the number of times she'd been shunted straight to voicemail.

At the next intersection the light turned green, but nothing budged. Luisa leaned forward in her seat, willing just a little movement, some feeling of momentum. All she felt was the seat belt digging into her shoulder. She turned up the volume of the police radio and listened for a few moments, hoping she wouldn't hear details of a bank robbery in progress on Pine. Apart from confirmation of the gridlock she was sitting in, there were no reports of major incidents. She let out a big breath, grabbed the handset and hit the transmit button.

'This is Rodriguez, can you tell me what's causing the traffic problem heading south on Bowery?'

The radio expelled a blast of static then a faraway muffled voice.

'There are reported disturbances on William, Liberty and Pine…' The dispatcher took a breath and carried on. 'Canal, Lafayette, West Broadway, plus—'

'What kind of disturbances? National security?' Luisa's grip on the radio handset tightened.

'No – just some people protesting.'

'About what?'

'Nobody's figured that out yet.'

'What the hell are they doing?'

'They're sitting in the middle of the road.'

'Why doesn't somebody move them?'

'Seems they've chained themselves to fire hydrants and each other. Nothing's gonna be moving on Bowery for a while yet.'

The line of traffic lurched forward another couple of feet and Luisa took her chance. She turned on the lights and the siren, turned the steering wheel hard right and drove the Crown onto the sidewalk. Pedestrians scattered as she braked sharply, just shy of the window of a kitchen appliance store.

She jumped out of the car and ran as fast as she could toward Canal Street.

Linus buzzed down the glass partition between the rear passenger seats and the driver.

'What's happening?'

'Traffic's a little heavy this morning, I guess.' The driver looked at him in the rear-view. 'Sir,' he added, as an afterthought.

'But we're not moving at all.' Linus peered out at the bumper-to-bumper line of vehicles stretching as far down the road as he could see.

'Would you like me to check for a traffic report?'

'Just do it quickly.' He buzzed the glass back up and dug a finger between the ankle of his right foot and his shoe. The shoes were fresh out of the box, the leather stiff and unyielding as he tried to ease the pain building in his Achilles. The collar of his shirt was scratching his neck, and despite the fierce air conditioning inside the car, expanding patches of sweat on his back and chest were threatening to seep into the fabric of his jacket.

The partition glided down again. 'Are you OK back there, sir?'

'Did you find out what's causing the problem?'

'Not exactly.'

'For God's sake.'

'But I can tell you nothing's moving south of Canal.'

Linus scooped up his bag. 'How far are we from Canal right now?'

'Next intersection.' The driver nodded toward the lights up ahead.

Linus thrust open the door, hitting a taxi in the neighbouring lane. He jumped out of the limousine and, without looking back, weaved through the stationary traffic to the sidewalk. Then he ran. He squeezed the satchel tight in his arms, his eyes focused on the next intersection. His legs felt as if they might give way beneath him, the muscles soft and weak as he pushed one foot in front of the other. The skin around both his ankles was raw, rubbing hard against his shoes with every stride.

As he approached the corner he saw someone running just as fast on the other side of the street. A short, curly-haired Hispanic woman. She was staring right at him. Then she started to holler, reaching inside her jacket. She pulled something out, it glinted in the sun.

'NYPD!' she shouted. 'Freeze!'

Luisa had been running with her head down for most of the way, but as she got closer to the corner she looked up.

And saw him.

The boy definitely looked older than the picture she'd seen on the English woman's phone, but the similarity was too striking to ignore. He was running, just like her, clutching what looked like a lady's purse to his chest.

She grabbed her shield from her belt and shouted at him to stop. But he continued to run, reaching the subway steps and disappearing underground. Just as she stepped off the sidewalk a courier on a bicycle swerved around her, missing a direct collision by fractions of an inch.

'Look where you're going, lady. You could get yourself killed!'

She took a breath and ducked around the traffic, then skipped down the subway steps three at a time. Before she reached the bottom a loud alarm started up: the perp must have forced his way through a metal gate. She waved her shield at an exiting passenger and yelled at him to push open the emergency barrier.

She got to the platform just as the subway train doors slid shut, the perp smiling at her from the other side of the glass. She collapsed onto a wooden bench and tried to suck in some deep breaths before attempting to call for back up. She hadn't run so far or so fast since patrol officer training.

'You reading that?'

She looked up to see a stooping man pointing at a discarded newspaper on the bench beside her. She glanced at the headline and large photograph on the front page. The image didn't fit the message. It made no sense at all.

# 55

Jean stood completely motionless, a cup of coffee in one hand and the paper bag of donuts in the other, watching the cop who'd arrived only minutes before take charge of the line at the counter, waving his night stick at anyone who so much as murmured at him or the tellers. Even Hal had been cowed into submission.

Stanley and the young security guard were still attempting to turn Ethel. But Ethel wasn't budging. Jean hoped the woman wouldn't suddenly open her eyes and wink, or give her the thumbs up, thrilled at her convincing performance as a near-death heart attack victim.

A metal clang sounded from the entrance. With intense relief, Jean turned to see Simon at the door struggling to push an extra wide gurney through the narrow gap. She shoved the paper bag under her arm and hurried to him, yanking the door wide to allow the gurney through.

'We have a slight problem,' she whispered to her son.

Simon glanced over to the counter, saw the uniformed cop and tensed. 'Someone called the police?' he said.

'No – he's not even on duty. He just happened to be passing.'

'Great.'

Jean looked down at the cop's bag of donuts and cup of coffee and wondered how he'd managed to get past the man guarding the entrance. 'When you came in, did you see someone outside wearing a yellow vest and hardhat?'

'I didn't see anyone outside.'

'So we could have all sorts wandering in off the street.'

Simon was still clutching the metal frame of the gurney, shifting from foot to foot, the long pants of Clarence's paramedic uniform folded over several times at the ankle.

'Get over there,' Jean whispered. 'Just play it by ear.'

'Fine, I'll do that, then. I mean – what's the worst that could happen?'

Simon wheeled the supersized trolley to the other side of the bank and lowered the bed as far as it would go. It remained a good foot and a half above floor level.

Jean turned back to the counter and froze. Mrs Kim and her two friends had made it through to the teller side of the counter. They hadn't yet spotted the policeman. Thankfully, neither the policeman nor the security guard had spotted them. Jean rushed over to the cop.

'Excuse me,' she said. 'The paramedic's arrived. Can you help?'

He looked at Jean then at the gurney parked next to Ethel's seemingly lifeless body. 'I should stay here.'

She pointed at the guard. 'I think this nice man has everything under control.' She hooked her free arm through the policeman's and steered him to the inner door.

The cop looked at Simon. 'Shouldn't there be two of you?'

Simon looked at Stanley, who didn't respond. Jean prayed her son would remember to speak with an American accent. Initially all he managed was a feeble clearing of his throat.

'I… um… my partner's in the ambulance. He's ah… preparing the equipment.' He raised a hand to his shaven head. 'The er… defib-u-lator.'

The policemen nodded slowly, and narrowed his eyes. Jean worried whether either her son's unconvincing explanation or his shaky accent was raising suspicion.

At that moment two of the people who had headed for the safe emerged from the corridor carrying more bulk under their coats and sweaters than they had on the way in. They stepped carefully over Ethel.

'Hey – what were you doing back there?' the cop asked.

'Just using the restroom,' one of them said.

Stanley grabbed the cop's shoulders and turned him away from the door. 'I think we're going to need all the muscle we have to get this lady on the stretcher here. Think you can manage it?'

The last of the safe group emerged, carrying a large shopping bag. She turned her head to Jean as she passed.

'I'm so sorry,' she whispered. 'There was practically nothing left in the safe by the time I got there.'

Jean had no idea how much money the bank kept in their safe. What if there wasn't enough to save Jimmy's house? And what about Simon?

The cop shrugged Stanley's hands from his shoulders. 'Course I can manage it.'

'OK. Are you all ready?' Stanley looked at the cop, Simon and the young guard in turn, each one acknowledging his question with a brief nod. 'First we've got to get her out of the doorway.' He glanced up at one of the septuagenarian doctors, who shuffled back into the corridor, keeping a firm hand on the door, ready to hold it open when Ethel was removed.

Jean glanced quickly toward the counter. Hal had started on the guard again, wagging a bony finger in his face. The tellers behind the glass screen were busy trying to herd Mrs Kim and her friends back through the door. Every time they attempted to touch one of them the women shrieked hysterically as if they'd been prodded with a hot poker.

'OK,' Stanley said loudly, 'on the count of three we heave upward and sideways.'

Having already managed to pull her clear of the door, the four men adjusted their grip on Ethel's various garments and flexed their knees.

'One… two…'

Jean closed her eyes.

'Three!'

With a succession of grunts and an alarming creaking of metal, Jean reopened her eyes to see Ethel lying on the vinyl mattress of the gurney. She quickly stepped forward and thrust the coffee cup and bag of donuts at the cop.

'I think you've earned these now!' she said.

'Yeah – thanks buddy,' Stanley said. 'No point in letting your coffee go cold.'

But much to Jean's dismay, the policeman reached for his belt instead and removed a walkie-talkie. 'Sure – but I'll call for back-up first.' He shot a look at the scuffle that had resumed at the counter. 'Seems like you could use it.'

'No need – we got this under control. Right son?' Stanley patted the acne-faced security guard on the back. 'You helped save a life here today. I'll be sure and put it in my report.'

'Better to be safe than sorry,' the police officer said and proceeded to relay the nature of the incident and the location into his walkie-talkie.

Jean pressed the cup into the cop's free hand, crammed the bag under his arm and nudged Simon with her elbow. Her son strained to push the gurney. It didn't move.

'Let me help with that.' Stanley stepped forward, kicked off the brake and grabbed the metal frame. With Jean's help they managed to steer Ethel through the main door and out onto the sidewalk.

A faint wail of sirens sounded in the distance.

Simon flung open the back of the battered second-hand ambulance and they pushed the gurney inside. They slammed the doors shut then clambered into the cab,

Simon behind the wheel, Jean next to him and Stanley squeezed in on the passenger side.

They only made it three blocks down the road before they hit stationary traffic.

'Looks like our protests are holding firm,' Stanley said. 'Pull over.'

Simon parked up as soon as he could and retrieved a smartphone from his pocket. He swiped a finger across the screen.

'What are you doing?' Stanley said. 'We gotta get out of here.' He and Jean jumped out of the ambulance and opened up the back doors.

Ethel was sitting on the end of the gurney smiling broadly at them. 'Did I do good, or did I do fantastic?'

Simon joined them, still staring down at his phone. 'I *really* need to get out of here.'

'What's happened?' Jean grabbed his arm and tried to see what he was reading.

'Conner's making a statement to the press outside company HQ in the next half hour.' He jumped into the back of the ambulance.

'Let's get down there,' Jean said. 'I want to see his face when he announces to the world Fisher Krupps is ruined. I want to see him suffer in the flesh.'

'I can't go anywhere near there.' Simon was peering under the gurney, then looked up at Ethel. 'Would you mind?'

Ethel slid off the end of the stretcher and Stanley helped her down onto the road. Jean's son shoved the gurney to one side and started to rip open the square plastic containers attached to the floor of the ambulance.

'Where is it?' Simon said. 'It was supposed to be in here.'

Jean looked at Stanley.

'Where's what?' Ethel was still smiling.

'Mum?' He flung open the final container.

'What's wrong, honey?' Finally Ethel's smile faded.

'Where's my money?' Simon jumped down from the ambulance.

Jean put an arm around his shoulders and squeezed. 'Things didn't go quite as we planned.'

# 56

Luisa emerged from the subway still clutching the newspaper she'd picked up at the Canal Street station. She glanced down at the photograph on the front page and then scanned the street. The picture of Linus Conner had to be a couple of years old. The perp she'd chased into the subway was leaner around the jaw. She searched the crowds for a skinny boy dressed in a smart suit. Where was the back up she'd requested? She started walking north up Broad Street, toward the tall columns of the New York Stock Exchange, into the heart of the Financial District, checking faces all the way.

She had called for assistance just before boarding a train at Canal Street, unable to provide much information about the location of the boy she was pursuing other than he'd jumped on a J train going south. He might have jumped straight off again at the next stop or transferred to another line for all Luisa knew. He could be headed anywhere on the subway system by now. Even though she'd been vague, she'd still expected to see at least a handful of transit cops waiting in the subway station.

Where was everyone?

She stopped walking and turned a full circle. Not a single uniformed cop anywhere. She checked her watch. Dolores had told her about Stanley over an hour ago.

Luisa scanned the street one last time for Linus Conner then dumped the newspaper in the nearest trash can. He'd have to be someone else's problem. Right now she needed to focus on stopping Stanley.

She headed further north, crossing Wall Street into Nassau, trying to convince herself she wasn't too late to save him.

She started to run.

A crowd of journalists and cameramen had already gathered outside the marble and glass building.

'I can't see anything from here,' Jean said and started to squeeze through the tightly packed bodies jostling for the best position. 'Are you coming?' She wrapped her fingers around Stanley's hand and tugged.

'Are you really sure you want to do this?' Stanley said. 'What are we gonna do about the money?' He let out a sigh. 'Or lack of it.'

'Did the teller say how much they kept in the safe?' Jean continued to weave through the crowd, taking Stanley with her.

'I figured I shouldn't ask – I didn't want to sound that interested. I was there to check security, not cash flow.'

'Well we emptied it. If it wasn't enough, there's not much we can do about it now.'

'What about your son?'

Jean couldn't really answer that. She'd tried to help him, but whatever money they had managed to liberate from Fisher Krupps should all go to Jimmy.

She pushed and pulled and wriggled some more until she and Stanley emerged at the front of the pack, standing just a few feet from a makeshift lectern, a selection of logo-embossed microphones duct-taped to the top.

'Should we at least be checking in on the…' Stanley lowered his voice. 'Operatives? Make sure everyone got away OK?'

Jean linked her arm through Stanley's. 'Someone would have called me if there was a problem.' She smiled up at him. 'Let's just appreciate this historic moment, shall we? Enjoy the fruit of Simon's labours.'

'You sound almost proud of what he did.' He wrinkled his eyes, the corners of his mouth turning down.

'Of course not.' Jean turned her head, in case her expression gave her away. She wasn't proud exactly. But she couldn't help feeling just a little smug.

A glass door to one side of the main entrance was pulled open by a well-built man in an ill-fitting suit. He stood on the sidewalk, holding on to the long steel handle, occasionally touching an earpiece lightly with his other hand. A few moments later Chuck Conner appeared, followed by his entourage. He strode purposefully to the podium and held up both hands to quieten the assembled crowd.

'As you know, my family is going through somewhat of a crisis at the moment.' The reporters immediately started shouting questions at him. He raised his hands again and looked straight into the lens of the most prominent of the news cameras. 'I'm afraid I have no news about my son. I know he's in your prayers.'

'Not mine,' Jean muttered. It was all she could to stop herself stepping forward and confronting Conner with the truth about his son right there. She'd insisted on calling the police as soon as she found a functioning phone box, but the woman who'd taken her call had sounded so sceptical about her tale of Linus Conner's crimes, by the time Jean had hung up she wasn't at all convinced the police planned to do anything about it.

Meanwhile Linus Conner was still roaming the streets.

'I'd like to take this opportunity to appeal again for information about my son's whereabouts,' Conner continued.

Jean clenched her jaw and both fists and silently urged the tan-faced man to get on with his announcement, wondering just how much of the bank's troubles he would take responsibility for.

'Earlier this morning I informed the Fisher Krupps board of directors that I shall be stepping down as CEO of the company, with immediate effect. Though I have steered the bank through difficult years since the crisis, I feel it is time for me to look for new challenges.'

Again questions were shouted from the assembled journalists.

'I have enjoyed my time here and wish the company future prosperity. I'm sure they will go on to flourish without me.'

Jean dug Stanley in the ribs. 'He's not even going to mention the losses. We can't let him get away with that.' She took a step forward, but Stanley held on to her blouse and pulled her back.

Just as she turned to unfasten his hand she heard a cry from further up the street, louder and fiercer than the shouts of the reporters.

Acting as a single organism, Conner's security men all turned their heads toward the noise, their attention snagged by sudden movement along the sidewalk. They reached under jackets and retrieved an armoury of weapons, aiming them at the perceived incoming threat.

'Put your weapons down!' Conner stepped from behind the lectern. 'That's my son.' He flung his arms wide.

Jean tugged her blouse from Stanley's grip, pressed forward to get a better view and found herself staring straight at the boy from the grocery store. He reached for a small bag slung over his shoulder and fumbled with the fastening, struggling to yank it open, then shoved his hand inside and shook the bag free.

When his hand emerged, the fingers were wrapped around the handle of a gun.

He straightened his arm and pointed the revolver at his father. Conner's bodyguards raised their guns again.

'Don't shoot!' Conner shouted.

Jean lurched forward. 'Stop him,' she hollered.

Instantly the boy's arm swung toward her. He hesitated, looked at his father, looked back at Jean.

Jean's breath stalled. She felt Stanley's hands on her shoulders.

The gun swung back toward Conner.

'On your knees!' the boy yelled.

In an instant, Conner's men surged forward and surrounded their boss. He disappeared behind a wall of dark suits.

'Don't hurt him,' Conner cried, as the guards dragged him away into the building.

Stanley pulled Jean backward, stepping forward at the same time, his hands raised in submission. 'Come on, son. Put the gun down.'

The boy turned back to Jean and aimed.

The crowd standing around them scattered.

'Hey, it's OK, just lower your weapon to the ground.'

The boy steadied the gun with his other hand.

Stanley leapt forward, shoved Jean hard and knocked her to the ground.

A sharp crack echoed off the tall buildings. Then another.

Stanley dropped. He crashed onto the sidewalk right next to Jean.

Luisa heard the gunshots and pulled out her gun as she ran, willing her exhausted legs to move faster.

She saw the English woman first, on her knees, rocking something in her arms. A few steps closer and she saw what it was. Her throat constricted and her vision blurred.

Mrs Henderson looked up. 'Go after him,' she said, 'he's getting away.' She turned her head and Luisa followed her gaze. About thirty yards away the boy in the smart suit was half running, half staggering up the street.

Luisa sucked a breath into her burning lungs and started to run. She shouted a warning, but either he didn't hear or he chose to ignore her. She pumped her arms and pushed her leaden legs harder.

'Police! Stop! Drop your weapon.'

As she ran, she frantically checked both sides of the street, looking for the promised police presence. Where were they?

'Linus Conner. Drop your weapon!'

Still he ploughed on, knocking pedestrians out of his way as he went. He was pulling away from her, she raised her gun, but there were too many people on the street to risk taking a shot. She shouted another warning. The perp glanced over his shoulder and stumbled, arms flailing as he tried to regain his balance, the gun waving around in his hand. He fell onto his knees and scrambled back up. But instead of running again, he turned and stood perfectly still. He pointed the gun at her.

The sidewalk around him emptied. Luisa slowed to a walk.

'Put the gun down. Come on, Conner.'

Still the gun remained high in his hands. He widened his stance.

'Linus! Lower your weapon to the ground and put your hands on your head. Nice and easy.' Luisa stopped, her gun pointing right at him. Her hands were sweating. She gripped the gun tighter.

He heaved in a breath and started walking toward her. 'Nice and easy? How easy is this?' he shouted.

'Stop! I'm warning you. Put the gun down.'

Still he came.

Luisa swallowed. 'Lower your weapon or I'll shoot.'

His pace quickened.

Her heart pounded in her chest and in her ears.

He started to run at her.

Luisa fired.

# 57

A three feet by two feet television was mounted high on one wall in the reception area of All Saints hospital. Luisa stared blankly at the talking heads. Though the sound was muted she had a pretty good idea what was being said. All the news channels were running the same three stories in a loop and speculating on the connections between them.

On any other day a double shooting in the Financial District would have filled the available airtime on its own. Today it was squeezed between reports covering the imminent collapse of Fisher Krupps and the occupation of the streets by scores of protesting seniors.

Luisa knew for sure that two of the stories were linked. The protests had stopped the 1st Precinct officers responding in time to arrest Linus Conner when she had requested back up. If they'd come, there wouldn't have been a firing line for Stanley to step into. And Luisa wouldn't have had to shoot a seventeen-year-old boy.

She opened her eyes wide, trying to get the image of the boy's limp body lying on the sidewalk from her mind. It faded for a moment only to be replaced by an equally disturbing vision of Stanley. She tried to focus on the TV screen as the picture changed again to show customers waiting in line outside branches of Fisher Krupps right across the country, eager to withdraw their cash before the bank doors were shut in their faces. That image was followed by an extreme close-up of Chuck Conner moments before his son appeared waving a gun. Luisa had to look away. She knew the next image would show Stanley pushing the English woman out of harm's way and taking two bullets in the chest.

The perp's last two bullets.

She looked at her hands. They were still trembling, hadn't stopped since she'd discharged her own weapon. She'd aimed for Linus Conner's shoulder, but he'd swerved as he ran at her, taking the full force of the shot in the middle of his chest.

Luisa had never fired her gun in the line of duty before. Now she had killed a boy. A boy with an empty gun. A moment's action she'd have to live with every day for the rest of her life.

She'd heard tales from other cops who had killed suspects, mostly in self-defence, sometimes not, but all of them, even the battle weary, hard as nails tough guys, said it was something they never got over. No matter how many years went by. According to them, she could look forward to weeks of sleepless nights, constant nausea and the threat of dishonourable dismissal hanging over her head.

A figure appeared at her shoulder. 'How are you, love?' An English accent. Luisa turned to see Mrs Henderson smiling sympathetically at her. The woman's eyes were raw with crying, mascara smudged in uneven half-circles underneath. One of her arms was encased in a dark blue sling. Held tight in her other hand was a transparent plastic bag. Inside Luisa spotted Stanley's retirement watch. A sob escaped from her mouth and she struggled to catch her breath.

Mrs Henderson nudged Luisa's arm with her good elbow. 'It's OK, love,' she said, 'you let it out.' She nodded to a row of seats bolted to the wall. 'Shall we sit down?'

'What happened to your arm?'

'Dislocated shoulder. They popped it back in.'

'Sounds painful.'

'Oh, it's nothing. I've been through worse.'

Luisa sniffed and rubbed a hand across her face. 'I should get back to the station house. They need me to file a report about what happened. I've got to hand in my shield.' She swallowed. 'They already have my gun.'

'You're not in any trouble, are you? I mean… after all that boy did. Then with what happened to Stanley…' Saying his name made her throat catch.

'It's just protocol – something I can't avoid. I'll be suspended while the investigation takes place.'

'If you need me to speak on your behalf, I can tell them exactly what happened.'

Luisa looked into the earnest face of the English woman.

'Thanks – but that won't be necessary.'

The woman shifted her weight away from Luisa, her feet turned toward the exit. 'About that other business – I'll come down to the station in a day or two and make a full statement. I'm fully prepared to face up to the consequences of my actions.'

Luisa wasn't sure which 'other business' she was referring to.

'I know what I did was wrong. I'll admit everything. Guilty as charged.'

Luisa dug an elbow into Mrs Henderson's ribs. 'Keep it down. This place is crawling with cops. No need for them to know anything about it.'

'But I want to do the right thing. I—'

'Do you really think that matters now, in the circumstances?'

The English woman looked down at the small plastic bag and sighed. 'I suppose not.'

'And neither does what happened on West Broadway this morning.'

'I'm sorry?'

'I know it had to be you. And Stan.'

'I really don't know what you're talking about.'

Luisa wasn't sure if the woman was playing dumb to protect herself or Stanley's reputation. She decided to give her the benefit of a doubt. She lowered her voice. 'In the confusion no one's even sure just how much was taken from the safe and how much was withdrawn legitimately by customers. With what's happening with Fisher Krupps right now, I'm not sure anyone will ever know. From what I hear, the descriptions the tellers gave of the people in the bank were very vague.'

'I suppose all old people must look the same to them.'

'I'm guessing they used that to their advantage.'

'It's possible.'

Mrs Henderson suddenly took a keen interest in the news programme on the TV screen.

A photograph of a blond-haired man was smiling down at her. The caption read: *Malcolm Oliver – rogue trader*. 'Isn't that the guy you identified at the morgue?'

Mrs Henderson nodded. 'By all accounts, he was the one responsible for Fisher Krupps losing almost a billion dollars. He caused the run on the bank single-handed.'

Luisa shook her head. 'One man can do that much damage all on his own?'

'Apparently. Hard to believe, isn't it?' The English woman looked away. She took a deep breath and after a moment turned back to Luisa. 'I meant what I said, before. If I can help in any way at all, please don't hesitate to get in touch.' She sighed. 'I'll be staying at Stanley's. There's a lot to organise.' She gave her a sad smile. 'I'll let you know the details when everything's arranged.'

As hard as Luisa tried, she couldn't manage a smile of her own.

# 58

The latest heatwave finally broke just as the cortege of mourners was assembling around the grave. A flurry of flapping umbrellas broke the silence and Jean let out a long slow sigh. She lifted her face to the sky and closed her eyes. Fat cold drops of rain hit her cheeks and mingled with her tears before sliding off. She felt herself toppling forward.

A firm hand gripped her shoulder and pulled her back.

'Hang on in there, Mrs H.'

Jean opened her eyes to see Luisa Rodriguez staring at her, a troubled expression on her face. 'I'm fine, no need to worry about me,' Jean said, the words sounding hollow. She tried hard to force a smile, but her mouth just wouldn't cooperate.

The past seven days were as uneventful as the previous ten had been frantic with incident. She still found it hard to believe all the things that had happened since she'd first arrived in New York. Most of it she would readily have gone back and erased. But there had been one or two moments that she would never regret.

The priest started reciting something Jean vaguely recognised from Sunday school. She tuned him out and concentrated instead on the sensation of Stanley's first kiss. Had she kissed him or was it the other way around? She decided it was best to remember a joint endeavour, both of them having the same impulse in the same instant. There was a definite minty freshness to his breath, as if he'd brushed his teeth in anticipation.

The priest's voice rumbled on, without feeling, without meaning. Just going through the motions, making it obvious he knew nothing about the man he was burying. Jean lowered her gaze to her feet, the tension around her mouth relaxing a fraction as she pictured Simon's face when he'd first laid eyes on Stanley. Wearing *his* dressing gown. It was worth a photograph.

She'd hoped her son would make an appearance at the cemetery. It would have been nice to have him standing next to her, to rest her arm on his. But he'd said his goodbyes the previous evening, the bag slung over his shoulder crammed with the ten and twenty dollar bills Jean withdrawn from her own bank account and those she'd begged and borrowed from Glenda and Mrs Kim and a few of their friends. The remaining cash from the robbery had either been promised to specific projects or had already been donated to a dozen or so soup kitchens and food banks across the city. In the circumstances, keeping any of the cash for Simon now seemed entirely inappropriate. There had been talk of a memorial fund, but that was considered too *high-falutin'* for a man who grew up on the wrong side of the tracks, and the notion was quickly rejected.

Simon had been unable to hide his disappointment at their measly haul, certain a larger sum would have convinced Cindy she should up sticks and follow him to the ends of the earth. Though he never told her the exact details of their meeting, Jean had a shrewd idea of how it would have gone. No doubt ending in a tearful Simon being escorted from Cindy's parents' apartment. Jean knew full well all the money in the world wouldn't have persuaded Cindy to exchange a secure and stable Upper West Side existence for a life on the run.

Her son hadn't been explicit, but she suspected by now he was sitting on a bus halfway across Pennsylvania en route to Mexico. Putting as much distance between him and his creditors as possible. Simon was still convinced the FBI would be on his trail just as soon as they dug a little deeper into the bank's records.

Jean sucked down a deep breath, and wondered whether she'd ever see him again. She felt Luisa's grip tighten, as if the detective feared Jean might lose her balance completely and tip forward into the open grave. She patted Stanley's old partner on the hand and took a step back, glancing up at Glenda on the other side of the gaping hole. Glenda nodded back and threaded one arm through Clarence's to her left, and hooked her hand around Mrs Kim's slim waist who was standing on her right. Clarence continued to avoid eye contact with Jean, convinced that not playing his part in the heist had somehow contributed to what had happened to Stanley, no matter how many times Jean tried to persuade him otherwise. How could he believe it was his fault when she knew the blame was all hers? She should never have dragged Stanley along to watch Chuck Conner's public humiliation.

The priest had stopped speaking. The low mechanical hum of the winch started up and the coffin slowly disappeared into the ground. Jean couldn't bear to watch and turned her face away, inadvertently glancing up at the mourners standing at the foot of the grave. Dolores stared back at her, the woman's mascara-streaked face a mask of indignation. Jean held the woman's gaze and reached out to the wheelchair parked next to her to steady herself. Finally Dolores looked away and with a clank the coffin hit the bottom of the grave.

If the plan had panned out the way it was supposed to, they would all be celebrating with Jimmy right now, thrilled to have saved his house, with enough money left to pay for an operation and his ongoing medication.

But Jimmy had told no one about his worsening symptoms. The first anyone knew that his hernia had ruptured was when the phone call came from the hospital in Queens. They'd left a message on Stanley's cell phone, which Jean discovered when she had been handed his things at All Saints.

In the end Jimmy's bull-headed stoicism had cost him his life.

Jean slipped her hand from the back of the wheelchair and laid it gently on Stanley's heavily strapped shoulder. He raised his good hand and squeezed her fingers. He didn't look up, but she could see both his cheeks were damp. She said a silent goodbye to Jimmy and wrapped her fingers around Stanley's.

She reached into her handbag and found a handkerchief. She slipped it into his hand and gently kissed the top of his head.

Then she whispered something he wasn't supposed to hear.

'I should damn well hope you do,' he whispered back.

# About the author

Eva was born and raised in south London. She's been a local government worker, singer, dot com entrepreneur, portrait artist, project manager, web designer and content editor.

In 2011 Eva won the inaugural Lucy Cavendish fiction prize for her first novel, *The Loyal Servant.* The novel was also shortlisted for ITV's People's Novelist Award. Eva lives in Sussex and London.

For more information about Eva's other books, please visit her website at evahudson.com/books. You can also follow her on Twitter: @Eva_Hudson.

15233452R00210

Printed in Great Britain
by Amazon.co.uk, Ltd.,
Marston Gate.